THE OLDEST LIVING VAMPIRE *In Love*

Joseph Duncan

cobra e-books

Originally published under the pen name Rod Redux.

2014 Trade Paperback Edition
Published by Cobra E-books
Metropolis, IL

ISBN-13: 978-1495388415
ISBN-10: 1495388417

Also By Joseph Duncan

The Oldest Living Vampire Tells All
The Oldest Living Vampire on the Prowl
Menace of Club Mephistopheles
Mort
Hole: A Ghost Story
Indian Summer
House of Dead Trees
Nyal's Story
Apollonius
The Oldest Living Vampire Betrayed
Frankenstonia

For my true love
And
For all my readers,
This long love letter.

Vesuvius
December 29

1

I felt the music penetrate my flesh even before I entered the building, the thump of its bass like a second heartbeat. They call it "techno", but it has a primal quality that belies its modern label. It conjures memories of my people's ritual chants, the drumming of bare palms on hollow logs, men and women shouting as they leap and spin around a roaring fire, their bodies moist with sweat, their faces tilted to the heavens in ecstasy.

I closed my iridescent eyes to drink in the music. I can feel it in my flesh, in my mind.

For a vampire, television and cinema are irritants. My thoughts fly faster than a mortal human's thoughts, and so I am aware of each shuttering still image. They whirl like life itself for your human eyes, but for me they are still images, ticking steadily through my consciousness.

But music... *Ah, music!*

Music has the power to seduce me. A world without music would be a world without color, without dreams.

But I am not here tonight simply to enjoy the

music, as attractive as the idea may be. No, my motivation for coming is far more malevolent.

I intend to murder a man.

And so I opened my eyes and stepped to the red velvet rope and waited for the doorman to admit me.

The bouncer was a veritable Goliath, arms thicker than my thighs, chest twice the breadth of my own. He had a shaved head and artfully groomed facial hair and wore an electronic listening device in one ear. It looked like a plastic insect feeding from his ear canal.

I had to wrench my eyes from the throbbing blue vein in his ox-like neck. The hunger was burning in my guts, squeezing my intestines between its taloned claws. Young men and women pressed behind me, drunk and loud, eager like me to gain entrance to this temple of sound. Innocent souls, they were ignorant of the very real danger they had stumbled upon tonight. They rubbed their plump, sweating bodies against me, making me squeeze my hands into fists for fear of turning and ripping their throats out.

Throughout the millennia, I have lost control of myself more than I care to recall. I have devoured entire tribes in the hot red grip of my bloodlust. Some vampires can easily move among our human prey, pushing aside the bloodthirst without too much difficulty, but not I. I have always been far too easily tempted, prone to bouts of savagery in spite of my gentler nature.

For a moment I felt like I was drowning in a sea of human smells: their salty human sweat and sex pheromones, the coppery scent of human blood sluicing through all that succulent flesh. I wanted to bite them, rend open their throats and suck them dry--

Get a grip on yourself, monster!

The bouncer finally deigned to notice me.

"Namen?"

"Valessi," I replied.

The name I use in this modern era is Valessi. Gaspar Valessi.

He consulted a clipboard, began to shake his head.

Impatient, I hissed, *"Let me enter!"*

"Sorry, friend. You're not on the list."

I was a little surprised he refused to admit me to the nightclub, as I had pitched my voice to influence his mind. It is a trivial skill. Any vampire can master it, if that is something that they care to do. It only takes a few of your mortal lifespans to get the hang of it. He should have obeyed me without thought. Instead, he crossed his ridiculously muscular arms and scowled down at me like I was a child.

I realized then that it was the music. The music coming from inside the club had interfered with my carefully pitched tonalities, so I adjusted the frequency of my voice to accommodate the bass thumps pulsing through the steel doors—a bit trickier —and gave it another try.

"Step aside, you oaf. Let me pass!" I demanded.

The man's eyes fluttered. For a moment he looked confused, then he unhooked the velvet rope with a blank expression and gestured for me to proceed.

I slipped through the door, feeling somewhat guilty. The temptation to abuse one's preternatural abilities is a powerful one, but it is a danger I strive to resist. I need only remind myself of the Dark Ages, when the Catholics very nearly harried my kind to extinction, and I am duly chastised.

I passed though a brief antechamber decorated in the Roman style. Reproductions of Pompeian art—most of it quite raunchy-- adorned the walls of small alcoves, evenly spaced between faux marble pillars. I was impressed. The Pompeians were a very open-minded and sensual people. This modern world is not so liberal.

Plaster casts of Mount Vesuvius's victims curled on the floor below the erotic frescos, bodies contorted in the throes of their final agonies. They were crude, cruel reproductions. Juxtaposed against the sexually explicit murals, I found it all a tad gauche. That's just one man's opinion, of course, but I was present when the volcano erupted. I lost a woman I loved when the great wall of burning ash came roaring down the mountain.

The lights in the corridor throbbed in synch with the music. I passed a group of giggling young women-- tight clothing, breasts exposed like French aristocrats, half spilling from their bodices. A couple of them gave me a quick appraising glance, then I pressed through an interior door, and the music swallowed me whole.

2

Inside, techno pulsed loudly enough to damage human eardrums. Patterns of light scintillated across the ceiling and walls, flashing red, orange, purple. Young humans threw their sweaty bodies around the dance floor or mingled together at the bar or the tables, hoping to find a mate to accompany them home for the night... Or, at the very least, a momentary distraction from an otherwise mundane existence: a fight, a thrilling bit of gossip, the flash of an attractive stranger's eye across the crowded chamber.

They waved plastic sticks filled with luminous fluid, sketching the air with serpentine streaks of pastel light. They snorted coca powder up their noses and poured alcoholic beverages down their gullets by the gallons.

It reminded me of the Bacchanal-- or any of

Rome's countless drunken festivals.

You humans...! Always yearning for distraction. I don't know how you can find your lives that tedious. They are so brief. So very, very brief.

Of course, such things are relative. To me your lives are fleeting sparks. They rise up from the fire, twirling like little stars, to wink for a moment in incandescent glory before dying away, lost to the winds of eternity.

And this club--! This seething nightclub, these celebrants-- so tame in comparison to the sights I have seen. I, who witnessed the gladiatorial games of Rome in its heyday, who can recount the pantheon of Haman, a country-- and the gods its people worshipped, which they called the *Vitae*-- lost now to time but for my undying memories. I marched in the Bacchanalia, and watched in wonder and disbelief as the Bacchae, the crazed female worshippers of the Roman god of wine, tore their clothes from their bodies and ran wild through the streets, raping the men and the boys... even the dogs!

My name in this modern era is Gaspar Valessi, and I am the oldest living creature on this planet. I estimate my age at 30,000 years, although I could be off by a millennia or two. For a being as old as I, there is no accurate stick to measure the span of my existence. I was old when Homo Sapiens shared this world with other thinking beings, all of them now long extinct. I was married to a Neanderthal woman. I warmed my cheeks by the light of civilization's first sunrise.

Do you know who I am?

You, butterfly child, you press your body against mine as I cut through the thrashing crowd, smiling with your blood-colored lips, arching your breasts toward me, so full and soft to the touch. Don't you feel the lifeless chill that emanates from my flesh? Don't you see the strange luster of my skin, or notice its unnatural inflexibility? Do you not know how you tempt the monster inside me? You run your fingers across the front of my trousers, laughing at your own audacity. Do you think you can shock me with your forwardness?

You have no idea!

If you knew the thoughts that burned through my mind at your touch, like falling stars streaking across a blackened sky, you would run screaming from this place. Join a convent. Dedicate your life to the Christian god.

I seize you by the throat. My grip is cold steel. Irresistible. I push you down on the floor as you struggle in vain to pull my fingers from your neck. Your eyes bulge, your bloody lips split open to loose a scream of disbelief and terror. I tear open the front of my trousers, releasing my totem like a beast from its cage, and then I rip away your garments, sweep them from your flesh as if they were made of tissue. I penetrate you, make you cry out, and then, even as you claw at my back, trying to force me off you, I penetrate you again, my fangs hooking into your flesh as savagely as my organ hooks into your sex, fucking you, feeding on you, until you're as cold and lifeless as I am.

I would never do such a thing, of course! Not to someone as innocent as you. Not unless I was starved for blood. But your youth, your beauty... it tempts me. It tempts the monster that dwells within me. My soul is a terrible pit of ravenous vipers. Be careful that you don't fall in!

Yes, that's right. You've guessed my secret.

I am the vampire Gon.

No ordinary vampire, I am the Most Ancient One. The ghost god of the blood drinkers. For many thousands of years I have kept my identity a secret, but loneliness has driven me to publish my memoirs, to reveal myself to the human world, if only in the guise of gothic fiction.

Others of my kind have taken notice.

Have I told you that?

I have gotten very angry electronic mail from some of them. They are surprised by my revelations, and filled with self-righteous indignation at my reckless disregard for our secrets.

They speak of laws. They threaten retribution.

Bah! I do not fear them—not even the eldest!

My kind are too few now to have any real society. We have no laws for me to break. And even if there were a multitude to rise up en mass to silence me, who would carry out my punishment? Who among my brothers and sisters has the strength to challenge *me*?

Heed this warning, my immortal brethren! Gon has set up house in Belgium. This city is off limits to all of you, save those I have loved or made into immortals. You throw away your life if any of you dare venture into my territory!

My race is most rare, and yet I am singular. The oldest. The most powerful.

Indestructible, they whisper, in whatever dark crypts those self-righteous demons choose to haunt, and they are correct.

Many have tried to kill me, even my own vampire children, yet I am still here, the hoary grandfather of a deathless race.

But I don't like to brag.

Of course, I must appear to you, butterfly child, like any other human male. Early middle-age, handsome, longhaired and bearded. You have not guessed my secret yet, have you, little one? You see me here in this club, my white flesh disguised by cosmetics, and you think that I am just another 30-year-old "dude", too old by your standards to be in this thundering place. I should be home with my wife and my children, you probably think. You believe you play a game with me, torturing some prosaic family man who has not the good sense to retire from this sport.

I could-- I should-- kill you for your presumptuousness.

No!

Damn this hunger! It is so hard to maintain my self-control in this place, with so many warm bodies writhing up against me. All this hot, blood-filled flesh, squirming against me from every direction.

You play with fire, little girl! The way you place your hand on my shoulder, the way you lean your face into mine, your silky hair-- smelling oh so clean and fine-- swirling like a dark cloud, your neck so near to my teeth.

Your ripe red lips part. You mean to speak.

I smile at you suddenly, baring my fangs.

Surprise! Fear!

I see the blood drain from your cheeks, your eyes grow wide, even as your body shrinks instinctively away from me. Your hands rise to your defense, and then I use my preternatural speed to flit through the crowd away from you, vanishing from sight, leaving you shaken, and with the unspoken admonition:

Careful, little butterfly! The world is full of spiders!

3

It had been five days since my last feeding: the pornographer and sadist Hans Loen.

Now there was a meal fit for a vampire king! Betrayed by his associate, who I've been holding captive in my penthouse, he was a giant of a man, well over six feet tall. Vigorous. Full of hot, delectable blood. And beautiful, too, despite the injury that had claimed his right eye and scarred the flesh of his face. In his form could be found the ultimate romantic expression, handsome prince and furious beast, all wrapped up in a single mouthwatering package. Body of an Adonis, face of a Frankenstein's Monster. I have to confess, he was lying in pieces when I was through with him!

Oh, spare me your reproof, you tutting guardians of propriety, you waggers of fingers! The man was as much a monster as me. A deceiver. A child rapist. Delivered to me by his business partner, who is even more morally repugnant than Hans himself, if you can imagine that! Right to my door, just like you mortals order out for pizza.

I have made many moral capitulations throughout my unimaginably long life, driven as I am by this thirst for human blood, but perhaps I can win your sympathy by assuring you of this: I feed only on the wicked.

At least, I try to.

Oh, like any human addict, I have my slips. Just this previous August, I had gone to the Monos Gallery to take in a new showing. Local artist, lovely paintings. Reminded me of Cezanne. As I glided through the galleries, drinking in the sights, I was approached by an ethereal beauty, an art critic who wrote for one of the local newspapers.

She engaged me in conversation, and we talked at length about art. Her specialty was modern art. I, of course, impressed her with my knowledge of the classics.

Would you expect anything else?

She seemed quite taken with me, laughing at all my *bons mots*, nodding at my insights, stroking my chest and shoulders. She couldn't keep her hands off me, and my desire for her swelled with every passing moment.

I knew I should withdraw. Flee from her presence, lest I poison her with the venom of my desires, but I was too fascinated by her—by her beauty and her intellect. How can a man be rude to such an erudite admirer? I was helpless to resist her graces.

Before I was even aware of her intentions, she had swept me into a deserted stairwell, piercing my soul with a quiver of compliments, whispering that she had nearly fainted at the sight of me, she was completely enamored with me and that I must take her now, right here in this filthy stairwell like an animal, she wanted me so badly!

I covered her in passionate kisses, her head falling back in delight, her tiny warm fingers tangling in my hair. The flesh of her neck rashed with goosebumps at the touch of my tongue, so soft, so warm, and I thought: *Just a little drink, as I press myself inside of her...*

Yes, vampires can make love! The Strix, the black blood which animates us, has no quarrel with our cocks. Sex with us is dangerous for mortals, and not always pleasant if we—in our passion—let slip the reins of our true strength, but it can be done, and she wouldn't even realize I had fed from her, if I took the utmost care!

All vampires must learn this trick if they wish to go undetected by mortals: how to bring the black blood up from their gut, how to slather it on the wound after drinking their fill. Just a drop, delivered on the tip of the tongue, and the wounds stitch right back up. And our teeth are so very, very sharp! In the throes of passion, even little pains can be a pleasure when delivered by an amorous lover. She would think it a love-bite.

"Yes! Now, Gaspar, I must have you inside me!" my beautiful art critic whispered in my ear, and so I slid myself inside her, and then I slid myself inside her.

She latched onto me as I fastened onto her, and I lost myself in the pulsing red pleasure of feeding and fucking. We could hear the low murmur of the art show attendees just beyond the door. I think it enflamed her knowing we could be caught at any moment, her reputation sullied. She wrapped her legs around me as I held her in my arms, filling her, draining her.

It was only after the ultimate moment that I realized she was dead.

Cold, pale, limp inside my encircling arms. A lifeless China doll, arms flopping at her sides, the legs she'd clamped around my hips only moments before swinging flaccidly around.

Oh, the horror--!

One little drink, I'd promised, before granting myself license to indulge. I'm sure no small number of alcoholics have thought that very thing.

I made off with her body to a nearby wilderness, ashamed, furious with myself, and buried her in a lovely, remote location. I'm sure she would have appreciated the beauty of her final resting place, though not the untimeliness of her demise.

Still warm with her blood, I proclaimed: Never again! Never again will I feed from the innocent!

Though I'm sure every addict has sworn off their weaknesses in just such a manner, as well.

As I said, I try to feed only on the wicked, and such was my aim this night.

I don't ordinarily hunt nightclubs. Such garish gathering places are favored more by those with a mind for mating than the morally deficient that constitute my diet. No, my shadow most often falls upon the back alley brigand, and those who haunt dimly lit riverside bars. The irredeemable. The insane.

And don't think I prey only on the lower class, as I've been known to take a corrupt *marquess* or *marquise* from time to time as well... though it's become much trickier to steal them from their gilded halls in this modern age.

There are just so many damned security cameras!

Here, in this nightclub called Vesuvius, I feel as if I'm drowning in a sea of horny children. There are a few blackguards to be found. They're easy enough to spot for a creature like me. That one standing by the bar, plying a female with drinks—he's no stranger to a prison cell. I can tell by the stocky muscularity of his figure, the way he constantly peeks over his shoulder, as if he suspects someone might shank him in the back at any moment. And that woman there? She's a professional thief. See how she appraises the men who come to court her? She doesn't look them in the eye, but assesses their belongings: their clothes, their jewels, the timepieces on their wrists.

But I'm not hunting just any generic villain this evening. I have a target, a very specific victim in mind, and I've been assured he'll be somewhere in this club tonight.

Thinking about him makes the Hunger leap and snap inside my stomach. I would salivate as I press my way through the bounding mob if that is something that I was still able to do. The music, the smells, it makes my mind reel. I slip between the revelers like a lion stalks his prey through the high savannah grass, eyes alert, every sense humming like a high voltage wire. I feel alive, rooted in the here and now, vital and relevant. I so often feel unanchored, like flotsam drifting in time's slow tides.

All this hot bloody flesh pressing in around me: it threatens to distract. But I ignore them. Even if they were all great villains, I would stalk my prey no less single-mindedly.

You know how it is when you have a taste for something in particular.

Nothing else will do!

4

His name was Maurice Fournier. He was a half-French, half-Jewish money launderer and pornographer. Worse, he was an accomplice in the rape, torture, and murder of a young woman named Amelie, whose body my captive intended to dispose of in the Meuse.

That is where I encountered him-- my hostage, my confessor. Of course, I'm speaking now of Fournier's business partner, the murderer Lukas Jaeger.

Poor Maurice... You've been betrayed!

You remember Lukas, do you not? I wrote at length about him in the second volume of my memoirs. Lukas Jaeger, the sociopath I've been keeping imprisoned in my suite. He is chained in one of my spare bedrooms right this very moment.

How is he?

Still alive. Still vicious and depraved, but much more desperate and conniving, I warrant, than he was when you previously met him.

I snatched Lukas from the wharves only moments after he had killed my tragic beauty, my Amelie.

Amelie... I've wept bloody tears for you, little angel!

Such a fragile, naïve creature. When her parents disapproved of her love affair with a young man named Bertrand, they ran away from home together — she and her young paramour. Took a train to the city of Liege, and wandered right into my captive killer's embrace.

Lukas offered them shelter and food—and the

only payment he took from them was their lives.

Lukas and his cohorts, Hans and Maurice, murdered her lover, and then they raped and tortured her for days, filming every depraved act for distribution on the black market. They call it "kiddie porn". When she was of no further use to them, Jaeger put her in the trunk of his car, drove to a deserted section of the city, and murdered her on the quay, intending to roll her steaming carcass into the river.

Is it a wonder that a monster as ancient, as jaded, as I have become can feel such agony for the murder of a single mortal female? Perhaps. But I assure you, I have wept for her.

I hope you can rest in peace, knowing that the men who used you so badly will pay for what they've done. Hans, I have already dealt with. Lukas... well, I suppose you could say he's still working out his penance. I have plans for my hostage Lukas. But Maurice... tonight, Maurice, too, will pay.

Lukas was all too willing to betray his cohort, just as he betrayed Hans, offering their lives to me in exchange for his own.

When I rose with the dark this evening, it was with the agonies of the Hunger chewing on my guts. The bloodlust was upon me, my body in agony, even to the marrow of my bones.

I shall feed on him tonight, I said to myself when the sun had sunk and I awoke. Even as my gleaming eyes snapped open in the febrile gloom of my bedchamber, I thought this. *Enough with all your foolish schemes, you old monster! You are hungry, and he is here... just a few paces away.*

I rose from my bed and took off all my clothes. I was wearing very expensive silk pajamas, and I did not wish to ruin my garments. Gliding silently from my bedroom, I crossed the parlor and traveled down the short corridor to his bedroom door.

It is time to finish this, I told myself sternly. *He is not a pet. Kill him now before you do something you will regret.*

I could hear him grunting on the other side of the door, and below his breathy gasps, the rhythmic clink of metal on metal.

I smiled.

What surreptitious endeavor is he up to tonight?

He jumped when I threw open the door, but he did not cry out. He was not the type to easily startle.

"Are you trying to escape again?" I demanded.

"No!" he lied, but I could see the abrasions on his wrist. He had been trying to wriggle his hand free of his manacle.

He was sitting upright on his bed, dressed in only boxers and a pair of socks. His flesh was flushed and sweaty. A handsome man, my Lukas. Not handsome in the current fashion, all gaunt and disheveled-looking. More like an old-fashioned aristocrat. Well-fed. Powerful and arrogant.

He was a bit short, a bit on the stout side. Not fat, just big boned and muscular. Square, masculine features, silky dark hair, dark eyes. I hadn't allowed him a razor for fear he might injure himself, and he'd begun to grow a very fetching beard.

"You could free yourself from that manacle very easily," I said, striding further into the room.

He looked at the metal cuff encircling his wrist, returned his gaze to me.

"Oh, you won't be able to wiggle out of it. I know you've been trying to lose weight, thinking you will get thin enough to slip free," I said.

His face darkened with blood.

"Of course I took that possibility into account," I chuckled. "Do you think you are the first mortal I've ever held captive?"

He pushed the chains off his bed with an angry

sweep of his hand. The heavy steel links slithered to the floor with a purring sound, and then he gathered his pillows and leaned his back against them.

"Have you come to tell me more stories?" he sneered.

I shrugged.

"You're naked," he said, his eyes narrowing. He had just noticed.

"Yes."

"Why?"

"Why do you think?"

He thought about it a moment, then the color faded from his cheeks. "You've come to kill me," he whispered.

"Correct. Mortal blood is terribly difficult to wash from one's clothing." I grinned, showing him my fangs. "In the past, I often disrobed before feeding. Clothes were much more valuable then. Now they are mass produced. Almost disposable. They might as well sell them in cardboard boxes like tissues, but old habits die hard. I hate the thought of being so wasteful."

He didn't laugh at my humor. I can't say I blamed him.

"The weather is much too cold to venture out tonight, so I decided--"

"What if I give you Maurice?" he said quickly.

My grin widened. I must have looked like a ravening wolf. "Your father's best friend? The man who smuggled you out of Hamburg? Set you up here in Liege with such a cushy job, fucking little girls?"

"My father was a drunk bastard," Lukas hissed. "He used to sneak into our bedrooms and make us suck him off at night."

I flinched from his words. Not so much from surprise as disgust. I was a father once. Long, long ago.

"We were his personal harem. Me, my brother

and my sisters."

"You never told me this."

"I have many horrible stories I can tell you," he said, mocking a thing I had said to him previously.

He fixed me with his dark eyes. For a mortal, his stare was powerfully hypnotic.

"That's why you keep me alive here, isn't it?" he asked. "To feed off my soul? But you don't see that, do you? You don't just feed on blood, Drac. You feed on lives. You want to devour my life force. You want to devour the terrible things I've done, and the terrible things that have happened to me. You feed on misery." His heavy brows knitted together, and then he said, "I think it... distracts you from your own misery, the pain of living for so long."

I could feel my smile wilting.

Such a dangerous man!

"Am I right?" he asked.

I narrowed my eyes. "Perhaps. There's more to it than that, but..."

"If you kill me tonight, you'll never be able to find him. You think he should be punished, too, don't you? You think we should all pay for the terrible things we've done. Me, Hans, Mo."

"You wish to be punished?" I asked.

He laughed. "No! But that's what you think. Don't deny it. You might be thirty-thousand years old, but you're a terrible liar."

I nodded. "So be it! But have no illusions... I will kill you, Lukas."

He smiled back. "Will you?" he asked softly.

And so he sacrificed his second compatriot on the altar of my appetite. Maurice Fournier, his father's best friend. He pulled up a photo of the man on his cell phone. Maurice, Hans and himself. The three of them in a pub, mugging together in a booth. He told me where I might find Maurice. "He likes to hang out at the Vesuvius when he's in town," he said. "He travels a lot, but before you, uh, kidnapped me, he told me he wasn't planning to return to Germany until after the New Year. He should be there tonight. Scouting for chicks. He rents a private booth that's up over the dance floor so he can look for fresh talent. He's friends with the club manager, so when someone catches his eye, he has Jules—that's the manager's name—he has Jules go and invite them up to party with him. Mo's kind of old and ugly, but he passes out coke and ecstasy like it's Halloween candy."

"Charming," I said, but I was already growing excited.

The hunt is always exhilarating!

I had reached the center of the dance floor now. Youthful revelers leapt and gyrated all around me. Their bodies sometimes bounced against me. I had to be careful not to injure anyone. Leaping up against me can be like flinging your body against a marble statue if I am not careful to make myself more pliant.

I squinted my eyes against the strobing lights. All the flashing was making my brain ache. There were projectors everywhere. They cast video loops onto the walls of various volcanic eruptions. Clouds of ash and lava billowing from ruptured calderas. Red flowing magma. Then depictions of the aftermath: cities buried in ash. Forests burnt to blackened matchsticks. I tried to avoid looking at them. Video images are horribly irksome to me.

Well, that and my memories. I was there, in Pompeii, with my vampire companion Apollonius. We survived, but we lost a confidante we were both madly in love with.

Painful memories. A tale I have no time to tell you. For now.

A young woman danced in front of me, smiling. She slid her body against mine, staring seductively into my eyes, and then she spun away and was lost amid the crowd.

I scanned the balconies that overlooked the dance floor. One was full of dancing, drunken women. The second was empty. The third, I thought, was empty as well, but then I saw a shadow stir, and my quarry leaned over the railing.

There you are!

Maurice Fournier stood with his elbows on the balustrade, watching the seething crowd below with a predatory expression. At the sight of him, the hunger leapt inside me: the black blood, the Strix, clamoring to be fed.

Yes, yes, be patient! I said to the monster. *You will drink your fill soon enough!*

I watched as a lanky gentleman approached Maurice from behind. Maurice straightened and turned toward the man, and they conferred for a moment, standing cheek-to-cheek. I couldn't hear them over the crashing of the music, even with my preternatural senses, but the subject of their discussion was obvious enough, as Maurice pointed to someone in the crowd a moment later, and his attendant nodded, then leaned over the rail to get a better look at the person the old man was pointing at.

Keeping my eyes on my prey, I started forward again, pressing myself carefully through the mob.

The man Maurice had spoken to—the club manager, I presume--withdrew from the booth, and Maurice returned to his vantage, staring down on the celebrants like a spider in its lair.

I waited at the edge of the dance floor, watching him.

Lukas was not being unkind when he described my quarry earlier tonight. Maurice Fournier was indeed an ugly old man. Large hawkish nose, curly gray hair and sallow skin. He was as thin as the stereotypical mortician, replete with sunken cheeks and a small, disdainful mouth. Not an imposing figure by any means. Cruel, wily looking, but not the great villain I had hoped for.

I prayed his blood was more robust.

Jules reappeared, exiting from a stairwell onto a ground floor dais. I watched as he spoke to two other men, pointing into the crowd. His two lackeys broke away, headed toward the dance floor, and the manager returned to the stairwell. Shortly after, the two men the manager had dispatched, accompanied by two very young looking women, followed.

I followed, too.

Have your fun while you can, old man, I thought. *It ends for you tonight!*

I smacked my lips as I crossed to the stairs. I could taste the Frenchman's blood already!

5

"Mon frère!" I cried, as the door banged off the wall.

"*Merde*!" the old Frenchman exclaimed, leaping halfway from his seat.

His two young guests ogled me guiltily as they crouched over a glass table, their nostrils powdered, their eyes shining. They had the look of grade school tarts: thigh-high stockings and very short skirts. Their faces belied the lasciviousness of their garb, however. They were young, innocent, ashamed of being caught in the midst of such repast.

"Who are you?" Fournier demanded. "What are you doing, barging in here like this?"

"Je suis desole!" I apologized, putting on an expression of surprise. "I am looking for my friend Louis. Louis Chevalier? Have you seen him?" I moved

as if to lean against the doorway and stumbled further into the room.

"There is no Louis here, you fool!" the old man snapped. The nightclub manager raced across the booth to intercept me.

The girls began to giggle at my antics, charmed, I'm sure, by my looks and drunken clumsiness.

"This is a private room, *monsieur*," the manager intoned. He put his hands on me, trying to hurry me away from his client. He did not seem to notice the chill that emanated from my flesh.

"I apologize for my rudeness," I said, trying to appear embarrassed and confused. "I thought I saw Louis come in here. I think, perhaps, I've become disoriented. This is such a large nightclub."

"Well, he's not here!" Maurice said scornfully, then to the nightclub manager, "I don't even know who he's talking about! Get him the fuck out of here, Jules!"

"Yes, yes," Jules hastened. "*Monsieur!* Come with me... No, this way, *s'il vous plait!*"

I allowed myself to be diverted, tottering against the manager as he led me down the corridor. I spewed incoherent apologies in French, patting the man on his shoulder. All an act, of course. In my mind, I was an errant young aristocrat who had indulged a bit too much tonight before becoming separated from his friends. I had no intention of attacking Fournier in the club, but my playacting had gotten me what I needed: a whiff of the old man's scent.

Someone should tell him that even the most expensive cologne can only go so far covering the stink of old man's flesh. But I had his scent now. There'd be no escape for him tonight.

"Again, I feel I must apologize," I said to the manager as he escorted me down the stairs. "If you see my friend Louis, could you tell him that I'm looking for him? Louis Chevalier? Short, skinny man. Large ears." I held my hands to the sides of my head, making *Dumbo* ears, enjoying myself a little too much.

"Yes, yes," Jules humored me. "I will have someone look for him immediately."

"*Merci*!" I slurred. "You are a true gentleman!"

"Yes, sir. Here, let me get you another drink. On the house. Gunther?"

"Ah, good man!" I trumpeted as a beverage was placed in my hand. I took a hearty swig.

The manager hurried away. I watched him disappear upstairs, and then I spit my drink back into my glass, my expression of feigned drunkenness fading from my features.

The bartender saw me spit out my drink, and I placed the glass down on the bar.

"Too much vermouth," I said dryly, and cast myself once more into the sea of human flesh.

Now that I had the old pervert's scent, I contented myself with haunting the nightclub's more dimly lit corners. A shadow among shadows, I stilled my thoughts and waited, untouched by the revelry surrounding me. I watched the stairs and tried to ignore the flashing lights and crashing music, the writhing bodies and shouts of merriment. At last the old man appeared, a young tart clutching each of his elbows. Escorted by the young women, he bid his friend Jules good night and pressed through the crowd toward the exit.

He didn't see me follow him out, or notice my dark form scaling the alley behind him.

It's one of the few details your popular media gets right when it comes to vampires. The ability to crawl up vertical surfaces is something almost all vampires can do. Our bodies, unlike the bodies of mortal men, are very light. When we are made into a blood drinker, the Strix crystalizes our cells, purging them of all bodily fluids. We are hollow shells, all the way down to the cellular level. Unless we've just gorged ourselves on mortal blood, that lightness, coupled with the rasp-like texture of our fingertips and palms, allows us to shimmy up just about any porous surface.

Also, it's very fun.

A sparse snow was falling when Maurice exited the Vesuvius. Tiny spicules of ice, more like grains of sand than snow, swirled through the streets between the tower blocks and high rise buildings. It made a sensual sound as it descended, a sibilant susurration. The girls, now in furs, ducked their heads as they accompanied Maurice, complaining loudly about the weather and trying not to slip on the icy sidewalks, wobbling drunkenly on their high heel shoes.

I leapt nimbly across the alley to the next building and scurried to about a twelfth floor height. The frigid winter wind tried to peel me from the wall as I ascended, hooting as it whipped through the icy canyons of the street. I pressed my belly closer to the cold bricks, my long hair whipping to and fro, and followed Maurice as he walked with his underage escort to a nearby parking garage.

One of the girls slipped and fell, landing hard on her rump.

The other one laughed, calling her friend a clumsy bitch. Her voice was cruel and taunting.

The fallen one cursed back.

"Ladies, please!" my Frenchman pled. "This icy wind is making my bones ache!"

I slithered around the corner of the building like a gecko, climbing higher so that I might pass unnoticed by any passersby. There, just ahead of my quarry, a street light was out. An entire block was mired in night. I shifted on the wall until my head was pointed earthwards. I had to crane my neck all the way back to keep an eye on my prey, my hair dangling below me, but at least the wind, on this side of the building, was not blowing so hard.

My victim was only meters from our rendezvous in the dark! I waited, my body tensing, as the Frenchman helped his tart to her feet, and then they continued on, their voices echoing down the street.

"We'll warm those old bones for you, *grand-pere*!" one of the girls declared.

"Old *bone*!" the other snorted. "Singular!"

Laughter.

"So long as he has more blow!"

"Yes, we want more blow, *grand-pere*."

"Give us some blow and we'll give *you* a blow."

"At the same time, if you wish."

Chuckling at their ribaldry, Maurice stepped into the darkness.

Finally--!

I pushed from the wall with all of my might, spreading my arms to guide my short flight to the street. The wind screamed in my ears. Icy snow struck my cheeks so hard it felt like little chips of broken glass were slashing across my face. I landed only inches behind him, unseen, unheard, and, encircling him in my arms, I took back to the air with such speed that the Frenchman was instantly knocked unconscious by the sudden, brutal acceleration.

The young women yelped as a powerful gust of wind blew up their skirts. It took them several seconds to realize that their naughty *grand-pere* was no longer walking between them.

I heard them call out to him, wondering aloud where he had gone, completely befuddled, but their voices were already growing faint.

I raced across the rooftops with my supper in my arms.

Maurice groaned and tucked his brow to my chest, blood seeping from one of his ears, instinctively shielding his face from the blistering wind.

I leapt from the ledge of a twenty story apartment complex and landed several seconds later at the southern perimeter of the Parc d'Avroy, which was always deserted at this hour, especially in the winter months.

"Wake up, *grand-pere,*" I murmured with a grin. "We have reservations for dinner."

I carried him into the park.

6

Parc D'Avroy has been here in the center of Liege for 130 years. It was once a tributary of the Meuse, but the city filled it in 1835 to make way for a plantation of trees. It continued to expand until 1880, until it had become the largest and most decorated park in the city.

During the warmer months, it is a tourist attraction, its multitudinous paths winding through broad green lawns and shady coppices, Greek statuary and monuments, but in the winter, blanketed in snow and ice, Parc D'Avroy is all but forsaken. A perfect retreat for a monster like me, one whose needs require a bit of privacy.

I shifted Fournier in my arms and carried him into the park, walking until my booted feet vanished into virginal white drifts, and the insulating snow had silenced the sounds of traffic from the Boulevard D'Avroy and Rogier.

In the woods near the lake, I placed Fournier on the ground and waited for him to rouse.

I was trembling with desire.

The old Frenchman looked frail, almost tragic, lying in that bank of virgin white, cheeks and eyes sunken. His features were made all the more gaunt-looking dominated as they were by that big French nose. I watched the snow fall onto his body while I waited for the cold to revive him. I was intrigued at how slowly the snow melted on his skin. It was almost like he was already dead. But for the puffs of vapor blowing from his enormous nostrils, I might have thought my violent abduction had done him in. I had been careful to cushion his body against mine when I took off from the sidewalk like a rocket, but it is still terribly jarring to be snatched into the air like that. I knew from bitter experience.

Snowflakes drifted down all around us. Some of them landed on the old man's eyelashes and clung to them. I stared, enrapt by the sight. If I looked very closely, concentrated on the image, I could just make out the fanning fractal patterns of those tiny, delicate crystals.

The old man stirred, groaned. His eyes flashed open, dislodging the snowflakes, and then he struggled to sit up, croaking, "Wha--? Where-- Where am I?"

He noticed me squatting nearby and scrambled a short distance away. I put my hand up, smiling to sooth him.

"You!" he accused. "You are the drunken Englishman from the club!"

"Actually, I'm German," I replied in French, "but I've travelled quite extensively. It's why my accent is so strange."

"Where are we? What happened? I remember stepping outside..."

I looked around with a pleasant smile. "We're in the Parc d'Avroy. Lovely, isn't it? The lake's right over there."

He followed my finger, looking toward the icy lake, which was just visible through the copse of trees to the east of us. His head swiveled back toward me, his upper lip peeling back from his teeth. He had large, ugly teeth, stained brown from nicotine and coffee. Snow accumulated on his wiry gray curls like a sprinkling of stardust.

"What happened? Why are we here?" he asked. He pulled a sour face. "Did those sluts rob me? Is that what happened?" He checked his skull for lumps, thinking someone had snuck up behind him and knocked him unconscious with a blackjack.

I shook my head.

"Then what happened?"

"You died," I said.

"I... died?"

I nodded.

Fournier snorted. "I don't feel dead!"

I spread my hands. "Whoever *feels* dead, *mon ami*?"

He still thought I was joking—or mad. He chuckled. "And I suppose you are the angel of death, *n'est-ce pas*?"

"*Effectivement!*" I said, giving him a wink. "I *am* the angel of death!"

His grin faded by degrees. I smelled the fear sweat begin to seep from his pores.

"I am here to take you to hell, Maurice," I said, and my smile faded—also by degrees.

"Who are you really?" he whispered harshly.

I waited a beat before answering. "I am a friend of your business partner, Lukas Jaeger. He has contracted me to kill you."

My confession rocked the treacherous old pornographer. "What? Why?" he exclaimed. "I have only been kind to that arrogant little bastard! Why would he hire someone to kill me? I don't understand!"

I shrugged. "It's complicated. We have an arrangement."

I rose and went to pick him up. The old man squealed as I lifted him bodily from the snow.

"Wait! Wait!" he squalled. "How much did he pay you? I will double it-- triple it!-- if you kill him instead!"

I paused as if to consider it. "Triple?" I asked, cocking an eyebrow.

"Oui! Oui!"

I laughed.

"He does not pay me in money," I said, and then I dipped my fangs to his throat.

The old man howled, stabbing me in the chest.

I stepped back, looking at the front of my shirt in surprise. I didn't see him retrieve the knife from his pocket.

"Die, you cocksucker!" he yelled triumphantly, and he lunged toward me and stabbed me twice more.

The third time he stabbed me, the blade caught in my chest, wedged between two ribs. It slipped from his fingers and he stumbled back from me, eyes wide, his skeletal frame quaking from head to toe.

I looked at him blandly.

He stood slightly hunched, puffs of white vapor billowing from his mouth.

"Well... die already," he said after a moment.

I sighed. I couldn't believe I'd let the old man ruin a perfectly good shirt. It was one of my favorites—my black turtleneck sweater.

I pulled the knife from my chest and examined it. A switchblade. How droll.

I bent the blade forward until it snapped back into its hilt. The old man watched with disbelief as I stuffed the weapon into my front pocket. Holding his gaze, I pulled the front of my shirt up. I wanted him to see my wounds heal, watch them fade away to nothing.

"*Mon dieu!*" he whispered, his eyes growing

wider.

"Not exactly," I smiled.

Mother always scolded me for playing with my food.

I took him then, leaping upon him like a blood-crazed animal... which is actually what I am. Let's be frank. He screamed as I knocked him to the snow, tried to push me off. I paid little attention to the fingers clawing at my face. He did not have the strength to scratch my marble-like flesh. I pushed his chin to one side and lowered my mouth to his throat.

Ah! That smell!

I took a moment to savor it: that aroma. I inhaled him, filled my lungs with him, the scent of his blood; his sweat, his fear. I imagined his entire body pulsing beneath me like a slug, sloshing with all that thick, hot, nourishing blood. I would make a bloody fount of him and drown myself in it!

Then my lips split back from my razor sharp teeth and I surrendered to my hunger. I tore into the flesh of his neck, severing his carotid and jugular with one quick snap of my jaws. He stiffened, then began to buck beneath me, struggling with renewed vigor, one last futile burst of strength. He grabbed a handful of my hair and tried to pull my mouth from his throat. I fastened onto him, making of seal of my lips. I was careful not to let any of his blood squirt on me, as I had one further errand to complete before I retired for the night. Finally, he surrendered. His hand flopped to the snow. His last breath rattled from his throat.

I only paused in my feast once: when the old man voided his bowels.

Hey, it happens.

A long and gassy purr emanated from his posterior. I drew back from him, wrinkling my nose. Disgusting old fiend! I shuddered at his rudeness and finished draining him, taking my time, drinking my fill. He had snorted a lot of cocaine tonight, and the stimulant rushed to my brain, giving me a sensation of euphoria before the Strix neutralized the chemical, as it does all poisons and drugs.

I finished with a sigh, sitting back in the snow with a satisfied smile. Eyes closed, I enjoyed the rush—the drugs he had ingested and the sustenance surging through every cell of my body.

As sometimes happens, I felt a distant echo of his personality as his blood coursed through my veins. Ghost voices murmured in my mind, like the mutterings of lost souls in the winding corridors of a dark and deserted manor.

It is never anything distinct, the voices. Not with mortals. Not for me. Just a sense of *otherness* as their universe slowly darkens, absorbed into my body, and then their souls (if that is what they are) dwindle to a single point of light in my awareness like an old television screen fading to black.

I brought the living blood up into my mouth and spat some of it onto my fingertips. It was marbled red, his mortal blood mixed with mine. It takes the Strix several minutes to fully absorb a meal. Before the fluid could oxidize, I smeared the glittering substance onto the Frenchman's savaged neck and watched as his wounds began to close. The ragged edges of his injuries softened like melting wax. The lacerations filled in, then quickly faded from sight. Within moments, you couldn't even tell that he'd been injured. Apart from the being dead part, of course.

I helped myself to the cash in his wallet, my belly sloshing, and then I leapt to the treetops and made my way out of the park.

As I returned home, I stopped at a diner to pick up Lukas's meal.

"Your shirt is torn," the waitress said. She had a

jowly face, bags beneath her eyes.

"So it is," I replied, peering down at my turtleneck.

"You should dress more warmly, love," the plump old frau advised. "On a night like this, you'll catch your death. Here you go. Your dinner's ready."

"Oh, it's not for me," I smiled. "I've already eaten."

Dinner Conversation

1

"*Scheisse!* It's cold!" Lukas complained. He scowled at me as he explored the contents of the Styrofoam containers I'd returned with, as if I'd allowed his meal to get cold on purpose. He crumpled the paper sack and tossed it aside, his chain clinking.

"It's very cold out," I said.

"Don't you have a microwave?"

"I'm not reheating your dinner," I growled, and he grinned at me, amused by my annoyance.

I chastised myself for allowing the cretin to goad me. *I really should kill him,* I thought, but I was too full to dine again tonight. For such a skinny man, his cohort Maurice had been very filling. To kill Lukas now would simply be a waste.

I watched him stuff his mouth with frites, what you Americans call "French fries", eating with his fingers.

I enjoy watching mortals eat. I suppose it's something that I miss: the variety of food you mortals dine on. Fruits. Vegetables. The seared flesh of animals. The pleasure of ingesting blood, for vampires, is almost orgasmic, but it is still the same thing every night. Blood, blood and more blood. I think that is why older vampires feed only when they are compelled to by their hunger. You would grow bored if you had to eat the same thing every night, too. Regardless of how pleasurable it might be.

"I wish I had some beer to drink," he said wistfully. I had forgotten to bring him anything to drink.

"I can only offer you some water," I replied.

"No, wine?" he asked.

I shook my head.

"If you're going to keep me here like some kind of pet, you really should stock up on some wine, at least. Beer would be preferable, though. To deprive a man of beer and wine...!" He shuddered. "Inhumane!"

I caught his eye. "I do not plan to keep you much longer."

He swallowed thickly, eyes wide, then he smiled again as if to show me that he was unafraid, but I could smell the lie of it. He smelled desperate. Aside from the sour smell of his unwashed flesh. He smelled desperate and unhappy.

I left the room to fetch him something to drink. My penthouse was dark, all the lights turned out but the lights in my captive's chambers, but I do not need electric lights to find my way around the dark. The shadows do not veil my preternatural sight as it veils the eyes of mortals.

My captive sneered when I returned with a mug of tap water, but he took it and drank before returning to his cold frites. I watched his jaw move, the muscles in his cheek bulging rhythmically. I could almost taste the frites from the smell that arose from the container. Grease, potatoes, spices and salt.

"There's something I can't quite figure out about you," he said casually as I crossed the room to a chair.

"And that is?" I asked. I moved the chair near his bed and sat.

Speaking with his mouth full, Lukas said, "Whether you're a faggot or not."

I chuckled. "Does it matter?"

"Of course it does," Lukas replied. "I don't like faggots. I spent half my childhood fending off my papa, and then in prison... always there was some faggot offering me his ass or mouth. It sickens me."

"I do not plan to force myself upon you, if that is what you fear," I said.

"I'm not *afraid* of anything," Lukas declared.

"When I was a mortal man, our marriage customs were quite different than they are today," I said. "My people were polygamous, and our group marriages often included more than one male member."

"Your butt buddy Brold," he grinned.

"Brulde," I corrected him. "And he was not my 'butt buddy'."

"You fuck him?"

"When we were young, we engaged in sexual behavior," I answered. "It was not considered a shameful act, as it is so often regarded in this repressed modern era. Our people called it 'good practice'."

"I bet you practiced a lot," he mocked.

Ignoring his derision, I said, "In those days, we believed such behavior contributed to the wellbeing of the community. Mated tribesmen were more successful at hunting than a single male would have been, more apt to survive in times of war. It was a way for the men of the tribe to bond, and it also afforded our females more time to mature before they mated so that they were more likely to survive the act of childbirth. Childbearing was a hazardous endeavor in those primitive times. I do, however, prefer females when I am in need of sexual gratification."

"Must feel like they're getting poked by an icicle," Lukas smirked.

"My flesh is warmer and more pliant when I am well fed," I replied. "But the act of sex with a member of my kind is always fraught with danger for mortal women. For mortal men, too, I suppose, though there are more male vampires than female vampires. Or there used to be. Regardless, I have made love to a great many mortal women since I was made the monster that I am. The number who did not survive the experience, though small, is a constant source of shame for me. Yet, I am a man, just as surely as I am a monster, and I can be seduced just as easily as any mortal man can be."

"Speaking of well fed," Lukas said, changing the subject. "You're looking very plump and ruddy. I take it your hunt was successful tonight?"

I smiled faintly. "Of course it was. You still live, do you not?"

"Poor Maurice..." Lukas said, looking down at his dinner with a grin. He glanced up at me suddenly, asked, "Will you tell me how it happened?"

His eagerness revolted me... and pleased me at the same time.

"If you like," I answered.

"Yes," he said, nodding. "Yes, tell me! Did he realize what you were? Did he beg you for mercy before you drained him of his blood?"

"Your sadism is repulsive, even to a creature like me," I sniffed.

"Yes, yes," he muttered, waving my condemnation aside. "That is why I fascinate you. Now, tell me. Give me all the details. I want to know if he cried. I want to know if he pissed his pants."

I sighed, pretending to be exasperated with his wickedness, but I have sworn to speak only the truth in these memoirs, and so I must confess to you that it was also gratifying. I have lived so long in self-imposed exile, here in the city of Liege, and abroad. I have hidden from the worlds of mortal and immortal alike, eschewing even the simplest pleasures of human companionship. It felt good to relate my experiences to another sentient being, to be heard by ears other than my own.

"He was at the Vesuvius, just as you said," I began. "The skinny Frenchman with the big nose..."

I have fed on enough mortals to populate a small nation, yet even the most unremarkable events are brightened by their sharing. I found myself warming to the story of the Frenchman's final hours. I could not help it. My captive was so eager to hear it.

2

Lukas laughed when the telling was told. "I wish I could have seen his face when you told him it was I who had betrayed him," he said. He had finished dining and sat propped against the headboard of his bed, his stomach bulging. I could hear his intestines gurgling as digestive fluids liquified his meal.

"Have you no remorse for the deaths of your former companions?" I asked. It was not an accusation, simply curiosity. "No guilt for your complicity in their murders? Maurice was your father's friend. He helped you to escape from Hamburg, when you were arrested for your crimes."

Lukas sat forward, his dark hair falling across his brow. "Let me tell you about Maurice Fournier," he said, his amusement giving way to sudden fury. "He may have helped smuggle me from Germany, but he was no friend to me! When I was a boy, my father would order my sisters to fuck him. Sometimes Maurice would have me join him in the act. My father pimped us all out— my mother until she was so old and ugly no man wanted to put his dick in her-- and then his own children. Can you imagine what that is like, you monster? My father and his friends had no regard for us as human beings. They thought only of the warm orifices they could shove their disgusting cocks inside! And Maurice was no better than any of the others. He took me in when my papa died, but it was only because I was useful to him. I had been well-trained by Papa and his cohorts. I did whatever Maurice told me to do. Fuck. Kill. If I am monster, it is because of the horrors that my father and his filthy friends subjected me to when I was too young to defend myself. They made me what I am."

"So why repeat their evils? Why not strive to rise above your sordid past?" I asked.

"It is the only life I know," he said, leaning back. His eyes rolled toward the window, devoid of emotion, concealing the memories that squirmed in the lightless depths of his awareness. "I do not derive pleasure from anything else in this world," he said softly. "Rape, murder, they are the only things that move me. Perhaps I should kill myself, remove the corruption that is my soul from this world of death and decay, but I do not wish to die. Why should I? I did not ask for this life, and the guilt for the acts I have committed do not stain these hands alone. I am merely a product of my environment."

I felt pity for him suddenly.

"When I kill you, I will not make it unnecessarily painful," I promised him.

He glanced toward me and smiled.

"No," he said. "I want you to. It is the only way I will feel it when it happens."

I stared at him in mute shock, taken aback by his need to be abused, his desire to die in pain. Then I thought: perhaps he only plays another game with me. This exhibition of vulnerability may simply be a ploy, one designed to evoke pity in me.

"I think we are like the opposite poles of a magnetic field," I murmured. "Fated by our nature to be drawn together."

I observed his demeanor as only a vampire can: the workings of his facial muscles, the tiny involuntary movements of his limbs. Even his smell. My instincts told me that he was not being deceptive, but I could not trust my instincts when it came to this mortal monster. His mind was like an onion; each layer I peeled back revealed yet another layer, and another.

He returned my stare and smiled, his mirth failing to reach his eyes.

"I have to shit," he said.

3

"Don't you want to stay and watch?" Lukas inquired as I rose to give him some privacy. He pushed his underpants down his thighs and sat on the portable potty chair I'd purchased for him several days ago. "You can experience my bowel movement vicariously," he taunted me, "just as you did when you were watching me eat."

"That won't be necessary," I said, stamping down on my outrage. Keeping my face neutral, I slipped out into the hallway.

"Wait a minute--! Oh, here it comes--!" he grunted toward my retreating back.

I shut the door firmly, ignoring his mocking laughter.

Vile cretin! I thought. Then I felt amusement, and I had to stifle a chuckle. No mortal man had ever challenged me so thoroughly.

I moved down the dark corridor.

I wanted music—if only to drown out the sounds of his elimination, which I could still hear through the intervening walls. I turned on a lamp, idled through my collection of phonographic recordings, settling on Brahms' *Tragic Overture, Op.81*.

No one knows for what exact purpose the *Tragic Overture* was designed—some thought *Faust*-- but the sonata is rich and energetic. I set the needle into the groove and retired to my sofa, closing my eyes to drink in the music.

To kill or not to kill, that is the question, I thought, paraphrasing the Bard.

Better yet: "Know yourself, vampire. When you strip away all vanity, you will find that your questions are only the truths you are unwilling to accept."

That advice from a mortal princess I once loved, many hundreds of years ago. Her name was Nina, after the Babylonian goddess of fertility. She is gone now, of course. Gone like all the others. Gone now to dust, like the lovers of my mortal span: Eyya, Nyala. Yes, even Brulde. Gone like my radiant Julia, who died with the city of Pompeii. Gone like my first vampire child, Ilio, and the blood drinker he made after his heart, his gentle bride who was called Priss. All of them dead and gone but for Zenzele, devoured by the insatiable maw of time.

And what strange continent did my Zenzele now roam? What music was she listening to at this very moment? If I know her, it is the piping of the wind or a chorus of crickets, or perhaps the rhythmic crash of ocean waves on some distant moonlit beach.

Zenzele, who is as hard and timeless as I. My soul mate. My female counterpart in this dark and empty universe. If I could move to her by some flourish of magic, I would fly to her with open arms. I needed her counsel, perhaps more than I ever needed it before. She might have been able to reason with me, talk me out of the mad schemes that kept whirling through my mind. At the very least, her company would distract me from my dubious contemplations.

To kill or not to kill... but who did I plan to kill?

That was the question.

If only my love were here to guide me. But Zenzele is lost to me, no less than all the others. She had begged me, two hundred years ago or so, to release her from the chains of my love for her. This was just before I settled here in Liege. She needed her freedom, she'd said. Some time apart. She promised to return. And I let her go. Of course I did. And she had drifted out of my life just as she so often drifted into it, always with her the need to be free, even from the bonds of adoration.

She would return to me. In another hundred years, another thousand. When her loneliness outweighed her desire to wander unfettered through the world, she would return. To me. To the home I kept for her in my heart.,

But would it be too late this time?

Perhaps... it was already too late.

You see, a terrible, selfish plan was incubating in my mind. I was about to do something wicked and evil, and though I pretended to debate this mad and half-formed scheme, I knew.

I had already committed myself.

Yet, I prayed that Zenzele would come... that she'd come and save me from myself!

4

Brahms had finished. The needle rose from the grooves of the phonographic record and returned to its cradle with a click. For a moment the music reverberated in my mind, but then I put it aside. I rose and returned to the my captive's bedchamber. I did not want to be alone with my thoughts. They were too melancholy, too desperate and unnerving.

I paused at his door to listen. I could hear nothing on the other side. Only his breathing. The beating of his heart.

For some odd reason, I felt compelled to announce myself, to ask his permission to enter the room.

Ridiculous! I thought.

I let myself in.

Lukas leapt toward me with a howl, throwing his chains over my head. He meant to garrote me!

He sprawled on the floor, but was on his feet a moment later, spinning around with a frantic expression.

"Really?" I asked from the other side of the room. I was standing casually beside the frosted window, nary a hair out of place.

"Ha!" he yelled, and then he raced across the floor toward me, his fingers curled into claws. He ran until the chain jerked taut and his feet shot out from beneath him.

"Let me know when you tire of this foolishness," I said-- back at the doorway now-- taunting him with a grin.

He rolled onto his hands and knees, panting raggedly, his long bangs hanging in front of his feverish eyes. "I'm going to kill you," he wheezed.

"You cannot," I replied, speaking gently, as to a child. "Don't you understand? You cannot choke me to death. I cannot drown. I do not burn." Frustrated, I strode toward him.

He cringed, expecting me to retaliate.

"Get up," I commanded. "Stand!"

He rose, his body trembling.

"Hold out your hand, Lukas."

"Why?"

"Hold it out!"

He extended his palm toward me.

I took his cohort's switchblade from my pocket. It was the knife Maurice had stabbed me with in the park. Lukas's hand twitched back when he saw it, then he pressed it toward me eagerly. I placed the weapon into his palm.

"Stab me," I said.

Grinning, he pressed the button on the hilt that unleashed the spring-loaded blade. It flashed out with a snick, then he eyed me up and down, licking his lips, trying to decide where he wanted to stick it. At the periphery of my vision, I noticed the front of his boxer shorts beginning to tent out.

"Go on," I encouraged him "Perhaps you will believe me if—"

He shoved the blade into my throat.

I stumbled back, knocked off balance.

"Die, you fucker!" he hissed at me, his eyes avid and insane. His flesh was flushed with excitement, his male organ fully erect.

I couldn't speak with the blade lodged inside my windpipe. Hoping to impress on him the futility of any further attempts on my life, I squared my shoulders and gripped the handle of the blade. Meeting his gaze, I shook my head, and then I used the blade to slice my throat completely open.

He blanched in disbelief, retreating a step, as I sawed the knife in and out of my flesh. I worked it all the way around to my right ear, and then I tilted my chin back to open the wound. It hurt tremendously-- I might be immune to death, but I am not immune to pain-- but I gave no outward sign of my discomfort. I kept my expression bland as I displayed the interior of my larynx.

"Jesus Christ!" he exclaimed.

I lowered my chin. I could already feel the Strix knitting the wound. The living blood shifted inside my body, racing to the region that had been injured. It frothed at the edges of my slashed throat, tingling, as fibrous white tissue went zigzagging back and forth across the gash. The edges drew together like a pair of gruesome lips. Finally, the injury faded from sight. It took-- at most-- four seconds. I swallowed experimentally. Cleared my throat.

"Do you see now?" I asked, slightly hoarse.

I judged by his expression that he was having trouble believing his eyes.

I held my free hand up, palm toward him, then sawed off one of my fingers. I sliced through the flesh, then snapped the bone with a grimace. It was only then, at the sight of the black tendrils wavering from the stump, that he accepted what he was seeing. He covered his mouth.

"Stop, please," he said with a belch, struggling to keep his dinner down.

I held my finger near the stub. The Strix snatched ahold of the severed digit and drew it back into place. In less time than it took me to saw off the appendage, my body was whole again. I flexed my hand to show him.

"I cannot die," I said. "Nothing you can do in your present form can possibly harm me. The light of the sun will not incinerate me. A stake through the heart will only annoy me. I do not burn. The strongest acids will not etch my skin. I am the deathless hostage of time... just as you are mine."

My captive sank onto his bed, his chain clanking on the floor at his feet. "So what do we do now?" he asked softly.

"Just talk," I said soothingly. "I only want to talk."

Exodus of the Neirie
23,000 Years Ago

1

Twilight resolved slowly into night as my vampire child and I watched the Neirie from afar. The band of escaped slaves had traveled all day through intermittent showers, a group of some fifty-odd, work-hardened souls. They had marched relentlessly, even through the lashing rain, pausing only to care for their wounded, the sick and the old.

The clouds had lifted shortly after we arose, hurried on by a westering wind, and it was as if a heavy gray blanket had been swept away from the sky. A multitude of glittering stars winked down at us, a milky river of them, flowing from horizon to horizon.

I was just as exhausted as the Neirie below. My body ached where I had been pierced again and again by the arrows of the Oombai. The living blood had healed me, of course. Healed me without a trace of the injuries I had sustained, but even vampire flesh remembers its wounding, and in remembering, throbbed tiresomely in the night's moist air.

The sight of the Neirie exodus raised my spirits, however. If not for me, these people would not have had the opportunity to win their freedom. I had killed the leaders of the tribe that had subjugated them, decimated its army, allowing the Neirie to rise up, to free themselves from tyranny. The pride I felt in their liberty lifted some of my weariness from my shoulders.

If you are there, father, I hope that you are pleased with your son, I thought, glancing toward the heavens.

I once believed the stars were the campfires of my forefathers, that the night sky was a dark inverted plain that hung suspended over the world. I know now that the stars are really distant suns, much like the sun that warms this busy world. They appear tiny, like flecks of diamond strewn across black satin, but only because of their distance. Still, sometimes I think about my people's myths, and there is a part of me that takes comfort in those old fantasies.

The stars dimmed and brightened like the distant fires of the Neirie camp. If I squinted, I could just make the wayfarers out, moving among their crude shelters, huddling around their glimmering fires for warmth. The refugees we followed had camped for the night in the middle of a glade. How they had managed to find enough dry wood to make their fires, I could not say.

I recalled the pitiful living conditions they were forced to endure in the village of the Ground Scratchers. Worked until they fainted from exhaustion, whipped at the slightest hint of disobedience. Raped. Reviled. Butchered for sacrifice, and sometimes just for sport. Their Oombai masters had kept them in pens like they were animals. Disposed of them without even a modicum of human compassion just as soon as they were too old or worn out to be useful anymore. I was glad they'd escaped, and I intended to escort them to the lands from which they'd been stolen.

Those wicked, greedy Oombai!

Ilio had spotted pillars of smoke rising from their settlement earlier.

"Good! I hope the Neirie razed that cursed village," I replied. "I hope they burned it to the ground!"

I didn't expect to encounter a people so cruel when we came down from the mountains. Ilio still lived then, a mortal child on the cusp of becoming a man. I'd wanted him to have a natural human life, to know a woman's love, to have a family, and so we went to the village of the Ground Scratchers hoping to find him a wife. But the Oombai stole my mortal child from me, made a mockery of all my hopes, and in my wrath, I visited complete and total destruction on them.

"Can you hear them singing, Father?"

Ilio squatted in the high grass at my side, a short, stocky lad with round cheeks and long dark hair woven into braids. He would forever be a halfling, made immortal just at the cusp of manhood, neither fully a man, nor completely a child.

I cocked an eyebrow at him, thinking, *How many times have I chastised you for calling me father?*

It was not that I disliked his familiarity. I loved him as I had loved all of my children, but I feared he had grown too dependent on me. What if something happened to me?

I did not know how utterly immune to death I was. Not then.

But if the boy was anything, he was persistent. He was much more stubborn than I, anyway! I did not have the energy to argue with him about it.

Besides, I reminded myself, *you yourself call him "son" in your thoughts. You have no right to reprimand him.*

Ilio watched the distant campfires, his eyes

glinting in the moonlight. It pained my soul to see him so changed. His form whitened, removed from time. An eternal boy-child. He had only been a vampire a handful of days, and there was still a hint of mortal softness to his flesh, but I knew even that would soon be gone, and then he would be like me—a creature of living stone, cast adrift on the listless watercourse of eternity.

It was all my fault. I should have let him die.

It would have been a mercy. A few moments of pain, fear, then release from his mortal shell, his spirit rising to take its place in the ghost world, or whatever afterlife his people believed in. But I was unwilling to part with him. I had grown to love the boy too much.

"I wish we could go and visit the Neirie," he said. "I would like to see them up close. Join them in their singing."

"It is a joyous music," I agreed. "They celebrate their freedom, but you know it is not safe for you to venture very close to mortal men. Your thirst for their blood would surely get the best of you. Perhaps, when you learn to control your hunger a little better, we might venture among the living. For now, you'll simply have to be satisfied with observing them from afar."

"I understand, Father," he said, dropping his eyes in respect. "Still," he said, peeking up at me with a smile, "I think it would be interesting."

2

I patted him on the shoulder as I rose.

"It won't be forever, Ilio," I assured him. "Though it may seem like that right now."

I scanned the surrounding plains, trying to decide which direction we should go.

"What are you looking for?" Ilio asked.

"You are just made a blood drinker, boy," I explained, squinting toward a distant copse. I could sense many small animals moving in its shadows, tiny warm-blooded creatures that had risen with the night, looking-- like us-- to fill their bellies with food. But I sensed no large animals. Not large enough to satisfy our hunger, anyway. "The living blood inside you must be fed often when you are newly made, or your hunger will torment you unceasingly."

"The Hunger," he muttered, his dark eyes grim. He already knew the relentless hunger of which I spoke. It is maddening in the first few years of immortality. In fact, it is pretty much all a vampire can think about, like a young man who's just had his first fine taste of sex.

"Yes, let us go hunt now!" he said. "I am starving!"

The urgency in his voice made me laugh. He had eaten just a couple hours ago-- filled his gut on the blood of one of the Oombai warriors who'd pursued us on the plains. If you've ever raised teenagers, however, you know how it is with young vampires. Their bellies are bottomless pits. Still, I didn't want Ilio to be tempted by the blood of the Neirie. We had sworn to protect them, not feed on them like parasites.

"We'll go in just a moment," I assured him. "I'm just trying to find some game so we do not wander the grasslands aimlessly."

"Trying to find some game?"

"Yes, now be quiet!" I answered, irritated.

Always so many questions!

I turned in a circle, sending my senses out like invisible tentacles. That is how I imagined them. My senses probing into the high grass, the dry washes, the shadowy copses. Like delicate antennae. I detected insects, hares, a solitary fox. Ilio waited impatiently, then interrupted me again.

"Do you sense anything?"

I sighed.

I decided to take the opportunity to educate him. Turning to address the young man, I said, "You know that your senses are more finely tuned now that you are a blood drinker. Do you remember the first night that I changed you? How the world around you became a whirlwind of sight and sound and smell?"

"Yes...?"

"I taught you how to close your thoughts to it that night," I continued, "but now you must learn something a little more difficult."

He understood. "Now I must learn how to master the whirlwind!"

"It would be a valuable weapon in your arsenal of skills," I said.

He nodded, stepping away from me and squinting into the distance.

"Take your time," I advised him. "Lower the barriers in your mind one at a time, but do it cautiously. Only let in the sensations as you are able to absorb them."

"All right."

Moving behind the boy, I said, "First, allow yourself to see to the full extent that your eyes are capable..."

Ilio gasped, squeezing his eyes shut.

I waited.

After a moment, he opened his eyes to narrow slits.

"I can see... *everything*!" he hissed.

"I know."

"Every star... every blade of grass..."

"I know."

"There is a cloud of mosquitos swirling above a pool of water. It is so far away... but I can see it like I am standing right beside the pond."

He groaned.

"I can see their wings flapping!"

Tears beaded his eyelashes-- the tarry black tears that blood drinkers weep. He jerked back suddenly, as if dodging a spear. "It is too much!" he exclaimed.

"It's all right," I said soothingly.

"I'm sorry, Thest. It is just too much!"

"You have an eternity to master your new skills," I said reassuringly. "You cannot expect to learn them all in one night. "

He nodded, wiping the black tears from his cheeks, but I wondered—I worried... Did he really have an eternity to master his new skills? I had survived the grinding teeth of the glaciers. How many millennia I'd slept in their dreamless embrace I could not say. But I had survived, and I did not look a day older than the moment I was made into this thing that I am. Ilio, however, seemed made of more fragile material. Perhaps it was because he was made so young—only half a man. Perhaps the gifts the living blood bequeathed weakened with each descendent generation. I only knew that Ilio was a far more delicate blood drinker than I. I suspected that he could die, just as my maker had died, and the thought of it was a horror to me.

To lose so fine a son--!

I slapped him on the back.

"Come. Let us fly on the wind. I spied a fine stag while you were trying out your skills."

Ilio nodded, looking morose.

"You can practice some more after we've fed," I promised. I grinned to cheer him, bending down to catch his eye. "I will even tell you tales of my most embarrassing failures. I was a clumsy fool when I was first made into a blood drinker."

Ilio smiled, peeking up at me. "You were?"

"Of course! Did you think I sprang from my maker's lair a master of all of these powers?"

Ilio laughed, and laughing with him, I took three running steps and leapt into the chill night air. "Come, Ilio! Follow me!" I cried back to him as the wind lashed through my great feathered cloak.

3

After we fed, I kept my promise to the boy and told him of my early days as a blood drinker.

My vampire child knew the origin of my parasitic nature. I had already told him of the fierce blood drinker who had attacked our neighbors, a tribe of Neanderthals, and how the warriors of my village had gone to battle the creature in his lair, afraid our community would fall victim to him next.

This the boy knew. That there were two of them, a master and a slave. That we had laid an ambush for the little one, unaware that there was more than just the one. I managed to slay the little one-- with a lucky thrust of my knife-- but his powerful master attacked us moments later.

I woke to find myself in a charnel pit, trapped like an insect in the web of a hungry spider. There, in that terrible pit, he made me what I am. The fiend changed me against my will, tried to break my spirit with violence. He wanted a replacement for the slave that I'd dispatched with my blade, but the living blood wrought a more powerful change upon me than the brutal old beast could ever have imagined.

"I thought only to return to my people after I slew the Foul One," I said. "My only thought, as I climbed from that pit, was to return to the wives and children that I loved."

Ilio listened gravely, the campfire gleaming in his

eyes, his belly full of stag's blood.

"I didn't think of the danger my lust for blood might pose to them," I continued, staring into the fire. "My maker knew only violence, so violence was all that he taught me. I knew nothing of our nature, nothing of our powers, or the hunger that so easily takes possession of us. I was an orphan blood drinker, ignorant and frightened. A danger to every mortal around me."

"What happened when you returned to your people?" Ilio asked, his eyes wide with trepidation. "You didn't hurt your children, did you?"

"No," I sighed. "Not my family, thank the ancestors! But I did hurt someone, I'm ashamed to admit. It was a man named Ludd, an old warrior. He had stayed behind to defend the village while the younger men went off to war.

"Gray-headed like my father he was, but always glum, always looking on the dark side of the world. He was standing guard when I returned. We had moved our camp to a place called Bubbling Waters, hoping to evade the demon-ghost who was preying on our neighbors, but the Foul One had found our village anyway, snatched away some children and a good mother named Pendra.

"Ludd was too excited at first to notice how I'd changed. We went to rouse the camp, walking side by side. We were about halfway back when he became suspicious of me. He'd finally noticed how pale I was, how my eyes seemed to catch the light of the moon, but it was too late for him by then. I could smell his blood, and I lost control of myself. I attacked him. I fed on his blood, and then I took his body and hid it in a bog.

"I knew then that I couldn't trust myself to return to my tribe. Even though I had slain the fiend who was preying on my people, my maker had defeated me, for

I lost the very thing I had fought him to preserve."

"So what did you do?" Ilio asked.

I poked a stick into our fire and watched the sparks swirl into the sky.

"I hid," I said. "I found a cave in a remote mountaintop—one that overlooked my village—and there I stayed, year after year after year. I protected my people, mostly from myself. I explored my new strength, my powerful new senses. I fed on game while I tried to master the Hunger. I learnt how to fly, how to scale sheer rock walls. I learned that I could stay underwater for hours at a time, and that my body would quickly heal itself no matter how terribly I was injured. I was never able to tame the blood lust, though. I attacked any warm-blooded creature that ventured too near to me. It was impossible for me to resist it.

"In despair, I watched my wives and children grow older. My male companion, Brulde, died, then my Fat Hand wife Eyya. Nyala died the following winter. My children married and had children of their own, and then their children married and had children.

"From time to time I came down from the mountain to defend them. When our enemies came slinking through the pass, intent on snatching away our children, I flew down from my cave like a howling god of death. I tore them apart with my bare hands, fed on them without remorse. Later, when I spied a flood that threatened to sweep away the village, I flew to them faster than the water could flow, and commanded them to retreat to higher ground.

"They called me Thest-u'un-Mann, the Man Who is a Ghost. It was many, many generations before I was able to move among them, and even then, when I appeared unto my children's children's children, it always seemed to be a very uncertain thing for me, the battle between my willpower and my hunger for their blood."

Ilio whined unhappily, "And how many generations must I wait before I can walk among mortal men? You are so much more powerful than I, Thest!" He tossed a stick into the flames. "Perhaps, for me, it is a hopeless aspiration!"

I laughed affectionately. "Don't be so dramatic, Ilio! You have one advantage I never had."

"What?" he demanded, overwrought by his imaginings.

I grinned broadly and thumped my chest. "Me, silly boy! You have me! I will be your teacher, your counsel and your guide. I will hurry you on your path to mastery."

"And will you also be a father to me?" he asked slyly, peeking at me from the corner of his eye.

"Yes, boy. Yes," I surrendered with a sigh. "If a father is what you require to be content, then I will be a father to you."

Ilio whooped and leapt across the fire to me. He was not as small a child as he believed, however, and his enthusiastic hug knocked me flat onto my back.

"Control yourself!" I laughed. "You are much too big to jump into my lap like that!"

Ilio rolled off of me, smiling up at the stars. "I am sorry, Father," he said. "It is just... I am blessed by the gods to have a guardian like you. You saved me from the blood drinker who stalked and killed my tribe. You raised me as your own child, and then saved me again when those terrible Oombai did their best to slay me. If it wasn't for you, I'd just be rags and bones by now. Instead, I have become a magic spirit. Or a god, like the ones my uncles spoke of when we gathered at night by the fire."

I turned on my side, looking at him sternly. "No, Ilio. You are not a god. Never think that! You can perish just like any mortal child. You are only stronger, more resilient, than our mortal brethren. Our kind can be slain. I've done it with these very hands-- and I was a mortal man when I did it. So do not deceive yourself. You are no god. You are only a blood drinker."

"I am sorry," he said quickly. "I only spoke in excitement."

"That is all right, Son," I told him, putting my arms behind my head. "If you promise to be careful, I promise not to coddle you. You must become strong so that you can care for yourself if anything should happen to me."

"I will work hard to master my new skills, Father," Ilio swore. "And I will work even harder to master this hunger for blood. I want to live among the mortals. I want to have a home."

He smiled then, his eyes twinkling at some inner rumination.

"And women," he murmured. "I would like to have mates. As many as you once had. Two. Maybe even three."

I chuckled, staring up at the heavens. "*Three* wives?" I asked. "No one can say you lack ambition, Son!"

4

As the world rolled round to the day side of the heavens, I took Ilio into my arms and wrapped us both in my cloak. It was a beautiful garment, that cloak, lined with sleek fur inside and out, and boasting a bristling collar of crisp raven feathers. It was regal and resplendent, and I was inordinately proud of that silly thing. It also made a good shelter for us during the daylight hours.

You should already know, my cherished readers, that Hollywood's depiction of vampires is something of a joke. How could any preternatural creature survive even a week if they exploded into flames at the slightest wisp of sunlight on their skin? I assure you, we don't! In fact, there's a sunlamp sitting less than a meter from my desk as I type this passage. It is casting its artificial daylight upon a lovely potted lily. But just imagine if I were a fictional Hollywood vampire. I'd be steaming pile of ash right now, destroyed by a lamp.

Actually, why don't we dispose of all those myths, right this very instant, especially for those of you who have just recently "tuned in".

First and foremost: crucifixes. No offense to you Christians, but I find crucifixes repulsive. Not because they have any kind of supernatural power over me. They don't. I find them abhorrent because of the atrocities they remind me of. If you've seen as many mortal men put to death on them as I have, you'd likely feel the same way. It is a terrible, painful way to die, one that was quite popular long before the followers of Christ made it a symbol of their religion. If I never have to see another soul writhing on one of those things, dying slowly of dehydration and exposure, I will be a happy blood drinker. For that matter, why a crucifix? Why not venerate some other symbol of Christ's purported miracles? And we are accused of being morbid creatures!

Let's see... The smell of garlic does not repel me. (Really? An herb?) I can see myself in mirrors just fine. I can walk right into your home uninvited—though I wouldn't, out of respect, if you are a good person. I cannot change into a bat or a wolf, although I think that it would be a wonderful power to command. I cannot turn to fog, or fold myself flat and slip through a door crack. It's all just rubbish, really, most of the legends that are associated with vampires. Hollywood hokum.

As for sunlight, the only reason we shrink from the sun is because it stings our sensitive eyes. We are nocturnal predators, after all, and roving about in daytime is like having two burning sticks shoved into our eyes. Thank the ancestors for Ray-bans!

That is the only reason Ilio and I retired as the first rays of the sun crept across the Pannonian Plains.

Simple comfort.

Ilio continued to talk, as all young men are wont to do, but I was tired. Not so much physically, as vampires have extremely hardy constitutions, but mentally. Like all living things we need to dream.

As Ilio prattled on about the Neirie slave women who had seduced him, asking me rather personal questions about my previous sexual experiences, I answered as briefly as I could, letting my mind drift. The last thing I remember him asking was, "But do they like it as much as we do, Thest? Our things going inside them?"

An instant later, it seemed, my eyes were flashing open in the dark.

5

I could tell by the light glinting through the seams of my cloak that several hours had passed. I don't normally awaken during the daylight hours unless I am disturbed.

Something was amiss.

It wasn't Ilio. The boy was sleeping beside me, still as a child's doll.

We were not in any immediate danger, but I felt a sense of urgency. Something was wrong, but what was it?

I lowered my mental barriers, reaching out with my senses. Almost immediately, a flood of sensory information overwhelmed my thoughts: sounds, smells, even tastes. The denizens of the plains deafened me with their chatter, their calls and yelps and buzzing and croaking. I could hear the wind blowing across the grassy hills. Smell wildflowers and earth, the coppery scent of mortal blood--

There!

Mortal men. Crying out in anger and pain. The whisper of arrows and spears, the clash of clubs and fists. A battle! And not very far away. Well within the range of my preternatural senses.

The Neirie were under attack!

I prodded the boy. "Ilio, wake up!"

"What is it?" he cried, almost throwing the cloak off in his surprise.

Restraining his arms, I spoke quickly. "The Neirie are being attacked. I must go and aid them, but it is still daytime. Your eyes are not yet trained to withstand the light of the sun."

"You go to make war again?" he said excitedly. "Please, Father, let me fight with you this time!"

"You cannot fight blind, Son," I said. "Now, cover your eyes. I rise to their defense."

I didn't wait for his acquiescence. Ilio cupped his hands over his eyes as I threw aside the cloak. He cried out a little as I rose, but I bent quickly and spread the cloak back over him.

"I will return as soon as I can," I said, patting him on the head, and then I surveyed the land to the south, the direction the war sounds were coming from.

I shielded my eyes with my hand, but sticky black tears began to dribble down my cheeks anyway. The sky was an open roaring furnace, the world around me baked in its glare.

I scrubbed the black tears from my cheeks,

blinking like a mole. I could hear them-- the howls of men fighting, the wails of men dying-- but my eyes were having a hard time adjusting to the light.

Then I saw them, very far away.

"Ancestors punish them!" I cursed.

"What is it, Father? Tell me what is happening!" Ilio called from beneath my cloak.

"The damned Oombai have sent warriors to recapture the Neirie!" I hissed. I looked east, then back to the south. "The Neirie have split into two groups. One half their number has turned back to engage their pursuers while the rest flee southeast in hope of escape."

"How many Oombai are there? Can you see well enough to help the Neirie fight?" Ilio asked.

"There are a great many Oombai warriors," I said, "but I will not stand idle while brave men die for their freedom!"

"Then go, Father," the boy said. "But take care! Don't make me an orphan again!"

I smiled grimly, eyeing the two armies who waged war in the distance. A moment longer and my eyes would be adapted to the light. Just a moment longer...

Then woe to the Oombai who thought to oppose me again!

6

I was disappointed I couldn't wear my cloak into the fray. What a frightening figure I would have made, swooping down upon my enemies like a monstrous bird of prey. Alas, Ilio needed the garment more than I! He was still too newly made to endure the glare of the sun.

I swiped at the tacky black tears the sun had

squeezed from my eyes. Even for me, the pain was nearly unbearable. It felt like my skull had been cleaved open and filled with molten lava.

Pushing my discomfort aside, I raced forward, pumping my legs faster and faster until the high plains grass hissed past me on both sides. My body cut through the field like the prow of a boat. I took two great leaps, each more powerful than the last, and then I threw my arms to my sides and catapulted my body into the sky.

My garments snapped upon my flesh. The wind whistled in my ears. My shadow leapt across the plains below like a fish breaching the surface of an emerald lake.

Flight... it is one of the few vampiric gifts that I unconditionally enjoy. All the rest of our preternatural abilities have at least one unpleasant drawback. Our penetrating senses often overwhelm. Our superhuman strength and speed can maim, even kill, if we are not careful to govern our movements. But flight... Ah, but I'm sure you've dreamed of it yourself! I revel in its sensations: being unanchored from the earth, the wind battering my cheeks, lashing through my hair. Glorious-- even when it carries me to war!

As the battleground swelled quickly beneath me, I surveyed the chaos. Just a few seconds had passed from the time I launched myself from the earth to my descent into their midst, but it was enough to take an accounting of the armies that clashed below. It was enough to see that the Neirie were desperately outnumbered.

I counted twenty-seven Neirie. They were fighting more than sixty Oombai soldiers.

It was easy enough to distinguish between the two groups. The Neirie were dressed in no finer garments than they'd worn in the Oombai slavepens.

Frayed rags hung from their wiry limbs, and those were the fortunate ones. Some of the Neirie men were fighting naked. And their weapons were just as poor as their clothing. A few of the Neirie were armed with knives or spears. Most, however, fought with crude clubs or heavy stones—and some even bare fists!

Brave men-- doomed, but brave. Already, many had fallen.

I came hurtling out of the sky from the north, so my shadow did not fall among the combatants. Still, two dozen pairs of eyes watched me descend from the heavens. I saw Neirie and Oombai alike fall back in superstitious awe, their eyes bulging, their jaws dropping to their chests in disbelief. I heard cries of horror. A few men shouted in joy, but only a few. Optimists. Or the pious, thinking their prayers had been answered.

I landed in the midst of them, the blood-speckled grass rippling outwards in an expanding ring. The confused and frightened warriors fell away on both sides. "What is it? Who has joined the fray?" the men in the back shouted as their brothers pressed against them, trying to retreat. Those who had kept their wits replied: "It is the white god from the mountains! The blood god who destroyed the Elders!"

Ah, now you flee, you wicked, wicked Oombai!

I rose slowly from my crouch, displaying my fangs with a fearsome hiss. If they were not already frightened, the sight of my razor-sharp grin must have frozen their hearts with terror. Tall, powerfully muscular, and with a great shaggy mane of dark auburn hair, I can strike an impressive pose when I want to—even without a fancy cloak!

The Oombai warriors on the front line turned immediately and fled, stricken with mortal fear... and rightly so! In their haste to escape, they actually began to trample the men standing behind them.

I couldn't let them go. I knew I had to break the backbone of the Oombai-- now, this day-- else they'd continue to be a thorn in the side of the Neirie refugees. If I didn't, they would pursue the bedraggled fugitives until they'd recaptured or killed them all.

The knowledge filled me with sadness for the killing I must do... but I wouldn't be telling you the truth if I didn't admit that it was only a *little* sadness.

Mostly I was pissed, to use the modern vernacular.

With a blood-curdling snarl, I launched myself upon the frightened phalanx of soldiers. I sliced into their ranks, loosing the reins of my careful control. Indeed, I pushed my powers further than I ever had before!

I moved in a blur, flattening skulls with my fists, sending heads, like startled crows, flapping from the shoulders they once had perched upon. I laughed, seeing some of the headless bodies continuing to run, though it was a terrible sight, and my laughter born more of horror than amusement. I tore the heart from the chest of one, and still clutching the bloody organ, punched my fist through the face of another. One Oombai warrior fell, and I seized his ankles and tore his body in half. Ten, I killed, then twenty. I ripped off one warrior's arm and swung it into the face of another, sending the mutilated man whirling bodily across the field.

In minutes I was covered in their blood, my chest heaving, my mind empty save one thought: *Kill!*

That single word drummed inside my skull, throbbing like a heart, or a hard cock: *Kill! Kill! Kill!*

I knocked a man down and stomped his skull flat. I grabbed another by the arm and flung him as high into the air as I could. He sailed into the sky, spinning end over end, as I blurred forward and threw another, and they collided at the apex of their flight.

Forty men I killed. In a whirlwind of bloody fists and feet, that number rose quickly to fifty.

The last few fell to their knees and began to beg for mercy. Crying. Clutching their hands together and shaking them.

"Mercy?" I snarled in disbelief. "I'll show you mercy! I'll show you the mercy that the Oombai showed their slaves!" Then I threw myself on them and sent their souls shrieking to whatever deity judged their race in the ghost world.

Dead. All dead, I thought, their blood dripping from my flesh.

And there was so much of it! I looked like I'd bathed in a river of it!

I brought my hands up, watched the blood trickle down my arms. The thirst for all that hot salty blood squeezed my insides, yammered inside my skull to be satisfied. I put my bloody fingers in my mouth and sucked them, my eyes rolling back in ecstasy. I licked it from my forearms. More! I wanted more! Desperate to slake my hunger, I seized the last man by his plated vest and brought his broken neck to my fangs.

That drumbeat of desire--! It pounded inside my skull, driving me to gorge myself. I had to silence it. I had to drown that fire or I'd be goaded to kill them all. I would turn on the Neirie and tear them to pieces just as surely as I'd destroyed their pursuers.

Blood! More blood! Must feed!

I tore the man's neck open with my teeth.

Oh, ancestors, yes! The blood! Still hot! Drink it all! Suck it out!

The mortal was still twitching. A faint spark of life lingered in his eyes, but I gave no thought to his pain or fear. I drained him, and then I squeezed his body against mine, crushing it to my chest to squeeze out every last drop. His bones crackled inside his flesh. Bloody shit spattered the grass beneath him. I drained the mangled corpse, and then I threw the empty husk aside.

The Neirie stood at a distance, moaning in horror and disbelief. I could hear them behind me. *Smell* them behind me. There was a part of me that wanted to kill them. Slaughter them like I'd slaughtered their enemies. I wanted to feed upon them until my belly sloshed with their blood--

No, monster! You have sworn to protect them!

I stood with my back to them, trembling, until I'd gotten myself under some semblance of self-control. It was no easy task. I'd never unleashed my lust for violence so completely, and like a ravening beast, the monster didn't want to go back inside its cage. I ground my teeth together, taking deep breaths like a mortal man would do. I squeezed my fists.

Finally I turned to address the Neirie warriors.

"No!" I cried out, horrified by what I saw.

The Neirie were down on their knees, their faces to the earth. They were worshipping me!

7

"No!" I cried. "Ancestors, no!"

The Neirie men had prostrated themselves. They were pressing their foreheads to the ground with their arms stretched out before them. I could not understand the words they were babbling, but the intent was obvious. They were chanting, praying to me, as if I were some incarnate deity.

I strode toward the emaciated men, shouting, "Stand up! What are you doing? Do you really wish to trade one master for another?"

The men nearest to me moaned, trembling at the fury in my voice, but none rose. I realized that, in my outrage, I had shouted at them in my native tongue, the language of the River People. I switched to the tongue of the Denghoi, the language spoken by Ilio's tribe, which the slave woman Aioa had known. Surely some of these Neirie must speak Denghoi.

"Stand! Stand! Up on your feet! You are not slaves! You are free men! Do not grovel in the dirt, you fools!"

A few of the men seemed to understand. They raised their foreheads from the ground, blinking at me in fear and confusion.

"Up!" I cried, gesturing with my arms. "I said 'up'! Would you trade one master for another?"

The few who understood Denghoi rose haltingly. They stared at me in disbelief, then called out to their brothers. I smiled and nodded my head as the rest of the Neirie men clambered one by one to their feet.

I recognized one of the men from the Oombai festival Ilio and I had attended. It was the giant with the curly red hair. The one who had been forced to mate publicly for the entertainment of the Oombai. I could tell from his bold gaze that he was the leader of these men... or would be soon, when they looked for one to command them.

"You there. What is your name?" I asked him.

"Tapas," he said. His voice was a deep baritone.

He stood two heads taller than I... and I was an unusually tall man. Nearly a head taller than most of my peers.

It was strange looking up at someone rather than down, as I was accustomed to doing. If I were a mortal, I might have been intimidated.

"Tell your men that I am no god, Tapas," I said.

I consciously softened my voice. I did not want them to worship me, but I did not want to sound as if I were giving orders either. I wanted them to regard me as an equal... or as near to an equal as a mortal can feel standing in the presence of a powerful blood drinker.

Tapas had a long, squarish face with crude, ugly features, his flesh riddled with scars, but his eyes were bright and intelligent. He called out to the others.

They crept forward uncertainly, looking to him for guidance.

Tapas talked to them in a rapid, sharp-sounding tongue. One of the men shouted out a question, and he replied sternly.

The one who had shouted glared at me with hostility, or perhaps it was simply hatred for my kind. He would try to kill me some time later, this man, but he was a stranger to me that day. At the time, I only thought it odd that he should glare at me so venomously, considering I'd most likely saved his life.

Tapas returned his attention to me.

"You are *T'sukuru,*" he said.

It was the Oombai word for "blood drinker".

I nodded. "I am called Thest."

The red-headed giant bowed his head. "I saw you sitting at the festival with Bhulloch and the other Elders."

"I was not there willingly," I told him.

"We suspected as much," Tapas said. "Though I was not there during the battle which ensued, there was much talk among the slave caste concerning the melee. It was said that the Elders slew your companion...?"

"My son yet lives," I said, and the giant looked surprised.

He absorbed that information for a moment, then leaned toward me with a grin. "I was watching from my pen two nights later when you flew down from the tree and killed the ancient one called Y'vort. It was quite entertaining."

"The Oombai Elders offended me greatly. I could

not let such a transgression go unpunished."

One of the men standing nearby tapped Tapas on the shoulder. The giant leaned down and the bearded man whispered into his ear. He needn't have covered his lips with his hand, however. His words were a mystery to me... though his language sounded oddly familiar.

Tapas nodded to the whisperer, then stood straight again.

"This man says the name 'Thest' is known to his people," Tapas said, regarding me with keen interest. "He says it is the name of one of their gods."

The bearded whisperer ogled me with religious awe.

"A Neirie god?" I asked, confused.

"Do not call us Neirie!" Tapas snapped, anger flushing his cheeks. He wrestled with his temper, then smiled at me contritely. "I apologize, but Neirie is the Oombai word for 'taken'. I am from a tribe called the Vis'hantu. There are Pruss and Tanti and also Grell among our numbers. We were stolen from our homelands by those Oombai whoremasters, but we are no longer 'taken'. We are free men!"

"It was not my intent to offend," I bowed. "I am a stranger to this region. Neirie was the only word I knew to call you."

Tapas spread his open palms, a gesture of acceptance.

I placed my hands on my hips, looked past Tapas to the wounded and dead lying sprawled across the field. "I can help your fallen, if they are not too badly injured," I said. "My T'sukuru blood has healing properties."

Tapas looked suddenly appalled. I think he was ashamed he hadn't thought of it himself. "Yes... yes, of course! If you would grant us such a favor--!"

Of the two dozen men who had engaged the

Oombai in battle, nearly half that number had fallen before I joined the fray. Of those, only three were strong enough to recover from their injuries. The rest were either dead or too far gone into the ghost world to be summoned back to the land of the living.

I moved from man to man, hunkering down over the wounded so that I could examine them. I was no medicine man, but I could tell the living from the dead, especially with my enhanced senses. If I did not hear the heart beating inside a man, I moved on. There was nothing I could do for them. Those I found still clinging to life, no matter how grievous their injuries, I tried to heal.

To do this, I summoned the living blood up from the pit of my stomach, then spat it onto my fingers and smeared the glistening fluid onto their wounds. I had learned the trick of it from the Oombai. It is always painful to summon up the Strix. It is easier to slice my tongue with my teeth, but that only renders a few drops of the precious liquid, and the injuries I tried to heal that day required more than just a drop or two. I was trying to heal men who had been gutted, their throats slashed, their heads bashed in. I worked my way across the field of battle as the Neirie observed with superstitious awe, anointing the injuries of their wounded with my blood, then waiting to see if the flesh would respond.

Sometimes it did. If they were not too far gone, their injuries melted away. Vitality returned to their bodies with shocking abruptness, and then they rose, grinning and blinking in disbelief, their compatriots rushing in to embrace them.

One man fell to his knees and began to kiss my feet, sobbing, "Thest! Thest!" over and over.

The awed whispers of the Neirie circled the open field like a swarm of buzzing insects, a low susurration of worshipful voices.

And the carcasses of the Oombai who'd attacked them?

Already the vultures were circling.

8

Tapas invited me to travel with his people, which I graciously declined. "My son is waiting for me back at our camp," I explained. "He is young and inexperienced, not yet strong enough to resist our hunger for blood. I would not be able to trust his restraint around your people, and I cannot abandon him."

"The boy is a blood drinker?" Tapas asked, raising his eyebrows. "I thought he was a mortal child."

He was confused. These men did not understand how a blood drinker was made, not completely.

"He is T'sukuru now," I replied. I was reluctant to say more to the giant, to reveal the mysteries of our vampire nature. I feared I might provoke the desires of these long suffering men. Who wouldn't covet our powers, especially if they didn't understand the cost? I did not like the way his companions were watching me either, as if they were ready to drop to their knees and worship me at the slightest indication that I might desire it. I did not want to be worshipped, nor did I wish to fuel their messianic fantasies.

Tapas sensed my reservations. "I am happy your boy lives," he said. "I had a family of my own before the Oombai captured me. A wife, two young daughters. I doubt my wife still waits for me. It has been years since I was taken, but I would like to see them anyway. I would like to know if they still live."

While we conversed, some of the Neirie warriors were picking through the bodies of the Oombai I had slain. They were taking what they could salvage:

clothing and armor that was not too bloodied or broken by my rampage to be of use to them, the dead men's weapons and shields. Others hovered near us like sycophants, watching me with awestruck eyes. They whispered to one another when they thought I wasn't looking.

"What are your plans? Where do you go from here?" I asked.

Tapas squinted toward the southeast, his upper lip peeled back from his teeth. "We travel first to the land of the Tanti, the home of these men who stare at you so worshipfully." He nodded to our whispering attendants with a twinkle in his eyes. "They are a spiritual people, and you have the good fortune of sharing a name with one of their gods," he said.

I glanced toward the men who continued to hover. "I don't know if I'd call that good luck," I murmured. "My people did not believe in gods. We revered our ancestors. From what I've seen of gods, they're much too generous with suffering in exchange for all this bowing and scraping."

Tapas laughed. "That could certainly be debated," he said. "My people also had little use for gods. The Tanti's gods certainly did not free us from the Oombai, despite all their prayers. Except through death, perhaps... but what good is that?" He sighed, looking away pensively. Remembering, perhaps, the indignities he had suffered. Finally, he blinked, resumed our conversation. "When we reach the Tanti homeland, we shall all rest for a while," he continued. "The Tanti might bore you to death with talk of gods and fishing, but they are a generous people and do not turn away foreigners. Once we have recovered from our journey, those who are not Tanti will continue on to their own lands. The Grell. The Pruss. Their lands lie to the north of the Tanti. I and my fellow Vis'hantu will journey south, to our lands." He glanced at me, curious. "Where lies your homeland, T'sukuru? Do you live in the east, where the other blood drinkers dwell?"

"No," I answered quickly. I didn't want to be associated with such brutal creatures. "I come from the northwest, from a land far removed from these climes. My people, however, are long departed from this world. I have become a wanderer. Alone, but for my adopted son."

"It is a hard thing for a man to be without a home," Tapas mused. "Are you certain you will not accompany us on our journey? You are T'sukuru, but my people would welcome you. It might take a while for them to trust you fully, but we have played host to your kind in the past. Other wandering blood drinkers, I should say. Not the T'sukuru of the east. You could have a home again. Men you could call brother." He grinned slyly. "Maybe even a wife-- or many wives, if that is your custom."

I laughed. "You tempt me, Tapas! I will consider it. My son and I watch over your group from a distance. We have sworn to protect you during your journey, but once you are safely home..." I shrugged. "I know not where we will go after that."

I did not tell him that I was tempted to continue east, to find this land of the blood drinkers that everyone spoke of. If not for the reputation they had among the mortal men of this region, I would seek them out for certain, but I feared for Ilio's safety. The blood drinkers of the east had such a fearsome reputation!

The fiery globe of the sun hung suspended over the horizon, casting a gold, slanting light across the great open plains. It would be dark in a couple more hours. I needed to return to Ilio. He would be worried, no doubt, of the outcome of the battle. Also, once it was dark, he would be free to move about on his own.

If I did not return soon, he'd come to investigate, and I did not want him to chance across any of these mortals, not without me at his side to help guard his behavior. Mortal blood is always so tempting!

"It's encouraging to know that we have such powerful guardians looking after us," Tapas said. He looked as if he wanted to clap me on the back, but he restrained himself, hesitant to take such a familiar attitude with me. "Know that you have our gratitude, Thest. If not for you, the Oombai would have slain every man on this battlefield today. And they would have caught the rest shortly after. Dragged them back to those horrible pens. Or worse. I have no doubt of it."

Glancing at the Oombai corpses, I said, "I do not think you need worry about them anymore."

The Neirie scavengers were fighting with the vultures over the bodies now, waving their spears and clubs at the birds and cursing them. The vultures did not seem overly concerned with the mortals, however. They merely waddled away, wings spread out, or flapped to a less disputed locale. There were plenty of dead bodies.

More scavengers would come soon, though, I thought. Larger animals. Dangerous ones, perhaps.

"I think the threat of the Oombai has passed this day, as well," Tapas said, looking in the same direction, his face unreadable. "We are truly free now."

9

"Father?" Ilio called. "Are you unharmed?"

I had landed several meters away and approached the boy from the south. As I suspected, Ilio had remained awake, anxious of my return.

"I am unharmed, boy," I said, trying to contain my amusement.

The young man sat beside the ash of last night's fire, my cloak still draped over his body. As I drew near, I saw him quake. "I smell blood," the lad whispered urgently.

I looked at my arms, which were covered in a veneer of glazed blood. Much of the blood had been absorbed through my flesh, but not all. What remained was black and crusting, falling away in flakes. My clothing was stiff with it. Ruined, I suspected.

"I need to bathe," I said. "I wear the blood of many Oombai warriors."

"I heard the cries of your enemies in the distance," the boy said. "Screams of fear... then the sound of them dying." The cloak shifted as he turned his head toward me. "You killed them all, didn't you?"

"Every last one," I said.

It was not a boast. I was simply speaking the truth. Now that the battle was over, I felt only weariness and remorse. I do not like to kill. Or perhaps I should say, my higher spirit does not like to kill. There is a pit in every man's soul wherein lies the most ancient part of us, the reptile spirit, which revels in violence and mayhem and the satiation of our basest desires. I am no exception. It is what makes war so terrible for the men who partake of it: remembering the part of their spirit which reveled in the killing. It is enough to give a man nightmares... and an immortal an eternity of them.

I looked to the west, where the sun was melting upon a scrim of blue-gray mountains. The clouds above were the color of lacerated flesh. I wiped tacky red tears from my cheeks, squinting into the molten sky, then turned to my young companion.

"The sun is setting," I said. "Why don't you

remove the cloak? Let's see if you can tolerate the light."

Ilio eased back one edge of the cloak. He yelped and jerked it closed. I waited while he gathered his resolve, and then he surprised me by tossing the entire thing off.

He sat cross-legged, his eyes squeezed down to slits. I saw his fingers curling into the folds of the cloak. Black tears streaked down his cheeks, but he endured the pain. "It burns!" he hissed, but he did not relent.

My brave, strong son!

I hauled him to his feet. "Can you walk? I would like to bathe. I want this repulsive blood off me. Then we can hunt, if you'd like."

Ilio nodded, his lips split back from his teeth. He had very fine, very white vampire fangs. He wiped his cheeks, smearing tarry blood.

"Yes... I'm starving," he said.

His flesh was like mine: milky white and with a faint crystalline texture. Glints of orange and yellow and blue winked upon the contours of his face when he turned his head to look at me.

"Can you see?" I asked, pushing through the grass beside him.

"The pain is abating a little."

"The light will always sting your eyes, but a man can learn to put aside his pain if he sets his mind to it. It is a simple skill to master, even for a mortal."

"Yes, Father," Ilio murmured, opening his eyes a little wider. His pupils had constricted to tiny pinpricks, but he suffered without complaint.

"Good, good. Never surrender to pain. Embrace it. Defy it."

I sniffed the air, then angled away to the north.

"This way."

Ilio stumbled over a hummock, not yet

accustomed to the daylight, but I did not have to tarry for him.

Not far from our camp, a shallow rill of water meandered through a sodden flat choked with reeds. We removed our boots and tiptoed across the slurping mud. Ilio washed his hands and face in the idle stream while I stripped off my stiff clothes. As I hung my bloody garments upon the bulrushes, I told him of the battle, and the invitation the Neirie had made to us.

"Perhaps we could visit their camp after we feed," Ilio suggested. "I would not be so tempted by their blood with a full belly. You see how well I am able to endure the sunlight. I can endure my thirst for blood as well."

I came across a human ear in the pocket of my breeches and threw it away with a grunt. "We shall see," I said.

Ilio sighed and splashed his hand through the water.

"Don't pout," I said. "It is not becoming."

"Easy for you to say. You make all the decisions," Ilio complained.

"True," I laughed, shucking off my breeches. I squatted in the middle of the stream and began to splash the water up onto my arms and chest. Ilio twitched, his nose wrinkling at the smell of the blood that swirled toward him in the current.

"What if I leave the decision to you, Ilio? Can you judge your self-control honestly, despite what your desires urge you to do?"

"Yes!"

"So tell me true. Can you resist the lure of their blood? Have you the strength to endure the hunger if we should go and walk among them?"

I sidled closer to him as I spoke, allowing the blood of the Oombai to drip from my skin. The moistened blood trickled down my abdomen and limbs.

Ilio's eyes flashed at me, and his body began to tremble. I could see the desire welling up in him, seizing control of his mind. He wanted to throw himself upon me and lick up all the blood. Perhaps he even fantasized of biting me.

He scrambled away with a cry.

"Ilio...!" I called after him.

"No," he moaned, crouching amid the reeds. He hung his head in defeat. "Not yet. I am not yet strong enough to resist it."

"Take heart, Son. You see your weakness and confess it aloud. That is a good thing," I said proudly. "A man cannot address his weaknesses if he refuses to see them. We will try to strengthen your will. Tonight, when we hunt, you will only drink half your fill of blood."

10

It was many night's journey to the land of the Tanti. We followed the slave refugees from a safe distance, staying close enough to aid them in the event of some threat, but far enough away that we were not tempted to prey upon them.

In the evenings, when we roused, we enjoyed the simple music the people made around their fires, though from time to time it also filled me with a great melancholy. Many of their songs reminded me of the songs my own people used to sing in the evening, when our bellies were full and our children were sleeping in our laps and we had gathered outside the Elder Siede for community.

It was enough to bring a black tear to my eye, listening to the melodies. I remembered laying with my wives to music like that, making love as our tribesmen sang at the cave of the elders, night not quite come but the evening insects chirruping, the flesh of my wives moving sinuously beneath my body, the heat and smoky smell of our wetus mingling with the scent of our sweat.

I wanted to reach out and grasp those memories, pull them to me and press them into my heart. I wanted to fly from this cold existence and take refuge in the arms of my old lovers, but they were gone to me now, never to return.

Ilio saw the melancholy come over me and would try to distract me with idle talk. He would talk about the gods of his people, the extinct Denghoi, or badger me with his endless questions.

Sometimes it worked. Sometimes my mood would lighten, and I forgot the past for a little while. Other times, he could not draw me from my gloom, and I had to leave him for a while.

I would run through the grassy plains at full speed, racing beneath the moon and stars, run so fast my passage ripped the grass from the ground by its roots, run and run until I was far away and I could rage in solitude at my fate… or weep.

One night, Ilio looked up at me in surprise as he hardened the tip of a spear in the fire. "Do you hear that, Father?" he asked with a grin. "They are singing to you! They are singing to Thest!"

I had been listening absently to the melody but paying little attention to the words. I never knew what they were saying anyway. I craned my head so that I could listen more closely and was shocked to hear my name woven into their song.

"That must be the Tanti," I said after a while. "One of their gods is named Thest, too."

"I believe they sing to you, not their god," Ilio replied. "They are praising you for saving them from the Oombai."

"Your stick is burning merrily, boy," I said, nodding toward the fire.

"Oh!" he cried, and shook it out.

The next evening, we woke to find that the Neirie had left an offering to us. We smelled it immediately upon rising. A gourd was perched upon a stone a short distance from our camp. Inside was a small amount of blood. Cold, congealed, but human.

"Superstitious fools," I growled, after we had identified the source of the blood tribute. "Do they mean to tempt us to murder?"

Ilio stared at the gourd with wide, glittering eyes, his nostrils flaring. He looked like he was about to snatch the gourd from my hands. He had been trying to strengthen his willpower the last few nights, drinking as little blood as he could manage. The offering those silly Tanti put out for us—I was fairly certain it was the Tanti who left it—had nearly pushed the boy over the edge. He was trembling, his fingers opening and closing compulsively.

"Ilio!" I shouted.

The boy jumped, his eyes jerking from the gourd to my face.

"We cannot accept this tribute," I said. "It would only strengthen the temptation to feed on them."

"Yes, I... I understand," Ilio whispered. "But, Father... *the smell*!"

I held the gourd out to him. He jumped back as if I'd tried to strike him.

"Take it," I said. "Pour it out upon the earth."

"I... I don't think that I can!"

"Yes, you can," I insisted. "Pour it out. Then we will hunt."

He nodded, took the gourd into his hands. The blood inside was thick and dark. Several insects had drowned in the sticky fluid, tempted to their deaths by the rich, salty scent. I wondered if the boy could do it. Could he pour it out, as I'd commanded, or would he give in to his bloodlust and try to gulp it like a greedy child before I stopped him?

He made a noise that was halfway between a choke and a sob, his hands trembling, but he tipped the gourd and poured the scarlet fluid into the grass.

"I'm very proud of you," I said, patting him on the shoulder.

"Foolish mortals!" he snarled, throwing the gourd into the dark.

He threw it with his full vampire strength, and it shot away like an arrow into the night sky, hooting.

"Come, let us hunt. You shall drink your fill tonight. Your will has already been proven this evening."

As we continued to travel, keeping pace with the Neirie refugees, the featureless topography of the Pannonian Plains became increasingly hilly and forested. The hazy blue scrim of the mountains grew higher and more distinct with each passing night. We were nearing the lands of the Tanti… a region called Romania in your modern era. The mountains we were approaching were the Southern Carpathians. Rugged, their flanks swathed in thick pine forests, and beyond the Carpathians: the Black Sea. But we were not to reach that sea. Only I, many years later, would breach those waters. The home of the Tanti sat in a valley at the base of the Southern Carpathians, near a lake that no longer exists, in the middle of what is now called the Retezat National Park.

The lonely Pannonian Plains had fallen behind us. The region we passed through now was more densely populated. Twice, in the weeks that followed, the Neirie refugees crossed paths with small groups of roving hunters. Though Ilio and I watched nervously from afar, the encounters were relatively peaceful. It seemed, at long last, that the Neirie's luck had changed.

By day, the men hunted while the women gathered. There was an abundance of game to be caught—hares, deer, squirrels, birds. Plenty of forage on the hillsides and in the forests to collect-- herbs and vegetables, fruit and berries and mushrooms The Neirie began to look plump and strong once again. They were no longer the walking skeletons they'd been when they won their freedom from their Oombai overlords.

It was midsummer now, the weather hot and humid. Tapas, the leader of the refugees, left their camp one evening and walked a good distance toward us, torch in hand. I watched from our camp as he shoved the handle of the torch into the earth and sat. I waited to see what he would do next, but he did not move. He just sat there with the wind blowing his red hair to and fro.

"I think he wishes to speak with me," I said to Ilio finally.

"Are you going to meet with him?" the boy asked.

It was a blustery evening, cumulus clouds piling up in the sky like great black boulders. The dark base of the storm clouds gathering to the north of us flickered with lightning. The air felt energized. Judging by the wind, the deluge was headed our way, but I estimated that it would be hours yet before we needed to seek shelter.

"I suppose I should," I said. In fact, I was eager to visit with the giant. It had been weeks since I spoke with anyone other than my adopted son. I enjoyed Ilio's company, but Tapas was a man, and did not speak only in questions.

"Perhaps I could accompany you," Ilio suggested.

"I believe that would be allowable," I replied. "You have made good progress learning to control your hunger. I think Tapas would be safe from your appetite." I smiled at the boy. "Or you could hunt by yourself tonight. Bring us back a tasty meal to share beside the fire."

I had to restrain my laughter, watching him try to decide. Each option was equally tempting. His glinting eyes twitched swiftly to and fro. *Speak with a mortal... or hunt on his own.* His decision surprised me.

"I will hunt while you converse with the mortal," the boy said.

"Are you sure?" I asked.

Ilio shrugged, rising to his feet. "It is just a man."

I rose as well, dusting off my leggings. "Do not stray too far," I said, and then I yelled after him, "And do not bite off anything bigger than you can chew!"

Teasing him just a little.

"I'll be fine," he said, exasperated, as he hurried away from the fire. He grinned back at me, eyes bright. "Now watch me fly, Father! The wind is so strong tonight!"

He took several running steps and lifted into the air, his garments flapping. I watched his figure diminish into the distance, arms thrown out to his sides. The gusting winds tossed him back and forth a bit as he sailed through the dark, but he was right. I worried too much. He would be fine.

Smiling indulgently, I headed toward Tapas.

11

The giant rose as I appeared at the perimeter of his torch's dancing light. "Thest!" he greeted me. "I was beginning to think you hadn't noticed me!" He shouted to be heard above the gusting winds, but he needn't have bothered. I heard him just fine.

"Tapas," I nodded, showing him the palms of my

hands. "How do you fare?"

"I fare well," he answered. "We all have, under your protection."

He spoke true. His cheeks were no longer sunken, his eyes no longer pits. His body had grown plumper and regained the pink hues of good health. He was not handsome, not this great beast of a man, but he would no longer frighten women and little children if he should chance to cross their path.

"A storm approaches from the north," I said over the whipping of our clothes.

"Yes, and a powerful one, too, by the look of it."

He clasped my hand and I patted him on the shoulder. In another time, another place, I would have offered him my home, the comforts of one of my wives. I sat on the ground at his feet, and he joined me, crossing his legs. "What did you wish to speak of?" I asked. I was very curious.

"I have two things to tell you, T'sukuru," the giant answered. He was grinning so it must be happy news, I thought. He cast his gaze in the direction I had come. "Where is your boy? One of the things I come to tell you involves your son."

"Ilio?" I asked, surprised. "He is hunting on his own tonight. I am trying to wean him."

Tapas laughed, nodding in understanding.

"What news do you have of my son?" I asked. I worried: had he snuck away and caused these people mischief? I did not know how he might have done so. Perhaps, while I was sleeping...

"In due time. First, I wished to let you know that I will be departing from camp at sunrise."

"Departing? Where are you going?"

"The hunters we met a few days ago hail from a tribe very near to my people's lands. They are starting their journey home in the morning. I and my Vis'hantu brothers and sisters will accompany them."

"I hate to hear that. I'm sure the others will miss your wise counsel."

Tapas nodded, spreading his hands. "All things joined must also part," he said. "That is a saying my people have. I only wished to let you know so that you did not wonder when we departed. The Tanti camp is only a few days journey east from here, if you wish to accompany them the rest of the way... or you may join our party."

"I would have been curious. Thank you for keeping us informed," I said.

"No, Thest, thank you," Tapas said, his expression very sincere. "If not for your assistance... I... These people..." He choked on his emotions suddenly, his eyes growing misty. He looked embarrassed.

"No need for that," I said, feeling a great affection for the man. I hardly knew him, but there was something in his nature that reminded me of my father-- his sense of honor, perhaps, or maybe it was just the great frizzy mane of red hair. My father's hair was red when I was a boy, and just as unruly. I patted the giant on the leg. "I hope your journey is a safe one, Tapas. And I hope you find your wife and daughters in good health."

"Yes, I too," he said.

"Now... what of your other news? What must you tell me regarding my son? Has he done something that I'm not aware of?"

Tapas grinned very broadly. "Your boy will soon be a man. That is the other thing I came to speak with you about."

I frowned, thinking I had misunderstood him. Some Denghoi words had several interpretations. "A man? What do you mean?" I asked.

"One of the Tanti women is with child, T'sukuru. She claims the father is your son."

Ilio

1

"With child...?" Lukas interrupted. "I thought you said that vampires were impotent."

"Not impotent," I corrected him. "Sterile. There is a difference."

"You can fuck. You're just shooting blanks, right?" Lukas grinned.

"Vulgar as always, but yes. Our seed is as lifeless as the rest of the human cells in our bodies, incapable of striking the spark of life. A vampire is really only the transmogrified host of the parasite which dwells within him. A means to an end for the organism we vampires call the Strix. We function only to feed its hunger, and to carry out its natural desire to reproduce, which we do by spreading the vampiric curse to others."

"So how did...?" Lukas's voice trailed off, then his eyebrows shot up. "Oh!"

"Yes. Ilio, my adopted son, mated with a mortal female only once before he was made into a vampire. When we were visited by the Neirie sisters in the village of the Oombai."

Lukas snorted. "The kid must have been quite a marksman."

I nodded with a smile. "Bullseye."

2

Tapas embraced me as we parted. "Fare well, T'sukuru," he said. "Know that you will always be welcome in the lands of the Vis'hantu."

"Fare well, Tapas."

The giant plucked his torch from the ground and turned away, stormwinds tossing his frizzy red hair. I watched the big man walk back to the Neirie camp, the news he had brought me still bouncing around inside my skull.

Ilio, to be a father? I marveled.

The Oombai Elders had sent slave women to see to our ease when we first arrived at the village of the ground scratchers. It was just a ploy to get some of my T'sukuru blood, of course, and we had played right into their hands. Allowed ourselves to be distracted, seduced. Ilio had mated with two of them while I was occupied with the third-- their doomed sister, Aioa. He was still mortal then, a fecund man-child, his bow nocked and ready.

Ilio, a father! I thought, amused.

It seemed too soon for the woman to know she was with child, but then again, I did tend to lose track of time. It was midsummer now. An entire season had passed since we came down from the mountains. We had been trailing after the Neirie for weeks. Plenty of time for her belly to grow.

Truth be told, the news that Tapas just delivered pleased me to no end. As the giant's massive figure dwindled into the night, I stood in the darkness trying to contain my excitement.

From the moment I'd adopted the young mammoth hunter, it had been my ambition to give the lad a normal mortal life. The Oombai Elders had spoiled my plans, but not—as it turned out—without hope of redemption. If this Neirie woman carried his child to term, delivered it without complication, my son might yet know the joys of fatherhood-- a family, perhaps even a wife!

It would not be a simple thing. He would have to master his thirst for human blood to be able to enjoy any kind of interaction with his mortal offspring, but he did not seem to be ruled by his hunger as desperately as I was when I was first made into a blood drinker. In fact, he already seemed to have a firmer grasp on his lethal impulses than I ever had!

Perhaps it was because he was weaker than I, more human-like. Perhaps his will was stronger than mine. Or maybe I was just more self-indulgent. Whatever the reason, I could easily imagine him living alongside a human wife and child, having something very like a natural mortal life—despite the stumbling blocks fate had seen fit to throw beneath the lad's feet.

Ilio... a father!

Of course, it was possible the Neirie woman might miscarry. Both mother and child might die during childbirth. It was not uncommon.

Perhaps it would be wise to keep this news from him. If anything were to happen to either of them, the lad would be devastated.

I knew I couldn't do that, however. I wouldn't want someone to keep news like that from me, not even out of love.

Ilio... a father! I mused one more time, and then I went to find my fertile little brat.

3

I found him in a stand of conifers just to the north

of our camp, sobbing quietly.

I knew what he had done even before I saw him. I could smell the blood on the seesawing wind. Mortal blood, rich and fresh. The aroma was so strong it stopped me in my tracks, and I had to wrestle down my own hunger before I could continue.

"Ilio?" I called out gently.

His weeping wrenched at my heart. Such remorse! Such self-loathing! Despite all his training, his ambition to master the bloodthirst, he had chanced upon a mortal and surrendered to temptation.

"I'm so sorry, Father," he sobbed, crouching in the shadows. "I didn't mean to do it."

The pines creaked as the wind tossed them to and fro. The drumming of the thunder was louder now, the storm closer. I crept into the deeper shadows of the grove, moving silently over the blanket of pine needles, and found the boy squatting beside the body of a mortal man. Ilio had wrapped his arms around himself and was rocking back and forth. His cheeks were stained red with bloody tears. His lips and chin were smeared with blood, too. There was blood on his hands. Blood on his clothing. My stomach gurgled at the sight.

I glanced at the mortal the boy had killed. Even in the starless dark, I had no trouble identifying the man. It was one of the Neirie who had turned back to battle the Oombai-- one of the Tanti men who'd stared at me so worshipfully that day. An ill-fated fellow, he had survived the skirmish with the Oombai only to run afoul of my son.

He was a pitiful sight, his eyes staring fixedly, glazed and slightly crossed, tongue protruding from slack lips. The sad, confused expression of all dead creatures.

I saw that Ilio had broken his body. Shards of

bone protruded from his twisted left arm. His left leg had too many joints. He had suffered terrible violence at the boy's hands. I wondered: had he startled the lad, or had my son done this to him out of savagery?

"Tell me what happened," I said. I kept my voice neutral, neither condemning nor condoning.

Ilio snuffled. He was reluctant to answer.

"Ilio...?" I pressed him.

"I was tracking a deer," the boy confessed. "I guess the mortal was doing the same. I didn't even know he was there. He was crawling through the grass on his belly."

"You didn't smell him?" I asked.

Ilio shook his head. "The wind was blowing the other direction."

"What happened then?"

"I was making a game of it. I wanted to see how close I could come before the deer sensed that I was there. Then all of a sudden this mortal stood up out of the grass! He was just a few strides ahead of me, but his back was turned. He didn't see me. He nocked an arrow, took aim at the deer. I was so close I could have reached out and tapped him on the shoulder. I was going to leave him, but then the wind changed direction and the smell of him washed over me..." Ilio groaned as if the memory was causing him physical pain. "I couldn't stop myself. I leapt onto his back, tore his neck open with my fangs. He fell beneath me, screaming. I wanted to stop myself, but I couldn't. His blood tasted so good, and I was so hungry--!"

"All right, Son," I said. "That's enough."

"I can feel him inside me," he said quietly. "I don't mean his blood. I mean his mind. I can feel his thoughts inside my head. His memories."

A rash of goosebumps shivered up my spine. "What do you mean?"

"He's in here, inside my skull," he said, and then

he shrieked, grabbing coils of his hair and tearing them from his scalp. I froze for a moment, shocked by his outburst, and then I rushed forward and took ahold of his wrists.

"Stop it, Ilio!" I shouted. "What are you doing? Get ahold of yourself!"

"He's in my mind!" Ilio exclaimed, struggling, and then he collapsed against me.

"Tell me what you see," I said to the boy, pulling him to my chest.

"He had a son," Ilio murmured. "His son was my age when the Oombai took them."

Ilio looked up at me, the whites of his eyes very bright in the dark.

"I can hear his thoughts inside my own. He keeps saying a word. He says it over and over. *Gart. Gart...* I think it's the name of his son."

"What else do you see?"

"He was teaching the boy to hunt. The Oombai came across them in the middle of the forest. He knew who the Oombai were. He knew why they had come into his people's lands. He surrendered to them without a fight. Gart was his only son. He didn't want them to injure his son. He told the boy to surrender, to give himself up peacefully, but the boy wouldn't submit to them. He fought them. He fought them so fiercely! *No, Gart! Put down your weapon! There are too many of them!*"

The timber of Ilio's voice had changed. It sounded deeper, more man-like. I could feel him shaking in my arms, but there was nothing I could do to ease him. I did not, in truth, know exactly what was happening to him. I never experienced visions when I fed, and up until that point, neither had the boy. Probably because we mostly fed on animals. It never happens with animal blood. I know now that some blood drinkers see visions when they feed. It is a rare gift, but it was one I did not share with the lad, so I did not know how to comfort him, and to be honest, I was a little afraid he'd gone insane.

"Oh, Thest, they beat him so badly!" Ilio sobbed. "They took great pleasure in it. They beat him until he was unconscious. His father tried to carry him to the village of the ground scratchers, but the boy died the next day. He died in his father's arms. The Oombai made him put the boy down when they saw that he was dead. They wouldn't let him bury his son. They just left him. Left him behind for the scavengers."

I could see the boy's hair sprouting where he'd torn his locks from his scalp. It was strange watching the hair wriggle from his skin, seeing it wind down, serpent-like, across his brow. I hugged him tight to my chest. "Oh, Ilio," I sighed.

"*His son!*" he said in a grating voice. "He loved his son so much! How can a man live with such pain, Thest? It would drive me insane!"

"It is hard," I confessed. "It is always hard when you lose someone you love. But it is something we all must learn to do. Especially creatures like you and I, who live so much longer than mortal men."

"I do not think that I will be able to bear it!" he hissed.

"You will have to, Ilio," I replied. "You may soon have a child of your own to look after!"

4

Even with his accelerated mental faculties, it took a moment for my words to sink in. He frowned up at me, confused by what I'd said, still wrestling with the memories of his recent mortal victim. "What... what do you mean?" he stammered.

I laughed gently as his confusion. "You may be a

father soon," I repeated.

He pulled away from me, pressing his fingertips to his temples. "Please, Thest, no lessons tonight. My skull feels like it's splitting open. I don't even know which thoughts are my own, and which thoughts belong to the mortal that I've killed."

"I'm not trying to impart a lesson, Ilio. I am only acting as a deliverer of news."

He blinked up at me doubtfully. "What are you talking about?" he cried. "How can I be a father?"

"Ilio," I teased him gently, "we had this talk when we still lived on the mountain. Don't you remember?"

"I don't mean 'how' like that--"

"Do you recall the Neirie women the Elders sent to our tent? One of them is with child. She claims that you are the sire."

Ilio shook his head. "Me? A father? That can't be true!"

"I assure you, it is a distinct possibility."

"But I only did it that one time," he protested.

"All it takes is one time!" I laughed. I put a hand on his shoulder, smiling sympathetically. "Come now, man! I explained to you how babies are made. It is not a complicated process."

"No, it is not," Ilio said. He thought for a moment, head down, then looked at me with a tentative smile. "Can it really be true? Have I fathered a mortal child?" he asked.

I shrugged. "I cannot say for sure, Ilio. The Neirie man I conversed with tonight, Tapas-- you know, the giant that I told you about-- delivered the message to me. And he was only repeating what the slave girl claims. Only she would know if it is true or not, but she says that it is you. I do not know why she would lie about it."

Ilio scrubbed his bloody cheeks with his sleeve. "Can we go to their camp and see her tonight?" he asked.

I nodded to the dead man lying at our feet. "Do you think that is wise?"

His face crumpled. "Oh, Thest! What am I going to do? I failed miserably the very first time I was tempted!"

"As did I, remember?"

"Perhaps it would be best if I do not acknowledge this child. If I harmed the baby, or the woman who bore him, I would destroy myself out of remorse."

I nodded. "That was the course I chose when I was made this vicious thing we are," I said. "I abandoned my children, abandoned my mates. I did it for their safety, but it is a decision I have always regretted. Perhaps, with my help, you could have a happier fate."

"You would do that for me?" he asked.

I shrugged. "I will advise you," I answered. "I will do my best to train you, but ultimately your life is your own. Your decisions are yours, and it is you and you alone who will have to live with the consequences of your actions."

Ilio looked to the dead man.

"I suppose we should bury his body in some remote location," he said finally. "It would not be fit for the Neirie to learn of my failure. Not if we wish to live among them. Not if I wish to be a father to this child."

I nodded solemnly. Acts of deception have never set well with me, but I am enough of a realist to know that a lie is sometimes the lesser evil. As I myself have lied-- to the boy, from the very moment that I "rescued" him.

I am a father of lies, I thought, but aloud I said, "If that is what you think is best."

"I don't think any of this is 'best'," Ilio confessed, scooping up his victim's body. He stood, the Tanti dangling in his arms. "It is just that I see no other alternative," he explained.

He sounded so like me in that moment that I had a strange thought: that the man-child was more like me than could rationally be explained. He seemed more like a child of my flesh than an adopted son. Perhaps, when I had made him an immortal, the essence of my soul had been distilled into his own, as the essence of mortal men and women mix when they make a child together.

The clouds that had been massing all evening had finally overspread the heavens. Lightning flickered like the tongue of a serpent, followed by a great crash of thunder. We listened to the thunder reverberate across the plains, waning into the distance even as the echo rolled back upon itself. The rain began to fall with a sudden drumming in the treetops. Cold rainwater filtered through the piney boughs above us, drizzling down on our heads in purring rivulets.

Water running down his face, Ilio looked at the dead man in his arms. "Would that this rain could wash away the wrongs I have done tonight," he murmured.

"Such stains can never be washed away."

"As you know from bitter experience," the boy said. He looked at me, raindrops dripping from his curled lashes. "And now I."

I looked back at him, silent. Waiting.

"Let us bury this man tonight," Ilio nodded. "Then tomorrow we shall visit the camp of the Neirie. I would like to see this woman who claims I've fathered her child. I will know if she speaks the truth."

"As you wish," I nodded, and then he turned and walked into the open.

The boy vanished into the flapping gray curtain of the rain.

A moment later, I followed.

5

Ilio dug the Tanti's grave beside a stream, laying his victim to rest at the base of a willow tree. The tree was young and twisted by the stout winds that ripped through the region, but I thought it was probably a very lovely spot when the weather was not so miserable: the stream, the willow, the gently sloping hills.

"I can still feel him inside me," Ilio said as the rain beat down on us. He shoved his hand into the earth like a spade, wrenching out a great divot of muddy sod. A mortal would have been impressed by the strength such an act required, but not I. I was only wet.

I'd offered to help the boy dig his victim's grave, but he had refused. He said he wanted to do it himself. I approved of the sentiment and so I did not press him. Instead, I walked a little distance away and sat on the bank of the stream.

I watched the water race by as he dug, dangling my feet. Leaves and small branches went whirling past, hurried by the downpour. My hair was hanging in wet strands, my clothes soaked through, but it did not bother me overly much. Cold hasn't bothered me since the night I was made into a blood drinker.

"It is like his ghost is whispering inside my mind," Ilio said later, taking a break from his labors. "His words are foreign, yet I understand them without effort."

"What does he say to you?" I asked.

"He does not blame me for his death," Ilio answered. "He says... his suffering was no greater than the beasts he killed to feed his own belly. He says that all living creatures must eat to live. That life is a great circle, and even we T'sukuru will return to the earth someday, to be devoured by the grass and the trees and the flowers."

"That is a comforting thought," I said.

Ilio returned to his chore. He tore another chunk of earth from the mortal's grave, the roots in the soil snapping. The drumming downpour cleaned the boy as quickly as he muddied himself, which I thought was very fitting. He had done a terrible thing, but not willfully, not with any malice.

"He asks me only to remember his life, and the love he had for his son," Ilio said with a grunt, pushing another hunk of earth aside. "And if I, by chance, ever come across the bones of his son, to give them a proper burial so that his son's spirit can rest in peace as well."

Ilio lifted the Tanti into his arms and placed the man gently into the ground. He laid the man to rest in the manner that my own people once favored: on his side, with his knees drawn up to his chest. Like a child in the womb.

Ilio climbed out of the grave. He knelt down and began to push the dirt in upon the dead man. He filled the hole quickly, pressing it down with his palms. When he was finished, he stood on his knees. He tilted his head back and held his arms out at his sides and let the rain wash him clean.

"He's gone now," Ilio sighed.

"Then let us go now, as well," I said, rising from my perch. "I'm soaked to the skin, and I need to fill my belly."

6

We camped that morning in the grove of pines where I'd found Ilio huddled over his Tanti victim. The rain continued to slash down from the heavens, so we constructed a crude lean-to and wrapped up in my cloak.

My vampiric skills were no match for the deluge. I could find not one dry stick with which to build a fire. My only solace was that the nearby Neirie, as resourceful as they were, had no fires either that night.

We rested together beneath the angled roof of our dripping lean-to, listening to the rain hiss down without respite. If we were mortal men, we would have been miserable. Cold, wet, shivering. As we were not mortal men, the storm was merely an inconvenience, but I did miss the comforts of a nice big fire, its light and warm. I have always enjoyed staring into the flames of a campfire, watching them leap and twirl like dancers. Much as you modern mortals enjoy staring into the cold blue light of your electric television sets.

Ilio talked interminably as the rain drummed down. He talked of the child he might have, and how a blood drinker might live among mortal men, and keep them safe from our cursed appetite.

I offered what advice I could, cautioning him against too much hope. "The woman may not even want you for a mate, Ilio," I pointed out. "Naming you the father is no proposal of marriage." To his credit, he understood, and confessed that he was only passing the time. I nodded, water dripping from the tip of my nose.

"Tapas said that he and his people will part with

the Neirie in the morning," I said, changing the subject. "The hunting party they met a couple days ago are from a region near his tribal lands. He plans to travel with them."

"You wish to see him off, don't you?" Ilio asked.

I nodded. "I think we should both go. He can introduce us to the group. He speaks the language of the Tanti, the tongue the mother of your child speaks. Once Tapas and his people leave, there may be few among the Neirie who speak the Denghoi tongue."

"I would like that," Ilio admitted.

He pressed up against me, quietly happy. I put my arm around his shoulders, wondering how long it would be before we parted, this boy and I. He was nearly a man, in thought if not in form. He might look like a child, frozen in time by the vampiric transformation, but he would soon yearn to be free of my rule. He would want to lead his own life, be the master of his own destiny... and that was as it should be.

What would I do then, I wondered. Where would I go?

Perhaps I would travel east, I thought. Seek out those Others we've heard so many rumors of. Their brutal reputation did not frighten me. I knew my power, and I was fairly certain I could protect myself among the blood drinkers of the east.

I spent the rest of the night thinking about those mysterious immortals, wondering what they were like, how many of our kind roamed the world. What strange customs did they keep? What deities did they worship? The questions swirled inside my head like a cloud of buzzing gnats. The prospect of meeting other members of my race filled me with great excitement.

I looked toward the east, but it was just as gray and featureless as any other direction in the downpour. The rain, like the mountains, guarded the secrets of the eastern blood drinkers.

7

At the first hint of dawn, which was little more than a lightening of the featureless haze that had enveloped the region, we set off for the Neirie encampment. It was still raining hard when we abandoned the conifer wood, but the rain slackened as we traveled southeast, ebbing at last to a slow drizzle as we rounded a hill and beheld the camp below.

Like us, the Neirie had slept beneath makeshift lean-tos constructed of tree limbs and foliage. They had fled the village of the Oombai with scant supplies, living off the land as best they could as they journeyed home. They had plundered a bit of clothing and weapons from the fallen Oombai army, but their settlement still looked quite poor. Once again I found myself impressed by their spirit and resourcefulness.

A good number of men and women had already arisen. They stumbled groggily about the camp, looking for a bit of breakfast, or ducked into the bushes to take care of their morning toilet. They had managed to build a couple smoldering fires, shielding the flames beneath the overhang of their shelters, and that's where most of them gathered once they'd visited the woods, boiling their morning tea or having their first smoke of the day.

None took note of our approach.

Ilio faltered at my side as we descended the hill toward their camp, his face purposefully neutral. I could see his nostrils flaring. I put my hand on his shoulder to support him.

"Are you sure you can endure this, boy?" I asked.

I could feel his muscles twitching beneath my

hand. His entire body had gone rigid, like a great cat preparing to spring upon its prey.

"I can… smell them," he whispered huskily. "Their... blood!"

"As do I," I said. "Try to put thoughts of feeding out of your mind. Do not even allow yourself to fantasize about it."

He swallowed, then nodded anxiously. "I am ready."

He strode ahead of me without encouragement then, moving purposefully. I hurried to catch up, putting a pleasant expression on my face. The ground squished soggily beneath our feet.

Where was Tapas? I wondered, searching the Neirie faces below. Had his group already departed?

At last someone took notice of us. A female voice rang out in fear. All through the camp, nervous Neirie eyes swiveled in our direction. Several men leapt to their feet, clutching spears or clubs. Others tried hurriedly to reassure their companions, explaining that I was the one who had killed the Elders, saved them from the Oombai's final attempt to recapture them.

I saw Tapas then. He came scurrying from a copse of spindly saplings, fumbling with the laces of his breeches. He raised his hand to me as he shouted at the others. *"Taian dow!"* he yelled. *"Sprecht ien d'tzau!"* Most of the men lowered their weapons, though a few continued to stare at us suspiciously.

"It pleases me to see you, Thest," Tapas called, climbing the hill to meet us. He was a little out of breath. "Have you come to see me off this fine summer morning?"

I embraced the soggy man with a laugh, and we continued toward the camp, walking side by side. "I have motives other than courtesy for visiting you this morning, I must confess," I said.

"If you've come to ask us for a favor, know that we are only too happy to accommodate your needs," Tapas replied. "We owe you more than just our freedom, T'sukuru. Many of us owe you our lives."

"You are very generous, Tapas. The favor I ask is very small."

"You have but to speak it."

I noticed that he kept peeking at the boy as we walked. "This is Ilio," I introduced them. "He is my adopted son."

"He is much changed from the last time I saw him," Tapas said, looking down on the lad with a friendly smile. "Ilio, is it? That is a Denghoi name. I saw you at the Oombai festival." Ilio nodded in acknowledgement, and Tapas turned back toward me. "He is a blood god now. I can tell by the pallor of his skin."

"He is T'sukuru," I confirmed.

I glanced at Ilio from the corner of my eye, noting the stiff gait with which he walked. I could see it was a effort for him to resist the song of the blood. I empathized. I, too, felt its seductive call. The living hunger twisted my guts into knots. It whispered temptations in my mind, seducing, cajoling. *Kill them... feast on their blood...!*

As it always does.

Never ceasing.

Even as I suffered, I kept a close eye on the boy, ready to restrain him should he lose control and pounce.

Tapas sensed that I was reluctant to discuss the boy's condition. He changed the subject. "So tell me, great warrior, what is this favor you seek?"

"You speak the tongue of these other tribes," I said. "I would have you make a way for us among them before you leave for your homeland."

"A formal introduction, you mean. So that they're

comfortable with your presence?"

I nodded.

"But of course, my friend! Such a small favor to ask!"

Ilio looked at me imploringly.

"Also," I said, "we would like to see the woman. The one who claims my son has sired a child in her belly."

"The Tanti woman Priss," Tapas said.

"*Priss?*" Ilio shouted, surprising us both. "Priss is the one who carries my child?"

Tapas absorbed the boy's excitement, grinning knowingly at me.

"So she claims," Tapas said mildly. He leaned toward me, muttering out of the corner of his mouth, "*No ass can proclaim a foal of his spraying 'til the babe is full grown and takes up his braying.*"

I tried to conceal my amusement, looking toward Ilio to see if he understood the jest.

But Ilio had retreated into his thoughts. He stared straight ahead as he walked, his brow furrowed.

I could see past his troubled expression, however. We had been companions for two whole cycles of the seasons. He was pleased, despite his worries, that this woman called Priss was the one who carried his child.

As for me, I could not recall which one was which. In all honesty, I had paid little attention to the slave women who tended to Ilio that day. Their eldest sister, Aioa, had commanded the lion's share of my attention. A fiery and self-possessed woman, Aioa had given me to drink of her blood, seduced me with her body, whispering sweet venom in my ears in hopes of setting me against her Oombai oppressors. I knew Ilio had mated with the two subordinate sisters, but I was deaf and blind to the rather vigorous activities on the boy's side of the hut that afternoon.

As we walked, I made small talk with Tapas. "I

wager you're excited to be headed home at last," I said.

Tapas nodded. "Excited, but weary. Leading these people has become a tiresome burden. Everyone worships a different god, and each man thinks his is the only true faith. Now that we are safe from the Oombai, thanks to you, these people have taken to bickering endlessly about their beliefs. It gives me headaches. I cannot wait to be free of such fruitless concerns."

We were walking through the outskirts of the camp now. The whole group had roused and moved to surround us. It was as if they shared a single mind, dogging our steps as Tapas led us to the center of the settlement. They whispered to one another fretfully--thin, dirty men and women, eyes round with curiosity and fear. The drizzle helped to subdue the smell of their bodies, the scent of their blood, but only a little, and certainly not enough for comfort.

I glanced toward Ilio nervously, but he still had control of his bloodthirst.

Barely.

Though I am sure the signs would be indiscernible to a mortal, I could see him wrestling with the impulse to attack them. I could see it in the dilation of his pupils, the tiny flutters in the muscles of his jaw. I heard his stomach gurgle, and then he swallowed.

So did I.

We were assailed by a multitude of tongues. Some of the words sounded familiar, but most of their talk was nonsensical. The babble of lunatics.

Tapas threw his arms into the air. He yelled for their attention and the crowd instantly fell silent. He had the voice of a natural born leader, deep and rich and carrying. In the village of the ground scratchers, he had been an object of scorn, employed as a sex performer because of his unusually generous endowments. Now he was the provisional chieftain of a large group of freed slaves. Even I was impressed by the man, and I worried what would become of the Neirie once he departed.

He spoke for a long time, switching between several different languages. A few men standing in the crowd translated his words even further, muttering under their breath to their own individual cliques. Every time the giant gestured toward us, the eyes of the crowd turned obediently in our direction, and each time they turned toward us, it seemed, their expressions were more and more awestruck. I could hear my name being whispered in the throng: *"Thest... Thest...!"* Some of the Tanti men standing in a cluster near the back of the crowd were jabbering at one another anxiously, gesticulating. I could see two women standing in their midst, though the bodies of their tribesmen blocked most of their features from my sight.

Tapas finished speaking and the crowd shifted toward us. Many of the men and women laid their hands upon us, their faces beaming with gratitude and acceptance. "Thest! Ilio!" they said, nodding their heads and patting us. Ilio made a low groaning sound, his hands twitching, and I grabbed ahold of him by the upper arm, yanking him nearer to my side.

A dozen languages, a hundred hands.

"T'sukuru gi onho!"

"Ilio on'n ma sumbun!"

"Che wheh? Ulg! Ulg!"

I could feel the boy trembling against me. *Endure!* I thought intently, as if that might somehow transmit the unspoken command to his mind.

Then the crowd parted and the Tanti strode forward in a group. They were stout, proud men--much like the people of my own lost tribe-- their chins thrust out, their eyes fervid and shining with what I surmised was some species of religious ecstasy.

Watching them approach, I again felt that nagging sense of familiarity. It was as if I recognized some part of myself in them. A modern person might call that feeling *déjà vu*, but it was not *déjà vu*... not exactly.

Something is different about these Tanti people, I thought. *But what...?*

I did not have time to ponder it further. The men in the front turned sharply on their heels, stepping aside with an abbreviated bow. From the center of their protective circle strode two young Tanti women. It was Aioa's sisters, the slave women who had seduced my mortal son.

Ilio gasped at the sight of them. "Priss!" he exclaimed.

The smaller one, the one who commanded Ilio's attention, stepped to the fore. She was as lovely as Aioa had been, though frailer, her features unspoiled by the passions that had tempered her older sister's looks, and though she was dressed in little more than rags, I found myself moved by her placid beauty. Priss's other sister (who, I learned later, was called Lorn) was a taller, more voluptuous woman, just as attractive in her own way, though not as finely featured.

Priss smiled at Ilio, one pale hand cupping the gentle curve of her bare belly.

"Ilio," she nodded, and then she said something to him I could not understand.

Ilio went to his knees in front of her, moving faster than I could react. For a second I feared he meant to attack her, that he had finally lost control of the bloodthirst.

Instead, he put his ear to her belly.

As if he could hear such a tiny thing! I thought. She couldn't have been more than two moons gone by!

As the rest of the Tanti watched, nervousness and wonder warring in their expressions, the young slave woman cupped Ilio's chin and urged him to his feet.

They were both small in stature. In fact, they stood almost eye-to-eye-- Ilio being a scant shade taller. Priss, still holding his chin, turned Ilio's face from one side to the other. She took in the changes the living blood had wrought upon his features. His skin: smooth and hard as stone. His complexion: white and bloodless. She stared into his gleaming jewel-like eyes, and an expression of sympathy stole over her countenance.

She smiled and spoke to him again. Soft words. A promise, perhaps? I could not understand their meaning, but Ilio could, it seemed. He nodded and replied to her in the Tanti tongue, and then stepped backwards—very formally-- to my side.

The Tanti slave women withdrew inside their ring of protectors. The men enclosed the females, then, bowing once more to us, they huddled the women away.

I looked from Ilio to the retreating Tanti, wondering what, exactly, I had just bore witness to.

8

The sky remained overcast all through the morning, the rain falling intermittently. Every leaf, every blade of grass, every mortal face around us was beaded with water-- dripping, dripping. It was as if the entire world had been dunked in a great pool. The sodden gloom was a blessing to us, however, as it kept our discomfort to a minimum. I doubt the Neirie would have been so welcoming if blood-streaked tears were dribbling down our faces.

I was curious to find out what Ilio and Priss had

said to one another, and how the boy had understood the Tanti tongue—even spoke it himself!-- but I did not press him for details. We had plenty of time to speak of it later, when we weren't so tormented by the smell of mortal blood.

The Neirie continued to accost us after the Tanti hustled away. Most of the escaped slaves spoke Oombai, which I was somewhat able to decipher, but they said little of import to this narrative. They introduced themselves to us. Thanked us for slaying the Elders, and for interceding when the Oombai warriors tried to retake them.

All around us shifted grinning mortal faces, eyes gleaming with superstitious awe, their soft mortal flesh flush with pulsing blood. Dirty hands clutched at our clothing, patted our arms and backs. I don't think I've ever been groped so much in my life, not even when I was a mortal man, and the tribe I hailed from had engaged in ritual orgies!

Ilio was trying his best to follow what they were saying, but there were too many people talking all at once. He was starting to become overwhelmed.

"He says that he prayed every night for deliverance," Ilio translated for me as some toothless old man gabbled in my face. "He thinks the gods sent you to strike down the Elders. He says that you're… *Ne w'ae*?"

Someone stumbled against the boy then, and he hissed, baring his fangs.

"Kwa Wa'elah!" he snarled, a Denghoi pejorative.

I grabbed Ilio by the arm as quick as I could. As he brought his free hand up to strike the clumsy mortal, his fingers curled into claws, I yanked the boy from the throng, moving to a safe distance at superhuman speed.

"Father!" Ilio cried out breathlessly, shocked by the speed that I had moved us from the Neirie. His

knees went weak and he fell against me.

"I'm sorry, Son. I had to get us away from that crowd. Are you unhurt?"

He nodded as I helped him to his feet. "Yes... I-- I am fine."

He recovered quickly, turned to look at the horde in the center of the Neirie camp. I had swept him just beyond the furthest lean-to, away from all the chaos, the maddening smell of blood.

"I almost lost control," he confessed shakily. "If you hadn't pulled me away—"

"I know."

"We should go now!" he said.

"I agree. We've done what we came here to do. They have seen us, laid hands on us. You've spoken to the woman who claims to bear your child. We should retire to our own camp before we push our luck too far." I glanced to the sky, which was showing a few patches of blue. "The storm has nearly spent itself. The sun will come out soon. Let me bid Tapas farewell, and then we will fly away from here. Can you hold on just a moment longer?"

"Yes, just... let me wait for you here."

Tapas was looking for me in the camp. Moving at great speed, I appeared at his side. He started, his red hair lifting at the swirl of wind that accompanied my arrival, then he chuckled in appreciation of the trick.

"Your sudden disappearance has sealed your reputation," he said teasingly. "Now they are certain of your divinity. Was that your intention all along, T'sukuru?"

"Not at all," I said. "The crowd was making us uncomfortable."

Tapas noticed Ilio in the distance. The man-child stood slouching with his elbows in his hands, watching us impatiently. From where we stood, he looked like any other teenage boy. Short, slim, just on the cusp of manhood, his chest and shoulders developed, but his waist narrow, his legs gangling. As he was now, so would he remain forever.

"They cannot figure out where you've vanished to," Tapas said with amusement. The Neirie were milling around aimlessly, everyone babbling at once. I moved subtly to put the giant between us. I didn't want to be spotted before we could make good on our escape.

"We are returning to our camp momentarily. I just wanted to bid you farewell, Tapas. Perhaps I will come visit you when my chick has flown the nest."

"I would welcome that, Thest," Tapas said, turning away from the Neirie with a grin. "The Vis'hantu territory is but two fists walk to the south of the Tanti village. Come see me if you tire of fables and fishing stories. And good luck with that boy of yours. I have a feeling he's quite a handful."

I smiled and nodded my head, and then I was away. I moved at full speed to where my vampire child awaited. "Come, Ilio!" I said, pausing at his side only long enough to speak, and then I was in motion again, the wind whistling in my ears. I sped to the top of the hill, and then I threw my arms out and flew.

9

The sky was clear when we arose, the moon a bright sickle skimming the rugged peaks of the Carpathian Mountains. We had found a relatively dry location in which to sleep the remainder of the daylight hours. It was a sandy crevice tucked beneath a shelf of stone, one that looked as if it might host a waterfall during the spring season, when snowmelt sent torrents of icy water coursing down the mountains. The falls were all but dried up now, just a serene pool standing below the rocky recession we'd slept in, the water green and full of wriggling tadpoles.

I slipped from beneath the overhanging rocks, dropping lightly to the ground below. We were in a lush wood not far from the Neirie camp, a beautiful location with ferns drooping from the stony ledges and flowering plants crowding around the evaporating pool. I noticed soapwart among the crocuses and lilies and decided to scrub my filthy clothes. But first I needed to build a fire.

There are many different methods of making a fire, most of them terribly laborious for mortal men. For a vampire, however, it is a simple thing to do. Our great speed allows us to generate enormous friction, which in turn creates heat. I can rub two sticks together fast enough to make them burst into flames in just a couple seconds. It might take a mortal hours to do the same.

I gathered some stones, then dug a shallow pit in the earth. Ilio rose as I was placing the stones in a circle and I sent him off to collect some firewood.

We did not need a fire. We had no fear of animals, nor did we need it to cook our evening meal. We did not need its light to see by, nor its heat to warm our flesh, but a campfire has always comforted me. I enjoy watching the flames curl and lap at the wood, the smell of the smoke, the pop and crackle of the glowing embers. It connects me to my mortal life in a way few other things do, reminding me of a home that no longer exists, a family long returned to the earth. The memories ache like the bones of the elderly, but I hold them close to me nonetheless.

Ilio returned, dragging an enormous log behind him.

"Will this do?" he grinned.

"*Ilio...!*" I sighed, and then I had to laugh.

I rose and helped the boy break the log into useful sized pieces. It wasn't difficult. The log was half-rotted. We positioned the remainder near the firepit as a place to rest our backs.

"So tell me, Son," I said, arranging tinder in the middle of the pit, "what did you speak of with the slave woman down in the Neirie camp?" I hadn't had time to ask him earlier. The sun had come out and we were preoccupied with finding a comfortable place to rest. I plucked the fluff from the seedhead of a cattail, placing it into a small mound of birch bark and dried grass.

Ilio looked embarrassed. "She didn't really say much."

"So tell me," I badgered him. "Or have you suddenly grown bashful?"

I got my kindling ready, then took up a long, sturdy stick and placed its tip upon the flat surface of a split log. Holding the stick between my palms, I moved my hands back and forth, pressing down. My hands moved in a blur, the wood squealing. Within moments, a curl of smoke was rising from the log. I tipped my ember into the tinder and blew softly. A tiny flame blossomed from the spark, hungry to devour the meal of cattail fluff and birch bark I'd prepared for it. I fed it kindling, watching it grow, then roofed it with larger pieces. Our campfire sputtered and hissed as the moisture from the morning's rains boiled out of the wood.

"Well?" I prompted the boy, sitting back.

The firelight glimmered in the vampire boy's eyes, red embers winking in their depths. "She said that I was acceptable," Ilio confessed.

"Acceptable?" I chuckled. It sounded like something one of the women from my tribe might have said.

He nodded. "She said she would take me for a

mate, but I would have to prove myself worthy first."

"Do you want her for a mate?" I asked.

He smiled and nodded his head. "Yes. I find her appealing."

"Do you realize how difficult such a marriage will be? Every moment you are around her, you will have to fight the urge to kill her. You will be like a wolf mated to a doe."

"I can resist the hunger," he insisted. "Look how well I did today."

"Yes, but... a *wife*, Ilio! Think about it rationally. You would be with her at all times. She would expect sexual intercourse. Ilio, she is a mortal. As fragile as a flower. One slip and you would crush her, and then how would you feel, especially if you've grown to love her?"

"I will be careful of my strength," he said. "It is not so hard to do. And you coupled with a mortal woman without harming her. I saw it myself. It is not impossible."

I could see that no argument would sway him from the idea. Though the complications of taking a mortal woman as a mate should have been intimidating to him, I let it go. He would do what he would do. I was not his master. Not even, really, his father. Besides, who could know the future? Perhaps he would succeed.

And if he could do it, did that not also mean the same could be said of me?

10

At that point in time, I had only just awakened from the ice. If you recall from the first volume of my memoirs, I had cast my body into a glacial crevasse, trying to end my immortal suffering. I had outlived my wives and children. My descendants had abandoned the valley that had been our home from time immemorial, fleeing before the advancing cold. In my loneliness, I was seduced by Death, and so I had climbed atop the largest of the icy floes clawing their way into the valley, and I had thrown myself into the deepest, darkest fissure I could find. My last thought had been a declaration of satisfaction and relief as massive planes of jagged ice crushed me to a pulp.

But I had not perished. I lay in the womb of the glacier, locked in dreamless slumber, preserved by the Strix until the ice retreated once again, several thousand years later. Cast out, crushed and senseless, I was a stillborn thing awakening in the middle of a desolate tundra.

For me, only a year or two had passed from the time that I cast myself into the maw of the glacier to that night, talking to Ilio about the complications of marriage for our kind. I was still haunted by the loneliness which had caused me to throw myself headlong into the void. I had Ilio, and if it weren't for him I might have tried to find some other way to end myself, but he was just a boy—my adopted son, yes--but his company could only go so far in filling the emptiness in my soul.

To have a female companion again... someone to provide for, someone to comfort me as only a woman can comfort. And sex... let's not forget about that! I no longer had the need for sex that mortal men are driven by, but my encounter with Priss's fiery older sister had awakened a new desire for the act. The overwhelming pleasure of our coupling still sizzled in my memory.

Still, I could not put the dangers of such an adventure completely out of my thoughts. Ilio was young. Inexperienced. He still thought only of his own wants, his own needs. I was much too old for such selfish self-deception.

Put it out of your thoughts, I advised myself.

But still, it remained: the ache.

I remembered my days as a young bachelor, living with my tent-mate Brulde. The era of my mortal life had been a time of plenty, a brief period of warmth before the final glaciation of Europe. Our lives were easy, and we had lived in relative peace with our neighbors. By day we fished or hunted small game in the valley forest. By night we dreamed moonily of all the young women in our village, debating who was prettiest, who would make the best wife, and who we'd just as soon club in the head.

My people had practiced fertility magic. Sex for our tribe was a sacred duty. It was used to heal, to strengthen the bonds of our community. For the River People, every occasion was an excuse for a ritual orgy! I had never lacked for sexual partners when I was a mortal man, and if I did come up deficient, I could always depend on Brulde. The men of our village coupled much like the Spartans or the Greeks.

But to have a wife! To have that special bond, to become one with another and bring forth new life--*that* was the holiest of holy to my people... not the petty rules and regulations of your uptight modern deities!

I suppose I should end this monologue before I offend you unnecessarily. I know how you modern folk cling to your new myths, your rigid rules and customs, preferring the comfort of fairy tales to the unflinching stare of reality, the tranquility of imprisonment to the fearful prospect of freedom. You've become timid pets, kept so long in confinement that the grass beneath your feet, the open sky above, even your own instinctive desires, freeze your hearts with terror.

Sometimes I think this willful ignorance, this fear

of liberty, is a symptom of another type of loneliness. *Racial loneliness.* You are a solitary race on a tiny, remote world, circling a massive black hole that is careening through an infinite freezing void at two million kilometers an hour. A single race, a silent galaxy, a vast and hostile universe. It should come as no surprise that so many of you seek refuge in fantasy. It must be comforting to believe some omnipotent Papa is watching your every thought and deed, guarding you from the big scary universe-- so long as you follow His rules.

Here is the ultimate, terrifying truth: your mother and your father are your Creator, and you are free to do as you will.

I'm sorry if that upsets you.

But I digress...

11

Lying on my belly in the grass, I turned to the boy and hissed, "Have you taken leave of your senses, Son? That creature is twice the size of you!" In the dale below, a herd of aurochs had bedded for the night.

The precursors of modern cattle, Aurochs were massive horned beasts. Powerful and foul-tempered, the bulls stood six feet tall at the withers and sported lyre-shaped forward-angled horns. Though the meat was delicious, and a single aurochs could feed an entire tribe for days, my people had not hunted the monstrosities with any regularity. The game animals of our valley forest had been too abundant, and much too easily killed, for us to bother with the fierce two thousand pound creatures, though our cousins to the south had sometimes hunted them, and traded their hides and meat to us for the fish and crustaceans we collected from the river.

This is how he intends to impress the girl? I thought with disbelief. The horns of those monsters were long enough to run two grown men straight through-- with room for another, at least. I was growing ever more certain the boy had gone mad!

In the vale below, the cows slept, their front legs tucked under their chests, their heads curved back toward their hind quarters. The much larger bulls dozed standing up, guarding the herd against predators.

I had suggested that Ilio take one of the smaller cows. There was enough meat, even on the small ones, to impress the Tanti, but he had scoffed at my counsel. He had set his sights on the biggest bull in the herd, and would settle for no less a glory.

"Please, Father, have some confidence in me," he'd said. "I am nearly as fast as you!"

We'd come across the aurochs the previous night, after bringing down an elk for our evening meal. We had just finished filling our bellies when we heard an otherworldly bawling sound echoing in the distance. Curious, we went to investigate, and spotted the animals in a marshy lowland area.

"Let's come back tomorrow night and hunt one of those great beasts!" Ilio had whispered excitedly. "After we've fed on its blood, we can take its meat to the Neirie. It will prove to Priss that I can provide for her and her family. *All* the Neirie will be impressed by our feat!"

"Why not bring them the elk we killed tonight as well?" I replied. It had never crossed my mind to bring the animals we had fed on to the Neirie, but now that I had thought of it, it seemed shameful that we had not done it before. It was a terrible waste to leave the flesh of our kills for the scavengers. The elk meat would appease many hungry bellies.

We had hurried back to the elk, frightening away a pack of hyenas that were gnawing on its belly, and then we'd dragged the carcass to the Neirie camp. It was a journey of several kilometers, but the animal's bulk gave us little difficulty.

One of the night guards saw us dragging the animal into camp and had cried out ecstatically, awakening the others. Rushing to us, spear in hand, he had circled the great beast with amazement, gesturing and gabbling in some language neither of us understood. Smiling back at the sentry, making hand signs so that he understood we were giving the kill to his group, we had retreated before the sleepy Neirie could rise from their beds to mob us again, even though our bellies were full and the smell of their blood was not so distracting.

"They will not go hungry tomorrow," I'd said to Ilio as we retired to our own camp, proud of our good deed. "I only wish we'd thought of it sooner."

Ilio had prepared spears for his aurochs hunt the rest of the night, burning their tips in our fire to harden them. I sat across from him, knapping a new-- and much larger-- flint blade, just in case we should need it to finish off one of the great urus.

I was fairly confident of our superhuman strength, but the urus were mighty animals, very strong, and very quick despite their great bulk, and I wanted to make sure we had the means to dispatch one of them should our vampire strength prove inadequate to the task.

Now, looking down into the glade at them, our spears and stone knives seemed laughably insufficient. I was no longer so comfortable with the thought of Ilio tackling one of the beasts on his own.

But he was insistent. He wanted to make the kill himself, without my help. He had made it a point of honor, saying I should assist him only if it seemed the task was too great for him.

I seriously debated reversing my decision. The boy was strong-- and fast, yes-- but the beast he'd pointed out to me was just so... *enormous!*

Before I could object again, however, Ilio wriggled forward on his belly.

He slid through the grass like a snake, stalking the aurochs in the same manner his Denghoi relatives had hunted the wooly mammoths. I waited, tense, as he slithered down the hill, closing in on the massive creatures.

Vampires have a further advantage over men in the hunting of wild beasts. Disregarding our strength and speed—not to mention our enhanced senses -- we give off very little body odor, only what smells cling to our clothing and skin from our environment. Before we left off to hunt the great aurochs that night, we had stripped down to our loincloths and bathed in one of the pools near our camp, using a diffusion of soapwart to strip away any scents that might give away our presence. Although the boy approached from upwind, I knew his odor would not alarm the dozing behemoths. But still, I worried.

Ilio crawled on his elbows through the grass, staying low, several spears clutched in his fists. I could see him quite clearly in the moonlight, the muscles in his shoulders and thighs flexing as he worked his way downhill. His smooth white flesh was very reflective.

Too reflective, perhaps.

We probably should have smeared mud on our skin, I thought. *One of those bulls is surely going to spot him!*

I started to crawl after the boy, hoping to warn him of our lapse. We might still withdraw and camouflage our pale skin, but only if I could catch up to him before he attacked.

Too late--! One of the bulls spotted the boy, and let out an alarmed bellow.

"Ilio, wait!" I hissed, but the boy had already launched himself at the herd.

Even as I rose in pursuit, I saw the lad fly onto the back of the startled bull. I leapt to my feet and ran down the hill as he thrust one of his spears into the aurochs's shoulder.

Please, ancestors, let it be a fatal blow! I prayed, but the wooden shaft snapped. The bull bucked an instant later, and Ilio was thrown from the great beast's back, landing in a sprawl directly in front of the enraged urus.

"Ilio! Fly!" I cried, but the entire herd was in a panic now. I dodged among the stampeding animals.

A subordinate bull charged straight at me, its massive horns leveled in my direction. I sprang easily over the animal, but was struck a glancing blow the moment my feet hit the ground.

The aurochs, a cow, plowed into me, eyes mad with fear, and I was spun completely around in a circle, thrown to my knees by the impact.

Shaking my head to clear it, I stumbled to my feet and continued after the boy, but I was too slow to save him. I watched in horror as the alpha bull lunged forward, running my adopted son through with one of its great curved horns.

Ilio cried out as the animal's horn penetrated his back, bursting out the front of him just below the ribcage. Ilio grasped the horn protruding from his torso, his face twisted with anguish, as the animal lifted him into the air and shook him violently to and fro. Black blood frothed from his lips and boiled from the hole in his abdomen.

I leapt into the air, delivering a fierce blow to the animal's shoulder, but the beast was so massive, its body so dense with muscle, that the animal barely stumbled. It bawled in anger and confusion. I felt pain in my fist and looked down to see a webwork of fine fissures in it. The impact had nearly shattered my hand.

The cracks healed even as I looked at them, and I leapt after the beast again.

I lunged onto its back, thinking to wrestle it to the ground, but I had no leverage, and the bull bucked me off, tossing me several feet away.

Ilio shrieked as the animal's violence sent several zigzagging cracks racing up through his chest and down across his pelvis. He was about to split in two!

Desperately, I went after the bull again. This time I did not throw myself upon it, but drove into it from beneath. I ducked against its hot belly and, planting my feet, shoved it up and onto its side.

It fell with a howl, and I felt the reverberation of its crashing body in the earth beneath my feet. I raced around to its head before it could rise back up and snapped the horn that impaled my adopted son.

All around us, the aurochs stampeded. The air was full of flying mud. The lowing of the panicked cows deafened. Some of the other bulls had seen us and were lumbering in our direction, horns lowered. I swept Ilio's limp body into my arms and leapt.

"Oh, you foolish boy!" I cried.

I landed and leapt again, getting us clear of the thundering herd.

I set him down on the moonlit hillside. The boy yelped in pain, still clutching the aurochs horn that protruded from his diaphragm. I could see the black blood bubbling from his wounds, trying to knit his damaged flesh back together. "Harden your spirit, Ilio," I hissed. "I have to pull this horn from your body."

"No!" he pleaded as I rolled him onto his side. "Please, Thest, don't do it! Wait!"

“It must be done,” I said. “Do you want your body to heal around it?”

But in truth, I had no idea if he could recover from such a wounding. I did not know the limits of his durability. Despite my own apparent invulnerability, the only other blood drinkers I’d encountered had perished easily enough— and at my own hands! I was almost certain the boy’s wound was fatal.

Please, Ancestors, give him strength! I prayed. *I do not want to be alone again!*

The very thought brought back the specter of my former madness, the unbearable loneliness that had driven me to suicide.

If he dies I will kill myself, I thought. *I will find a way to finish it!*

Already, the Strix was sealing his flesh to the aurochs horn. I seized hold of the thick end that protruded from his back and pulled. Ilio shrieked in pain, and I, in my love for the boy, felt his pain and shrieked with him. I had to tear the horn loose of his mending flesh, twisting it to and fro, his flesh cracking again.

It came free with a horrible ripping sound and I tossed it aside.

“It is done! I have it out,” I panted, examining the hole in his back. I could see his vertebrae, the pale curve of a fractured rib.

I rolled him onto his back and his eyes tilted up to the heavens. He was dying. The living blood inside him was trying to repair the damage, but as it knit the edges of his wounds back together, his flesh was turning a dull gray color, his cheeks and eye sockets were sinking in.

“No, no, no!” I moaned, and then I brought up the living blood within me and expelled it upon his injuries.

The tearing pain in my guts was bad, but the

thought of losing another child was unbearable. I summoned up the Strix and did it again, vomiting the living blood upon him.

I could see it bubbling, spreading across his injuries like some tentacled sea creature. It was healing his injuries, but would it be enough?

"Ilio? Ilio, can you hear me?" I shouted, shaking the boy. He flopped bonelessly and I clamped my hand over my mouth, thinking, *This isn't real! I am dreaming this, and I will wake up any moment now with the boy sleeping beside me, whole and healthy. We will rise and then we will range out and find something warm and full of blood and--*

Blood! I thought. *He needs living, mortal blood!*

The aurochs herd was rapidly dwindling into the distance, but they were still within range. I told Ilio I would be right back, and then I took off running toward the herd. The grass blurred beneath my feet. The wind whistled in my ears, and then I was among them. I searched through the stragglers and settled on a young and bawling calf. Something easy.

"I'm sorry, little one," I gasped, and then I scooped the calf into my arms.

The calf's mother wheeled around to charge me, but I had already snapped the aurochs's neck.

I returned to Ilio and slashed the cow's jugular with my eyeteeth. Holding the dead animal above him, I drained its warm blood onto his body.

Yes! That was it!

The Strix quivered as the blood pattered down. It shot out wavering tentacles to absorb the hot red fluid. The black blood within Ilio's body strained out through the wound in his chest, glistening pseudopods reaching toward the mutilated beast. I fed the aurochs blood to it, aiming the scarlet fluid toward the hole in the center of his body. Slowly at first, it began to shrink.

"Ilio, drink!" I cried, and I sat the boy up. I pressed his lips to the calf's torn neck. For a moment he hung limply in my arms, but then his throat convulsed. I heard the smacking of his lips. He seized the animal with sudden, desperate strength and began to suck great draughts of blood from it.

His wounds healed at a quickening pace. I watched all the little cracks shrink, then close and fade from sight. The hole in his chest dwindled, dwindled, then finally vanished completely. His skin regained its alabaster luster, veins pulsating rapidly. He fell back, groaning and weak, but I knew that he would live.

My son would live!

The Strix, which I had spat upon his wounds, crystalized after his injuries had healed. It turned to a fine, ash-like powder and fell away from his flesh. I helped the boy to sit up.

"Father?" he groaned, disoriented and weak.

"Here, Ilio, drink some more. You were terribly injured. You need blood to regain your strength."

"What happened? I can't remember."

"Drink first, then we will talk."

He bent his lips to the animal's neck, and I held the boy in my arms like a babe, making sure he drained the calf to the very last drop. I held him tight, shaken by how close to death he had come.

When at last the ordeal was over, and he swore he could drink no more, I helped him to his feet, asking him repeatedly if he was all right, if he was strong enough to walk.

"Yes! Yes, I am fine!" he exclaimed, pushing my hands away from him. He swayed drunkenly, but I restrained myself. He did not want me to fuss over him. He was ashamed, embarrassed, and my concern was only making it worse, but I could not help myself. I had nearly lost him.

"Come, let us return to camp," I said gently. "You need to rest."

Hanging his head in humiliation, he stumbled along beside me.

The mighty hunter… defeated by a cow!

12

Ilio was weak and withdrawn the three nights that followed. Though his physical body healed completely, his failure hunting the aurochs was a terrible blow to his ego. He moped. He was sullen and uncommunicative.

Though I was sympathetic, I hoped this experience would ameliorate his reckless nature. He had always been a headstrong boy, and he was much too careless when he got excited. Still, I was so shaken by his brush with death that I could not bring myself to lecture him overly much. Also, I couldn't help feeling I was partially responsible for his injuries. I was far too indulgent of his schemes.

He hobbled around our camp, moving like a mortal old man, wincing when he bent to pick something up and stroking his lower chest where the bull's horn had run though him. I held my tongue and tried not to let my irritation show. I've never had much patience for self-pity. Finally, on the third night, I decided enough was enough.

I began to mock him gently, hoping to draw him out of his malaise. Even back then we had idioms like "biting off more than one could chew", not to mention, "grabbing the bull by its horns", and I was generous with them.

At first he acted wounded by my teasing, thinking I was making light of his injuries, but then he let slip a chuckle, and by morning he was himself again.

As night gave way to morning's light, he confided in me how close he'd come to the spirit world. "It was like my body had become a great weight and it was dragging me down into darkness," he whispered breathlessly. He had a very intense look in his eyes, trying to impress on me the gravity of his experience. "It hurt, but at the same time, the pain did not seem to matter. I felt like I was being propelled toward some unknown destination, yet I knew I was not moving physically. And then you were there. Your presence. You were carrying me back to the living world."

"I used my *potashu* to heal you," I explained. "I brought it up out of me and spat it onto your wounds, much in the same manner that I changed you into a blood drinker."

Ilio nodded. "I could hear your thoughts, like the Tanti hunter I killed by accident."

"Is that so?" I said carefully, staring into the campfire. "And what did my spirit say to you?"

Thinking of my crimes against him. The terrible things I had done when I awakened from the ice. No thoughts. No memories. Driven by the Hunger.

Ilio shook his head. "You did not speak. I only had a sense of your presence, your emotions." He looked at me somberly. "Your spirit seemed very sad."

We spoke of the Tanti hunter he'd killed then. Somehow Ilio had experienced the man's memories, learnt the tongue of the Tanti people, by drinking the man's blood.

"And you've never experienced this before?" he questioned me.

"No. Nothing like that," I answered. "Sometimes there is an echo of their dying thoughts in my mind, but it is very faint. And I have never acquired knowledge or skills from the men that I have fed upon. Their thoughts are just whispers in a dark cavern. They fade away to silence even as I strain to listen."

It pleased the boy that he possessed a talent which I did not. He grinned pridefully, said, "Perhaps, I will explore this strange skill further the next time I feed from a mortal man."

It disturbed me to hear him speak of killing men, but I did not comment. I knew he would kill again, as would I. The call of the blood is just too strong. A vampire can resist, but our hunger for mortal blood can only be postponed, not denied. Eventually, all vampires succumb to that siren song.

I have since come to learn that the preternatural skills of vampires vary quite remarkably. While I was much more resilient physically, Ilio had mental capabilities which I did not possess—some of them quite astounding. It is no different from the talents of mortal men. Even womb brothers, I suppose. One may be an accomplished hunter, the other a fine musician. Apollonius, a vampire who became my companion many millennia later, was just as impervious to harm as I, and possessed all of Ilio's mental abilities and more! And my beloved Zenzele... but I will come to her soon enough!

We had not moved from the dried up falls since Tapas and his people parted with the main group. The Neirie lingered in the area for several days, combing over the hills and through the forests, looking for the hunter that Ilio had killed. They did not seem suspicious of us. They appeared to have no inkling that their brother had met his demise at the fangs of my adopted child. After all, we were not the only large predators in the area. There were wolves and bears, large cats and raptors. Any one of them could have killed the missing man.

Eventually they gave up hope of finding him and broke camp. As we slept through the daylight hours in our comfortable little cleft beneath the waterfall, they gathered their sparse belongings and continued east. When evening came, we rose to find their camp abandoned, and so we gave up our own little shelter and trailed after them.

That night we took down a red deer stag. We came across the large ungulate as it was drinking from a stream. I urged Ilio to slay the animal, hoping a successful kill would bolster his confidence, which had been flagging since our disastrous aurochs hunt.

Looking anxiously at the animal's great antlers, he hesitated, but I nudged him forward, nodding for him to go, and he flew down from the tree limbs we were perched upon, concealed by thick summer foliage.

The beast did not see him coming. Ilio threw his arms around the animal's neck as he swooped down, and he used his vampire strength to wrestle the animal onto its side. Quick as a snake, he jerked his flint knife from its sheath and gashed open the deer's neck, holding the animal down until it finished struggling. When we had drunk our fill of its blood, we carried the animal between us to the Neirie's new campsite.

It did not take us long to catch up to them, not even dragging the four hundred pound stag. The distance they'd covered that day took us only an hour to traverse.

We could not take to the air, not with such a heavy load, but we jogged tirelessly, following the trail of downtrodden grass, which was as clear as any modern road to our vampire eyes.

The Neirie had encamped near a thick evergreen wood. Their temporary settlement was quiet as we approached, the travelers subdued. Though many of the former slaves were awake and gathered around their fires, they spoke in low voices and eyed the darkness nervously. I suppose they felt smaller and more vulnerable now that the mighty Tapas and his Vis'hantu associates had departed. Several men saw us swim out of the dark, like divers emerging from murky water, and leapt to their feet. They cried out to their companions, pointing.

Of course they all gathered around us excitedly. Ilio spoke to several of the men in his newfound tongue, but I could still only understand a few words here and there. They were ecstatic when Ilio explained the deer meat was for them, and they took the animal away to skin it on the far side of the camp.

I could understand the men who spoke Oombai, and I nodded to accept their gratitude. They must all have been fluent in the tongue of the ground scratchers, being slaves to them for so long, but there seemed to be an unspoken consensus against speaking the language of their oppressors, as most of the people spoke only in their native tongue, and those who did converse in Oombai were frowned at.

Once again I was struck with a strange sense of familiarity, and I looked more closely at the Tanti men. They seemed to be of the same stock as the people who had birthed me. They were muscular and robust (now that they were free of the Oombai), and very egregious in their mannerisms. The men had thick, shaggy manes and curly beards. Their women were bold-- and by that I mean they did not scurry at the commands of the men or drop their eyes when I looked in their direction.

Could these Tanti be descendants of my own people? I wondered.

It was an idle thought. It snuck into my mind without fanfare, almost as if it had been hiding there in my subconscious all along, waiting for just that moment.

The answer came almost immediately after.

Of course, they were!

The realization stunned me, yet the logic of it was unassailable. It was no coincidence they worshipped a god named Thest. Thest was the name the River People gave me when I became their guardian blood drinker. Thest-u'un-Mann, to be precise. *The Ghost Who Is a Man.* By the time the River People abandoned their valley home, my name had been shortened to Thest, and its original meaning, "ghost", had long been forgotten.

It seemed incredible that my people had survived the last great ice age, and that I had unwittingly followed in their footsteps seven thousand years later, when the retreating glaciers cast my mutilated body upon the frozen steppes. Yet I had merely sought out warmer climes, traveling the pathways of least resistance... just as my descendants must have done.

My descendants... my *children...!*

I was paralyzed by the implications of this discovery. As Ilio laughed and spoke easily with the Tanti, I stood stock still and examined the men and women who had gathered around us.

I inspected them in exhausting detail, opening up my vampire senses to their fullest, taking in every mote and minutiae. There--! That man's beard was much like my father's beard once was, wiry and gray and curled in the exact same manner my father's beard had curled, even to the way the hair whorled underneath the line of his chin! There stood a man whose eyes bore the same somber shape and color as the eyes of my tent-mate Brulde. Was he some great-to-the-nth grandson of my long dead companion? I scanned the figures milling around me with ever more intense concentration. There was a dark-skinned woman who was full figured like my Neanderthal wife Eyya. Though she looked completely human, she had the prominent brow and receding chin of a hybrid Fat Hand woman. And there, a woman who was frustrated with her makeshift cooking utensils stood and stamped her foot, one hand on her hip, in the exact same manner that my second wife might have done.

I felt suddenly overwhelmed, as if I stood in the vortex of a stormwind. Faces from the past whirled before my mind's eye. My brothers, my father, my mates, my tribesmen. Their voices echoed in my skull, so real and so loud I wanted to clap my hands over my ears. I could not understand what the Tanti were saying, but I could imagine that their language had evolved over time from the tongue of the River People. It shared a similarity to my people's language, with its emphasis on plosive consonants and the abbreviated, almost careless way they made their vowel sounds. Though it was far from musical, the language of the River People could communicate a lot of information in a very efficient manner, and the Tanti had inherited this rapid way of speaking.

Ilio took notice of my distraction. "Are you all right, Thest?" he asked.

I nodded absently, waving away his concern.

I had magnified the Tanti in my awareness, taking in their sights, their sounds, even their smells, and all the evidence I collected pointed to these people being descendants of the tribe that I was born of, that I had protected for so many hundreds of years after I was made into a blood drinker.

One of the Tanti men gestured for us to sit beside him at his fire. Ilio was speaking to me again, but I could not understand what he was saying. His Denghoi tongue seemed foreign to me suddenly. I could make no sense of it.

I pushed the ancient memories from my consciousness, closed the floodgates of my vampire senses so that my thoughts were clear and quiet and solitary. The world around me seemed to leap into vivid relief. I returned to the here and now, where each man was the sum of his parts, rather than a swarm of sensory impressions.

"They want us to sit and share a meal with them," Ilio was saying, and I turned to him and nodded, patting him on the shoulder. He eased me toward the fire, concerned by my sudden distractibility, helping me to sit like I was an elder.

"Are you certain you are all right, Father?" Ilio asked, lowering himself to the ground beside me.

"Yes," I nodded, my eyes heavy-lidded, my mind still deep in thought, and then I smiled at him. I shrugged off my shock like a winter coat, grinned at him. "Yes! I am fine, boy. I am... very happy!"

The man whose beard curled like my father's beard sat down across the fire from us. He took a stick that was angled into the coals and put the hot tip to the bowl of a long-stemmed smoking pipe. His cheeks puffed in and then he exhaled a plume of sweet-smelling gray smoke. He coughed a bit, his cheeks ruddy in the firelight. Handing the pipe to the man seated to his left, he smiled at us and said, "*Merh*."

I recognized the burning herb by its scent, of course. Our people had once called it "merje".

13

The man who reminded me of my father—same curly beard, same great mane of fuzzy gray hair—was named Paba. He was a stocky man, late middle-age, with a comically round belly and skinny legs. He told Ilio he had been a slave of the Oombai for more than ten cycles of the seasons. He was taken captive with his two older brothers while fighting Oombai slavers who had raided their village. Both of his brothers were dead now, Ilio translated. One had died shortly after their capture, killed while trying to escape, and the other had died during the slave uprising following my battle with the Oombai Elders. Paba was the oldest of the escaped Neirie who still lived. He had assumed the mantle of leadership when Tapas and his group departed, though he shared the burden of that responsibility with some of the younger, more robust slave men and women, some of who hailed from other nearby tribes: the Grell, the Pruss.

Paba's pipe circled around the fire, and when it came to me, I puffed on it to be polite, though the redolent smoke could do little to enlighten my thoughts. The living black blood moves quickly to eliminate any drug-like or toxic substances I ingest.

Paba nodded in approval as I exhaled and passed the pipe on, his eyes reddening from the drug. He spoke to Ilio, gesturing with a thickly calloused finger, and Ilio translated his words to me.

"He says that he believes you are their god Thest, even though you deny it," Ilio said.

The old man spoke some more, then nodded for Ilio to relate what he'd said. The other men gathered around the fire listened to Paba with wide solemn eyes, then turned to see what I would reply.

"Why else, he says, would you have killed the Elders," Ilio translated. "Why protect the lowly Tanti, even feed them, if you are not one of the... *tessares*?" He frowned and asked the old man to explain what *tessares* meant.

The old man spoke for several minutes, gesturing to the ground and then to the sky and then waving his hand horizontally in the air.

Ilio listened, nodding his head, then explained, "Tessares means 'four corners' but it is also the word for their pantheon of gods. There are four, he says. Namames is Great Mother Earth, Tul is Great Father

Sky, Vera is their goddess of water, and Thest is their god of wind." He listened some more and said, "Vera and Thest are the children of Mother Earth and Father Sky. They are brother and sister, and their children are the little spirits that inhabit the living realm... minor gods and goddesses."

Paba jabbered some more, then spread his arms out.

"But of all the gods and goddesses," Ilio said, "the Tessares are the most powerful."

The old man fell silent, waiting for my answer.

I smiled. To Ilio, I said, "Tell them that I am the one called Thest, but I do not know these other gods and goddesses he speaks of."

The Grell and Pruss gathered around the fire were unimpressed, but several of the Tanti men gasped. They whispered to one another indignantly. The old man, however, burst out laughing. He put his hand on his bouncing belly.

He spoke to Ilio when his laughter had tapered away, and Ilio translated: "He says he has never seen the gods either. Only the one who sits before him tonight."

The old man spoke and Ilio added, "Perhaps you forgot them when you came to the world to free your people... in the same manner the spirits of children forget their past lives when they are born."

I smiled and shrugged.

Nuhnhe, I might have said in a bygone era, but I doubted the old man would have understood the word, or appreciated the sentiment behind it. The word meant "who knows" in the tongue of the River People, but it was more than that. It meant who can really know anything, the world is a mystery and we are nothing.

One thing I did know, however. I knew it would be useless to argue with the old man. He seemed as unflappable as my father. Also, I didn't want to upset these people any more than I had to, or make us unwelcome when we arrived at their homeland. These were the descendants of the tribe that had given me birth. Their great ancestors were my great ancestors. I had lost them long ago, when the glaciers enveloped our valley home, but now we were reunited, as unlikely as that might seem. If they wanted to believe that I was some kind of guardian spirit, an incarnate deity, well… it wasn't very different than what I intended to be to them anyway.

Once again, I become Thest-u'un-Mann, I thought. The Ghost Who is a Man. The god who watches over the River People.

Only now I intended to live among them.

As we conversed, Ilio acting as our translator, the fragrance of cooking venison drifted to our group. The women had already butchered the stag and were preparing a meal over one of the other fires.

The aroma of the sizzling meat was a pleasant one. It stirred up old memories, though it no longer stirred my appetite. I found myself wishing that I was a mortal man again, flesh and blood like the men sitting around the fire with me. I wished that my belly could ache for the flesh of the deer, instead of the blood of my tribesmen, that the smoke of the pipe that circled the fire could still turn my thoughts to dripping honey, that a woman waited for me in my hut when I tired of my brothers' company, that she would welcome me into soft arms, into her warm womanhood, and see me off to fur-lined dreams, sated from food and talk and sex. The wishing was suddenly an ache in my soul that was much more painful than my hunger for their blood. That hunger I could control now… within reason. The ache for my lost humanity was suddenly unbearable. I wanted to leap to my feet. I wanted to flee from these people, find some dark and hidden place far away, and curl around the ache in my heart until it killed me or drove away my mind.

The men were discussing their long years of captivity, the cruelty and decadence of the Oombai. They told me of their prophecies, that the gods would free them from bondage and punish the wicked Oombai. *And look,* Paba said to the others, pointing to me with his pipe, *you disparaged the gods of the Tanti, but who is scoffing now? Our God Thest has come, just as we prophesied. He has taken human form, delivered us from slavery, and punished those decadent Oombai, just as we told you would happen.* He said this to the Grell and Pruss men sitting around the fire, and they peeked anxiously at me, wondering—no doubt—if the old man was speaking the truth. Was I the incarnate deity Thest, or just a blood drinker who had stolen the name of the Tanti god? They couldn't make up their minds.

One of the Pruss men was glowering at me. He was a stout fellow with a face like the knuckled root of an oak tree, his hair shorn to the scalp, as many of the Neirie had been shorn, their hair used for wigs or rope by the Oombai elite. He was dressed in only a ragged leather loincloth and his muscular body was crisscrossed with thick hypertrophic scars. In some places, scars overlapped other, older scars. He must have been a very defiant slave.

When our eyes met, he did not look away, but sat up straighter and said, "I do not think he is a god, Paba. He looks no different than any of the other T'sukuru that came to the land of the Oombai demanding their tribute of blood." He spoke in the Oombai tongue so that I would understand him, but also, I think, to disturb the other men.

"Kuhl!" his Pruss companion hissed, embarrassed and a little afraid.

The rebellious man crossed his arms and said, "Twice the Oombai sacrificed my woman to feed those damned T'sukuru leeches! First, Heda. Then, three summers later, they came and took my woman Gehena from the pens. Tore her from my very arms. She had just given birth to my son. They took the baby from her breast and bashed its head against the post. To punish me for fighting them." Kuhl glared at me with unrepentant hatred. "Do you expect gratitude from me, false god? You are just a blood drinker who grew angry with the Oombai when they killed your little... *pet*!" He gestured to Ilio as he said "pet".

Kuhl rose and stomped away. His back was a nest of raised pink scars.

"Forgive him, Thest, he was never one to hold his tongue," Paba pleaded in Oombai. "His Oombai master whipped him every day."

"There is nothing to forgive," I said. "The truth can never be offensive."

Paba looked confused and unhappy, as did the rest of the men gathered around the fire. They shifted around uncomfortably, embarrassed by Kuhl's ill-mannered outburst. Some of them, I could tell, were also secretly wondering who they should believe—the hot-tempered Kuhl or the old Tanti zealot. Was I T'sukuru or the Tanti god of wind? Perhaps I was both. Who's to say a god couldn't take the form of a blood drinker instead of a man?

I could see the thoughts running through their minds. I could see it in the way their eyes moved, the way their muscled ticked and bunched, the smell of their sweat.

Before our conversation resumed, I noticed several approaching women. As I turned my head to look, the other men around the fire mirrored my movement. Ilio half-rose, a look of excitement on his face as Priss drew near. The women lowered themselves to their knees. Most of them carried long wooden trays upon which steaming venison wrapped in leaves had been arranged. Ilio's female, however, was carrying two hollow gourds.

The scent of fresh blood wafted from the gourds.

The women spoke. Though I could not understand their words, they seemed very respectful of the men sitting with us. Not subservient. Just polite.

Hot venison was distributed around the campfire, while Priss bowed low to Ilio and held out the gourds. She smiled as he tried to make conversation with her, fanning her eyelashes, but she did not respond to his words, and then she rose and hurried away with the other women.

Ilio passed me one of the gourds. I didn't have to look in it to know what it contained. It was the blood of the stag. They had hung it from a rack or a tree and drained the rest of the blood from its body before butchering it.

The men around the fire had unwrapped their venison steaks, were carving into them hungrily with flint knifes. They stuffed the food into their mouths with nods of approval and much *mmm*ing and *ahhh*ing.

I shrugged at Ilio, then tipped the gourd up and swallowed a mouthful of the blood. It was warm. The Tanti women had heated it over a fire.

I felt its heat slide down my throat, as rich and delicious as if I were sucking it straight from the vein. Pleasure rippled out from the core of my body as the blood suffused me. From the corner of my eye, I watched Ilio shiver as he followed my lead.

Smiling and nodding at Paba in appreciation, I thought: *Yes, perhaps this will work.*

14

The Neirie moved on the next morning. When Ilio and I rose that evening, we hunted and brought them the meat of our kill, just as we had the night before. We shared a late meal with them and gossiped for an hour or two. I noticed that Kuhl was absent from the campfire, and the old man explained that the Pruss had parted with the main Neirie group that morning, going their separate way with little more than a few terse condemnations cast over their shoulders to mark the end of their journey together.

Kuhl, the man who had been so rude the night before, could endure no further traffic with the Tanti and their blasphemous gods, he'd said, nor with the blood drinker who had so easily deceived their foolish leader. Paba told us this with an apologetic smile, but assured us that none of the Tanti shared the man's convictions.

"It is just as well," the old man said. "The Pruss are always quick in speaking ill of others. The only time they show restraint is when they apologize for their bad behavior."

Ilio translated most of our conversation, as the Neirie refused to speak the Oombai tongue, but I was picking up their language fast. I could already understand many of the words they used, and had figured out how they ordered them in their speech.

"We are at the western edge of the Tanti hunting grounds," Paba said happily. "If we keep a steady pace, we should reach our village by tomorrow evening."

"You should send a runner ahead to tell your people that you are coming," I suggested. "That way no one will be alarmed by the appearance of such a large group of strangers. It has been a long time since you were taken. They might not recognize you."

Paba nodded after Ilio translated. "That is wise," he said. "We shall do it in the morning." He laughed wistfully. "Would that we could all run home in the morning! Alas, so many of us are old and worn out by our years of captivity. Still, the skills we have learned may yet be of worth to our people. We have learned the art of herding plants. If we can offer our people nothing else, that is still a valuable thing. Our people may yet profit by our return, despite our poor health."

Ilio and I returned to our own camp shortly after and quietly enjoyed the rest of the night. We laid down to rest at dawn, sliding into a shallow cavity we had cleared beneath a jumble of fallen tree branches, the boy first, then I. "Good rest," Ilio murmured, wriggling around until he'd found a comfortable position. I bid him good rest, and watched as life seemed to flee from his body.

He went very still, his lips parted only the tiniest bit, the tips of his fangs showing. He quit breathing. His heart did not beat.

I lay awake, watching the sky burst into flames. The light strengthened, crawled into our retreat inch by inch. I watched the sunlight climb across my hand, my inhuman white skin glinting, and then I shut my eyes and dreamed of virgin snow.

I was a mortal again, slogging through snow to check the traps I'd put out the day before. It had snowed all night, covering the valley in a fluffy white blanket, but the sky had cleared by dawn, and the sunglare off all that glittering ice dazzled my eyes. Every time I blinked, I saw green afterimages. My breath steamed in the frigid winter air. My nose dripped. My cheeks stung.

"Wait, Gon! I'm coming with you!" Brulde cried out behind me.

The snow went *crunch-crunch-crunch!* as Brulde hurried to catch up with me, high-stepping comically. I waited, sweating beneath all the layers of clothing I had put on. "I thought you were staying inside where it was warm?" I said, and he laughed, his curly blond hair whipping out from beneath his badger-skin cap.

"They started cleaning," he explained, and I nodded.

"Ah-hah."

We continued on, walking side-by-side. Brulde said he hoped there would be a hare caught in one of our traps. He had been craving rabbit stew.

That would be good, I was about to say, but someone seized my tunic by the shoulders before I could, and I felt myself being dragged from my shelter.

I opened my eyes. Daggers of sunlight stabbed into them, blinding me. I hissed and tried to bring my hands up to shield them from the glare, but someone stepped upon my wrist and then a spear was plunged into my chest. Once, twice, three times, in rapid succession.

"Die, T'sukuru leech!" a man howled furiously. I knew that voice! It was the Pruss named Kuhl, the one who had been so angry and rude the night before last.

I rolled over, blind and in pain, and Kuhl's spear came down through the back of my neck, plunging into the earth beneath me. The blow severed my spinal cord and feeling fled from my limbs. My body went numb below the neck. I couldn't move.

"Where is the little one?" a second man asked, his voice shrill.

"Look underneath the deadfall. He's probably in the back of their den."

"Yes, there he is!"

"Is he awake?"

"No."

"Then pull him out. We'll deal with him after we take care of the sire."

"You pull him out! I'm not crawling in there!"

"Coward!"

I was confused, frantic. A part of my mind was still walking through the snow with my companion Brulde. Going to check our traps, our wives and children snug and warm at home. That muddled part of my mind mistook my sundazzled eyes for snowblindness, my paralysis for frostbite. Yet, I clearly remember thinking, *The boy! I must save Ilio!*

A foot pressed down on the back of my skull, grinding my nose into the dirt. The spear was unceremoniously jerked from my neck, vertebrae scraping against the wood shaft as it withdrew. Above me, the Pruss named Kuhl said, "Get the bowl ready to catch its blood, Omak. We will drink after we've cut off their heads, then share our blood with all of our tribesmen. The *ebu potashu* will make us strong. No one will enslave our people again!"

"I have the little one!"

"So pull him out!"

"Ugh! I'm trying! He's awakened! He's fighting—*AIEE!* He bit me!"

"Get out of the way...!"

"He BIT me!"

"Let me see--!"

"Spear him! Pin him down!"

I could hear Ilio hissing, the sound of spears stabbing into the brushpile. My extremities began to tingle as the Strix repaired my severed spinal cord. The men who had tracked us to our lair were no longer paying attention to me. They were distracted with Ilio, trying to spear him in our shelter beneath the fallen tree branches.

I blinked my eyes to clear them of blood and dirt. They had not yet adapted to the light, but I could not afford to wait. Now that I could move again, I had to fight back.

I rolled onto my back and leapt to my feet, landing in a crouch. Three mortals were standing around the opening of our shelter, their forms blurry and indistinct to my sundazzled eyes. One was nursing a wounded forearm, while the other two were stabbing their spears into the dark opening of our shelter.

"He's trying to dig his way out the other end!" one of the men shouted. I recognized that voice. It was the one named Kuhl. "I'll run around to the other side and spear him from there," he said, and then he turned and saw me crouching behind him.

His face was still too blurry for me to see his horrified expression in detail, but I could see well enough to tell that his mouth had dropped open in surprise and fear, that his eyes were bulging from their sockets.

I lunged onto his body with a snarl.

He fell back into the deadfall, yelling in dismay, and I pressed my mouth into the crook of his shoulder and did as much damage as quickly as I could. I chomped into his neck with my razor sharp teeth, his hot blood spurting onto my face.

I bit as deep as I could, and then I wrenched my head back and forth, tearing through the muscle and tissue and veins. A fatal wound.

Kuhl tried to speak, but I had ripped open his esophagus. The only sound he could make was a bubbly sucking noise. He slid to his rump, clutching his savaged throat. Blood pulsed from between his fingers, coursing down his chest.

"AAAIIIEEE!" Kuhl's companion cried out.

It was the one Ilio had bitten.

As I stood over his gurgling accomplice, watching the man bleed out, Ilio had grabbed the wounded man's ankles and was pulling him under our shelter. The unnamed man screamed shrilly, clawing at the dirt and grass, but his efforts to save himself were in vain. Our attackers had lost the element of surprise. They were doomed.

The wounded man grabbed ahold of one of the branches, trying to save himself, but he vanished beneath our shelter with a jerk. I heard Ilio snarl, and then the man's screams fell silent.

Only one left.

He had fled.

I licked Kuhl's blood from my whiskers as I listened to the last one's receding footfalls. He was running south through the forest, his feet swishing through the underbrush. It would be simple enough to follow.

Surrendering to the thrill of the hunt, I scanned the forest canopy. The trees were large and close enough to pursue the retreating man through the treetops.

I sprang into the nearest bough, then began to race after the one called Omak.

I could hear him crashing through the forest below, lumbering through the undergrowth like a clumsy aurochs. His breath whooshed in and out of his lungs. His heart drummed: *thud-thud-thud!* I could smell his fear sweat, the sharp ammonia odor of urine. He had pissed himself in his panic.

I flew from branch to branch. My eyes were growing accustomed to the light. Finally, I saw the man below. The one that Kuhl had called Omak.

Omak was running across a clearing in the forest, a spear still clutched in one hand. He was shambling, at the edge of exhaustion, his body slick with sweat.

I jumped down from the tree branches and pursued him across the open field, my body cutting a path through the chest-high grass and wildflowers.

Omak looked back, saw me coming and made a mewling sound of despair. Our paths angled together, became one. At the last moment, he spun around and tried to throw his spear at me, but I batted it aside with my hand and leapt upon him.

"Nooooo!" he wailed, holding me back with his forearm. I snapped my teeth, and he turned his head instinctively, squeezing his eyes shut. I pushed his arm aside and went for his jugular.

Oh, the blood...!

I drank from him leisurely then, amid the grass and wildflowers, and when my belly was full, I left him where he lay. I returned to our little shelter in the woods.

"Ilio?" I called.

"Yes, Father...?" The boy replied, rising from Kuhl's throat. He was on his knees, feeding from the man. He was covered in mortal blood.

"Ah... I just wanted to make sure you were safe," I said.

"Yes, I'm fine." He pushed back his braided hair and returned to feeding from Kuhl's savaged neck.

I watched Ilio feed in the sun-dappled shade with a growing sense of unease. It wasn't the violence that disturbed me, or the fact that we had glutted ourselves on mortal blood. Kuhl and his cohorts had tracked us to our lair. We had only killed them out of self-defense. No, what disturbed me was the motive behind Kuhl's foolhardy attack.

His hatred of the T'sukuru I could understand. He had lost two wives, sacrificed by the Oombai Elders as tribute to the eastern blood drinkers. Kuhl had made his feelings quite obvious two nights ago in the Neirie camp. If he had only tried to kill us out of hatred for our kind, I would not feel so anxious as I watched Ilio feed from him. What bothered me was that he'd planned to drink our cursed blood.

It had never occurred to me just how valuable our living blood might be to mortals, especially if they understood its nature. The Oombai had known. Their Elders had traded the blood of their slave stock for a dribble of the *ebu potashu*, the living black blood that animated our bodies. It had extended the life span of those old fiends, fending off the ravages of time—sickness, infirmity, senility. It had even amplified their senses to a degree. How much more of our blood, if I'd given them what they wanted, would it have taken to spark off the full vampiric transformation in their ancient bodies? Would my blood have made Kuhl and his cohorts immortals if they had somehow managed to kill us? Could our immortality be stolen in such a manner?

He had spoken of sharing his transformed blood with his entire clan. I suddenly envisioned the chain reaction that would have surely followed, the vampiric curse spreading from mortal to mortal like a virulent contagion. First, a whole tribe of blood drinkers, then an entire region, then, after that, the world.

But no, it wouldn't be like that, I thought. That was not human nature. There would come a point when men used their vampiric powers to enslave their weaker mortal brothers. They would withhold the living blood from all but their fellows. They would subjugate the mortals who remained, put them in pens, keep them as food animals. Humanity would be divided, the weak living only to satisfy the hunger of their ravenous vampire masters. The whole world would be cast in the likeness of the wicked Oombai culture—decadent, depraved, inhuman.

I thought of my simple mortal life, its joys, its pleasures, before I was made into this terrible thing that I am now. Such pure and simple happiness would be forever extinguished if the blood curse overran the world. Instead of love and friendship and the sweet joy of family, there would be only hardship and horror, pain and subjugation.

It must never come to pass!

The blood drinkers of the east must understand this, I thought, else the world would have been overrun by our kind long, long ago.

It was good that I had learnt this lesson.

Before now, I had only worried about my hunger when I imagined living among mortal men. Now I understood that I must be wary of the mortals as well. Kuhl had proven that it was possible for them to track us to our lair, to attack us. If I weren't so invulnerable to harm, he might actually have killed us.

If I still planned to live among the mortals, I would have to do more than protect them from my hunger. I would have to protect them from their own ambitions as well.

We must conceal the nature of our living blood, I decided. For their sake and for ours. We must guard the truth until the world of mortal men has forgotten it. Even if we must dress our nature in the clothes of myth and spirit-tales. Even if we must hide our true faces behind the masks of gods and monsters.

15

I think it was then that I first realized how ignorant I truly was. I was old, and yet, in many ways, I was like a babe fallen from his papoose. I was lost in a world I did not fully understand. I had been transformed by a cruel blood drinker, a demented creature that knew only hunger and the need to dominate, yet in destroying him I had made myself an orphan. Out of love for my mortal family, I had never ventured far from the valley of my birthplace. I had remained there, isolated, untrained, until the great mountains of ice came and swallowed everything... even myself. I had thoroughly explored my abilities in the years that I was a recluse, yet in all other ways, I was a child. As much as the boy I thought to father.

I shared these thoughts with my adoptive son that night as we trailed after the Neirie exodus: that we must safeguard the living blood we carried in our bodies, lest we infest the world with the curse of our blood lust. That we must play the part of gods or magic spirits until the truth about our nature is forgotten again by mortal men. That we must make no others like ourselves unless we are certain of their trustworthiness.

He nodded in agreement, confessing that he had taken Kuhl's memories along with his blood. He had experienced the subjugation of the Pruss as if it were his own life, he said. He had shared Kuhl's bitterness and thirst for vengeance.

"You cannot imagine what he lived through, Father," Ilio said gravely. "His masters were so wicked. I understand why Kuhl was so angry, yet in his hatred, he was no better than the men who owned him. In the end, he was just as cruel as they. We cannot allow men like Kuhl access to the powers the living blood has granted us. He would devour the world, thinking his suffering justified his actions."

The moon was bright in the sky, the weather balmy and pleasant. We walked peacefully side by side, following the trail of the Neirie exodus. I looked up at the trees shifting somnolently in the cool night breeze, listened to the insects chirring, the rhythmic croaking of frogs in some nearby brook, and I couldn't bear the thought of this beautiful world coming to ruin.

"I plan to live among the Tanti for a while," I said. "These people are my descendants. I will stay until your child is born, Ilio, and then I go to find the blood drinkers of the east. I would like to know our history, and learn the customs of our brethren. You may accompany me on this journey, or you may stay with the Tanti. You are free to follow whatever path you choose. I am not your father, no matter what you like to think. I am not your master either. You are your own man, Ilio. I only tell you my plans because I love you, and because I enjoy your company."

"I love you too, Thest," Ilio said. "You are as much a father to me as any mortal man ever was. I barely even remember the man who sired me, or my life among the Denghoi."

His words touched my heart, and I stopped on the path, turning fully toward him. My hands shot out of their own accord and grasped him by the shoulders. "I have committed terrible sins against you, Ilio!" I said with sudden vehemence. "I cursed you with this hunger for blood out of selfishness. You were mortally wounded, and I could not bear to lose you! I know you do not hate me now, but I fear you will someday. I fear you will curse the day you set eyes upon me!"

"You have saved my life again and again and again, Thest. How could I ever hate you? If not for you, we would not be going now to live among these people; I would not be expecting a child. I am going to be a father, Thest! My bloodline, and the bloodline of my people, will live on in the mortal world. You have not just guarded my life, you have preserved the Denghoi people."

His eyes lit up as a great truth suddenly occurred to him.

"*Thest!*" he gasped, seizing ahold of me back. "You say these people are your living descendants? Do you know what that means?"

"What?" I asked, startled by his excitement.

"If these Tanti are truly your descendants, then

you are the great great grandfather of the child I have made with this Neirie woman!"

I gaped at the boy, stunned by the revelation. I couldn't believe the thought hadn't occurred to me before. It seemed too incredible, and yet it was true! I felt the certainty of it in my soul. His woman Priss was just as much my descendant as the old chieftain Paba and all the rest of the Tanti.

Ilio danced in a circle, kicking his feet up and laughing. "I will have to call you grandfather now!" he cried.

He was right. I would be his child's most ancient grandsire.

Ilio dashed ahead, taunting me, "Hurry up, Grandfather! You've become much too slow in your old age!"

He leapt into the trees as I stood staring after him stupidly. I could hear him crashing through the canopy of the forest, his laughter receding into the distance. Finally, I followed.

Grinning, I gave chase through the dense network of limbs and leafy branches, jumping from tree to tree as the land rose steadily higher. He was a fast little monkey. His smaller stature gave him a slight advantage when we travelled through the treetops, but I finally caught up with him. He had paused at the apex of the ridge, hanging out from the trunk of a tree so that his body was outside the greenery. I stopped there too, standing with him near the top of the soaring oak, so high we swayed back and forth in the breeze.

"There it is," he said. "The village of the Tanti."

He was pointing down into a densely forested valley. There, on the shore of a great lake, stood the tiny homes of the descendants of the River People. *My people,* I thought, staring solemnly at all the winking torches that lit the settlement's avenues. I felt something lodge in my chest looking down on the village. The rugged gray peaks of the Carpathian mountains, capped in gleaming snow, loomed over the village, but it only reminded me of the great mountains that guarded our people so many years ago. A protective presence, those mountains, not oppressive or threatening in any way.

"The village of the Tanti," I echoed softly.

In truth, I felt as if I were looking through time, not space. I imagined that my family was waiting down there for me, that I might descend from this ridge and rejoin my mates and my children, and that all the years that separated me from that most precious moment in time would evaporate like a sad dream in the honey-colored light of dawn.

"What are you waiting for, *Grandfather*?" Ilio cried. "Let us go check on our new family!"

He flew from the upper boughs of the oak, making it sway violently back and forth for a moment. I watched him descend to the canopy of the forest below, his arms thrown out to his sides, his clothes flapping as he dived like a bird of prey, growing smaller and smaller. He disappeared in the lush green foliage with a resounding crunch.

I grinned, shaking my head with a mixture of amusement and consternation-- praying to my ancestors that the fearless boy hadn't impaled himself on some sharp tree limb—then, with youthful impulsiveness, I pulled back on the narrow trunk of the tree and used the forward momentum to launch myself into the wind.

Interlude

1

For a moment I was twice lost in time, dreaming of my home in the Swabian Alb as I descended into the valley of the Tanti-- *as I sat in the spare bedroom of my penthouse in present day Belgium, recounting all this to my captive Lukas Jaeger.* For a moment, I didn't know which was real. Was I in the past, dreaming of the future? Was I in the future, dreaming of the past? It was the sound of motorized traffic that finally snagged my floundering psyche. It caught in my mind like a hook, reeling me through the millennia to the present. One moment I was falling through the treetops, dreaming of my mates, my brood of squabbling children, as summer foliage whipped past me in a rustling green blur... and the next moment I was in my penthouse in the here and now. Liege. Winter.

I felt a constriction in my chest, as though my heart were being squeezed, as if I could no longer draw breath. Yet, I am a vampire. My heart does not beat. I do not breathe—unless I wish to speak.

I strove to still my mind. My soul was a gaping wound, spurting blood. *Staunch the flow with serene thoughts, old monster,* I counseled myself.

In the icy streets below: the rumble and burp of automobiles. Horns honked. A siren wailed.

Day was dawning on my beautiful snow-dusted city. Its pastel light glowed faintly on the bedchamber's frosted windows. I could sense the denizens of the city rising with the sun, attending to their toiletries, bundling up in fur-trimmed coats (faux fur, of course, in this "civilized" era) before rushing off to their jobs in their rude and fuming vehicles.

I shifted in my seat, wiped a tacky black tear from my left eye.

Lukas watched me from his bed, his body motionless, saying nothing. He didn't have to speak, however. He didn't have to move. He could not conceal his emotions from my preternatural senses. His faintly frowning lips, the way his eyes shone back at me-- the flat and emotionless stare of a crocodile—all but shouted his disdain. My nostalgia disgusted him. For this mortal, love was an alien concept.

"Are you aware of how horrible the present smells?" I asked.

I saw a flicker of confusion in those soulless, reptilian eyes.

"Of course you don't," I said with a smile. "Why would you? You were birthed in the fetor of this poisonous modern world. The stench of this age is as natural to you as your own skin."

Though it annoyed him to ask, I saw that he was too curious to resist. "What do you mean?" he said. He raised himself up on his pillow, trying to get comfortable. I'd been talking a long time. All night, actually. His body was probably aching from lying still so long.

If he weren't a ruthless murderer I might have felt some shame. Our original bargain was for an even exchange: his sad stories for mine. But I was the one doing all of the talking. How terribly egotistical of me!

His right knee was bent in the air, his left leg lying

flat on the mattress. He had crossed his arms.

I gestured vaguely. "The atmosphere has become a toxic haze in the last one hundred years. With each passing day, the atmosphere grows increasingly alien and repulsive. You do not notice because your mortal lifespan is so short, but for a creature like me, it is as if it happened overnight. The air of this world has become a wretched miasma of carbon monoxide from your gasoline-powered automobiles, of industrial pollution, insecticides and fertilizers. Human waste. Drugs. Humanity drowns this planet in artificial chemicals like a child playing carelessly at some new game. The rivers reek of sewage and unmetabolized pharmaceuticals. You bathe in noxious chemicals, then drench your flesh in pungent perfumes to mask your natural scent. Why mortals do this, I cannot fathom, as your natural scent is so alluring."

I laughed derisively.

"Better living through chemistry! Isn't that the motto? Modern man has bought into a lie, like an old fool who believes the snake oil salesman will cure all his ills, and now you drown in a sea of toxic chemicals! Even the taste of mortal blood is tainted.

"Soon, I fear, the scales will tip, and mankind will vanish from this despoiled land. Perhaps that would be the best thing for this planet, before humanity drags the rest of the world to the grave with it."

"It's a big planet," Lukas said. "There are still places untouched by humankind."

"You believe so?" I asked. "When I walked the earth as a mortal, I knew of only three or four hundred other men and women, and half of those were Neanderthals. Man did not dominate nature. We lived in balance with nature. For every human there were a million birds in the sky, a million fish in the waters. I have seen, with these very eyes, herds of bison stretching from one horizon to the other. I have seen the sky darken as if it were night with the passage of migrating fowl. What do you have now of any great number? Rats and cockroaches? Pigeons? If you venture into the countryside, the silence is deafening. Man has conquered nature, and left the carcass to rot in the sun.

"I once fought a war to save your race," I said to him. "I destroyed untold numbers of my own kind to preserve humanity." I looked to the frosted windows, which glowed now with a soft golden light. "I wonder if that was the right thing to do," I said softly.

"A war?" Lukas asked, his interest quickening.

Of course...!

He sat forward, his eyes avid. "There was a war between your kind? A vampire war, you mean?"

"Yes."

"When was this? Why don't you tell me about that, instead of all this soap opera crap? I don't care about Ilio's baby, or how you reunited with your descendants."

"You want action, is that it?" I asked. "Blood and gore and murder!"

"Hell yes!"

"Rest assured, I plan to tell you all of it. It's not much further along in this narrative, actually. I only tell you of Ilio and my grandchildren so that you will understand the decisions I made. You must love something before you will fight for it... or at least you should. What would be the point otherwise? To kill for the sake of killing?" I sighed. "I suppose there are men like that. Men who wage war simply for the sake of killing. For the thrill of it. But that is not something I would do."

The light was stinging my eyes. I was tired. Not physically tired. This immortal body does not grow weary so quickly. I was emotionally spent. I suddenly felt the need for solitude. I rose to leave the room.

"I think we are done for now," I said, moving toward the door. "Is there anything you require before I leave?"

"You're going to bed?" Lukas asked.

I nodded.

"Something to drink," he said. He raised his arm and shook his wrist. "Oh--! And unchain me from this bed!"

I smiled. "I will refill your glass."

2

He complained about the water again. I suppose I should stock a few bottles of wine. I do entertain guests from time to time. Not often. The last guest I'd had in my home before I became embroiled in this dance of death with Lukas and his vile compatriots was a man named Florian Gertraud.

Florian was a serial killer who stalked the nightclubs of Liege in the early 1970's. He seduced homosexual men, murdered them and took their hearts as trophies. The newspapers christened him the Valentine Killer. By the time our paths crossed, he had killed half a dozen men. I posed as a gay man, invited him to my suite. We shared a bottle of wine and listened to music, and when he stabbed me from behind as I stood listening to my phonograph record player, I turned and had my bloody way with him.

I found his address by going through his wallet, then carried his lifeless body to his bachelor's joyless flat and threw him from the roof of the building with a note pinned to his lapel. I AM THE ONE WHO TAKES THE HEARTS. That is what the note I affixed to his jacket declared. I had imitated his block-style handwriting, which I copied from the horrific journals he hid in a secret compartment in his bedroom closet.

I also found the hearts, which he kept frozen in his icebox. Though there was very little blood in the body when it burst upon the pavement, the police were none the wiser… or simply did not care to investigate.

I sat with Lukas as he drank. I did not leave the glass with him as I feared he would break it and use the shards to slice his wrists.

As he drank, he asked me what time was like for immortals.

"In most ways, I experience time no different than mortal men," I answered. "I exist, just as you do, trapped in the present as between two panes of glass. I can glimpse the future that lies ahead of me using my imagination. I can turn and look to the past through the impressions of my memory, but I cannot cross the invisible barrier that separates the present from the future and the past. In that, I am no different than you. We are all trapped in the glass corridor of the Now. I am time's prisoner just as surely as you are mine."

"But your memory is extraordinarily vivid. How do all those thousands of years of experiences fit inside your brain?" he asked.

"They do not. I can no more remember who I fed from exactly one hundred years ago this day than you can remember what you ate for breakfast on June Third, 1997. The little things, the unimportant minutiae… they drift away like flakes of ash upon the wind. Like mortals, I remember only the events that are important to my soul. They are so real I can close my eyes, and it is like I am living those days again. It is like I am there. All the rest… Dreams. Ghosts."

I glanced at him, the hint of a smile flickering across my lips.

"But why do you ask those things?" I said. "You do not care about them. I can see it in your eyes. The lie of your curiosity. What is it you really want to know?"

He took a sip of water. Swallowed.

"You do not plan to kill me," he finally said.

I laughed. "Really?"

He looked nervous, but he spoke his mind regardless. "Your long life has made you arrogant. You don't think a mortal man can grasp the workings of your thoughts, but I have been observing you just as much as you have been observing me. I am... getting to know you."

"So what is it you think I plan to do?" I asked.

"I think you're testing me in some manner. With all these tales. I think you plan to make me an immortal."

"You? An immortal?" I scoffed. "Why would I unleash such a horror on this world?"

Lukas's eyes narrowed. "I'm not sure yet. There's something you want from me. Something you see in me. Otherwise you would have already killed me. I can see how badly you want to do it sometimes. Your lust for my blood smolders in your eyes when you look at me, even though you try to hide it."

I laughed, rising. "You are right. If I were not so lonely, I would tear you limb from limb. I would drain you to the last drop and dispose of your body like the garbage that you are. You saw what I did to your giant compatriot. That is what I plan to do to you when I have tired of your company."

I reached for the doorknob.

"Let me go!" he said hurriedly, anxious to have his say before I departed. "There's no need to keep me in chains. I want it! I want you to make me a vampire! Let me return home. Let me put my affairs in order, and I will return tonight. You can tell me your stories. I will listen to them all, if that is what you need from me, before you change me into what you are!"

I stood glaring down at him in disgust, my lips curled back from my fangs.

"Are you afraid I'll go to the *gendarmes*?" he asked. "I am a wanted man! And even if I ran, you would have no trouble finding me."

"No, I would not--"

"Then release me! My sins are no greater than your own. You have no right to pass judgment on me."

He rose from the bed, and I stepped away from him. I *retreated*, and it infuriated me.

"I know you're lonely. I'll gladly be your new companion. I'll listen to all your tales. Hell, I'll even fuck you, if that's what you want. You can take me right now, right here on this bed. We can be together forever, you and I. Hunt together. Kill together—"

"Be silent!" I roared, grabbing him by the throat.

He retched, his eyes bulging.

Jerking him close to me, I stared into his eyes. "Do not presume to know what I do or do not desire from you," I snarled.

His fingers scrabbled at my encircling hand, but he could not loosen my icy grip. His face turned red, then began to purple.

"You are nothing to me," I whispered. "Less than nothing. A moment's distraction. An idle diversion. If I wanted to fuck you, I would fuck you. If I wanted to kill you, I would kill you. You offer me nothing I cannot take from you by force. You possess nothing that I need."

The vein in his forehead bulged. His eyes fluttered and went blank.

I threw him onto the bed with a snort of derision.

He rolled onto his side, wheezing and clutching his throat.

"You've spent your entire life preying on the weak," I said. "A predator, yes, but you are a hyena in the den of a lion. Do not forget that, Lukas Jaeger. I will devour you if you task me."

He did not reply, just laid there whooping and

holding his throat. I think, perhaps, he nodded a little, but it might have only been a twitch.

I picked up his glass and glided silently from the room.

I locked his door on the way out.

3

I do not sleep in a coffin, but I'm sure you've already deduced that, you should know me well enough by now. Some vampires do. Even in this day and age. It is a specious affectation, an ironic nod to the superstitions that have always surrounded our kind. I've never been one to put on airs, however. I have no delusions about my place in the grand scheme of creation. A bizarre mutant leech, that is all I truly am, but that doesn't mean that I don't pamper myself.

I sleep in a sumptuous four poster bed, a great custom-made bier of cherry and oak, with hand-carved columns and thick draperies of deepest red interwoven with gold threads. I commissioned the bed when I moved to Liege in the early 1900's, and I paid the craftsman lavishly when I saw the work that he had done for me. The columns are decorated with reliefs of leaping animals and delicate foliage, very detailed, in a swirling art nouveau style, which I find intriguing and lovely.

After leaving my captive so abruptly, I retired to my bedchamber. I snatched off my clothing and sought refuge in my covers. The room was dark and quiet, the thick drapes filtering out not just the light of the sun but the sounds of traffic from the street below. Despite the comfort of my dark, warm bed, however, I found that I could not sleep. I was too angry.

I was angry with my captive. Angry at his presumptuousness. And I was angry with myself, that I had allowed the mortal to upset me.

You should kill him now! I said to myself. He has begun to sniff out your schemes. If you allow this farce to continue, he may find some advantage.

He might be a mortal, but you cannot underestimate his intellect. He is every bit the predator that you have accused him of being, and you are not half as invulnerable as you like to portray yourself. He has already guessed part of your plans. You know it is only a matter of time before he discerns the rest!

Plans? I argued with myself. What plans?

I was lonely, that much was true. And I had allowed this wicked mortal to live, so far, because of that loneliness. All the rest was a jumbled mess of longings and half-formed strategies, a catalogue of what-ifs and do-I-dares. My mind pursued a faint possibility-- helplessly, against my will-- but my intrigues were a hopelessly elaborate house of cards, one that would collapse at the removal of any piece.

My captive mortal could no more guess my ultimate goal than he could conceive of some way to take advantage of my desires, I consoled myself. The fool actually believed I was sexually attracted to him! Alas, for him, all paths save one led to his destruction.

And only if I dared to try again.

My thoughts circled the prospect, a hungry fish eyeing a worm. It knew the worm dangled from a hook. It could see the bright, shining barb... but the meal was so tempting!

An end to this unceasing existence.

I have tried so many times before! I won't bore you by enumerating the methods of self-destruction I have experimented with over the eons. I've already told you how I've thrown my body from great heights, tried to drown it in the sea, burned it with fire and acids, poisoned it with man's deadliest drugs and nature's most lethal venoms. I have sent the cells of my flesh to the most advanced medical research facilities on the globe, hoping their scientists, and the tireless computers they man, might unlock the secret of my annihilation. I never sent a sample of the Strix, the living black blood that animates my flesh. No, never that! For the sake of the world! Only a scraping of my cold, white flesh. All I ever received back from them was a listing of my flesh's elemental components—complex structures of carbon and silicon—and inquiries begging me to divulge the origin of the material that I'd sent to them. Or more of it. In all my time here on Earth, I have only ever seen a true immortal like myself destroyed once, and replicating the circumstances of it are hopelessly impossible.

And yet...

Perhaps there is another way.

Thinking of death, I drifted into darkness.

4

My captive was dozing when I returned to his chamber, his body sprawled across the bed. He was sweating profusely, the fitted sheet untucked from one corner of the mattress and crumpled beneath him.

A restless sleeper.

I should think of him by name, I said to myself, *if I intend to set upon this course.*

I was reluctant to do it. A name is a terribly intimate thing to wield.

Every culture has its superstitions: that a name can bring good fortune or bad, that it can be used to curse or bless, heal or strike dead. The ancient Hebrews believed that a man's name was his soul. Even God bends his ear when called upon by name, or so some men believe. And yet the most powerful invocation is the intimate one, the lover crying out a partner's name amid the throes of passion, or whispering it lovingly, twined in compliments like the stems of hothouse flowers.

What responsibilities must I assume then, in the utterance of this monster's name?

Lover?

God?

My lips moved soundlessly: "Lukas Jaeger."

Jaeger meant "huntsman", an apt name for such a deadly human predator. An amoral beast-- child pornographer, rapist, murderer. His name gave testimony to the caprice of the fates. What man, woman or deity could have chosen a better name for this creature, or foreseen that our paths would one day intersect? It seemed preordained.

I stood over him, a silent revenant. Cold. White. Motionless. I examined him thoughtfully, looking for any flaw which might cause the Strix to reject him.

A stout man, his body was dense with muscle, fleshy and powerful, his legs like the trunks of two trees, his arms thick, biceps bulging, even at rest. He was a modern barbarian, with thick black hair and a tangled mat of curly hair on his chest and stomach. Square, rough-hewn facial features, handsome despite their severity. A smattering of moles and freckles. Birthmark on the meaty part of his left hip.

I opened my senses wider, probing his body more thoroughly. Diving through the surface, searching for defects or the telltales of disease.

His flesh was warm and pink, the whooshing of his heart strong and steady. I could not detect any odors which might indicate cancerous or malfunctioning tissues. He had no infestations of fungal, bacterial or viral organisms. His lungs did not wheeze. His intestines gurgled efficiently. He was the epitome of good health, a living indictment of karma.

What a monster he would make!

I envisioned him cold and white and eternal, and shuddered at the thought.

Dare I do this? Was I so desperate?

"Lukas," I whispered.

He lurched on the bed, coming awake with a cry. I watched with some amusement as he scrambled away from me, his chain slithering after him with a metallic purring sound. It was only when I noticed his blank stare, his head jerking to and fro, that I realized he was blind. It was too dark in the room for him to see me, though I could see him easily enough.

I flicked the light switch with the tip of my finger. The incandescent globes in the ceiling fixture swept the dark away. The tiny metal filaments inside the glass bulbs hummed.

I hate that sound. It permeates this modern era: the hum of electrons sweeping through molded metal conduits.

My captive—*Lukas!* – blinked at me like a mole. "Oh, it's you," he said, but his muscles did not relax. He remained in a semi-crouched position on the opposite side of the bed.

"The Strix may reject you," I said without preamble.

"What?"

"If I were to... *attempt* the thing you proposed to me this morning," I said, "the Strix might reject you. The living black blood which animates our flesh does not always accept a new host body. There is sometimes an... incompatibility. We have never discovered why this occurs, nor can we predict if or when it may transpire. If the living blood finds you unsuitable, you will die a slow and painful death. The Strix will devour you from within. I have seen it occur many times."

"How often does it happen?" he asked. "One in ten? One in a hundred?"

I shrugged. "Somewhere between the former and the latter. Vampires like myself-- the true immortals, I mean to say—have more success making new blood drinkers than our short-lived kin. In that you are most fortunate, but it is never a sure thing, even with a maker as old and powerful as myself. The results are always... wildly unpredictable."

"And if I survive?"

"You may become utterly invulnerable, like me. An Eternal. You may live for several millennia. Or your altered physiology may begin to deteriorate in a few hundred years."

"What's the worst case scenario, besides instant death?" he asked.

"You may become a mindless, bloodthirsty ghoul. If that is the outcome, I would be compelled to destroy you. The mindless ones are not allowed to exist. If I did not do it, my vampire brothers and sisters would do it the moment they laid eyes on you. We have an instinctive hatred for the failed ones, the ghouls. My kindred would destroy you, and then they would hunt me down and punish me for allowing you to live." I smiled. "Or perhaps I should say, they would *try* to punish me. I doubt they would succeed, unless I allowed it."

"Punish you how?" Lukas asked, his eyes narrowing. He had relaxed, had moved to sit on the edge of his bed.

He did not seem overly excited by the prospect of immortality. Not outwardly anyway. If I listened close, however, I could hear his heart beating more rapidly. I could hear the churning of his stomach.

"There are ways even one such as I might be punished. If I were to do something sufficiently outrageous, my brethren might be goaded to attack me en mass. I cannot be killed, but I can be overwhelmed, and then they might Divide me. It is how the Eternals are punished. But I will tell you more about that later. In this modern era, such a thing is not very likely to happen. Vampires are very rare in this day and age. You might even say we are an endangered species. We tend to be solitary creatures as well. Group endeavors are a very uncommon occurrence."

"So you do have laws," he said.

"In a manner of speaking, yes, but there are not nearly enough of us to enforce them in any practical way."

"No vampire covens? Like in the movies?"

"Our social groups tend to be very small. Two, sometimes three will travel together for a while. It usually occurs when one of us makes a new blood drinker, but the parental bond sours quickly. Sometimes it lasts a few decades. Sometimes even a few hundred years. Never much longer. Can you imagine being someone's companion for such a length of time?"

"No."

"If they do not part when the bond withers, any affection they may have had toward one another will turn swiftly to resentment, and then, inevitably, to bitter hatred. Even my own vampire children have turned against me once or twice, and I have never been a cruel or domineering maker." I shrugged. "It is simply human nature."

"Familiarity breeds contempt."

"Yes, and despite the changes that are wrought upon our physical bodies, our souls remain human. That is, perhaps, our greatest curse."

"That you still love?"

"And hate. And feel loneliness. All our human emotions—despair, envy, joy, disdain—immortality traps the human soul like an insect in amber."

I watched my captive killer absorbing all that I had said to him.

"So tell me… do you still want this curse? Do you want to live forever?"

He nodded-- slowly at first, uncertainly-- then more decisively, his shoulders squaring with his resolve, his eyes wide and sober. "Yes," he said.

"Even though the attempt may kill you? Slowly, painfully?"

"Yes, I want you to make me immortal. I've seen what you can do. I want your long life. I want your powers."

"Even though you must feed on the blood of the living?"

He laughed.

"And what are you willing to give me in exchange?" I demanded.

He thought I was implying sex again. I could see it in his eyes. The way they flicked down to my groin and back up. His muscles went rigid at the thought. I could tell the idea was distasteful to him, but I could also see that he would do it, if that is what I desired of him.

"Would you *please* stop thinking I want to have sexual intercourse with you?" I said, exasperated. "The idea of being intimate with you is revolting."

His face flushed and he looked away, the corner of his lip curling up on one side.

"I may decide to make you what I am," I said. "I have not completely made up my mind whether to kill you or make you immortal, but if I do, I would require one act of fealty from you. I am not ready to tell you what it is yet. I do not know if you are even capable of it, but I would bind you with one promise, and if you fail to carry it out to the best of your abilities, I will bring your vampiric existence to an abrupt and premature end. Do you understand?"

"You want me to promise to do something, and you won't even tell me what it is?"

"In exchange for a chance at immortality," I nodded.

He grinned humorlessly. "That's an awful big condition to put on it."

"It's a very rare offer."

He scratched his nose, then shrugged. "Sure. Why not?"

I started around the bed toward him.

"Now? You're going to do it *now*?" he squawked, scrambling away from me, his eyes bulging in sudden fear.

"Don't be ridiculous," I said. "We still have many things to discuss. Now give me your hand—*your other hand, idiot!*" I slipped the key to his manacle from my pants pocket and released him. As he rubbed his abraded wrist, free of his bonds, I stepped away from him and said, "I release you, Lukas Jaeger. You are free. Go. Do what you will tonight, but return to my home tomorrow at dusk so we can continue our discourse. I would like to finish telling you my story before I make you an immortal. It is the only way you will understand the payment I shall exact from you."

"I have no clothes," he said, looking toward the frosted windows. It was snowing outside. It had been snowing since I awakened.

"I have clean clothes laid out for you on the counter in the bathroom. There are fresh towels and toiletries as well. Make certain you avail yourself of them both. You stink."

He nodded. He gave me a wide berth as he moved to the door, afraid I would snatch him up and devour him, I suppose. Perhaps he suspected I was toying with him, teasing him with the prospect of freedom, of immortality, before cruelly taking his life. It was probably something he would have derived great enjoyment from were our roles reversed, but I had no such intentions.

"We have brokered a deal, Lukas Jaeger," I reminded him as his hand fell on the doorknob. "If you do not return to this penthouse tomorrow night, I will hunt you... and there will be no bargaining for your life when I sweep you into my embrace... no promise you can make to keep me from sending you to the afterlife, if such a thing exists."

He nodded, his back to me. "I understand," he said. "Don't worry. I'll be here when you wake up."

I was sitting in the parlor, listening to "Gloria" from "Mass for Four Voices" on the phonograph player when he exited the bathroom. He stopped in the middle of the parlor, waiting for some sign of dismissal from me. The clothes I had purchased for him were a bit snug, but he looked presentable. Quite handsome, actually. He would be a beautiful, perfect beast of a vampire. His hair, still wet, fell across his brow like the glossy black wings of a crow.

Aside from a couple fading bruises, he was none the worse for wear.

"Your wallet is on the table," I said. "I put some extra money in it for you."

He retrieved his wallet, flipped through the bills, stuffed it into his back pocket.

"I suggest you indulge whatever mortal vices you hold dear," I said. "Get drunk. Or high. Whatever you will. It will be the last time you are able to do such a thing. And you will miss it when the deed is done. Believe me."

He nodded, his face very grave.

"Your coat. It is cold outside."

He shrugged into his jacket.

"Where do you plan to go?" I asked.

I was merely curious.

"I don't know. Home, I suppose. For a little while. Then maybe the pubs. Or a club. I might even hire a prostitute." He grinned. "Or two."

I nodded. Gestured for him to leave.

He went to the door. Hesitated. When I did not rise to attack him, he let out his breath and stepped into the corridor.

"I will return," he murmured, and then he shut the door.

5

"Mass for Four Voices" ended with a mechanical clatter, and silence rushed to fill my apartment. Self-loathing propelled me from my seat. I put my forehead against the door, my eyes shut. I heard the chime of the elevator at the end of the corridor, the swish of its doors parting. Lukas stepped inside and pressed the button for the lobby. In the apartment below, my erudite French neighbors were enjoying a late supper. I could hear them speaking, their voices genteel and proper. Henri, the retired banker, complimented his wife on the waterzooie. His wife, Josette, replied demurely, "*Merci, j'ai juste fait.*" The scraping of their silver set my teeth on edge. Anxiously tapping a toe, Lukas Jaeger descended in the elevator cab, gliding smoothly past their suite to the ground floor.

I paced around my apartment then, trying to ignore the voices in my head. They shouted condemnations: *You have made a pact with the devil, Gon! You have fallen!*

If I believed in the Christian hell, I would have

trembled.

The condemnations swelled in volume, growing louder and louder until it seemed my skull would split in two.

I put my palms over my ears, though I knew it was a futile gesture.

Thirty thousand years, and I have never purposely committed an evil act!

Trying to defend myself, to silence the thundering critics.

I have done evil. Oh, yes! This curse has compelled me to do unspeakable things. My crimes are innumerable. But never on purpose, never with such cold-blooded calculation.

You will unleash a monster on this world, the voices accused.

"I know," I whispered. "I'm sorry."

So this is what damnation feels like, I thought.

I have never understood the Christian concept of damnation. My people worshipped their ancestors. We did not believe our mistakes clung to us like a stain, that they pursued us into the afterlife, where some stern and judgmental deity punished us for our shortcomings. It seemed rather hypocritical for a god to create flawed beings, then discipline them for the way He had made them, wouldn't you say? Yet, releasing the rapist and murderer had left me feeling sullied, unclean. I was horrified by my own ruthlessness. I would have prayed for forgiveness if I believed in the god of the Hebrews. Not even my ancestors, I feared, could forgive such a terrible transgression!

I ran to my phonograph player and stacked up my favorite recordings. I tried to distract myself by working on my memoirs. As Puccini's "Tosca" thundered in my apartment, my fingers flew over the keys of my laptop computer, but the thread of my narrative was hopelessly snarled with guilt and self-recrimination. I erased more than I wrote, and finally abandoned my efforts in frustration.

I tried to persuade myself to pursue the villain, to hunt him down and kill him, as I should have done the moment I saw him. He could not have gone far. It would be a simple task to track him down, especially at this time of night, when the streets were so deserted. I would take him quickly. Yes, that is what I would do! Snatch him at speed so that the impact rendered him unconscious. He would not even know that I had reneged on our contract.

Now! Before it's too late! Hunt him! Kill him!

But I did not do it. Instead, I cleaned his bedchamber. (Yes, I do my own housekeeping!) I stripped his stinking sheets, put fresh linens on his mattress. I vacuumed the carpet, disposed of the chain with which I'd bound him.

As I tucked in his fitted sheet, I discovered a spoon that he'd been sharpening. It was hidden beneath his mattress. *Naughty boy,* I thought, examining the shiv, and for some reason the whole situation struck me as being fantastically hilarious. Standing there beside his bed, sharpened spoon in hand, I began to laugh.

A shiv! It was so ridiculous!

I did not even notice it missing from whatever dinner tray he'd stolen it from.

I found the scrape marks on the frame of his bed where he'd been sharpening his makeshift weapon. He must have been doing it while I slept during the day. He was nothing if not persistent, I thought, still smiling in amusement.

I threw the spoon into the waste bin atop the coiled chain and empty food containers, then exited his room.

His room...

You should not think of him as a guest, I chastised myself. *He is a tool, nothing more.*

A means to an end.

6

He returned, just as he said he would. I could hear him waiting for me in the corridor. His footfalls, padding restlessly up and down the hallway. He paced like a wild animal in a cage.

Let him wait, I thought petulantly.

I bathed, put on some fresh clothes, watched the last light of day bleed out of the sky. The heavens had cleared while I slept through the daylight hours. The snowstorm had dumped its freight of ice upon the city and moved on. The wind, when I stepped out on my balcony, was as cold and sharp as the razor of a back alley killer.

In the corridor, Lukas paced.

Finally, lazily, I went and let him in. I was afraid he would accost some passing neighbor if I put him off much longer.

"I told you I'd come back," he said, grinning his shark-like grin.

"Enter freely, and of your own will," I said gravely. I did not ask him to leave something of the happiness he brought.

If he took note of my jest, he gave no sign of it.

"It's colder than a witch's tit outside," he said, edging around me into the apartment. "At least it stopped snowing."

I was somewhat taken aback that he could enter my lair with such seeming lack of concern. Perhaps he intended to put me off balance with a show of braggadocio. I half expected him to hand me his jacket as if I were some common *diener.*

“I have been debating whether I should renege on our agreement,” I said, closing the door behind him. “Your lack of respect for these proceedings does not argue in your favor.”

His eyes flashed toward me. His grin withered. “We had an deal!” he protested.

I shrugged.

“I am not sure you grasp the gravitas of our contract,” I replied. “If I do not feel confident that you will uphold your side of our bargain, I will dispose of you and look for someone more trustworthy. This is not a game. There are no rules for you to bend. If you do not take this serious, I will kill you in the most terrible and painful fashion you can imagine.”

And then I grinned, making sure he saw my fangs.

I stepped toward him.

He shuffled back involuntarily, visibly alarmed. I smelled his sudden fear. His heart skipped a beat and then began to race.

“*Nein! Nein!*” he stammered, holding up a hand. “Have no misgivings. I am very serious about the bargain we have struck!”

“I hope so,” I said. “For your sake.”

He fell into step behind me as I started across the apartment. “So… what’s next, Drac?” he asked.

“We talk,” I answered. “As we did before.”

We passed into the dining area. I sat at the table and he eased into a chair across from me, folding his hands in front of him. I could see out the window just past his right shoulder. Liege, surrounded by her forested hills. The Belgian city does not have the most impressive skyline. There are few truly tall buildings. Still, I enjoyed the twinkling of her lights, the way the hills enfolded them, like giant hands cupping something delicate and pretty. The intimacy of the city appealed to my reclusive nature.

“Do you mind if I smoke?” he asked, reaching into

his jacket. He slid a pack of Gauloises Blondes from his shirt pocket as I gestured my acquiescence. "I quit smoking for my health several years ago," he explained with a grin, "but I figure it doesn't really matter now. Our arrangement can only have two outcomes."

"True," I agreed.

He lit a cigarette and breathed out a cloud of redolent gray smoke.

"Ashtray?" he inquired.

"In the kitchen cabinet above the oven."

"*Danke.*"

When he had returned to the table, he tapped his ash and said, "So I suppose we continue with your story."

"Yes."

"You followed the escaped slaves to their homeland," he summarized. "During the journey, you discovered that your adopted son had gotten one of the slave women pregnant. Most importantly, you realized that the Tanti were descendants of your original tribe... your grandchildren to the nth degree."

"Yes, yes, and yes," I replied, oddly impressed with him.

Criminals are usually stupid. I am always surprised when they display some cleverness.

But his mind is broken in other ways, I reminded myself. He is bereft of empathy, not intellect. Do not forget.

I tried to decide how I should resume my narrative, but it was difficult. My present concerns overshadowed those ancient memories, made them seem less consequential.

"I would like to linger on the days I spent among the Tanti," I finally said. "It was a happy time for me. For the first time in several thousand years, I felt as though I belonged to a community again. I felt whole.

We are social creatures, after all. It is our nature to seek out the society of those who are like ourselves. Though I am a vampire, a cold white mutant monster, my soul has always been the soul of a mortal man, and I was happy among the Tanti. So indulge me if I linger on the season that I spent among them longer perhaps than its import to this tale deserves."

Life Among the Tanti

1

The Tanti were the descendants of the tribe I was born to millennia before, but a great gulf of time separated the Tanti from the people of the German valley from whence I'd come. Seven thousand years, to be exact.

Seven thousand years is nearly the whole of recorded human history, and yet the days I speak of now to you, sitting here in this snow-covered city, is four times that length receding into the past, and the bucolic summers of my mortal life yet another seven thousand years deeper still.

The Tanti were much changed from the River People who had occupied the forested valley of the Swabian Alb. So much so that I had only gradually come to recognize our familial relationship. The Tanti were shorter and stockier than they had been in the past, owing, I am sure, to the rigors of the last glacial epoch. They were no longer the lanky forest dwellers I remembered from my mortal life. Their forms had slowly adapted to the long chill that was by then only just loosening its grip upon the world. While I lay insensate in my prison of creeping ice, they had shrunk, gotten fatter and more muscular. The physical alterations were also influenced, I suspect, by the Neanderthal DNA that my unusual group family had thrown into the mix. My tentmate Brulde and I had both made babies with our Neanderthal wife Eyya, and those vigorous hybrid children had lived to make even more mixed species children. Seven thousand years later, the influence of those Neanderthal genes was faint, a weak chin here, a sloping forehead there, but it was easy enough to discern the lingering traits once I realized who the Tanti were. And there were even a few among the Tanti—throwbacks, I suppose you could call them—who resembled their Fat Hand ancestors to a remarkably large degree. Enough to give me pause when I first saw them among the others.

The noble race we now call Neanderthals, the people I had so admired when I was a young man—so much so that I'd taken one of their women for a wife —had strut and fret their hour upon the stage. They had passed from the world of living men but for a dwindling essence, which their surviving cousins, Homo sapiens, carried forward through time like a guttering candle. Their bloom had withered while I lay insensate in the ice, but they lived on in the Tanti, just as they live on to this modern era in many of you.

Height and weight were not the only physical changes the ice age had wrought upon my people. The sexual dimorphism of my descendants had become more pronounced. The women were fuller in the breasts and hips, their behavior more submissive. It was another ice age adaptation-- one that has only recently begun to reverse itself. The women of my mortal era were much like your modern females—assertive and athletically built. More so than the buxom and dutiful Tanti women. They were not masculine, the women of my day, simply more self-possessed and powerful. The Tanti men had changed as well. Their features were more crudely drawn, their bodies hairier. They were also much more aggressive than the men of my era, more confrontational and domineering. I suppose natural selection chose those traits—aggressive males, submissive females—over the more egalitarian gender roles I was accustomed to. Extreme environmental conditions breed extreme cultures-- even gross physical adaptations, given a long enough span of time-- and my people were no more exempt from this rule than any other race.

Physical appearance was not the only way my people had changed in the intervening millennia. In times of plenty, when there is less pressure on a group to reproduce and provide for their young, sexual mores become more relaxed. I was born at the end of a long interglacial period, a time of abundance and ease. When I was a mortal man, food was plentiful and there was little competition between my people and neighboring clans. Because of that, my tribesmen were lazy and laid back. There were few cultural restraints placed upon our sexuality. We had group families, traditions of wife sharing, ritualized orgies. Homosexual behavior was not only tolerated, it was an institute of our culture.

The sexual practices of the Tanti were much like the sexual customs of this modern era. Orgies were no longer a part of their religious celebrations. A man took only one or two wives, and homosexuality was frowned upon. Men no longer shared their wives with visitors. In fact, Tanti men and women had become quite jealous of their mates, and extramarital affairs had become a punishable offense. As I'm sure you've already deduced, jealousy and intolerance have distinct evolutionary advantages, especially in times of deprivation and hardship.

Their technology had advanced. They no longer lived in crude domed tents and caves, which was the standard when I was a living man. They lived in lodges made of wood and stone, with thatched roofs. Though they had rudimentary furniture—benches, tables and shelves—they still slept on mats of woven reeds, padded with fur and primitive textiles. In the center of the village was a community workshop, a freestanding structure with a central hearth. There, a variety of tools and weapons were constructed of wood and bone and stone by the Tanti men. To supply the large community with tools as efficiently as possible, the men sat in a line and passed the work down from man to man, each performing only one task in their production. An early assembly line! Other groups worked as boatsmen or hunters. All hours of the day, and sometimes into the night, Tanti fishermen plied the still waters of the lake, fishing with string and hook or with woven nets. The hunters stalked the dense forest that surrounded the village, armed with spears and bows.

The women were just as industrious as the men —perhaps more so. While the older women looked after the children, the younger women foraged for fruits and vegetables and nuts and berries and grains. They prepared meals together at the communal cooking pits that stood alongside the central lodge. They made and mended clothes in what I suppose you could call "sewing circles". They even tended to the community's livestock—goats and pigs, which they kept penned near the tannery, and a type of domesticated fowl (extinct now) which they called Nukku.

I realize you're thinking, "But, Gon, archeologists say mankind did not raise livestock or plant crops until much later." I assure you, however, neither of these things was invented by any particular culture at any particular time. They are technologies that were developed by man again and again-- lost, reacquired, and lost again—until the invention of written language some thirteen thousand years later. Until mankind learned to preserve its knowledge, mortals lived in a constant state of forgetfulness, a perpetual dream existence, its progress lost to disaster, disease and warfare like sleeping fantasies flee when one is woke abruptly. Before written language, all knowledge was passed down orally, easily lost should a single link in the chain of telling be removed. It also resulted in exaggeration, not to mention outright lies and misinterpretation.

In other words: religion.

The spiritual beliefs of my people had grown quite elaborate over the course of seven thousand years. Crossbred with the myths of all the other cultures they had encountered during their ice age wanderings, the Tanti had become polytheistic god-worshippers. They still believed the spirits of their ancestors resided in the heavens, but they now held that the journey to the afterlife could not be made by man alone. They insisted that the spirit must be carried there by one of their deities, and then only after his deeds had been weighed by his patron god, the good versus the bad. If a soul were not judged worthy of *Esselem*, the Tanti word for the afterlife, they believed that person's life-force remained bound to the physical plane, a miserable wandering spirit, until such a time as their suffering put paid to whatever misdeeds they'd committed while they were alive.

And there were certainly plenty to choose from. Patron gods, I mean. The Tanti had a god for everything, from the least little nature spirit—Tselbhe, the deity of small brooks and pools of water—to the most powerful-- Tul, Great Sky God and supreme ruler of the heavens and earth. They called their pantheon the Tessares, and I bore the name of their wind deity Thest.

Don't get me wrong. I don't prescribe to the notion that the souls of men must be judged at death by gods. It seems to me to be a kind of faulty logic. If man was created flawed, then the onus of responsibility for those flaws would fall upon the maker, not the made, wouldn't you agree? What God had any right to condemn His flawed creation for the very imperfections that He or She instilled in them? It would be like a sculptor dashing his sculptures to the floor, infuriated by his own inadequacies. Surely, a perfect being would be above such petty displays of self-indulgence. Who knows... Perhaps the gods are sadists.

All I can tell you is this: in my 30,000 years, I have never met a preternatural creature I might consider deserving of the title "god". I have met vampires-- and even some rare humans—who have displayed exotic and impressive talents, but no transcendent beings.

Whatever the case, I had no compunctions about assuming the identity of the Tanti deity of wind so long as it greased their acceptance of me and my adopted son.

Lack of faith can be very liberating.

Not all of the Tanti accepted my divinity at face value. In fact, a good number of them were suspicious of me. I was accused—and rightly so—of being a charlatan, a deceiver, a T'sukuru trickster. Remember, unlike the modern era we live in now, vampires were known to mortals then. Reviled, feared like any other lethal predator, but known. We did not fully camouflage ourselves in the raiment of mortal superstition until much later in human history. If not for the accolades of the returning Tanti slaves, Ilio and I would have surely been turned away, perhaps even attacked. In the end, however, we were accepted. Grudgingly, objects of fear and distrust, but we were accepted... and we lived for the first time among mortal men and women.

2

And what a wonderful living it was! I thrived among the Tanti, my true nature known to them all. I was no longer a wraith, drifting through a timeless dream-existence. I felt like a seed that had put down roots. These were my people, my descendants, but it was more than simple kinship. They were an industrious and hearty race, and I was invigorated by them. All through the day and night, I could feel their life force coursing around me, through me, and I soaked it up like the leaf soaks up the light of the sun. Life among the Tanti was nothing like the furtive existence I endure now. It was almost like being a mortal man again.

Yes, I live among humans in this modern era. How could I not? You have spread across the face of the Earth. Yet, the denizens of this modern world no longer believe that vampires are real. You dress the Strigoi in mythological costume, thinking us no more real than dragons or unicorns or fairies. Or worse, make us over into pop culture icons. White sparkly boy toys.

Oh, I'm quite aware of the fervid fictions of the modern adolescent female! The handsome, ageless object of desire... androgynous, all but emasculated. I understand why the fantasy makes you weak in the knees. I assure you, however, most of my kind are far more likely to rip out a girl's throat than accompany her to the prom! I'm probably the most civil immortal you'll ever meet, and that's not saying much. I'm just as bloodthirsty as the next.

This clandestine modern existence, all this hiding and creeping about... for nosferatu like me, it is like being imprisoned. We must conceal ourselves from the world, for our own protection and yours. Such secrecy wears on the spirit, a millstone grinding the heart to dust, but can you imagine the alternative? What would happen if some modern pharmaceutical company got a sample of our semi-sentient blood? What wars would be waged for the secret of our immortality! We would be hunted like animals, vivisected, turned screaming inside out.

If there is one law among my species, one universal rule that is adhered to by even the most incorrigible member of our secret society, it is this: we must never again be known to mortal man. We must ever remain the fitful shadow that trails mankind on his march through the endless ages. A boogeyman. A dark fantasy.

But the Tanti knew me. They knew of my nature. Some of them believed I was a god, some a vampire trickster, but most of them suspected I was a little bit of both, their wind god Thest, reincarnated in the body of a bloodsucking T'sukuru, and they were right.

They knew that I was not like them. They knew that I subsisted on blood. They had had dealings with the vampires of the east-- as recently as the winter before, when one of my kind appeared in the village and demanded a tribute of blood. Several of the Tanti had let open the veins in their wrists to appease the fiend, and he had passed on without harassing them further. My cold white flesh and aversion to sunlight was no mystery to them. They were only confused by my desire to live among them... and my congenial nature. The only T'sukuru they had ever met were arrogant and demanding.

After their initial distrust-- and when I didn't go on a killing spree, sucking the blood out of all of my neighbors while they slept-- they thawed towards me and my vampire son Ilio. Their curiosity gradually overcame their natural wariness. They allowed me to join them in their everyday labors. I sat in their tool-making lines, helped haul in their catch when the fishing boats came in late from the lake. I bartered for supplies or new clothing or crafts with the meat we brought back when Ilio and I hunted. They spoke to me as if I were a mortal man. The fishermen even gave me a nickname. *Shast'pa'ulm*. It meant "snow white"... referring to the color of my flesh, of course, not the fairy tale character. The moniker had feminine connotations, so it was a little bit of a rub, but a good-natured one, and I was proud of it. It symbolized their trust in me.

3

Ilio and I had built a hut at the edge of the Tanti village, constructing it after the Tanti method of homebuilding, with a thatch roof made of reeds and rushes and wooden walls and a stone hearth built in the center of the floor. We had traded meat for woven rugs and hangings to make it comfortable, and there we lived as the summer season withered into autumn, and the belly of the Neirie woman Ilio had got with child continued to swell with new life.

Priss and her sister Lorn were taken in by their parents upon their return. It was a joyous reunion, certainly, although I'm sure it was tempered by the grief they all felt for the death of Aioa.

Priss was not condemned for being with child. The Tanti did not censure unwed women for getting impregnated. They viewed marriage as a contract, and since she was unwed, no commitments had been broken. Priss's parents were a little taken aback that Ilio was the father, but only because it was strange that a vampire should mate with a mortal woman.

They only became more confused when Priss tried to explain to them that Ilio had been mortal when she laid with him at the command of her Oombai master. Her mother and father were simple folk, and did not understand how mortals could become vampires. They believed the T'sukuru were a separate, predatory race—a misconception I did not intend to cure them of, not after the Pruss warrior Kuhl had tried to kill me for my blood.

Ilio declared his desire to be a father to the child, and husband to the slave girl Priss (if she would have him), soon after we arrived, but his attempts to court her were stymied by her family, who politely—but firmly—turned him away whenever he went to call on her.

"Be patient, Ilio," I counseled him, when he threw himself about our lodge in frustration. "They do not disapprove of you. They are only hesitant because such a union is unknown to them. Give them time. Their hearts may yet warm to the idea."

I knew this because I had eavesdropped on the conversations they'd had in their home.

My enhanced vampire hearing.

"And what if they do not? What if they intend to bar me from seeing my child forever?" Ilio cried.

"Then that is what they will do," I said sympathetically. "Be wise. Do not defy her father. You will only harden his will against you. You will turn the whole village against us if you try to force yourself upon her family. You know what a fearsome reputation our kind has among these mortals. Would you be like the blood drinkers of the east?"

"No, of course not," he sighed, flopping down on his mat.

"If the girl Priss desires you for a husband, she will buzz at her father's ear until he surrenders in annoyance. It is how these things work. I know this from experience."

"You do?" he asked.

"When I sought to win the hand of my first wife, Eyya, her father was not very impressed with me."

'When you were a mortal man?"

"Yes."

"How long did it take her to convince her father to accept you?"

"Oh... several seasons," I answered, and the boy collapsed on his back with a howl.

4

Time passes quickly for mortal men, they say. How much more quickly, then, do you suppose it passes for an immortal? The season turned from autumn to winter in the blink of an eye—if you'll pardon the cliché. Ilio announced that he wished to live on his own, so I helped him to construct his own thatch hut. He wanted to show Priss's father that he was capable of providing for a human wife and child. And, I guess, he had begun to feel the need to strike out on his own.

I was cheerful and supportive, but it felt like someone had reached inside me and ripped out my guts. I'd always known the boy would one day leave the nest, but that day's coming was much too soon for my liking, and I worried that he would get into trouble without my constant supervision. He was such an impulsive young man!

Finally, one evening, Priss's father, accompanied by two of her male siblings, approached as we worked on the roof of the boy's new dwelling. With our vampire strength and speed, the construction of the home had gone quickly. We were all but finished, really, just adding a last layer of thatching to further insulate the structure. The roof had leaked the previous night.

A light snow was falling as we scurried about the roof, securing bundles of dried reeds to the previous layer of thatching. We would be finished with it within the hour, and just in time for the first snow of the season. A rainstorm had lashed across the village the day before, and the temperature had dropped precipitously in its wake.

Our visitors' torches whipped and crackled in the blowing wind as they marched across the village toward Ilio's new hut. All three men were dressed in multiple layers of clothing, their breath spilling from their lips in puffs of white vapor.

I was surprised they would come to visit on such a cold dark night. The entire village had retired to their homes early because of the weather. The village shaman had predicted a fierce snowstorm. I'd heard this from some of the fisherman earlier that evening as I helped them haul in their catch, and it looked like the seer's visions had proven correct. The sky was pitch black, thick clouds occluding both moon and stars. Even the jagged teeth of the Carpathians were veiled, a vague shape in the swirling dark.

We watched the men approach, sitting down to rest as spicules of icy snow whipped past. We had made a fire in the lodge's stone hearth, and the aromatic smoke billowed from the chimney opening, keeping us warm, though the cold is not much of a bother to our kind.

"I would speak to the father of the young man named Ilio!" Priss's father called up to us.

"Finish tying these bundles," I said to Ilio as he glanced at me anxiously. He nodded and I leapt nimbly to the ground, startling the three Tanti men.

They fell back a step or two at my descent, then drew themselves up. They were not armed, I saw, though their torches could be used as weapons if the need arose.

"I know you," I said genially. "You are the father of Priss. Your name is Valas." I bowed as I greeted the heavyset man. The Tanti way of speaking was still strange to me, but I was fluent enough by then to need no translator.

The father bowed back and said, "I know you as well. Your name is... Thest." It seemed to pain him a little to speak the name Thest. From what I could discern, he was a religious man and did not believe I was the literal deity, incarnate or otherwise. He had never spoken ill of Ilio or I when I was eavesdropping on his family, but I could tell he was not comfortable with my pretense of godhood.

His sons watched me with wary eyes, the wind plucking at the fur collars of their heavy winter coats. They were both stout men, with long hair and beards.

"I do not know how you can work on a night such as this," Valas said after a pause, switching to a more casual form of speech. "And with so little clothing for warmth! Does your species not feel the cold?"

He was trying to be friendly. That was a good sign.

I smiled faintly and shook my head. "We feel the cold, but it does not tax us as it does your people," I said. "And we can see in the dark."

"Yes, your eyes flash in the torchlight like the eyes of a large cat. It is... somewhat disconcerting."

"I apologize."

"No need to apologize... *Thest*. Does the snake apologize for its bite? In all honesty, I have sometimes wondered what it would be like to have the strength of your people. It must be a wonder to leap great distances or snap the trunk of a tree in one's bare hands."

"All living creatures have their strengths and

their weaknesses," I replied. "I have long envied your people. But you have come to talk about my son, not exchange idle pleasantries in the cold. Won't you accompany me to my lodge so that we may speak in comfort? I have a warm fire, and food and drink, if you desire."

"That would be greatly welcome, Thest," Priss's father said, bowing formally to me. "I have grown old, and this cold makes my bones ache."

"You are not old, Father," one of his sons said, and Valas shushed him.

"Bid your boy to follow, if he has time to rest from his labors," Valas said, and I waved for Ilio to join us.

5

Getting comfortable near the hearth, Valas surveyed my lodge. "Your home is very well made. Very warm." He had shrugged off his heavy outer coat and gloves, and was warming his hands by the fire. His sons had done the same. I was heating water in a wicker bowl across the fire from them, sprinkling in dried mushrooms and herbs. Ilio watched nearby.

"I constructed it in the Tanti way," I said. "It is a very sturdy design."

"The T'sukuru of the east do not build their homes in the same manner?" Valas asked.

"As I have told you all, I am not of that tribe," I said.

Valas smiled. "Forgive me. I am old. Sometimes I forget. Where did you say you are from again?"

My water was beginning to steam, and I leaned over the bowl to smell it. The scent was familiar and pleasing. I had felt a thrill of nostalgia when I found the leaves and fungi I needed to make this concoction, but I had not yet had mortal guests and thus the need to prepare it for anyone. Vampires can eat and drink like any human, but it literally runs right through us... explosively so, at times.

I stirred the liquid with a wooden spoon. The infusion needed to steep a few more minutes, but it would be done soon.

"I was born in a valley far north of these lands," I said, sitting back. "My people were the ancestors of the Tanti, before the great cold came and covered the world in ice. When the ice devoured our valley home, your forefathers fled to the south. Out of loneliness, I sacrificed my body into the jaws of a glacier and found myself reborn, far from the lands from which I was born."

It was the same story I'd told the rest of the Tanti when I was questioned about my origins. I had left quite a few details out of the explanation, but I would not soon forget the ambitious Kuhl. He had tried to kill me and my adopted son, planning to drink our blood and make himself immortal. I decided then that I would never reveal to mortals the secret of our living blood. I had explained the need for discretion to Ilio, and he had seen the danger and agreed to keep our secret. He glanced at me furtively as I explained to the man where I was from, but he did not add anything to my tale. The boy sat next to me, staring anxiously into the fire.

The old man squinted at me. "You say you sacrificed yourself out of loneliness. Why did you not accompany our forefathers when they fled from the devouring ice?"

"I gave myself to the gods so that our forefathers could escape," I answered smoothly.

That was a pretty big lie, but it could not be helped.

"And you emerged thus changed?"

I shrugged. "I do not understand the workings of

the transformation, or the reasons the gods must have had for it. I do not remember anything of the time I spent in the womb of the ice, nor can I tell you of the afterlife. I am what I am. What you see is all that there is. I was once a man like you. My people called me Thest. I died and then I was reborn."

Valas nodded, accepting my answers. "A miracle and a mystery," he said, "but life so often comes that way, does it not? Like twin children born with their bodies co-mingled. Mortal men also remember not the womb. I suppose it is fitting, though you certainly seem to have taken after your mother with that white and icy skin!"

He meant the glacier, I realized. He and his sons laughed.

My decoction had steeped long enough. I took my cooking bowl from the fire and poured the steaming tea into several cups. The Tanti used short, deep bowls of polished wood for drinking. I passed the steaming bowls around the fire.

"Careful, it's hot," I cautioned them.

Valas sipped loudly after sniffing the drink. "It's good. A bit bitter. What is this?"

"It's called framash," I answered. "Your forefathers drank it long ago. It can make you a little giddy, so drink it slowly."

"You are not drinking it?" Valas's son said suspiciously.

I smiled. "You know my kind only drink blood."

"Gibbus, don't be rude," Valas said, and the young man dropped his eyes.

We conversed leisurely as the snow began to swirl more thickly outside. All three finished their drinks, growing more at ease as the night wore on and the sedative in the infusion took effect. They took off a couple more layers of clothing, and stretched out on them, their cheeks flushed by the framash. Valas asked if I would teach his wife how to make the drink and I nodded. "It would be my pleasure," I said.

"So explain to me—and I don't mean to be rude," Valas said, his eyes glassy, "how your boy here became the same as you. My daughter insists that he was a mortal when they mated in the village of those accursed Oombai. She said she saw him struck down."

Ilio glanced at me, eyes wide, and I scrambled to come up with some lie that would assuage the man. It had to be plausible without revealing the secret of our living blood.

"There is no easy explanation," I finally said. "He *was* a mortal boy. He *was* fatally injured. He should have died. I do not know what happened. I prayed for him to live, and he was transformed."

"But you do not believe in our gods, or so you have said."

"Must the Tessares be believed in to intercede in the affairs of the living?" I countered.

"I suppose not..."

"If they rely on faith to exist, we could kill them with a thought. Then what kind of gods would they be? Nothing worthy of our respect, I would think."

"That sounds suspiciously like double-talk, my white-skinned friend," Valas said, but he smiled when he said it. His twinkling eyes asserted, *I will let it go, but do not think I am fooled.*

I did not.

"My father always said: take great care when asking the gods to meddle in your affairs," Valas resumed, looking into his empty cup with a frown. "Disappointment is always the result, he claimed. When they do not answer, which is most often the case, but also when they do. I never quite knew what to think of that... until now. You are either a very lucky man... or a very unlucky one!" Valas chuckled, his ruddy face crinkling.

Unlucky, I thought. Definitely unlucky.

"At least we know the seed takes root," Valas laughed, nodding toward the boy. I glanced at Ilio with a smile. I didn't know then that vampires were incapable of impregnating mortal women. I suspected it might be so. The glittery black fluid that issued from my organ seemed incapable of striking the spark of life in a woman's belly, but I didn't know for sure.

We shall see, I thought, worrying vaguely for Valas's daughter. If Ilio somehow managed to get her with child again... but my imagination shied from the thought.

Valas sat up suddenly, looking intensely into my eyes. "Priss said that you mated with my Aioa before she was murdered. That you went mad with rage when they killed her. She said that you slaughtered the Oombai's chieftains in vengeance. Every one of those bastards!"

"Yes!" I hissed, and I am fairly certain my eyes flashed at the memory. There is no word for the feeling that coursed through me right then, no modern equivalent for it, anyway. My people called it "kel'hrath", which was the joy you feel in avenging a terrible offense. Filled suddenly with *kel'hrath*, I spoke, my voice rough with emotion: "We met only briefly, but I was quite taken with your daughter. She was beautiful, and she had a fiery spirit, which is something I have always valued in a woman. I tried to bargain for her life, for the lives of all three of your daughters, but the Oombai killed her instead. So I killed them. I killed them all!"

He nodded, his eyes misty with tears. They did not fall—not the tears of a man such as Valas—but they glittered there at the edge of his eyelashes. "I thank you, Thest!" he said huskily. "Twice we tried to rescue our stolen ones from the Oombai, and twice their warriors turned us back. My family suffered greatly at their hands, but you have avenged our honor. If your boy wishes to be mated with my daughter, I would be proud to call him my son."

Ilio's head jerked up, his eyes bright. He looked at me with a grin, fangs exposed in his excitement, but no one seemed to notice, or if they did, they chose to ignore the unsightly display out of politeness.

We never did get the roof of Ilio's hut finished that night. Valas and his sons stayed to discuss the dower, and the details of the marriage ceremony. I poured them another round of framash and enjoyed the woodsy sweet smell of the merh they smoked when Valas's younger son produced a satchel of the dried leaves from one of his coat pockets. I partook of the merh when Valas passed the smoldering pipe to me, even though the drug in the smoke would only elevate my mood for a moment, at best, before the Strix eliminated it from my system, as it does all drugs or poisons. I didn't do it to be social, but for the nostalgia. Sitting around a fire, talking and smoking with my fellow tribesmen, recalled previous nights of like camaraderie.

Priss's dower was modest. Valas was not a greedy man. When we had agreed on the terms, her father and I discussed less pressing matters.

Valas was a family man, as I once was, and his thoughts turned to family and faith more than any other subject. He was frustrated that I could tell him nothing of the spirit world, but enjoyed my tales of the time before the ice, when our forefathers still lived in the valley by the river.

His two sons, Gibbus and Sephram, kept Ilio occupied.

"You are our brother now!" Sephram declared excitedly.

Though Gibbus was more reserved, he somehow managed to talk Ilio into showing them his fangs, and goaded him into demonstrations of our vampire speed and strength.

"Our grandchildren will be great warriors if they have even half his T'sukuru strength," Valas said as he watched Ilio stand upside down on one hand.

Our grandchildren...!

I felt a great upwelling of happiness as his words echoed in my mind-- for the man, for these simple people, and for the thought of having a family once again.

I also realized that I had not once thought of killing them and drinking their blood. The bloodthirst was there. It was always there. I was just so used to its clamoring, living among the Tanti, that I had put it out of my mind.

I was adapting to living in the world of mortal men.

6

Ilio and Priss wed shortly after.

When the first storm of the season had come and gone, the weather warmed back up for a few days. It was not what you might call balmy, but it was warm enough to melt the snow that had accumulated on the rooftops and in the avenues of the Tanti village. The sky cleared, the sun flashed off the lake and the air smelled earthy and pure. Spring fever spread through the village like a virulent contagion.

As melting snow dripped from the thatch roofs and the runoff coursed in gleaming rivulets down the hill to the pristine lake, the village women prepared for the wedding ceremony. I watched with amusement from the doorway of my lodge as groups of women tramped back and forth in the streets all day, paying little attention to the mud and muck.

The entire village was swept up in the excitement of the nuptial. Everyone was talking about it. It was very much like a modern celebrity wedding. Even the villagers who had previously been standoffish were coming up to me to converse about the wedding. They visited our hut to gossip and gawk under the pretense of bartering for goods. The village shaman and his protégé performed fertility rituals, good luck spells and came to our home to purify the boy's spirit with prayers and sweet smelling incense.

Ilio had not moved into his own hut, despite the fact that we had completed its construction. Now that the time had come for him to fly the nest, he was strangely hesitant to leave my side, but I didn't comment on his reticence. I really wasn't too eager for him to go either, even though I'd been preparing my mind for him to leave.

I had missed out on this human experience when I was first made into a vampire. In those early days, I was much too dangerous to go anywhere near my mortal family. I had been forced to watch my children grow up from afar, and had missed the sweet agony of my offspring leaving home to start families of their own.

I loved Ilio like he was my own, and I doted on him shamelessly. I made sure his lodge was outfitted with every comfort I could think of: mats, rugs, furs, hangings for all the doors and windows. I bartered for furnishings, all manner of utensils and dishware, spices and stores of food. I had new clothes made for him, and rebraided his hair so that his bride would find him more fetching. For his part, Ilio was especially attentive to his chores and, in general, was behaving much more maturely.

"Do you think I am ready to be on my own, Thest?" he asked one evening as we prepared to go out to hunt.

"As ready as you'll ever be," I answered lightly, showing no sign of my own concerns.

Then later: "I am so afraid I'll hurt them. What if I lose control of the bloodthirst, Father?"

He was talking about his wife and children, of course.

"I feared the same thing when I first took you into my care," I answered. "I'm certain your affection for your new family will stay your hand, as my love for you stayed my hand when I took you under my wing. You should be mindful of the bloodthirst, at all times, but you have always had more control of it than I. I think you will be fine."

"If I feel my restraint weakening, I will flee to the wilderness and hunt until I'm as fat as a tick," he said seriously, and I nodded in sympathy, laughing a little. Then we slipped out into the dark avenue and raced like pale revenants to hunt the forest for blood.

Twice, Ilio announced that he was going to move into his new home, and twice he reneged, but I did not comment.

One evening, Priss's brothers came and stole Ilio away. They were boisterous, as fresh young men often are. They said they were taking him across the lake to engage in some kind of pre-wedding tradition — the Tanti equivalent of a stag party. I grew bored waiting for him to return and began to straighten up my lodge, and that is when I found all the little toys I had carved for him when he was a mortal child.

I found them wrapped carefully in some hides beside his sleeping mat. They were pressed into the corner of the wall behind the rolled up fur he rested his head upon when he slept. I squatted and picked them up from the floor after they had tumbled from the hide. Turning them over in my hands, I examined them. Little wooden men, a carving of a wooly mammoth, a spear-tooth cat (one of the hind legs broken off). My eyes stung suddenly and I wrapped them back up and returned them where I'd found them.

You've become a sentimental fool, Gon! I berated myself, wiping black tears from my cheeks.

At least I could take solace from the company of Priss's extensive family.

As the nuptial drew nearer, Priss's father had become a frequent visitor in my home. He had taken a liking to my framash... and a liking to me as well. He enjoyed gossiping about his fellow villagers, especially who was coupling with who behind who's back. He had an inordinate amount of interest in the sexual escapades of his neighbors. He also derived great enjoyment from complaining about his wife, his ungrateful kids, and was not averse to the telling of tall tales—"big fish stories", the Tanti called them. It often felt as if we were co-conspirators in some plot I was only half-aware of, but I liked him. I enjoyed our conversations, especially with Ilio absent so much of the time now.

Nearly every evening, usually around sundown, Valas would yell from my doorway: "Oya, Shast'pa'ulm! Thest, you old bloodsucker! Rise and tend to your guest!" Sometimes he came with his sons or his cousins or sons-by-marriage, but usually he came on his own. When I swept open the door hanging to admit him, he strolled in without hesitation, giving my crotch a passing swat—a gesture of affection among Tanti men, somewhat similar to the way your modern athletes will slap one another on the rump during games. "Are you hiding a hogleg in there?" he would ask-- or something in that vein-- and then he would throw himself on a mat beside the hearth and wait for me to prepare some framash.

If Ilio was still home, the boy would roll up in his

bedding, complaining about the light. Usually he was gone by the time Valas came around, however. Ilio had begun to venture out before nightfall more and more frequently. Trying to get better accustomed to the daylight, he claimed.

"You'll never guess who I caught sneaking off into the woods with my brother Hale today, Thest," the old fellow grinned, running his fingers through his great frizzy beard.

"Who?" I asked, building up the fire in my hearth.

"Lettia! Tateron's new wife!" and then he proceeded to tell me of Lettia and Hale's longstanding affair, opining at length how calculating some women can be when it comes to their own satisfaction. "Hale is a lazy man. A terrible provider. He is my brother, but I am only speaking the truth. She would have been crazy to choose Hale over Tateron. Still, there are some things more important than a full belly and a warm hearth! While Tateron is out fishing on the lake, Lettia goes fishing as well." And then he burst out laughing.

The sons of Valbaulm, Valas's father, were renown in the village of the Tanti for their fertility... and their physical endowments. Valas, like most religious men I'd ever met, was inordinately obsessed with carnal things. He took great pride in his family's reputation as cocksmen and the number of children he had sired—sixteen, at present count, by two wives, the first of whom was (unsurprisingly) dead. Yet he was strangely prudish about subjects outside his experience. He acted appalled when I asked him if Tanti wedding rituals included a celebratory orgy, as his forefather's had practiced when I was a mortal.

"Great Tul, no! How would we know what children were ours if we all just humped in a pile? And you say our forefathers indulged in such rituals? Ha! I'd be afraid some nearsighted fool would mistake my fat rump for a woman's hindquarters!"

He was scandalized when I revealed that my group marriage had included a co-husband-- my lifelong companion Brulde, who raised our children after I was made into this thing that I am.

"Sometimes our young males will dabble in such behavior, but we try to discourage it whenever we can," Valas said. "It is not productive for a man to lie down with a man." He snorted. "Although I have heard some pretty lurid tales about those fishermen! Sometimes we see the boats rocking, but none of the men hauling in nets! They say they're napping-- ha!"

"There are advantages to such a living arrangement," I countered.

"Oh, I'm certain there are!" he exclaimed merrily. "There would be less children to tend to, for one thing. And a lot less haggling for sex!"

That wasn't really what I meant, but I didn't bother to debate the matter with him. Most people will not tolerate ideas foreign to their upbringing. I merely steeped his framash and let him ramble until he left.

In the meantime, Ilio was staying very busy himself.

Tanti marriages were often arranged, although allowances were made if the betrothed were irreconcilably incompatible, or a woman became pregnant by another man. The Tanti also tended to discourage intercourse between the prospective bride and groom before the wedding ceremony—socially as well as sexually. This was supposed to make the couple pine for one another, but I believe it was really just to make sure both parties had less of a chance to find fault in their mate and spoil everybody's plans. Ilio had only been allowed to visit with Priss a few times since our arrival in the village, and once the two of them were officially betrothed, he was not allowed to see her at all.

He spent his days adding the finishing touches to the home he had built for her, and gathering the dower we had all agreed upon (mostly foodstuffs, but also animal hides and trinkets for her mother and father and all her brothers and sisters).

He was restless and uncertain, and constantly sought my advice on everything from lovemaking to childrearing.

Childrearing I could tell him about. I had fathered six children. Lovemaking was the topic that neither of us were quite certain of.

I had plenty of experience with human sexuality. My people had been very casual about sex. But sex between a vampire and a mortal... that was a different matter altogether.

I knew it could be done. I had made love to Priss's sister Aioa when we visited the village of the Oombai. But it was the first and only time I'd made love to a mortal woman, and she had allowed me to drink of her blood in the midst of our congress. It had been a rapturous experience for me, my spirit soaring to the peak of sensual ecstasy, but I could not in all honesty encourage the boy to do anything but approach the act with the utmost care.

"I would discourage you from making love at all while she is with child," I counseled the young man. "With your strength, you could easily injure your bride, and your unborn child. If you wish to have congress with her after the child is born, do not use your hands on her until you are certain of your self-control. Allow her to make love to you."

I also advised him to depart from her temporarily during her monthly cycle. The blood that issued from her body, I feared, might tempt him to unsavory behavior.

"Blood?" he asked. "What do you mean? Why

would she bleed every cycle of the moon?"

"It is her estrus," I explained. "Have I never told you of the female cycle?"

"No."

"No? I'm certain that I did."

He shook his head, eyes wide.

His ignorance did not surprise me. He had been raised almost exclusively by men in a tribe of nomadic mammoth hunters. The Denghoi were quite circumspect about their sexual practices as well. He had been ignorant of even the rudiments of human sexuality when I adopted him.

So I had to educate him about the monthly cycle of the female reproductive system, how blood would issue from her sexual organ once a month unless she was with child, and that childbirth, too, would be a rather bloody affair.

"When the child comes, you must leave her to the care of her mother and sisters, and then come here immediately. You'll have to stay with me for a while afterwards as well, I should think. The mother of your child will bleed for several weeks after the child is delivered."

"Ancestors, they bleed an awful lot!" Ilio said with a nervous titter. It was obvious he was overwhelmed by all that I'd just told him.

"It is just the nature of things," I replied. "Birds fly, fish swim and women bleed."

7

Finally, the day of the wedding came, and the entire village, it seemed, turned out for the ceremony. The rite took place at the edge of the lake where meadow gave way to a swath of powder soft sand. The warm weather had lingered, though the sky was sodden and gray with clouds, rain's moist promise, and the wind came whipping in from the choppy surface of the lake, wet and chill. But at least the sun was occluded, and my cheeks were clear of the tarry black tears that vampires weep in bright sunshine.

Valas had tutored me in the procedures of the Tanti nuptial ceremony for the past several days, and I stood with him behind the village shaman, who would perform the bulk of the ritual to bind our two children in matrimony.

The rites would be somewhat altered for this unusual wedding, as the gods of the Tanti were invoked in the ceremony, and there were many who believed that I was the physical incarnation of one of those deities, but it did not seem as though it would be a problem with the majority of the Tanti people. They had an abundance of deities, and they were not overly concerned with those they had not dedicated themselves to.

The shaman, a leathery old thing name Padtuk, invoked the gods of the Tanti, calling out the name of each one in the order of their rank in Tanti culture. The villagers, who sat in a broad semi-circle before us, echoed back the name of each deity he entreated.

"...And we call upon the god of the hearth, Moab, the goddess of the threshold, Anavetrazeesi, the god of tools, Heb, and the goddess Yenaulba, who sanctifies the food that we put into our bodies," the old man droned.

"Moab... Anavetrazeesi... Heb... Yenaulba..." the crowd reverberated gravely.

So many mortals—I could feel them staring at me with avid curiosity! I searched the crowd with my gaze, taking pleasure in picking out the ones who bore the features of their ancient ancestors. There was the one who looked like my Eyya. She was sitting beside Paba, fussing with his clothing. There was a young man who favored Nyala, my second wife, and another fine fellow who had Brulde's somber eyes. I spied yet another, a lanky woman, who had my auburn hair and long, narrow face. How many generations separated the two of us, I wondered, this long lost granddaughter? And what a miracle I had found her across such vast gulfs of time!

Babies cried and children ran freely through the congregation, some of them playing in the sand, as Padtuk continued to call out to their deities. Finally, he finished. Either he'd run out of breath or run out of gods. When his voice fell away, Ilio approached from the village, decked out in his finest attire. He grinned at me as he passed through the assembly, then lowered himself to his knees in front of the shaman.

"Valas, father of Priss, this man Ilio petitions you for the hand of your daughter in marriage. Do you approve of this union?" Padtuk asked.

"I do," Valas bellowed, speaking loud so that everyone could hear him.

"The father of Priss approves of this man!" Padtuk cried. "Summon the woman this man would take for his bride!"

Priss appeared shortly after, escorted by her eldest brother. She was decked in a long braided dress, her features obscured by an ornate tasseled veil. At the sight of her, Valas's wife and daughters began to weep inconsolably.

Ilio turned to watch his betrothed approach, his eyes shining worshipfully as she descended to the beach. Despite the flowing garments, her pregnancy was quite evident. I had not glimpsed her since shortly after our arrival, and I was shocked how big she had gotten with child. She looked like she might burst at the slightest misstep.

She made her way gingerly across the sand, Gibbus holding onto her elbow to steady her. The wind coming off the lake made her garments flutter. She pushed the tassels of her veil from her eyes so she could better make her way through the crowd, and I was struck by her prettiness. She was lovely like her sister, but her features were more delicate, gentler. Light complected skin, freckled cheeks with long honey-gold eyelashes perched upon them. Her hair had grown out since she escaped from slavery, and it curled at her cheeks and around her lithesome neck. Some of the villagers who had come to honor the ceremony reached up to touch her hand or stroke her swollen belly as she passed, and she smiled down at them.

Ilio stared at her fixedly as she crossed the beach to him, his eyes wide, almost frightened-looking. I knew that look: disbelief that such a woman might want him, and fear that she might snatch back her affection at the slightest provocation.

She took his proffered hand, lowered herself to her knees, her movements ponderous. I narrowed my eyes. She was so big! Too big to be carrying just one baby. I lowered my mental barriers and probed her body with my enhanced vampire senses, trying to ignore the scents of all the mortals gathered around me, the delicious odor of their bodies. Sights, sounds and smells assaulted my consciousness, but I narrowed my focus, concentrating solely on the bride.

There!

I heard the steady, somewhat anxious *thud-tump* of her heart, but below that, softer and more rapidly paced, two additional hearts, beating almost in tandem: *tud-tud-tud-tud!*

Twins! I realized, the wonder of it flashing in my eyes. Ilio's betrothed was pregnant with twins!

I was so distracted I almost forgot my part in the ritual.

"Thest, father of Ilio, this woman Priss petitions

you for your son's hand in marriage," Padtuk said. "Do you approve of this union?"

Valas nudged me when I did not immediately reply, and I stammered, "Y-yes...I mean, I do!"

"The father of Ilio approves of this woman!" Padtuk cried out.

The shaman called on the Tessares to bless their union, turning to the four corners of the heavens as he invoked their names: Great Father Sky, Tul, to ensure they coupled frequently and with equal pleasure, Great Mother Earth, Namames, to ensure that they had many strong babies, the goddess of the waters, Vera, to ensure they lived without strife, and finally the god of the winds, Thest, to deliver their prayers to the heavens.

All eyes turned to me as the shaman called out the name I shared with their deity, and as we had prearranged, I bowed as if to accept the shaman's entreaty.

"Rise before your fathers, Ilio and Priss. You are bound now, one to the other, in the eyes of the people, and in the eyes of the gods." And then to the villagers who'd come to witness the ceremony: "Let us celebrate this blessed union together!"

Twins! I thought with delight as Ilio helped his protuberant new wife to her feet.

8

"Twins?" Valas exclaimed. "Are you certain, my friend?"

I had just told him the good news.

We were in the broad avenue that marked the center of the village, standing near the cooking pits. Tanti men and women packed the boulevard from one side of the village to the other, eating, dancing, playing music. The women had put on their finest garments. There were contests of strength and marksmanship. Tanti children chased one another between the legs of the adults, their laughter and shrill cries punctuating the buzzing air. Though it was late in the afternoon, the wedding celebration was still in full swing. Had been from the very instant the ceremony ended. The frenetic activity made my senses reel, but I was enjoying the festivities nonetheless, the sensual pleasure of all those mortal bodies pressing so close around me, their excitement and all the brightly colored dress.

The trilling of bone flutes and thumping drums played counterpoint to the throbbing hunger in my belly. I would have to hunt tonight, fill myself near to bursting, or risk temptation.

I nodded distractedly. "Oh, yes. My hearing is quite sensitive. There are two tiny hearts beating in our daughter's belly. I noticed during the ceremony."

"The gods do favor this union then!" Valas laughed. "I had my doubts, but there can be no question now! We are twice blessed, Brother. Have you told the children yet?"

"Not yet. I've barely seen them," I answered, scanning the crowd for the newlyweds.

"Let it wait then. These fools will drop from exhaustion soon enough," Valas replied, a steaming hunk of venison in his hand. He began to unwrap the leaf the animal flesh had been cooked in, stuffing the hot, greasy meat into his mouth. "Come, Thest. Let us go and watch those wanton hussies dance. I think it won't be long before they throw those skirts up over their heads!"

"Beware of jealous ears, my friend," I laughed, nodded to his right.

"Wha--?" He whipped around with a guilty expression, but it was too late. His wife was already stomping toward him, storm clouds gathering on her brow.

"Yorda!"

"I heard that, you horny old dog!"

"I was only making a jest. Right, Thest?"

Yorda's head snapped toward me, her fists sunk into the fat of her hips. I tried to blunt her wrath. "Only a joke, Yorda. You know how tongues wag."

"It's not his tongue I'm worried about!" Yorda growled.

It was obvious the happy couple needed a moment or two of privacy. Yorda was already beating her fists against his chest. I bid the stammering Valas a sympathetic good-bye and pressed through the crowd in search of Ilio and his new bride.

I found them near the boy's new lodge, accepting gifts from cheerful well-wishers. Priss was sitting on a low wooden bench, cradling her stomach, weary but happy. Ilio stood attentively at her side, looking after her needs.

They seemed relieved when I asked to speak to them alone, and we walked a short distance away, Priss limping a little, her feet swollen. Ilio held her by the elbow.

In a quiet alleyway between a couple homes, I embraced them both and told them how happy I was for them.

"I have tidings which I trust you'll both find joyous," I said. I was quivering with excitement. "I have been meaning to tell you all morning, only I have not had the chance."

"What is it, Father?" Ilio asked.

They were stunned. Ilio dropped to his knees to listen to her swollen belly. "It's true!" Ilio gasped after a moment. "It is hard to hear it because their hearts beat almost as one, but there are two babies growing inside your womb, wife!"

Priss's eyes glimmered with tears as she stared down at her stomach. "Oh, Ilio--!" she sobbed. "It is too good to be true! If one of the babies is a girl, let me name it after my sister, Aioa!"

"Of course!"

Priss smiled up at me. "And if a boy, we should name him Tu'Thest, in honor of our deliverer!"

The prefix "tu" meant "small" in the Tanti language. It was their way of naming someone "junior".

The Tanti didn't kiss as modern people do, pressing their mouths together. They would have thought such an act unhygienic. Instead, she threw her arms around me and put her cheek to mine.

"Thank you, Thest!" she murmured in my ear. "This is the most wonderful gift of all!"

Her flesh felt so soft and warm against mine. I could feel the heat of her blood as it coursed just below the surface of her skin. It made the hunger leap inside my belly, but I thrust the monster back inside its cave and rolled a stone in front of it, horrified by my instinctual reaction.

Have you no shame, monster? I berated myself.

I embraced Ilio again and told them they could find me in my lodge if they needed me further today. "I am going to my bed. It has been a long day and I am weary to my bones."

"I understand, Father."

"I will see you—" I almost said "tonight", but of course, I would not have his company tonight. Tonight, he would retire to his new home, and to the care of his new bride. Perhaps he would join me for the hunt, I thought, but I did not put the question to him. I did not want the boy to feel torn between us. I smiled at them awkwardly, then bowed and walked away.

9

I took the long way around the village, hoping to avoid the boisterous crowd. I really was weary to the bones, and the daylight was making my head ache, despite the overcast sky. Behind one of the huts, a mangy-looking mongrel was scrounging through castoffs. He looked so skinny and forlorn, I instantly took pity on the animal. "Here, boy," I called, kneeling down. The mongrel jumped in surprise at the sound of my voice and pelted away down the alley, tail tucked between his legs, scraps forgotten.

I rose with a faint frown, looking after the animal for a moment or two, then continued to my hut.

The dark inside was a relief to my stinging eyes. I felt the tension drain out of my neck and shoulders. *At last-- rest!* I built up the fire in my hearth until my little lodge was hot enough to roast meat, and then I undressed and slipped into the soft embrace of my sleeping furs, rolling up in them, wiggling around until I'd found the most comfortable spot in which to lie. My own flesh felt cold and foreign to me. And heavy. So heavy.

Listening to the drums banging outside in the avenue, the laughter and loud conversations of the celebrants, the trilling of the flutes, I closed my eyes and gave up the mortal world.

It was like skidding down a dark passage.

I had two dreams that afternoon.

In the first, I was standing at the edge of an icy crevasse, the whole world stretched out around me-- the mountains of my native land, the vast flat plains beyond, caught in winter's white teeth. Bitter gales buffeted my body, whipping my clothes, making my hair billow like the tentacles of a sea creature. I was staring into the jagged maw of the creaking abyss, thinking, *This will end it, surely. Please, ancestors, let this end it! I cannot stand this loneliness anymore. Everyone I love is dead and gone.*

As I stared into that dark maw, squinting in the blasting wind, I realized there was someone standing beside me.

I knew who it was before I even looked up.

Brulde--!

We faced one another, two fleas perched upon the back of an icy leviathan. My lifelong companion. Brulde regarded me with pitiless eyes, silent and grim. His curling blond hair lifted and fell. His beard had frosted over, icicles depending from his scruffy chin. A lifetime of memories streaked across the dark walls of my mind-- the boy, the father, the old man. I wanted to reach out to him, but I held back, fearful, though I could not articulate the reason why I should feel that way. Suddenly, his lips split open, a leering grin, revealing a pair of curving, wolf-like fangs. "Jump!" he snarled, and I came awake in my lodge, biting back a cry.

A dream! Just a dream.

I closed my eyes and drifted off again.

In the second dream, I was in some unfamiliar forest. It was night. Pale moonlight filtered through a lattice of bare tree limbs.

I was not alone.

Something smooth and cold caressed my upper arms. Fingers, delicate and thin. The palm of a hand. I felt breasts-- small, round, firm—press against the middle of my back. And then a woman's voice, purring with amusement... or perhaps contempt.

"Surrender to me, beautiful one," the unseen woman murmured, and I wanted to obey her. With all my soul, I wanted to submit to her. To that husky, purring voice. "Surrender," she said, "and I will let him live…"

I awoke, the touch of my dream seductress lingering on my flesh. I was staring at the roof of my hut, watching the shadows twitch between the beams of the roof in the low red light of the hearth. The village was silent, the flash of the sun absent now from all the little chinks in the roof and walls. Night had come. All the day's celebrants had retired to their beds in exhaustion.

I rose, my belly clamoring for sustenance.

To the hunt.

"Well, hello there!" I said, looking down with a bemused expression.

My cock stood out rigidly from the fuzz of my lower abdomen, a pale and turgid cucumber.

"What's aroused you from hibernation?"

When I was a mortal man, my organ had always awakened before I. It had every morning I can recall from the day that I became a man. So dependable was it, in fact, my mates had nicknamed it "the daily prod". Not so once I became a cold-blooded immortal, but don't think the male organ merely ornamental after a man is made into a vampire. Even the undead can be enflamed by passionate feelings. Still, it was uncommon to awake in such a state now, and I wondered at the dream that had stirred the sleeping beast.

It was easy enough to recall the dream's particulars. I always remembered my dreams. The husky purr of the unseen temptress. The soft press of her breasts against my back. My recollection was so vivid that my cock stiffened even further.

This was certainly strange!

Because I was alone, I gave the proboscis a experimental clout. It bobbed up and down a couple times as if sniffing at the air, and a tingle of pleasure rippled throughout my body.

"Just a dream, my friend. We have no lover in whose embrace we may retreat." Not without a twinge of disappointment.

Leave it alone and it will go away, I counseled myself. *It is time to feed.*

I did not dress. I did not want my garments to get bloodied or torn. Besides, it was not nearly cold enough outside to be bothersome to me.

Slipping out my door into the darkness, I considered entreating Ilio to join me in the hunt, but I was reluctant to disturb him on his first night as a married man. Besides, this damned erection still had not subsided! I could not summon Ilio from his home in such a state. What would the boy think of me?

Chuckling under my breath, I hopped to the thatch roof of my hut. With my penis pointing the way, I ran lightly across the roof and leapt to a nearby tree.

10

I fed upon a mountain lion that evening.

Like me, the great cat was hunting for her sustenance in the moonless wilds. A beautiful creature-- sleek, powerful-- but the Hunger is blind to aesthetics. It knows only Prey and Not-Prey. I leapt upon her tawny form from the canopy of the forest and dispatched her with a quick jerk, snapping the predator's neck before she even realized she had become the hunted. I tore into her fuzzy throat, slicing through the big veins in her neck with my teeth, and gorged on her pungent blood.

I released the reins of my control, slurping, grunting, snarling. The Hunger had been clamoring at my thoughts all day, throughout Ilio's wedding ceremony and the rowdy feast that followed. I drank until I felt near to bursting, and then I slung the warm carcass across my shoulders and hiked leisurely back to the Tanti settlement, my stomach sloshing.

The animal's flesh had no value as food—the Tanti did not eat the flesh of predatory animals-- but its pelt, as well as its teeth and bones and some of its organs, would make good barter.

Back at the village, I suspended the carcass from a tree behind my hut, hanging it so that it would be out of reach for any scavengers that might be attracted by the smell, and then I walked down to the lake to clean the blood and dirt off of my body.

As I splashed myself, standing thigh deep in the bracing water, my thoughts returned to the mysterious woman in my dream.

As if my musings had summoned her spirit, I felt the cold caress of her fingertips on my biceps, the firm pressure of her breasts upon my back. It was real enough to make me spin around, but there were no phantoms wading in the lake behind me. The beach beyond was dark and deserted, the village silent as a tomb.

I saw that my erection had returned with a fury, all the little veins in it standing out like braided cords. I scowled down at the protruding organ, my previous amusement curdling.

I certainly hope this does not become a common occurrence, I thought. It would be a terrible inconvenience!

What strange malady has afflicted me? I wondered. This was not a natural thing! I stood in the icy water and reached out with my vampire senses, sending them into the moonless night like wavering antennae. I do not know what I was searching for exactly. A ghost? A lurking prankster? To be honest, I did not expect to find anything with my mental probes, and I cannot begin to describe to you just how shocked I was when I sensed a nearby presence.

It was a vague sensation, directionless, but it was most definitely feminine. Its femaleness made itself evident to me through a flurry of impressions, almost abstract in their fundamental nature: the image of a body, modest curves, dark skin, an identity, fleeting memories.

It recoiled in surprise and confusion as if it had felt the touch of my consciousness as well. Our thoughts brushed briefly, and then the presence was gone.

I stood in the icy lake, bewildered.

What was this strange presence? Was it a real person? A spirit? And how had our thoughts touched thusly? Was this some strange new power, like Ilio's ability to perceive the fading thoughts of his human victims? If so, what had triggered it? I had never sensed another's presence in such an unusual manner!

I searched again with my preternatural senses, but my efforts were in vain. Whatever it was, whoever it was, the presence had withdrawn.

I am going mad! I thought.

No, I reasoned with myself. You are alone again, after devoting yourself to the boy for many seasons, and anxious of your new solitude. Dreams have lingered in your thoughts, fueled by fear of loneliness. Nothing more.

Put your worries aside, old bloodsucker, I thought. You need never again go mad out of loneliness. Ilio is but a stone's throw from your door, and you are surrounded by mortals who know you. Perhaps they may even come to love you, if you can avoid fouling your own bed for a change.

At least the beast had gone back to sleep, I saw. My organ had dwindled along with the presence, dangling limply now between my thighs.

I finished cleaning myself and slipped through the dark avenues of the village, a wraith, a bone-white interloper. I did not even rouse the dogs to barking.

Outside Ilio's lodge, I paused and listened for a moment. I felt like an intruder, loitering at his door in the dark, but I couldn't help it. I needed to reassure myself the two were still okay.

Had the boy hunted tonight? I wondered. Was he being careful of his fragile mortal bride? I prayed to my ancestors that I had trained him well enough to resist temptation, that his new bride, Priss, would never have to suffer the cruel sting of our rapacious appetite. The boy would be devastated if he hurt his young wife. The Tanti would despise us. They would hound us from the village, and rightly so. But if tragedy came of this experiment, the fault lay squarely on me. Out of selfishness, out of my need for community, I had placed every one of these mortals in danger.

I listened, but for the soft sigh of the mortal woman's breathing, the hut was silent.

Perhaps the boy was hunting.

Without me.

I sighed and continued home.

11

Inside, I clothed myself and built up my fire, then tried to find something to occupy my mind. I was restless and melancholy, and more than a little bored.

What would I do with myself now that the boy was grown?

That was my conundrum for the next couple of weeks. When I was not worrying that Ilio would murder his new bride, I looked for something to keep me busy. I loitered at the lake, aiding the fishermen with their labors, sometimes even venturing out in the daylight to help them, though the sunlight flashing off the waves was like thorns stabbing into my eyes. I looked forward to Valas's evening visits, and even called upon him at his home when he did not show up for his nightly gossip and framash. I befriended Priss's family, ingratiating myself to them by bringing them the remains of my nightly feeding. When Ilio came to call, joining me to hunt after his bride had gone to sleep, I hung on his every word.

For a while I sent my thoughts out nearly every night, hoping to encounter the ghostly presence again. I had decided that I'd sensed another of my kind that evening at the lake, that our spirits had briefly entwined, drawn together perhaps by mutual loneliness. The idea of finding a female of my kind restoked my interest in the vampires of the east, but the time was not yet right to set off on a new adventure. I was not quite ready to give up the comforts I enjoyed living among the Tanti. Though I tried many nights to sense the spirit of the mysterious siren, my efforts were in vain, and I finally began to think that I had imagined her completely.

The unseasonable warm spell broke shortly after the wedding. Another snowstorm sprang up over the Carpathians to blanket the village in glittering white. The knee-deep ice and snow brought all activity in the little settlement to a sudden halt, and loneliness and boredom plagued me even more fiercely than before. Valas, who hated getting out in the cold, visited less often, so I took up whittling, and crafted little toys for my adopted son's children.

One of the toys, the likeness of a plump Tanti woman, was recovered in 1957 during an archeological dig and is on display in a natural history museum in France. Can you imagine my surprise when I saw a news article about the find-- and recognized my handiwork-- some 22,000 years later? The archeologist who uncovered the relic opined that it was some type of religious fertility idol, but it wasn't. It was just a little doll that I had carved for one of my grandchildren.

12

Priss went into labor after the snowstorm passed, her water breaking as she squatted at the hearth preparing her morning meal. I had gone to my bed shortly after the sun winked over the rim of the world that morning, and was fast asleep when Ilio flew across the village to summon Priss's mother and sister to his wife's side. I was dead to the world as Ilio and his excited in-laws rushed to the young ones' home, or else I would have heard their babbling and gone to check on her as well. As we'd discussed, after seeing that his wife was well attended, and making sure she was in good spirits, he retreated to my hut to await the birth of his children.

"Wake up, Thest! It is time! The babies are coming!" he cried, and I rolled wearily from my furs.

"It is time?" I asked groggily, stumbling to my feet, then his words sunk in and I smiled in excitement, clasping his arms. "It is time, Ilio! Your children come!"

But he was not so enthusiastic. He paced around my hut all through the morning, growing more and more pessimistic. By afternoon I was checking the floorboards, sure he had worn them smooth. As his wife struggled to deliver the twins, he fretted and despaired, certain of calamity. The boy's lodge was near to mine and we could hear her every gasp. Ilio froze in his steps each time she cried out in pain, his eyes wide, his lips twisted down, then turned to me for reassurance.

"All new life comes into this world in blood and agony, Ilio," I told him. "Her pain will be forgotten when she holds her babies to her breast."

I did my best to soothe him, but my words fell on love-deafened ears.

"What if she dies, Thest?" he moaned. "I do not wish to live without her!"

"She isn't going to die, Ilio," I said. "Come. Sit by the fire. Try to calm yourself."

"I cannot!" he wailed, his eyes full of imagined horrors. "Oh! Did you hear that? I think something's gone wrong! Maybe I should go over there!"

"That would not be wise. The blood—"

"But if something bad happens, I could save her. I could heal her with the *ebu potashu*. I could make her like us." He ran his fingers through his hair, tugging at his locks. "Or perhaps you could do it, Thest. I don't know if my blood is strong enough, but yours is. I know it is! You snatched me from the very jaws of death!"

I quailed inwardly at the thought, but if it came down to it, I would do it. I would make her a blood drinker if it meant preserving her existence.

For Ilio.

What terrible crimes we are willing to commit out of love, no? Or was this selfishness too?

But his fears were groundless. Priss birthed both babies without undue injury, and though her labor was difficult, our resolve to safeguard her life was not put to the test. We heard the cries of Ilio's babies shortly after nightfall. At the sound of their bawling--first one, then minutes later, the second-- Ilio collapsed to the floor in relief, weeping black tears into his hands.

Yorda came to summon us some time later.

"Come, Ilio," she said, her face lined with

exhaustion. "Your daughters await their papa." She looked at me then with a weary smile, strands of gray hair clinging to her round, careworn face. "You too, *grandfather*."

Yorda and her daughters had cleaned Priss and the babies and disposed of all the soiled linens. The smell of blood and amniotic fluid still lingered in Ilio's home, and it gave us pause at the threshold, but the odor was not overpowering. We were able to ignore it.

Priss lay propped up near the hearth. Her face was gaunt and there were dark crescents beneath her eyes, but she smiled at us as we entered. Yorda had piled clean furs upon her and wrapped both babies, one of which was suckling at the young woman's breast. Priss's sibling was sitting beside the new mother, cradling the second of the pair.

"Come see, Ilio," Priss sighed. "We have two daughters."

"Are you well?" Ilio asked, rushing to her side.

"Tired," she said.

He kneeled beside her and embraced her, then looked to the baby feeding at her breast. Black tears glittered at his eyelashes, threatening to spill down his cheeks. He scrubbed them away, grinning broadly (fangs showing, but no one even noticed, all eyes upon the babes). His fingers hovered at the edge of the child's swaddling, afraid to touch the fragile creature.

"I'd like to name this one Irema," Priss said, stroking the top of the baby's fuzzy head. Irema was the name of Priss's birth mother, who had died many years ago.

I glanced toward Yorda, but she didn't look upset. Priss's mother, Irema, had been Yorda's eldest sister. The Tanti often married the siblings of a deceased mate.

"Yes, of course, whatever you want," Ilio babbled.

"Lorn is holding Little Aioa."

"Aioa and Irema," Ilio said and laughed joyously.

I sidled forward and peeked at the two babies. "They are beautiful," I said. "They have your dark hair and skin, Ilio."

"Yes, they do!" he said, laughing softly.

Lorn approached me with Little Aioa. "Would you like to hold your grandchild, Thest?"

"I'm afraid my cold flesh will upset the child," I objected, but Lorn pressed the tiny bundle into my arms.

"There... See? She likes you," Lorn said, smiling up at me.

I held the child as carefully as possible, afraid even to twitch. *I must make the most delicate gestures,* I thought, more frightened than I had been in seven thousand years. Cautiously—oh, so cautiously!—I touched the child's plump cheek with a fingertip. Rather than cry out at my icy touch, Little Aioa seemed to find it pleasant. She turned her face toward my cool caress and made a suckling motion with her perfect little coral lips.

I was instantly, madly, in love!

"I think she's hungry," Lorn said, caressing my back as she peered into the baby's swaddling.

"I'm sorry, Little One, I have no milk to give you," I said, nearly swooning in my affection for the tiny thing.

This helpless, beautiful creature was a descendant of my people—a descendant of the children I had made with my wife Nyala; I was certain of it!—and sealed the bond between my adopted son and I. I was joined now to all of them by ties of blood kinship.

The thought made me dizzy with happiness.

Such an unlikely wonder could only have been

wrought by the scheming of the ancestors, I thought. I glanced toward the heavens, thanking my forefathers for their generosity. I had sacrificed much to safeguard my people. I had lost even my humanity. But this moment… these tiny creatures… were all the recompense I needed to put paid to all that I had lost. To have a family again! To have a life, after so many long years of suffering and solitude! It was all that I could ask for. It was more than I deserved. I was magnificently happy in that bright shining moment. Perfectly content. My life had come full circle, bringing me back to joy.

It would only last three cycles of the seasons.

The Vampire Thief

1

Do you know what it is to love?

When you are young, and if your parents are kind, you know love as a child knows it: uncomplicated, unconditional, all-encompassing. Love, for a child, is like a primary color, bright and without nuance. Mama hugs you and tends to your boo-boos, Papa plays with you and protects you from harm. They are your world.

But it is a needy love. A helpless love.

Later in childhood, as you grow older, love for self develops. You chafe at the boundaries of your parents' safekeeping. You wriggle from their arms, seek out the world on your own terms, exploring, testing, tasting, thinking you are the first person in the world to discover this thing or invent that game. You take great pride in your accomplishments. "Look what I made, Mama!" you cry, holding up your pie of mud and twigs. "Watch me throw this rock, Papa! See how far I can throw it?" But it is a selfish love. This love sees only itself, knows only its own needs. It is egotistic. Narcissistic.

As you mature, so does your love. It is flourishing, growing more complex. There are gradations in its coloration now. Subtle shadow if your path has crossed with tragedy. Patches blanched by violence or betrayal. Wearying parents teach you empathy. Perhaps one of them sickens. You must care for them. These are lessons in compassion. Lessons in self-sacrifice. It is still a simple love. It is still a selfish love from time to time, but it is evolving, transforming—perhaps into something truly magnificent.

When the bud of youth gives bloom to passionate love, it is once more all-encompassing, dizzying in its heat, reckless in its hunger. It is the enslaving love, binding you by the shackles of carnal desire. You become a driven thing, searching desperately for fertile soils in which to sow your seed, or flinging wide your bloom to tempt the passing bee, obsessed, *possessed,* by the overriding, undeniable prerogative of all living things: to be fruitful and multiply, to increase the number of your kind.

And when those seeds burst forth with new life--

Love achieves its crowning glory. Selfless love, the love of mother and father for child--unconditional, fiercely protective. This is the love that sacrifices, that leaps upon the jaws of savage beast, that starves so that the children can all eat, that toils without rest, that treks to any length, even to hell and back. This is the most profound love, and in its fading days, as blossoms wither and fall away from stem, crinkled, singed by wind and sun, it becomes the most beautiful love of all.

In the seven thousand years I had lived thus far, I'd known all loves but one. I was a baby, and knew the helpless love of a child. I was a reckless boy, and knew the rebellious love of self. I knew passionate love. Oh, yes, I was a lover! When I was a mortal man, I was a dynamo of lust. My libido was so fervid it is almost a point of embarrassment to me now, but that passion was nothing in comparison to the love I felt for my children. That love did not wane when my humanity was stolen from me. It only became tragic. I pined for my mortal family in the early days of my immortality, but I could not trust myself to venture too near to them. I was a ravening monster, a bloodthirsty beast. And so I haunted them, watching over my children from afar, and then my children's children, and their children's children. But it was only in Ilio's daughters that I was able to experience the joy of being a grandfather.

Such a profound and glorious love!

With the birth of my granddaughters, Irema and Aioa, I knew all that it was to love, but I found that the joys of grandfathering were much different than the joys of fathering, which I knew already. In grandfathering, there is not the exhaustion of constant supervision, the midnight cries, the conflicts with one's own selfish desires. I could play with my granddaughters to my contentedness, then hand them back to their exhausted parents. I could dote on them without fear or guilt of spoiling them. I was, after all, their Grandpapa! It was my job to spoil them!

And in spoiling grand-babies, I found in Valas an equal, eager accomplice. Priss's earthy father was as fond of children as I. There was many a day, when the season had returned to warmth, that we paraded our babies proudly through the village, grinning like fools as the women all cooed and made babble-talk and remarked how beautiful our granddaughters were and oh-my-how-quickly-they-are-growing! Side-by-side, my partner-in-crime and I.

I wish I could tell you everything, every little detail, of those joyous times, but I know domestic bliss does not a thrilling story make. Just know that I was impossibly happy and bear with me as I detail my final days among the Tanti. My happiness, as always, would prove unfairly short-lived. It seems to be a recurring theme of my existence. I only beg your indulgence for a little while longer so that I might immortalize my twin beauties in the pages of this tome, and then we'll get on with all the killing and the fucking.

I promise.

Irema and Aioa were uncommonly beautiful. I say this without bias, *of course*. They possessed the olive complexion of their father, with silky black hair and great fanning eyelashes, but the delicate features and startling blue eyes of their mother. Yorda, Valas's wife, was of the opinion their eyes would change color as they grew older, but they never did. Their eyes retained that lovely shade of winter blue until the day that I last saw them, two fine and powerful women, huntress-goddesses who fought at my side against the vampires of the east. But we are talking right now of the days before the great vampire war, when they were just two inquisitive and affectionate toddlers, always eager to climb into the lap of their cold white grandpapa.

They were so similar in appearance that people often confused one for the other, but I could always tell them apart. Irema was slightly more robust, bolder, while Aioa was the more delicate, the demure one, tenderhearted. They were so similar in appearance that Valas made necklaces for the girls, one with stones of blue for Irema, the other with stones of milky quartz for Aioa, and that worked fine until the clever little things got older and began to make a game of swapping their necklaces.

I was in love with them both, my loneliness forgotten. I had even forgotten my dream seductress. I visited Ilio and his wife every evening, playing with the little ones until it was time for them to retire. Some nights I even rocked them to sleep in my arms, sitting on the floor beside the hearth.

I witnessed Irema's first tentative steps. I thought my heart would break when Aioa called me grandfather for the first time—*adda*, in Tanti. I watched them play with the little dollies I made for them of wood or bone or stone, sometimes for hours, and never once did I feel the urge to kill them and drink their blood.

They grew quickly, the seasons whirling past. In the three years that followed, the old shaman who performed Ilio's wedding ceremony passed on to the spirit world, and his protégé, a young man named Kuhnluhn, took over his duties. Yorda gave birth to a little boy, and Lorn got married to a fellow named Honch. Paba, the old Neirie I'd escorted back to his Tanti homeland, died that first winter, but he died contented in his sleep beside a grandson's hearth.

One summer evening, just a few months before the vampire thief came, Irema climbed into my lap. After tangling my beard for a little while, she looked up at me very seriously, and asked, "Adda, why is your skin so cold and white?"

"I am T'sukuru, like your papa. We are different from the Tanti," I answered.

"But why?" she asked.

"That is just how it is. Why is the sky blue, little one? Why do the birds sing?"

She scowled at me. She didn't understand. "When I grow up, I want to be cold and white like you," she said, and I embraced her, sighing, "No, you do not, my beloved. No, you do not." And her chubby little arms went around my neck to hug me back, so tiny and warm, her curly black hair tickling my lips and the tip of my nose.

My beautiful grandbabies. They were my life. My love.

And then the raiders came.

2

I call him the vampire thief because he stole away two children, and in so doing, he also stole the happiness I'd enjoyed living with the Tanti.

Though I would not know it for another day or so, the blood drinker's name was Hettut. He came in the night, in the winter of my third year with the Tanti, and snatched two sleeping children from beside their dozing parents.

We found his tracks leading in from the forest to the east. From the eastern edge of the wilderness, where the great pines gave way to open meadow, he circled around the north side of the lake and struck the first lodge that he came unto.

His victims were two Tanti boys named Pudhu and Emoch. They were only a little older than my darlings. I shudder to think how easily he might have taken Irema and Aioa, and I thank the ancestors that he did not. Cruel, I know, but a grandfather cannot help such merciless thoughts.

The vampire's icy touch woke the boys as he eased them from their sleeping furs. Both of them began to scream, first Emoch, then Pudhu moments later, and their parents leapt from their bedding in horror. Though their father, a fisherman named Iltep, reached immediately for his weapons, Hettut was T'sukuru, and he flew from the lodge with unnatural speed after grinning toothily at the children's' frightened parents, head twisted strangely to one side. He vanished into the night before the man's blade could even clear its sheath, a plump squirming child tucked in the joint of each of his arms.

If we were home, Ilio and I might have been able to save Iltep's children, but we were far away when the blood drinker attacked, hunting in the snowy forest to the northwest of the village. If we had been home, Hettut might have even passed around the Tanti village, confused by the presence of other blood drinkers.

Yes, I know: *if and if...!* Who can really say what might have happened? The ancestors might know, but not this man.

I did have a strange sense of foreboding when I rose that evening, the sky crowded with dense gray snow clouds, or maybe I just made that up later, to spice the stew of self-recrimination, but really I think that I did. It was just a tingle in my guts. A sense that something unpleasant was bearing down on the village, and not just the storm heads creeping over the eastern peaks. I remember standing in front of my hut, sparse white flakes drifting down around me, the sky starless and thick with freight of snow, thinking there was some odd quality to the atmosphere that evening: the air was too heavy, the cold more cutting than it normally was. I dismissed it after a moment or two, and went on to Ilio's home. I wish I had investigated further, but I did not.

There was no way I could have known. There had been no sightings of the blood drinkers from the east since the fall of the Oombai three years before. Though they came up in conversation from time to time, the Tanti had forgotten about the eastern vampires just as surely as I. They didn't even really think of Ilio and I as T'sukuru anymore. To them, we were only Tanti.

It wasn't until we were returning from our hunt, our bellies sloshing with the blood of a boar, that we realized something was amiss.

"Look at that, Father!" Ilio said, pointing toward the village as we rounded the white hump of a hill. "Why are there so many torches? Everyone's running through the streets!"

(There were not actually *streets* in the village, just muddy strips of open ground running between the buildings—filling in with drifts of snow that night—so please do not lecture me on linguistics. The Tanti called the avenues between their homes *leptruff'u*, which mean throat or open passage. I simply use the modern approximation.)

I had been listening to the crunch of my feet sinking into the snow, enjoying the sound of it, the sensation of my feet punching through the crusty surface of the ice. The boar we had killed was slung across my shoulders, the warm tingle of its blood pulsing through my limbs. At Ilio's exclamation, I looked up with a frown, following his pointing finger to the sparks of light winking between the tree trunks.

"Something bad has happened," I said.

We both went still for a moment, lowering our mental defenses so that we could hear what was going on in the village. The hiss of the wind through the trees, the clatter of bare branches brushing against one another as they stirred, even the snap and flutter of the torches twinkling down there in the village, made the Tanti's voices an unintelligible babble. I filtered through the extraneous sounds, pushing them out of my consciousness until only human voices remained.

What I heard turned my heart to ice.

Women were crying out, sobbing, calling after their husbands in fear. Someone was keening, "My babies! It took my babies!" And the men, speaking in loud, angry voices: "Where is Thest?" and "Its tracks head toward the mountains!" and "We have to set after it at once!"

I heaved the boar off my shoulders. "Come, Ilio! Someone has violated the Tanti while we were away!"

I flew down the hill toward the village, my bare feet kicking up great fans of snow. Fast as I was, however, Ilio was faster. Fearing for his mortal family, he raced ahead of me through the darkness, his passage whipping snow back in my face in a sudden icy flurry.

3

Pudhu and Emoch's mother screamed shrilly at the sight of us, which is completely understandable, as we were moving at full speed, and it must have looked to her as if we'd suddenly melted from the darkness. Worse, we were buck naked and splattered in pig's blood. We were lucky the Tanti men, who were working themselves into a fury, did not start chucking their spears at us immediately. If not for Valas, they probably would have.

"It's him! It's him!" the boys' mother wailed, a trembling finger pointed our direction. Her eyes rolled in the torchlight, empty of all thought save for her children.

"Calm yourself, mother!" Valas snapped. "It is only Thest and Ilio!"

Priss was standing nearby, her stepmother Yorda fretting at her shoulder. Ilio ran to his wife and grasped her upper arms. "Are the girls safe?" he demanded, and when she nodded he closed his eyes in relief.

As did I.

"What has happened, Valas?" I asked, after the spears and bows and knives pointed toward me had lowered.

Before Valas could answer, Iltep, the boys' father, shouted, "You fucking T'sukuru stole my babies, that's what happened! From my very hearth!" His voice cracked as he shouted at me. His cheeks were wet with tears. Several men had taken hold of his arms--to restrain him from chasing after the blood drinker, I assume. "Let me go, you cocklickers!" he snarled at them, twisting his body back and forth. "We can still save them!"

"There is nothing you can do, Iltep! You know it!" one of the men restraining him said, not without sympathy, and Iltep railed against him, cursing profusely.

"No man can prevail against the T'sukuru, but we are not all men here," Valas said. All eyes turned to him, and then, when his meaning was understood, toward me. Valas squinted at me. "Will you aid us against your kindred, Thest? Will you help us to save Iltep's children?"

"Of course, Brother," I said. "I told you before. I've told you all before! I have no allegiance to these blood drinkers from the east. They are no kin of mine."

Valas nodded, smiling grimly, while Iltep and his wife looked at one another in sudden hope. They all knew of my prodigious speed and strength, if not the full extent of my powers.

"Then let us be after this craven fiend, before he does harm to good Iltep's sons!" Valas declared. He hesitated, glanced down, then leered back up at me. "You might want to put some breeches on first."

4

I had little hope we could rescue the children, but I was more than willing to make the attempt. I had helped Iltep with his labors many an evening. We were not close, but his rough tongue and bawdy humor had always amused me. The others tried to persuade the man to remain behind—saying he was too overwrought to be of any help—but he refused. I understood completely. I wouldn't have been able to stay behind either.

I think most of the men who took off in pursuit of the stolen children were about as optimistic as I of the boys' safe return. I was confident of my abilities. I had no fear of being harmed. But I knew the Hunger. The beast we hunted would have no mercy for his victims—not even for children so young and innocent.

The Tanti were well acquainted with the cruelty of the T'sukuru. This was not the first time a blood drinker had abducted someone from the village, though it had been many years since the last time a vampire had preyed on them. Long before our arrival. If not for my presence, and the trust they had in my strength, I doubt they would have pursued the T'sukuru into the wilderness. Like Valas said: no man can prevail against the T'sukuru. And for the most part, that was true. I had killed one such creature when I was a mortal, but only with the aid of four other men, not to mention a good deal of luck. And it had been a weak one. And day when the battle took place.

At least the beast was keeping to the ground.

So long as he stayed on the ground, it would be easy to track the creature. The snow was deep. In some places, the drifts were knee high. The beast's tracks were plain to see in the jumping gold light of our torches, but I could see in the dark, regardless of moonlight or torch.

I wasn't certain why the villain had not taken to the treetops. It was what I would have done, rather than leave such a plain trail for vengeful villagers to pursue. There were plenty of trees to which the creature could take flight. The forest to the east of the village was dense, full of great old oaks and soaring pine, acacia and beech. Perhaps the vampire could not move into the treetops with two squirming children in his arms, or maybe he just wasn't accustomed to flying through the trees as I was, or he didn't believe the mortals were a threat to him. Whatever the reason, I was grateful the creature had not taken flight. I might have been able to track him through the canopy of the forest, but it would have been a much more difficult task.

"Why do we hold back, Thest?" Ilio asked as he jogged through the snow at my side. "We're much faster than these mortals. We should race ahead, catch the foolish blood drinker before he has a chance to harm the children!"

"And what if there is more than one of them lurking in the forest?" I asked. "What if the one we pursue doubles back on us? He could slaughter our entire party in moments."

Ilio's eyes widened, and then he looked grim and nodded. "I understand. I apologize for questioning your wisdom."

"No need," I replied. "Just be on your guard."

As I raced through the snow, the Tanti villagers at my back, I was helpless but to recall my people's battle with the fiend who made me. I do not know the name of my maker, only that he was powerful, cruel, and insatiable. He had glutted himself on the blood of our neighboring tribe, and would have killed them all if they had not fled from the region. When we went to make war on the beast, marching to the land of the Gray Stone People, my powerful maker and his strange vampire pet had killed nearly every single member of our war party. Only two had survived, my uncle and my companion Brulde, and I... I was made into this.

I would not let the same fate befall my Tanti brethren. And if I got my hands on the leech that had raided my new home, I would rend the bloodsucker limb from limb!

No! First, I would question him! Where are you from? Are there others nearby? We needed to know if there were more of them. And if there were, I would make him tell me if they were just passing through, or did they intend to make war? It would be nice if I could make him answer some of my own questions, things I'd always wondered about—where do we come from, how many more of us are there, is there some way to undo this cursed affliction—but I knew this was no time for selfish concerns. Not with so many lives at stake.

I smelled blood.

Freshly spilled mortal blood!

I faltered and saw Ilio, a moment later, do the same. We exchanged an anxious glance. The smell of blood, so strong... it did not bode well.

"It's close," I said to the boy, and he nodded.

It had begun to snow again. Heavy flakes, like puffs of cattail fluff, spiraled down from the lowering heavens. Far to the east, a sheet of ice broke loose from some steep mountain slope with a reverberating crack: an avalanche on the distant Carpathians. The rumble of all that falling ice thrummed in the still winter air as we rounded the hill.

There, on the far side, lay one of the children.

It was Emoch.

The boy sprawled in a shallow ditch, a gully carved into the hill by spring runoff, empty now but for pebbles, the snow, and the little boy's body. His clothes had been rent from his bruised white flesh, his throat torn savagely as if by a wild animal.

As soon as his father caught sight of the boy, the fisherman fell to his knees. Iltep threw back his head and howled at the sky, the hundreds of little muscles in his neck standing out like ropes, his face turning purple. I and a few other Tanti men approached the pitiful corpse as the rest of the group encircled the bereaved father, trying to comfort him, to shield him from the sight.

"Oh, that poor baby!" Valas murmured.

The snow around the boy was splattered liberally with blood, still steaming. A spiral of tracks circled the spot where the boy lay, then continued east. I went to my knees beside the child, wrestling with my own blood hunger, and put my hand on his pale, bruised chest. There was no need of it. I could hear, even from a distance, that his heart no longer beat. I only did it to comfort the boy, should any awareness linger in his mind.

"May the ancestors guide you to the Ghost World, little one," I whispered.

The tracks of the T'sukuru angled away to the northeast, trailed by splashes of errant blood. Not far away, at the base of a gnarled oak, the footprints vanished. The killer had taken to the trees.

I gestured to Valas. I needed to confer with him. We needed to change our tactics. Before we could speak, however, Iltep broke away from his comforters. He pelted through the snow, falling, rising, then collapsing to his knees beside his son.

"Menoch!" he sobbed hoarsely. "Oh, Menoch, my son! I am so sorry! Look what that monster has done to you!"

He pulled the mangled child into his lap and began to rock him, stroking the lad's curly bangs from his brow. I had to look away. The sight of the boy's arm flopping lifelessly as his father cradled him was too heart-wrenching.

"The raider has taken to the trees with the other child," I said to Valas in a low voice. "There will be no catching him now, unless Ilio and I take to the trees after him. Your men won't be able to keep up."

The others had gathered around-- Gibbus and

Sephram, Valas's sons, the men who fished on the lake, our strongest and fiercest tribesmen. Some of them listened in on my conversation with Valas. The others were trying to sooth Iltep. Snow whirled around us, falling more thickly now.

"Do what you must," Valas said, his words steaming in the cold. "We will follow."

I told him what I'd already discussed with Ilio, that I feared leaving the group unprotected, that there could be more of my kind lurking in the snowy wilderness, that the blood drinker might double back and slaughter them in my absence.

"So we are slowing you down," Valas sighed. He shivered, snot frozen to his mustache. He looked back in the direction of the village, eyes narrowed, thinking, then announced, "Then we will turn back... for the other boy's sake."

Several of the men objected.

"How can we trust him to continue the pursuit?" one of the men demanded. This was a fisherman named Gilt. He'd always been suspicious of me. "How do we know he won't let the fiend go? Or join the foul thing in feasting on poor Pudhu? They are kin--!"

Before he could finish what he was saying, Valas stomped forward and clouted the man, sending him stumbling back into the fellow behind him.

"Bite your tongue or spit your teeth on the ground!" Valas hissed.

I was shocked. I did not expect Valas to defend my honor to such an extent, and with the revelation, a fierce love for the man swelled in my breast.

Gilt lurched upright, wiping blood from his lips. For a moment I was afraid the two men would come to further blows, but Iltep intervened.

"For my son's sake, don't fight," he said. Though he did not speak loudly, the ragged pain in his voice froze us all. He looked up at me and said, "Go on,

Thest, if you think you can save my little Pudhu. I trust you. You have never done us harm. We will return to the village so you do not have to worry about us. We will take my poor Emoch home to his mother."

I glanced at Ilio and he nodded.

"I will save your son," I told the man. "If I fail in that, I will bring back the villain's head so that you may spit upon his face."

Iltep nodded, his dead son in his arms. Valas and Gibbus helped the bereaved father to his feet. "See that you do," Iltep said hoarsely, clutching the boy to his breast. "See that you do!"

"What if the beast kills you first, Brother?" Valas asked.

"Then know that I die content," I answered. "For the first time in many, many years."

The men turned and began to make their way back to the village. I watched them shuffle through the snow for a moment, their torches glittering on the snowdrifts, impressed by the way they closed around Iltep in a protective circle, their hands going out to the dead child's cheek, the father's shoulders. They were good men. As compassionate as they were brave, and then it struck me again that they were my descendants, all of these men, and I felt such pride and love for them that I thought my heart would burst. The children of my children's children. Recompense for all that I had suffered.

"Come, Ilio!" I called, my voice tight with emotion, and then we were away.

5

We raced through the snow to where our quarry's footprints vanished, then leapt to the nearest bough. I landed in a crouch, grabbing the limb above my head to keep my balance. A moment later, Ilio was perched beside me. The limb bobbed beneath our weight. Clumps of snow plopped to the ground below.

"How will we follow him in the trees?" Ilio asked quietly, glancing back at the withdrawing Tanti. They were too far away to hear him now. Their torches winked between the tree trunks. Shadowy claws raked the hillside as if trying to erase their tracks.

"There will be a trail to follow, even up here," I answered. "It won't be as obvious as those footprints in the snow, but... Ah! There! Do you see the bark scraped away from that limb? And there: a broken branch."

"Yes!"

"This way!"

Perched upon the limb I had pointed out to Ilio, I cast my gaze about. The canopy of a nearby tree looked as though it had been disturbed recently. The snow had been jarred from its branches so that the patterns of light and dark did not match the whole.

Calling out to Ilio, I leapt across the space between the trees. I moved quickly through the maze of leafless tree limbs, ducking some, climbing over others, following the faint trail with my eyes.

The limbs were icy and slick, and twice I nearly lost my purchase and fell to the ground below. The next tree over, I picked up the scent of the mortal child. I found a scrap of torn clothing on a sharp pointed branch, a droplet of blood where the limb had gouged his skin. Poor little Pudhu... I had been dragged through the treetops like this once when I was a mortal man. It is not a pleasant experience.

I quickened my pace.

The land sloped down, the trees more closely spaced. It was becoming easier to follow the child's scent. We were closing the gap. I heard tree branches snap in the valley below, the sound echoing in the snow-padded hush. I froze, gesturing for Ilio to halt, and listened intently. Another snapping tree branch. And then the child whimpered. Faint. Distant. The boy was still alive!

I slithered forward through the trees, Ilio at my heel, moving as quickly and as quietly as I could. As we drew nearer, the sound of the vampire's flight through the forest grew more distinct, the boy's scent stronger. I wasn't even paying attention to the fiend's trail now. I was following him by ear. By ear and by nose.

"We've almost got him!" Ilio whispered at my side, and I hissed, holding up a hand to silence him.

But I knew it was too late the moment the words left his lips. If I could hear the Tanti child's whimpers, our quarry could certainly hear Ilio.

I listened. Our quarry listened, too. The forest was silent but for little Pudhu's whimpers.

A voice called out somewhere to the north of us, not far from our position. It was not speech-- not any kind of speech I understood, anyway-- but a series of rapid clicks that echoed within the encircling hills.

What was the meaning of such a sound?

I did not know, but I did not intend to respond to it. I stayed still, and made sure with a gesture that Ilio did not reply to it either.

Again, the strange clicking. It was the sound a man can make by popping his tongue against the inside of his cheek, but what did it mean?

The other blood drinker let out an inquisitive

grunt, and then I heard him scrambling through the treetops again, racing away from us. The child yelped, began to wail.

I shot forward, careless of any noises I might be making. It didn't matter now. The other blood drinker knew we were pursuing it. He might have even guessed that we were T'sukuru, like him. I had no idea how keen his senses were, or the meaning of the strange sounds he had made, but he had surely heard us flying through the treetops, and no mortal man could move in such a manner.

He was fast. He raced through the trees like a storm wind, breaking branches, limbs still swaying as we followed in his wake, but we were faster, and we narrowed the gap between us even further.

Suddenly, our quarry stopped. I heard a soft snapping sound, and the vampire's young captive let out a piercing howl. A moment later there was a thud, as if a large fruit had fallen to the ground, and then the blood drinker was racing away through the forest again. I could hear the swish and crackle of his flight, growing ever fainter, but the mortal child's wailing did not wane.

I flew forward, grinning with sudden optimism.

Thank you, Ancestors...!

Little Pudhu lay at the base of an alder, sprawled in a hump of snow.

He was crying loudly, his left leg bent unnaturally just below the knee, but he was alive. The vampire had broken his leg and abandoned him—or the boy's leg had broken when he fell from the tree. Thinking of the snapping sound I had heard, and the child's immediate cries, I deduced it was the former, and our quarry had done it to distract us from further pursuit, but no matter. The child lived! That was all I cared about.

Ilio and I descended from the trees.

The child wailed even louder as we approached. He could not see who we were in the dark, only our shapes closing in on him. He clamped his hands over his eyes, his lower lip quivering.

"It's all right, Pudhu," I said gently. "It is Thest. We're going to take you back to your mama."

"Mama?" the boy snuffled, his chest hitching.

"Yes, Mama is waiting for you at home," I crooned, kneeling down beside him. I examined his leg without touching him, scowling at his injury. I had seen my father set bones when I was a boy, but I'd never done it myself.

"Thest, he's getting away," Ilio hissed at my shoulder, looking to the north.

"I know. It does not matter."

"Is Pudhu going to be okay?" Ilio asked, coming around to the other side of the boy. He kneeled down and tried to sooth the child. "Ssshhh, Pudhu. You are safe now."

"Ilio?" the little boy sobbed.

"Yes, it is Ilio."

"I want my mama, Ilio! I want to go home!"

"I know."

"Will you take me home now?"

"Yes, yes, just lay still for a moment."

Ilio stroked the little boy's hair, looking at me with a fretful expression. I was digging through all my pockets, then the satchels attached to my belt. I pulled out medicinal herbs, sharp flakes of flint, which I used for cutting, some bone fishing hooks, an awl, but no string. I sat on my butt and took off my shoes, then pulled the laces out of them.

"What are you doing?" Ilio asked.

"I am going to set the bone," I said. "It is a long way back to the village. We can't have his little broken leg flopping the whole way back."

"Can't you use the Blood?"

"And have the bone heal crooked?"

"Oh."

"His injuries are not serious enough to use the living blood. Just comfort the child," I said, rising. The snow and wet mulch of the forest floor squelched between my bare toes, but it felt good. I listened for the retreating raider-- the vampire thief-- but he had passed out of earshot. He was no longer a danger to us or the child. Putting the T'sukuru out of my thoughts, I broke off a couple tree branches and returned to the child.

"Pudhu, are you listening?" I asked, kneeling back down.

"Yes," the boy sniffed.

"This is Thest. Do you remember me?"

"Yes."

"That bad man hurt your leg. I have to fix it before we take you home."

"Okay," he said shakily.

"It is going to hurt," I told him. "Can you be brave for a few moments longer?"

"Yes."

"Good. You're a good boy."

I used my superhuman senses to determine how the bone was broken underneath the flesh, and then I grasped the boy's limb and repositioned it. He screamed and went limp, fainting from the pain, and I placed the wood splints on either side of his leg and fixed them in place with the laces of my moccasins.

I scooped the trembling child into my arms and rose. His head rolled back limply and I cupped the base of his skull in my palm.

"Can you find your way back to the village from here?" I asked Ilio.

"Yes, but why?"

I put the boy into Ilio's arms. "Return with the boy quickly. Protect his body from the wind as you go."

"Thest--! What are you planning to do?"

"Don't argue with me," I said sternly. "Return the child to his parents. Tell Valas what has transpired, and that I have gone on in pursuit of the T'sukuru."

"Come back with me, Thest," Ilio pled. "We can chase after the blood drinker together, after we have returned Pudhu."

"If I return to the village with you, our enemy will escape. Don't worry, boy. I will be careful."

Ilio sputtered and complained, but he was a good son. He obeyed. "Keep to the ground," I called after him as he pelted away. "Do not drag that poor child through the treetops a second time tonight!" I saw him nod as he reached the top of the hill, and then he rounded it and vanished, and I was on my own.

I looked in the direction the vampire thief had fled, smiling faintly. Narrowing my eyes, I dropped my mental shields and searched for the little beast with my powerful vampire senses. *There!* The greedy thing was far away now, moving at great speed... but not too far away! Not fast enough to escape me!

With a great lunge, I flew to the very top of the alder, and set off in pursuit.

6

In truth, my pursuit of the vampire thief was motivated by curiosity as much as it was by a desire for revenge. Menoch's death was an outrage. I was not close with the child or his immediate family, but he was a member of my tribe, and more than likely another of my descendants. Or, at the least, a descendant of one of my ancient tribesmen. A cousin, if not a grandchild. His murder could not go unanswered. Yet, I was excited by the thought of meeting another of my kind. I had been a blood drinker for untold ages, but in all those years, I had only known three other vampires: Ilio, my maker, and my maker's twisted pet. Of the rest, I knew only rumors—the name Zenzele, a fabled city, gossip of foul deeds and cruelty. I wanted to catch this blood drinker. I wanted to lay eyes upon him. I wanted to question him, if we spoke the same tongue, and find out what he knew about our kind. Where did we come from? Was there truly a city in the east where our kind lived together as mortals do? Only then, when I had sated my curiosity, would I destroy him.

If I could.

I flew through the treetops as I had never flown before, racing recklessly across the wooded valley, the wind roaring in my ears, the cold snow cutting across my cheeks. I paid little attention to the injuries I sustained in my headlong rush through the wilderness. My skin was sliced open a dozen times by cold-stiffened tree branches, but the living blood healed the injuries almost as quickly as I inflicted them upon myself.

In the middle of the valley was a river, a winding black ribbon in the starless night. I plunged down to the forest floor and made my way to the edge of the water. There, on the opposite bank, were some footprints, left behind by the fleeing blood drinker. I straightened my winter coat—it was hanging askew, tattered by my flight through the forest—and then I leapt across the burbling river, a distance of about thirty meters.

I knelt down beside the tracks and examined them, then stood and glanced up and down the watercourse. If I were the one who was fleeing, I would try to use the water to throw off my pursuers. It was an old trick, but I saw no sign that he had changed course. The mounds of snow to either side of the waterway were undisturbed. There were no tracks on the river's rocky banks either—so far as I could see.

I listened. All was still but for the chuckle of the river. Then, from the south, the snap and rustle of movement in the treetops. Distant, but closing fast. I was certain the blood drinker had not circled around behind me, and besides, what would be the point of that? It was most likely Ilio, though I thought I had told him to stay in the village.

Perhaps I had not.

I waited while the noise of his approach grew increasingly louder. Finally, he sprang from the treetops and landed on the other side of the river. He grinned at me guiltily, then jumped across the water to my side.

"I thought I told you to remain at the village," I said.

"Did you?" he asked. A little too innocently.

I cocked an eyebrow at him. "I am almost certain I did."

"In either case, I am getting too old for you to shelter me so much," he replied airily. "I am no longer the child you rescued on the steppes."

I laughed. "You will think again when I turn you over my knee!"

He grinned.

"Did you return the child safely to the village?" I asked, all humor aside.

"I carried him to his father," Ilio answered. "They were almost back when I caught up to them."

I nodded, turning in a circle.

"Do you still sense him?" Ilio asked.

"Yes, but he has taken cover. I'm having trouble pinpointing him exactly." The land on the north side of the river rose steeply to a high and thickly wooded ridge. If our quarry had been a mortal man, I could have sensed him easily. I would have heard his heart beating, smelled his blood, sensed the heat given off by his flesh. But he was not mortal. Like Ilio and I, his heart did not beat, and the only odor I could detect was the faint scent of the mortal children he had abducted clinging to his skin. I listened closer, shutting my eyes, then cupped my hands behind my ears. I sniffed at the wind. I could smell the residue of poor Menoch's blood, probably smeared across the blood drinker's lips, but it was faint.

And something else. A scent I did not recognize.

"What is it, Father?"

I shook my head. "Curious... I sense a large animal in the wilderness ahead, a creature I've never encountered before." I lowered my hands, looked at Ilio grimly. "I don't like this. I think there may be more blood drinkers up there. Not just the one we've been chasing."

"What do we do?"

I stroked my beard thoughtfully. "To be honest, I would like to see them. There is much we do not know about our kind. I doubt if any of them can harm me, but you are not so resilient."

"Don't order me back to the village, Thest!" Ilio objected. "You shelter me too much!"

I shushed him, peering into the silent woods.

I stood indecisively, stroking the whiskers on my chin. I was terribly excited, but my excitement warred with wariness, and even a smidgeon of fear. Not fear for myself. If these vampires knew the trick of killing one such as myself, then I would fly happily to join my lost loved ones in the Ghost World. No, I feared for Ilio, and for my Tanti tribesmen. We were so near to the village. What if these T'sukuru decided to make war on my Tanti brethren? How could I possibly protect everyone, besieged by multiple foes?

I scanned the dark ridge again with my vampire

senses. Again, I felt that there was more than one being lying in wait for us there, but I couldn't pin any of them down. My suspicion was little more than an intuitive thing.

I did not know their numbers. I did not know their strength. And might they not have strange talents as well, like Ilio? Ilio could learn things from the blood of his mortal victims, an ability I did not share. What might these mysterious blood drinkers be able to do? Yet, I could not retreat now. They might think it a sign of weakness, and pursue us back to the Tanti village.

I cursed my own foolishness.

"There is nothing to do but go forward," I murmured to Ilio. "Stay close to me, and be on your guard."

Ilio nodded, his eyes gleaming with excitement.

We started up the ridge.

7

The attack came from multiple directions, sudden and shocking in its ferocity. There was nothing we could do but strive to defend ourselves as each new challenger threw himself at us.

We were halfway up the ridge when our enemies sprung their trap. Ilio and I were creeping as silently as we could through the treetops, alert to any sign of movement. The forest was dead silent. All I could hear was the distant chuckle of the river, and the intermittent plop of snow falling from overburdened branches.

I heard a rapid rustling sound and caught a blur of movement from the corner of my eye. A moment later, a pale form tackled Ilio and carried him to the forest floor below.

"Ilio!" I cried out, and I threw myself from the tree limb on which I was perched.

Ilio and his attacker struck the ground with terrible force, but the boy wriggled from the grasp of his gangly opponent even as I fell earthward in pursuit. Ilio scrambled back and then flung himself to his feet, then shifted to higher ground so quickly he seemed to melt in one spot and reappear in the other.

I was impressed. The man-child was *fast!*

I hit the ground in a crouch and was about to spring at my son's attacker when I was struck from behind by something large and powerful and shaggy.

I rolled down the slope, wrestling with my opponent. Long yellow fangs snapped in my face as my attacker loosed a stream of blood-freezing snarls.

A wolf--!

But this was no ordinary canine. It was too strong!

I hooked my fingers into its bushy pelt and tried to fling the creature away from me, but it resisted, driving forward, jaws snapping.

Its body was dense with muscle. Its teeth clacked shut just a hair's breadth from my cheek, and that was when I noticed the chill of its flesh and realized why the animal was so powerful.

It was T'sukuru!

For a moment, I was paralyzed by surprise. I had never imagined an animal might be changed in the same manner that I had been transformed, but I could think of no reason why it could not be done. Someone had trained this beast, and then infected it with the living blood!

The wolf dug its paws into the wet soil and drove its snapping muzzle closer to my face. Its fangs sliced into the skin of my cheek.

Roaring in pain and rage, I heaved the animal upwards. It might be strong, but it had no fingers to anchor itself to the ground. It took sudden flight, crashing through the canopy of the forest overhead with a yelp.

I jumped to my feet and touched my hand to my face, but the living blood was already stitching the wound back together.

Where was Ilio?

Up the slope, Ilio and the thin blood drinker were dancing together, hand in hand. His opponent was a slim blond-headed male dressed in fur leggings and boots. The boy's foe was a little taller, a little more muscular, but they seemed equally matched in strength. Neither was able to overpower the other.

Ilio twisted to the right, his teeth gritted. His opponent jerked Ilio to the left. Their muscles writhed beneath their pale flesh as they tried in vain to throw one another off their feet.

I took a single step toward him, intending to jump into the fray—

And was struck again.

The blow was devastating. It took me off my feet and sent me spinning through the air. My body collided with the trunk of an oak tree hard enough to fissure my flesh. A multitude of zigzagging cracks opened on my back and across my ribcage where my body had plowed into the tree.

I fell to the ground, twitching in pain. Snow plopped down around me. Some of it landed on my head, obscuring my vision. The living blood repaired my injuries again, and I started to rise, clutching my aching ribs. I shook the snow from my head and turned to face my opponent.

The blood drinker who had attacked me from behind was a giant. Two heads taller than me, at least, and half again as broad. He was bald, with flat features and a wide fanged mouth. Full lips. Flaring nostrils. Eyes like two black pebbles.

As I rose unsteadily to my feet, he cocked an enormous hammer back over his shoulder, preparing to bludgeon me again.

It was a massive weapon: a thick wooden club with an enormous stone head lashed to the end of it. It would crush my skull like an egg if it connected.

I saw it coming, though, and pushed down with all my might.

I propelled myself into the treetop, that big hammer whistling past below me. It struck the trunk of the oak tree with a resounding crack, and a great spray of bark and splinters went flying in all directions.

A spear came whistling toward me, even as I landed in the tree branches, and I could do naught but sling myself earthward again to get out of the way of the projectile.

On the way down, the gargantuan caught me in the hip with his hammer.

The blow sent me flying up the hill past Ilio and his opponent. I hit the ground rolling, then jumped back to my feet, snarling.

I looked down, watched the fissures in my flesh fade away.

I was starting to get angry.

I flashed down the hill and caught ahold of the blood drinker who was wrestling with Ilio. Jerking the two of them apart, I lifted the skinny fiend over my head and flung him down the hill at his partner.

They crashed together cataclysmically, went rolling down the slope in a tangle of limbs.

Another spear came whistling out of the dark. I caught it in mid-flight and sent it back. The vampire who had thrown it let out a cry, gawping down at the shaft protruding from his chest. It didn't kill him. He was too powerful for that, but judging by his howl, it did not sound like it felt very pleasant either. He mewled and tried to pull the lance out, but the spear was stuck in the tree behind him and he didn't have the sense to simply walk forward and unimpale himself.

I heard a strange clomping sound behind me and spun around to meet my next foe, but the creature pelting down the ridge toward me was so bizarre that, for a moment, I was too distracted trying to figure out what it was to mount any kind of defense.

It ran on four legs, and was nearly as tall at the shoulder as I, with a muscular, barrel-shaped body and two heads, one elongated and animalistic, with a great tossing mane of black hair, the other human... female to be exact.

As I stared at it, trying to figure out what the strange hybrid thing was, it struck Ilio and I with terrific force, knocking us into opposite directions.

I collided with a tree. Ilio went rolling down the slope.

The creature reared over me, making a high-pitched wailing sound. I ducked, trying to avoid its flailing hooves. It landed on all fours, and then the human half of it fell off —or rather, leapt off. It was no human-animal hybrid, of course, but a woman riding a beast. A sight I had never beheld.

The woman, flesh as dark and glossy as the beast she rode upon, came around the animal's neck as sinuously as a snake. She drew a knife from her belt as she straddled my sprawled body, then grabbed me by the hair and thrust the blade against my throat.

"Surrender, stranger, or we will kill your little pet," she hissed, speaking the Tanti tongue.

I glanced down the hill and saw Ilio struggling in the grip of the gargantuan. The giant blood drinker had my son in a headlock, was dragging the boy up the hill with him. The skinny blood drinker followed, crawling on all fours.

As they drew near, the one who'd been pierced through with the spear stepped out of the bushes, fussing with the hole in his sternum. It was closing up, healing, but slowly.

There were four of them… but was that all? How many more were lurking in the shadows? I tried to decide if I could free Ilio before the giant blood drinker could do him harm. They were drawing nearer. If I could fling this female off me, fly down the hill to where the two of them struggled…

The female sensed the workings of my mind and pressed her flint blade deeper into my flesh. "One word from me, and Bhorg will tear the little one's head off," she warned, eyes flashing. She was grinning, teeth bright and sharp, eager for me to press her to further violence.

"No, no, don't harm him!" I said quickly.

"Father--!" Ilio yelped, and I squeezed my eyes shut in defeat.

The female looked at Ilio, surprised, then returned her gaze to me. "Father?" she echoed, and a menacing little laugh slipped from her sensuous mouth. Her eyes searched my face, her thighs clasped around my hips, and then she growled, "Surrender to me, beautiful one. Surrender and I will let him live."

The words shattered the last of my resistance. I recalled the dream I'd had the night that Ilio was wed. The feminine presence I had sensed at the lake. The way our souls had briefly intertwined, and I found my body responding to her, just as it had that night. Helplessly. Against my will.

This was the siren who had called out to me in my dreams. Of that, I had no doubt.

The female blood drinker felt the stirring of my loins and laughed at me in contempt. If I could blush, I would have.

"Bhorg…" she called, eyeing me with terrible

amusement. Ilio's destruction trembled on her tongue.

At her call, the giant tightened his grasp upon Ilio's head. His arms were thick with muscle. I had no doubt that he could tear the boy's head from his shoulders.

Ilio grunted, and I heard a crackling sound. The flesh of the boy's neck began to fissure.

"No! Ancestors, no! Please!" I pleaded with her. "Please, don't hurt the boy! He is my son!"

"Then submit to me!" the female blood drinker hissed, looming over me. She pressed her knife to my throat, squeezing her thighs around my waist. "Swear yourself to my service, and I will set your child free."

I nodded, the knife digging into the flesh beneath my chin, and she leapt to her feet in exultation.

"You are my slave now!" she proclaimed, then, pointing to the ground beneath her feet: "On your knees, dog!"

I hesitated, then moved to all fours in front of her, my head hanging. Laughter rang out from the woman's male companions.

"Let the boy go, Bhorg," my vanquisher commanded.

Ilio rushed to my side, kneeled down beside me. "Father, do not do this! Rise up! Fight!"

"I gave my word," I said to the boy.

"No!"

"Go home, little one," the female blood drinker crowed. "Your father has traded his freedom for your life. Do not let his sacrifice be in vain."

Ilio pressed his forehead to my temple. "No, Thest! No!"

"Go, Ilio, return to your wife and children. Love them and protect them with all of your strength. Tell the Tanti what has transpired here tonight." I peered up at him, tried to smile encouragingly. "Do not act so overwrought, boy. I am defeated, but these blood drinkers cannot end my life. I have flung myself from mountaintops and lived. I will return. Have no doubt of it."

"No—!"

I grabbed the boy by the shoulders and pulled him into my arms. Hugging him to my chest, I bent my lips to his ear. "Tell the Tanti they must flee from these lands," I whispered in Denghoi, praying the T'sukuru could not understand. "Make certain that they do it, Ilio."

The female stepped toward me, lips curling back from her teeth, and I pushed him away from me.

"Go, boy!" I said sternly, and the lad rose to his feet. He hesitated, shot a look of complete and utter hatred at the woman standing over me, and then he turned and pelted quickly down the wooded ridge.

"What did you say to him?" she demanded, watching the boy flee.

"Only that I love him," I said. I had returned to my hands and knees.

She looked down at me, arching an eyebrow, but did not challenge my lie.

One of the male blood drinkers spoke in an unfamiliar language. The trio of men walked past me, headed up the ridge. Each glanced at me as they passed: the giant with amusement, the little one with curiosity, the one I had speared with disdain. I remained on all fours, staring down at my hands, while the female blood drinker walked to her mount and returned. A thick braided rope was placed overtop my head. The woman cinched it around my throat and then gave my leash a tug.

"Up!" she said in Tanti. "On your feet, beautiful one. The night wanes. We return to camp."

I stood, pulling my hair from the tightly cinched rope, and she leapt nimbly to the back of the great ebon beast. She clicked her tongue against the side of her cheek and the vampire wolf came trotting from the underbrush.

"Vehnfear," she called to the animal. "*Wuhat lot*!"

The shaggy gray canine glowered at me as it limped by, its black upper lip curling back from its fangs, then it tossed its head and went trotting up the slope, its tail held arrogantly erect.

The female blood drinker gave my leash another tug. "Come, slave," she said, and with a gesture of her thighs, the beast she rode upon turned around on the path and started up the ridge after the rest.

Zenzele, My Captor

1

With Ilio out of harm's way, I felt more sure of myself. I allowed the female blood drinker to lead me up the forested ridge, observing the woman discretely as we travelled.

She was a comely creature, my captor, small of stature, with a lithe and muscular body. She had small breasts, a narrow waist, but full hips and powerful thighs, which I found quite sensual. I had always been attracted to voluptuous women when I was a mortal man (and such things were all consuming) and the sight of her body, full hips rocking on the back of her powerful beast, rekindled desires I had thought long gone to ash.

The color of her skin intrigued me. It was dark, almost black, and lustrous like obsidian, which is a glasslike igneous rock that was used to make cutting tools in those days. Humans with very dark skin often take on that glossy black appearance when they are made into vampires, in stark contrast to mortals with more lightly colored flesh, who unerringly turn the color of sun-bleached bone.

It was the first time I had ever seen such a dark-skinned immortal, and I imagined how she must look in the moonlight, limned in its quicksilver glow.

She glanced in my direction as if she felt my eyes

on her.

"What is your name?" she demanded.

She had a round childlike face, with full lips, a broad nose and large expressive eyes. Her hair, like Ilio's, was black and styled into braided coils, swept back from her brow like the plumage of some exotic bird.

When I did not answer, her nostrils flared and she gave the rope around my neck a sharp yank.

"Answer!" she snapped. "Or would you prefer I call you slave?"

I stumbled forward a little at her tug. For such a petite creature she was surprisingly strong!

"Thest," I croaked. I wriggled my fingers beneath my leash, trying to loosen it.

She looked amused. "So, you are the blood god who destroyed the Oombai." She shrugged when I met her eyes, surprised that she knew my name. "Do not think me impressed, Thest. Those craven fools had long lost any good sense they might once have possessed. And they had even less honor, if that is imaginable. You should have seen the way they groveled at my feet. How they lapped my spittle from the dirt. They would fight over it like dogs!" And then she laughed, her eyes flashing with contempt.

"And might you be the blood drinker Zenzele?" I asked. My lover Aioa had described one such creature when I was a guest of the Oombai.

Their chieftain is a female, Aioa had said, *with skin like volcanic glass. She is very beautiful, but cruel and full of spite.*

"The Goddess Zenzele!" my new mistress corrected, holding her back very straight.

"The goddess of death," I said, echoing my dead lover's words.

My beautiful captor did not reply. She merely chuckled, looking away to the north.

I wondered what she would say if I told her that I'd dreamed of her, If I told her of that night at the lake, when it seemed that our spirits had intertwined. I was certain this woman was the seductress of my dreams, though how I had dreamed of her I still cannot explain.

The words trembled on the tip of my tongue: *I have dreamed of you.* But I knew she would only make light of them.

Of course, dreams and prophecy have long been closely related. It is a phenomenon common to all human societies, from modern times to the most ancient civilizations. I myself have dreamed the future. Once. When I was still a mortal man. I dreamed of my doom, personified by the snake god of the Grey Stone People. Was my dream of the vampire Zenzele a premonition of doom as well? I had dreamed of my maker's coming. Was this spiteful beauty, then, fated to be my un-maker?

O, Ancestors, let it be so!

If death was come for me, it could not have bore a finer countenance.

We had come to the peak of the great wooded ridge. The ground here was open and strewn with slabs of weathered granite, frosted in ice. Far below, in the distance, the forest gave way to a rolling plain, and there, twinkling like distant stars, the lights of many small fires. Torches, I realized, squinting to bring them into focus; a procession of torches wriggling eastward like a snake.

"How is it you speak the tongue of the Tanti?" I asked, returning my attention to the mounted woman.

She rode silently for several minutes. I did not think she was going to answer, but then she sighed and said, "I speak all the tongues of this region, beautiful one. These lands are my keeping, as they have been for many cycles of the seasons. The Tanti are known to me. We have many Tanti slaves in Uroboros. They are strong, obedient workers."

"Uroboros?" I asked.

"The city of the gods!" the woman shouted in disbelief, wheeling around on her animal. "*Yahi*, beautiful one! Do you know nothing of the world? Who is the blood god who made you immortal?"

"My maker taught me nothing," I said. "He made me a blood drinker against my will. For that transgression, I took his life. I am far from the lands where I was born a mortal man. I know nothing of your blood drinker ways."

I saw a flicker of compassion in her eyes. It was fleeting—there, then gone an instant later—and then she merely looked annoyed. Perhaps I'd only imagined it.

"Do not expect me to be your wet-nurse," she said, sliding back around on her animal. "We are returning to Uroboros. When we arrive, I will present you to our ruler, Khronos. He will decide your fate. Until then, you are bound to me. You have sworn on your honor."

I nodded.

She knew that I could escape her. It was the promise I had made to her which restrained me, not the rope around my neck. She had spared the life of my son, and in return, I had made an oath to serve her, and I intended to honor that oath—for the time being.

Until we were far away from the Tanti. Until I felt sure that Ilio would be safe.

When we had travelled far enough away, when I was certain that my loved ones were safe from retribution, then I might think of... *renegotiating* the conditions of my surrender.

Until then, I would be her obedient slave.

Also, I wanted to see this "city of the blood gods".

Uroboros.
Just the sound of it excited me.

2

We left the forest behind and started across the plains, headed toward that wavering line of torches. The snow had begun to fall more heavily, the wind blowing fiercely east to west. The great beast that Zenzele rode upon snorted and shivered, its breath coming out of its wide nostrils in puffs of steam, but the woman did not seem bothered by the whorls of cutting ice, despite the fact that her legs and arms were mostly bare. No more than I, walking barefoot at her side. She was a powerful blood drinker. I knew this the way all vampires know the strength of other blood drinkers. It is an instinctive thing. From the moment I saw her, I knew that she was every bit as powerful as I.

Our going was slow in the plains. The snow had bent the high grass into great white humps, and the ground was a soggy morass. If I were free, I would have taken to the heavens, crossing the snowy field in great bounds. But my mistress would not allow it. The animal she rode upon was a mortal creature, and she showed no inclination of abandoning it, though the poor thing was having as much trouble walking in the muck as I.

My captor seemed to have a great affection for her beast. She stroked its thick neck and murmured words of encouragement into its ear, speaking in a tongue I did not know—the language of the T'sukuru, I assumed. When the animal's legs became mired in the mud, she slid down from its back and helped to pull them free.

"I shouldn't have ridden her through all this mud

and snow," she said, and then her eyes flashed at me meaningfully, as if to say that this was all my fault.

I suppose it was, if she had ridden to the assistance of the little blood drinker.

"Why don't you give the living blood to this beast, too?" I asked, after we had moved on.

"It kills the horses," she answered. "Only the wolves can be transformed as men are transformed, and then only a few survive. Vehnfear was a gift from our god king. In honor of my service to him."

"So it is called a horse. I have never seen a horse before," I said, stroking the haunch of the beast. It twitched at my touch, snorted in complaint. "I have never seen a person ride an animal in such a manner either. The children in the village where I was born would sometimes play at riding the dogs, but—"

"You talk too much," Zenzele snapped.

I held my tongue.

It was merely my excitement. I had long wondered about others of my kind. What they were like. How they had come to share my fate. What strange powers they might possess. Their myths and social customs. I had planned to seek them out after Ilio struck off on his own, when I tired of living among my mortal kin.

Only they had found me first.

But in truth, I did not feel as though I were defeated. I wanted to be taken to the city of the blood drinkers. I wanted to feel the dust of its streets with my feet, to see its sights, smell its odors, good or bad, harken to the chorus of the creatures who peopled it. Only there would I find the answers to all of my questions. They would know the secret of our beginnings... and perhaps even the method of putting this life to an end, if that was something that I decided again to do.

That was my hope, anyway.

And this woman, to whom I'd sworn myself to servitude... I wanted to know her as well. She was the first female blood drinker I'd met, and what a vampire she was! Fiery. Confident. Regal. Cruel. She *was* a goddess of death, and I could not help but wonder what it would be like to worship at her altar. I would do it! By her leave, I would commit myself, body and soul, to glorious veneration, despite her harsh nature. To lie down with such a woman...! I would not have to guard my passion as with a mortal woman. Her flesh, every bit as resilient as my own, could withstand the ferocity of my lust, and no doubt respond in like kind.

I felt a stirring in my loins at the thought. It had been four years since the last time I'd made love to a woman, and that was with a mortal. Before that: a seeming eternity. Vampires might not be driven by the physical need for sex as mortal men are driven, but I was still a man, and I still had a man's desires.

A billow of snow and ice stung my cheeks, and I hunkered down and tried to put such trivial thoughts out of my mind. Now was not the time for idle fantasies. We were approaching the column of torches that I had glimpsed from the clearing: the procession of the blood drinkers.

No column now, the phalanx had come together at both ends, forming a circle. The storm was growing more severe, the windblown ice hissing across the plains, flying almost horizontally. If not for the storm's increasing fury, I might have sensed the mortals sooner and would not have been so horrified when I suddenly laid eyes upon them. But I did not sense them, not until we were nearly upon them, and then I could do ought but gape at them in dismay.

There were at least four dozen of them.

They huddled inside the circle of fluttering torches, men and women in tattered garments. They were tied to long wood poles, bound around the neck and wrists by intricately knotted cords. Grouped by sixes and eights, the poles running along the right and left shoulder of each group, they hunched their backs against the scathing wind, their bodies packed closely together.

Captives of the T'sukuru, being marched to Uroboros.

Moving among the slaves: several unbound mortal men. Perhaps a dozen of them. Brawny, cruel-faced brutes, servants of the blood drinkers no doubt, warmly dressed and tending to the captives. Some of them were throwing furs upon the shivering prisoners. Others distributed food and drink, or worked at erecting shelters alongside their vampire masters. One of the slave-tenders was beating a man with a whip, flogging him across the back and shoulders without mercy.

Anger subsumed my horror. My head began to throb. Slavery infuriated me. What, save greed, gave one man right to claim ownership of another? I had destroyed the Oombai Elders for this very offense, and here I was, confronted by the same outrage! I was sorely tempted to renege on my bargain with the vampire Zenzele. To cast off all pretense of submission and throw myself upon these cursed slavers!

But I was outnumbered. And I had already been defeated by them once. Would the battle go any different if I revolted against them now? And what would they do to the Tanti, to my adopted son Ilio, if I did not honor my bargain with their mistress?

My captor took note of my shock and revulsion. One of her delicately shaped eyebrows rose, and she grinned as if to say, *Well, what did you expect?*

The other vampires had spotted us and paused at their labors. One of them waved Zenzele over.

"Come, beautiful one," she said, and with a jerk of

my leash, she delivered me into the hands of the blood gods.

3

I had yet to meet the one who'd waved her over. This one had been absent from the battle in the forest. As Zenzele's horse stepped into the circle of torches, he left off from his toils and met her halfway across the grounds. He appraised me with a scowl-- from my tangled hair and muddy face to my torn clothing and bare feet-- and then he turned his attention to the woman. He spoke in the tongue of the T'sukuru, the words still gibberish to me, but it was obvious that I was the subject of their conversation.

He was a tall man, broad across the shoulders, and with features that could only be described as beautiful. Large, pale blue eyes, a small upturned nose and dimpled cheeks. He might have looked childlike but for his powerful jaw and jutting chin. He had shoulder-length brown hair, pulled back by a leather thong, and wore intricately inscribed bone-plated armor.

Zenzele answered him, her voice purring with mockery—yet, I detected an undercurrent of defensiveness in her tone. Her posture was stiffly erect, as if she did not fully trust the man.

The handsome blood drinker looked at me again, clearly unconvinced by whatever it was she had said to him, and she snapped at him.

He ran a tongue along the tip of one of his upper fangs, the corner of his mouth curled into a smirk, then he shrugged and ambled away. I watched as he returned to his labors, helping several mortals to erect a high-peaked frame tent.

Zenzele sighed, then urged her mount forward. A

mortal attendant came trotting toward us, and my captor slid from the back of her beast. She turned the horse over to the care of the mortal, then led me toward their captives.

"That one is Palifver," she said in a low voice, nodding toward the handsome blood drinker. "He is my second-in-command."

"You do not trust him," I murmured.

Her eyes flashed at me. "Khronos is his patron."

I glanced at the man over my shoulder, impressed that he could unnerve such an imperious woman.

Most vampires are like my adopted son Ilio, stronger and faster than a normal human, more resilient, able to survive physical trauma that would kill a mortal man-- but not completely invulnerable. Decapitation, dismemberment, grievous injury... these things will kill most vampires, and we can all sense those vulnerabilities in one another. Palifver was strong. He was a bit more powerful than my maker, perhaps, but not much more. He was not a true immortal like me... or my beautiful obsidian mistress.

Khronos must favor him greatly, I mused, to make a true immortal so wary.

I thought for a moment that she intended to bind me with the rest of the captives, but she did not. She inspected them, paying particular attention to the bite marks on their necks and wrists. I guess she was checking them for disease. A vampire's bite can transmit infection just like any other animal's bite.

I followed Zenzele as she circled the captive mortals. The sight of them filled me with great pity, yet what could I do? If I defied these ruthless blood drinkers, they would surely visit retribution on my loved ones.

The mortals were haggard, their bodies bruised and riddled with teeth marks. They were filthy and tattered and hollow-eyed. Hopeless. Pushed to the brink of collapse. I wanted to save them. I wanted to deliver them from bondage, but I was as much a prisoner as they.

Some of them looked at me, their eyes beseeching. Others sneered with revulsion or contempt.

I turned away, ashamed.

At least they had shelter: a crude lean-to. Several fires blazed near enough to keep their bodies from freezing. They would survive this howling blizzard... but to what end?

My mistress finished her inspection. She gave some orders to the mortals who tended the slaves, then ducked from their shelter and led me toward the big tent that Palifver had been laboring over.

It was fully erect now, its peaked roof shaking in the whistling gales. Zenzele bent through the flyflap and surveyed the interior. Waterproof skins had been laid out on the soggy ground. In the center of the tent, Palifver was working to build a fire. A couple mortal attendants dashed to and fro, putting down sleeping furs and woven mats. Soon the shelter would be cozy and warm, while the captives of the blood drinkers shivered outside.

Palifver's glinting blue eyes followed us as Zenzele led me to a particularly luxurious pile of furs. She took the rope from around my neck and put it aside. She watched me warily for a moment, as if she thought I might attack her or try to escape. Like my flimsy leash was anything more than symbolic! When I did not immediately revolt, she smiled and called out to the domestic slaves.

They were still readying the tent for occupation, but at her summons, they came scrambling to assist her.

They were small males. Young. Androgynous.

More finely attired than their slave-tender counterparts. Their faces were painted white with red lips and dark-circled eyes.

"Hold my hand," she said to me, and when I took her tiny cold fingers in mine, she lifted her left foot and allowed her attendants to wash it. She smiled at me, her teeth very sharp and white in the dim interior of the tent, then she lifted her other foot, her perfectly formed toes slightly curled.

They helped her out of her body armor and cleaned and dried her flesh, then eased more comfortable garments onto her.

I stared into her eyes, trying to ignore her nakedness, trying to will my body not to respond to those brief glimpses of bare flesh.

I should feel only hatred for this woman, I thought.

She represented all that I found repugnant in this world. Arrogant. Cruel. She was a slave trader. A killer.

And yet, the sight of her small breasts, the smooth curve of a flawless thigh, made my stomach flutter like an adolescent boy. I wanted to circle my lips around her nipples. I wanted to lick my way down her body, part the coarse fleece of her maidenhood with my tongue.

She belted the bright red frock they'd put on her, grinning at my studied neutrality, then lowered herself onto her furs and gestured for the mortal attendants to clean me.

One of them asked her something, and she replied curtly, looking annoyed. With a flick of her fingers, she sent them hurrying away. I watched as the little mortals crossed to the other side of the tent and started searching through a large sack.

While the attendants were digging through the bag, Palifver stared at Zenzele. He had built up the fire to a crackling blaze and his eyes glowed in the dancing yellow light. She ignored him, looking after her attendants. Finally, she grew annoyed and called out to them in a sharp voice. The fussy little men rushed back to us, one of them clutching a long strip of cloth.

They cleaned my feet, then relieved me of my tattered clothes, curling their noses in distaste as they handled my mangled garments. Zenzele appraised my nakedness as they cleaned me. I cupped my genitals in my hands, submitting meekly to their care as they swabbed the mud from my flesh. Some of the other blood drinkers pushed through the flap of the tent as I stood there exposed and I endured their mockery without expression. I still did not understand what they were saying, but their amusement was quite evident. They pointed and laughed. Made crude gestures with their hands.

"Ifv ever d'moii?" one of the little mortals asked, looking up at me. When I didn't reply, he glanced toward his mistress.

Zenzele nodded and flicked her finger at me.

I jumped as he slid his forearm between my legs.

"D'moii," he said, smiling up at me.

I raised my arms to allow the attendants to clothe me. The garment they'd taken from the sack was a loincloth. It was made of tree bark, cut into a long, narrow strip and beaten soft. While the first man held one end up over the front of me, the second twisted his end into a rope, yanked it between my buttocks and passed it around my waist. They circled the strip around to the back again and knotted it, cinching it tight. When they had girded my loins, Zenzele dismissed the two mortals to tend to the other blood drinkers. The little men bowed and scurried away, and she gestured for me to sit.

"Are you comfortable?" she asked in Tanti, and I shrugged. In truth, I wanted to pick that prickly cloth out of my buttocks. I kept my features devoid of expression, however. Emotionless. She smoothed her bedding as if she did not notice and said, "It will be dawn soon. We sleep during the day, of course, while the slave-tenders look after our captives. When night comes, we continue to Uroboros."

"How far is it?" I asked.

"Many nights past the mountains. We can only travel as fast as the slaves can walk. Alone, I could make the journey in two nights, but only if I ran without stopping. With as many slaves as we have this time: three fists, maybe four."

Fifteen to twenty days.

"Your eyes flash with anger when I mention the slaves," she said. "I saw pity in your gaze when I inspected them earlier. Are you truly so fond of mortals?"

"You were a mortal once," I replied.

She scowled. "I was also a slave once. What does that matter now?"

I wanted to ask her how she could be so callous. Did she not have a mortal family at some point in her life? Was she not loved?

Before I could give voice to my thoughts, however, the other blood drinkers laughed uproariously. Judging by the way the big one was gesticulating—swinging his big stone hammer, which he'd brought inside the tent—he was recounting our battle in the forest. The giant—Zenzele had called him Bhorg—pointed at me and grinned, his teeth big and square, with long and wickedly curved fangs. Palifver glanced in our direction. His laughter was shrill with hatred.

"They don't believe that you will honor our bargain," Zenzele said.

I glanced at her guiltily.

Maybe I won't, I thought.

"I told Palifver what I promised you. That I would spare the Tanti in return for your submission," she said, staring into my eyes intently, as if her words had some hidden meaning. "I sent Hettut to spy on them tonight. He was only supposed to count their numbers, but he is... easily tempted. I had planned to raid the village at nightfall tomorrow. Since the fall of the Oombai, we have been forced to raid the villages of the Western Dominions ourselves. It was simpler before, when we bartered with the Oombai for our slaves. You have caused us quite a bit of aggravation."

I absorbed what she had just confessed to me, wondering at the kindness implied by her words. She had lied to her second-in-command about the terms of my surrender. She knew that I cared for the Tanti, but why be merciful now? I was defeated.

And then I thought of my beloved Tanti. I imagined them bound and shivering in the cold. I thought of my Irema and Aioa, Valas and Yorda and their whole extended family, all their sons and daughters and grandchildren. I thought of the fishermen, the huntsmen, the craftsmen, and their wives. Good, dutiful, cheerful women. I pictured the village destroyed, the streets full of the dead, my Tanti tribesmen conquered, and all the tattered survivors marched away to Uroboros.

And what could they look forward to if they survived the arduous trek?

To be enslaved?

Devoured?

"I will honor our bargain," I said gravely. "Spare the Tanti, Zenzele, and I am yours. Whatever you will do with me."

4

In one night, I had met more of my fellow blood drinkers than I had in the entirety of my immortal existence, and I hated them.

While the storm raged outside and their captives huddled in the cold, the blood drinkers relaxed in warmth and luxury. Zenzele sat apart from the male members of the vampire raiding party. She did not partake of their revels, though she did not act as if she took offense at their behavior either.

After their domestic slaves had attended to the T'sukuru raiders, they made the two little men battle, and placed wagers on who would be the victor. Zenzele watched without expression as the two slaves wrestled, pummeling one another with their fists until both were bloody and one lay on the ground unconscious.

The men roared their approval (or dismay) at the outcome of the contest and then snatched up the little mortal who had won, biting him on the wrists and drinking his blood. He yelped as their teeth sliced through his flesh, but he did not try to escape them. He squeezed his eyes shut as they jerked him back and forth. Finally, bled nearly white, the servant's eyes rolled back in his skull and he went limp. They passed him back and forth a while longer, slurping and grunting as they sucked at his dripping wounds, then they discarded him near the fire beside his battered fellow.

Zenzele glanced at me, noting the strained look on my face. The smell of the blood was tormenting me. "Do you wish to feed?" she asked, and I shook my head no. But it was an effort.

The flap of the tent flew open then, letting in a

swirl of icy snow. Zenzele's wolf trotted in, tongue lolling, followed by the final member of the group I was to meet that night.

"Goro!" the others shouted as the blood drinker strode inside.

He was a short, stout man, dressed in furs, with a large nose, a prominent brow and a receding chin. I recognized the newcomer's race immediately. The blood drinker was a Fat Hand-- a Neanderthal vampire!

A mortal female hung limp in his arms.

The Neanderthal placed the woman on the ground, then stood upright and shook the snow from his parka, grinning at his companions. He said something—probably some remark about the weather—and the other men laughed.

Intrigued, I examined the blood drinker more closely.

Like all vampires, the Neanderthal blood drinker had glossy stone-like flesh. There were tribal scars on his face, designs typical of his race: concentric circles on his cheeks, dots running across his forehead, just above his eyebrows. The tribal scars must have been cut into his flesh when he was a mortal, during some sort of manhood rite, because vampires do not scar visibly when injured. He had large, glimmering brown eyes, a great mane of shaggy red hair and freckles. In all ways but one, he looked like any other human blood drinker. The only thing that set him apart was his fangs. He had prominent lower fangs. You could almost call them tusks.

Zenzele paid little attention to the Neanderthal. Her pet wolf had leapt into her lap, and she hugged him, laughing without reservation as he lapped at her face. The canine's thick pelt was wet and dusted with ice. His tail swooped back and forth in excitement, spattering us with flecks of melting snow.

"Down, Vehnfear!" she gasped. "Down!"

I could see it took an effort for the animal to restrain himself, and I smiled, remembering the dogs I'd played with as a boy. You have not truly known unconditional love until you are loved by a canine.

The wolf settled beside her, hind legs crooked to one side. He looked around the tent with a human-like expression of happiness, tongue hanging out, tail thumping the mat beneath him. These blood drinkers are his pack, I thought, and I realized something else: this creature was highly intelligent. I could see it in his eyes. The glimmer of self-awareness. The living blood had amplified the animal's intellect.

Once the Neanderthal had gotten settled in, he conferred with Zenzele. They talked for several minutes, and then he retired to the other side of the tent with the others. They roused the female he had captured, who immediately began to scream, then ripped off her garments and had their way with her--all but Hettut, who had gone to sleep. Her desperate struggling only incensed the vampires. They broke her bones in their enthusiasm. They bled her as they fucked her. When it was his turn, Palifver leered at my mistress, cock in hand, but Zenzele would not meet his gaze. He frowned, glanced toward me, then shoved himself brutally inside the woman, making her shriek.

It was only during the woman's rape that Zenzele betrayed her revulsion for their cruelty. As the male blood drinkers took turns assaulting the woman, Zenzele's lips curled back in disgust, and Vehnfear, sensing his mistress's mood, snarled softly.

I sat, staring down at my hands as the woman cried out. Would that I could have saved her, but I could not. For love of my son, for love of my people, I could not intercede.

And then it was over. They tired of their sport and began to bite into her flesh in earnest, and within moments of that she was dead.

Naked, his chest and groin smeared with mortal blood, Bhorg dragged the corpse to the tent flap and tossed it outside in the snow.

Seeing the swirling gray light outside, Zenzele said, "It is dawn. Time to sleep, beautiful one."

I lay back where she indicated, then tucked some rolled up furs beneath my head and covered my body. The furs smelled like wet dog, but the odor was not wholly unpleasant. My beautiful captor watched me for a little while, hands on her knees, her expression inscrutable, and then she lay down nearby. She stared up at the roof of the tent for several minutes, listening to the snow hiss against the leather canopy, then she turned on her side away from me.

Vehnfear whined, and she reached back to caress him. She curled her fingers in the wolf's plush fur, scratching the back of his neck. He lapped her hand, then laid his head down between his paws.

On the other side of the tent, Palifver laughed cruelly.

I closed my eyes.

5

"Wake!" Zenzele exclaimed, and then she smacked me with some sort of braided leather strap.

I lurched, my cheek stinging where she had struck me. I was disoriented, unsure where I was or how I had gotten there, then it all came rushing back. I was not home in my lodge in the Tanti village, as I had been dreaming. I was in the camp of the vampire slavers. I was a slave, sworn to the blood drinker who had vanquished me. The life that I had enjoyed the last three years was gone now. Lost in a single disastrous defeat.

My mistress stood over me, glaring. "You are the last to rise," she said. "Are you going to be a lazy servant?"

"No, no," I mumbled, and I started to sit up.

"I did not tell you to stand," she said, pushing me back down with one of her bare feet. She glanced around the tent, making sure that we were alone, then used her toe to push the covers off my body.

I lay staring up at her, uncertain what she wanted of me, but I need not have worried what I should do to please her. Hers was the dominant role. She intended to take what she desired from me.

Her toe slid up my inner thigh and caught against the fabric of my loincloth. She wriggled the tip of her toe beneath the edge of it and pushed it aside.

"Make it hard," she commanded, gazing down at my organ, and her sensuous lips quirked up a little at the corners.

"Well?" she said after a moment.

She sighed as if with annoyance and then used the silky pad of her foot to stroke the belly of my cock. It leapt quickly to attention. I gulped, then grasped ahold of my bedding as she stepped across my thighs and squatted down over me. She took hold of my organ and stood it upright, then lowered her body upon it.

I groaned.

"Quiet," she hissed.

The opening of her organ was tight. I would have said unnaturally tight if she were a mortal woman, but I had never coupled with a female vampire. Perhaps they were all this resistant to intrusion. I tried to peek between her thighs, but she was still dressed in the red tunic she had put on the night before. Her genitals were hidden from my sight. Still, I could feel that there was something abnormal about her organ. Her vulva was too smooth. The opening too small.

She pressed down, making a soft sound of effort, and then her body enveloped me all at once. She sank down upon me, cold and silky, swallowed me to the hilt.

She closed her eyes and rocked her hips, riding me as she'd ridden her beast the previous night-- the creature she'd called a "horse". I moved to caress her thighs and she smacked my hands away, and then she leaned forward and settled her palms upon my chest.

Head down, eyes squeezed shut, she impaled herself on me again and again. Her movements grew increasingly forceful as if she sought to do violence to herself, and then she groaned, and I felt the walls of her pussy begin to rhythmically convulse. She dug her nails into the flesh of my chest, her arms and legs twitching, and then she opened her eyes and looked down at me.

"Cum inside me," she commanded. She ground her groin upon me, wriggling her lower body back and forth. "Do it now! Like a mortal man!" she hissed.

I arched my head back, jaw dropping open, and she clamped her palm over my mouth.

"Do it!"

I howled into her palm as I exploded inside her, but she didn't stop, she kept twisting her organ around and around, and the pleasure surged with each rotation, wave after dizzying wave. *I dreamed--! I dreamed of you!* I thought incoherently. The words echoed inside my skull, sounding over and over. The lake. Ours souls entwined in chilly starlight. *I dreamed of you. I dreamed of you.*

And then she ducked her head down and put her lips to mine, her mouth as cold as ice, but it was soft, too. Yielding. Our fangs scraped lightly together. Her tongue flicked out, and she tasted what she'd kissed.

"I dreamed of you," she whispered, and then she

rose, my cock sliding out of her abruptly. I yelped, startled by her brusqueness. I did not want to be released so quickly, but she was finished with me.

"Do not speak of this with any of the others," she said over her shoulder. "You are woefully ignorant of the troubles you have caused."

6

In a slave culture, it is not unusual for a bondman to be used for his or her master's sexual gratification, and so I cautioned myself not to see more in her actions than she actually intended. She was desirous, and she had used me for her satisfaction. And yet she had brushed her lips to mine, and she'd confessed that she had dreamed of me, and that had a profound significance to me. I could not stop thinking of it. I also could not bring myself to feel offended by her use of me, though intellectually I knew I should.

We changed quietly into outside clothes.

She had produced new garments for me to wear, borrowing them from one of the other men. The new clothes lay folded near the stone hearth. I dressed, and then she bid me to assist her with some of the straps of her breast and shoulder plating.

As I fumbled with the ties, I inclined my nose to her nape and breathed in her scent.

"Stop that!" she snapped, elbowing me in the stomach. I chuckled, falling back a step, and she turned suddenly and began to whip me with her leather strap. Two, three times, she brought it down across my shoulder and chest, her lips peeled back in fury. "Don't you understand?" she hissed at me.

I retreated from her, stunned, raising my hands to ward off her blows.

She stared at me in disbelief for a moment, and

then she snarled, "You are a fool!"

She turned abruptly and stalked away, ducking through the flap of the tent.

Her flurry of blows had not harmed me, of course, but I was duly chastised nonetheless. She was right. There was much about the culture of these vampires I was ignorant of. I had taken a very tiny liberty of her to my way of thinking, drawing close to her, smelling her hair. But I had laughed when she commanded me to stop. Perhaps my lack of respect was the reason for her violent reaction. Perhaps sexual relationships were frowned upon among the blood drinkers of the east. She might even be bound to another, and our coupling an illicit affair! There was too much I did not know, too many lives dependent on my actions.

You *are* behaving like a fool! I thought, rubbing my stinging chest, and with that I followed her outside, and into the glittering white world that awaited.

7

The atmosphere had an amazing clarity. The storm had passed and the stars were out in a glorious abundance. The moon perched upon the distant Carpathians, and the image of it was so clear, the illusion of its nearness so perfect, that I imagined I could reach out and grasp it, pluck it down from the heavens like some pale fruit and take a bite of it.

The slave traders rushed about as I walked to the center of the camp. They were too busy at their labors to give me any thought. Some of them were tearing down shelters. Others were piling gear upon the backs of their riding beasts. Two of the slave-tenders were ladling food and drink into the mouths of the slaves. The captives of the blood drinkers had been lined up in preparation for their march to Uroboros, and as the slave-tenders moved quickly through their ranks, they groaned and slurped at the nourishment the men splashed impatiently into their mouths. Some of them pleaded for more and sobbed when their appeals went unanswered. The sight of the mortals, so desperate and exhausted, tore at my heart. Finally, I could watch no longer. I turned around, taking in all the activity, and I thought how easy it would be to slip away in the chaos.

I knew I would not do such a thing. So far, Zenzele had kept her promise to spare the Tanti. The blood drinkers gave no sign of mounting a raiding party upon my people. The thought of escape only came because it was evident, but I had no intention of acting upon it.

The groans of the slaves drew my attention again. Something about their moaning sounded out-of-place. It was not a sound that despairing men might make, rather something more akin to carnal pleasure.

I observed the slave-tenders feeding the prisoners.

Both of them were large and powerfully muscled, with crude features and dim, pitiless eyes. Each bore a bulging sack from a strap around the shoulder, which they dipped from as they moved from slave to slave. Every prisoner received a hasty splash of gruel and a dipper of water as the slave-tenders moved along the ranks. The captives gulped down the water without any unusual behavior, but when the man with the feedbag came around, all the mortals made the same curious expression. They gobbled the swill down greedily when the wooden ladle pressed to their lips, and then their eyes rolled back in their heads and a shiver passed through their bodies. It was a convulsion of orgasmic bliss, out of all proportion to the meager amount of food they had received.

What, I wondered, was in that gruel?

Scowling, I moved a little closer, and then I smelled it.

Blood.

It was not the coppery tang of mortal blood. I would have noticed that immediately. It was the tarry scent of vampire blood, the *ebu potashu,* the living black blood.

And they were feeding it to their mortal captives!

"Thest!"

Zenzele approached from the other side of the camp, stalking toward me purposefully. She frowned when I did not scurry immediately to her summons.

"I see I am going to have to train you to be a proper attendant," she threatened.

"You feed it to them," I said.

She followed my gaze to the bulging feedbag.

"It is only a few drops," she replied. "Just enough to enliven them."

"To keep them healthy for the journey?"

"Would you prefer our prisoners suffer? Their fate has already run them down, beautiful one. It is a kindness."

To that, I had no reply.

"Come," she snapped. "There is no place for pity here. The others will interpret it as weakness."

She leaned toward me.

"A weakness that will reflect upon me as well," she whispered, staring at me meaningfully.

I nodded, and followed her to my labors.

8

The raiding party set off shortly after. Of the blood drinkers, Zenzele, Palifver and Tribtoc took the forward position, riding upon the backs of the great snorting beasts they called horses. The little one named Hettut scurried along at our flank, running on his hands and the tips of his toes in a dog-like manner, which I reluctantly found amusing. The giant blood drinker named Bhorg took rear guard, sauntering after the group with his big hammer slanted across his shoulder. I had not seen the Neanderthal blood drinker since the previous night. He was the party's scout, and had set off well before everyone else. The captives marched between two columns of the blood drinkers' mortal guards, and Vehnfear ran alongside his mistress.

As Zenzele had said the night before, the raiding party could only travel at the pace set by their captives, and the mortals—who were headed for sale in the city of the blood drinkers-- were understandably reluctant to meet with their fate. Despite frequent lashings, they trudged forward like arthritic old women, delaying all they could. The sodden ground and mounds of crunchy snow did not ease our travel either.

I expected the slave traders to be impatient with our slow pace, but they didn't seem to mind. If vampires share one universal trait, it's a love of travel.

(Wouldn't you, if you had all the time in the world?)

I walked alongside my mistress's mount, taking care to project an air of submissiveness. I still did not fully grasp the intricacies of her relationship with Palifver, but Zenzele had intimated that her second-in-command was an influential figure in their society, and that I should be careful in his presence.

The leaders of the raiding party ambled along on their horses, conversing idly, though mostly they wanted to know about me. Palifver was especially interested in my past. He spoke to me in Tanti, as their T'sukuru tongue was still a mystery to me, asking me the name of the blood drinker who had made me into a vampire, what tribe I hailed from, and the circumstances that had delivered me to the dominion of the T'sukuru.

I answered his questions as respectfully as I could. I didn't even bother to deceive him. I told him about my maker, how I had tried to end my life, and how I had awakened on the frozen steppes. I told him of my battle with the Oombai, recounting the slaughter of the Elders. They listened with amusement, but their entertainment didn't matter to me. All I cared about was getting as far away from the Tanti as possible. Their safety, and the safety of my vampire child Ilio, was paramount in my thoughts. The further away we got, I knew, the safer my loved ones would be. For that, I was probably more impatient of our pace than the slave traders themselves.

I gleaned just as much information from his questions as I gave to him. I learned that the T'sukuru considered this whole region, from the steppes where I had encountered the mammoth hunters to the city of the blood drinkers, part of their extended domain. They called it the Western Dominions. I also learned that, in their society, the making of new vampires was a highly ritualized thing and subject to the approval of their god king Khronos.

Zenzele's second-in-command seemed amazed that I did not know the name of my maker, and was disturbed when I confessed that I had killed him shortly after he changed me, saying that it was a terrible crime in their culture, one that Khronos would judge me for shortly after our arrival.

"And how will this be done?" I asked.

"Khronos will look into your soul," Palifver said with a forbidding grin. "The blood is the soul, maker-killer, and it will tell him if your creator deserved to die by your hand." Judging by his expression, he did not seem to think it likely, but he went on: "If your actions were justified, Zenzele will be allowed to keep you. You have sworn yourself to servitude in her house, but such things depend upon the blessing of Khronos."

"Khronos is the First One," the other vampire interjected-- the one I had speared during our battle in the forest. Tribtoc spoke with a wondering expression, staring off toward the moon-limned peaks. "The Great Father will judge your heart, foreigner. He will judge you as he judges all."

I waited for him to elucidate, but that is all he said.

Palifver looked annoyed. He turned away from Tribtoc and said, "You are lucky in one regard."

"What is that?" I asked.

"Your mistress was a stray like you. She has no clan, other than her own house. She answers only to Khronos."

Palifver's observation stank of prejudice. I glanced up to Zenzele, but her face betrayed no emotion. She merely rode, her luminous eyes set on the distant mountain peaks.

A stray like me... I ruminated.

I wondered then how she had come to be a vampire. Was her maker as cruel as mine? Was she made an immortal against her will? What strange paths had delivered her unto the city of the blood drinkers, and how had she risen to a position of such authority?

I would have loved to ask her all those questions, if only we had some privacy in which to speak, but she had made it clear that she was reluctant to confide in me with so many other vampires around. Considering our enhanced senses and our skills at observation, I could certainly understand, especially if her position in their society was not secure, but what if we were alone? What if we could speak without the risk of being spied on?

I must remain alert for any opportunity.

The land gently rose as we marched. The peaks of the Carpathian Mountains grew almost imperceptibly. By the time the sky had begun to lighten, the rugged mountains dominated the eastern horizon.

Palifver and Zenzele discussed the pass we were headed toward. Palifver wanted to press on through the mountain pass, but Zenzele thought it would be wise to make camp early, so that we would be at a safe distance in case of any avalanches.

"What good is it to hurry, Palifver?" Zenzele said. "Frozen carcasses have little value in Uroboros."

As if on cue, we heard a distant rumble. A great sheet of snow had broken away and went crashing down the side of one of the mountains.

Zenzele glared at Palifver smugly.

He did not reply, just scowled and turned away.

Zenzele called a halt to the procession. The captives were given food and drink while fires were built and tents erected. Goro returned and reported that he'd come across a small settlement of mortals just to the north of our position.

"Several homes. Not very well guarded. I think they are Grell."

Zenzele nodded. "We'll have a look at them tomorrow night. If there are any old ones or sick among their number, we will take a few of them to feed on. Else we'll have to bleed some of the slaves, and they've been bled enough already."

Goro bowed and sauntered away. He ducked inside the main tent.

Zenzele glanced toward me. "Do you hunger?"

"I prefer to hunt on my own," I replied.

"I know you feed on animals," she said, and at my look of surprise, she smiled and added, "I can smell it on you. It's... not unpleasant, but it's strange."

I waited.

"Regardless, I cannot let you hunt on your own," she said with a sigh. "The others think I give you too much liberty as it is."

"What do you care what they think," I asked.

Zenzele looked at me darkly. "I am without clan, beautiful one. I must be above reproach if I wish to remain that way. Our laws are very strict. Those who do not abide by our ways are placed under the supervision of a clan master. I would lose my standing, my house... my very freedom."

"Then run away," I whispered to her fiercely. "Run away with me! We--!"

She slapped me—hard enough to turn my head.

"Hold your tongue!" she hissed. She looked around with a worried expression before returning her attention to me. "There is no escape, fool! Khronos *is* a god!"

She could see that I was wounded, that I did not fully understand.

"Do you know what they do to our kind when we do not obey his law?" she asked.

I knew she meant blood drinkers like us, the true immortals.

"Khronos will select five clan masters," she whispered. "Those five will take hold of your head and all four of your limbs, and then they will pull you apart. Not even this can kill us, not the eternal ones, but when it is done, each of the five will take a part of your body and they will ride in five different directions. They will hide the pieces in the most remote locations they can find, and none will ever say where they have hidden them. Khronos will keep the head, of course. Until he tires of playing with it."

I stared at her in horror.

She smiled at me, but there was pity in her eyes. "Your old life is over, beautiful one," she said. "It is better, perhaps, that you accept it now."

Zenzele, My Love

1

"Despite what Palifver has said to you, Khronos is not likely to order that you be divided," Zenzele said. "But he must find no rebelliousness in your soul. You must surrender to him as you have surrendered to me. You must put all thought of defiance out of your mind. Now. This very night. And think no more of it, or the life you've sacrificed to protect your loved ones."

She said this to me as we traveled north, toward the small settlement that Goro had spotted the night before.

Rising at dusk, Zenzele had announced that she was feeling restless and wished to hunt the mortals herself. She sent Goro ahead to check the safety of the pass, and informed Palifver he was to lead the raiding party in her stead until she returned from the hunt.

"Unless you have any objections," she said to him archly. "I assume you have no fear of leading our caravan through the pass tonight, if I do not return in time."

Palifver had answered with a scathing, "Of course not! Go! Have your sport!"

Later, as she was preparing to depart, he returned to the tent and stood with his fists upon his hips. "Why don't you take your little pet with you?" he sneered. "I'm certain his cock can further serve to distract you from your boredom!"

Bhorg and Tribtoc, who were standing nearby, had snickered—but nervously. They moved subtly toward her as well, I noted. As if to protect her.

They all knew, of course, that Zenzele had had her way with me the day before. You cannot hide a thing like that from creatures who can hear a fly rub its legs together.

"I had already decided to bring him," Zenzele replied airily, "though I fear his cock would prove too large a distraction from my plans tonight. I need to hunt, not fuck. Nevertheless, what I do with my slave, or his cock, is none of your affair. And I certainly don't intend to leave him at the mercy of you four beasts. I don't need a slave whose arse whistles every time the wind blows!"

Bhorg and Tribtoc had laughed uproariously at that, but Palifver took insult yet again. He whirled on his heel and stalked away, but I had seen the tiny muscles around his eyes twitching. He was jealous of me. I must be even more watchful of this one.

We set off north shortly after the raiding party started marching, traveling by foot so that we could move quickly and quietly. At first, we crossed the terrain in great leaps—the icy wind roaring in our ears—neither of us speaking, simply enjoying our liberty, flying beneath a sky milky with stars, our bodies launching us again and again into the heavens. Zenzele reached out to me and I grasped her hand, our fingers interlocking, and then we leapt together, and she smiled at me as we flew, and I laughed. The earth rushed up at us, and she let me go and ran ahead, blurring down a snow-covered hillside. I watched her grow small, and then she launched into the sky again. Hoping to impress her, I followed, running faster, leaping higher.

When we were out of earshot, we slowed to a normal walking pace, then stopped.

There, near a thicket of conifers, Zenzele gestured for me to come closer to her, and then she embraced me unexpectedly, pressing her cheek to my chest, a little sigh of relief escaping from her lips.

Her eyes closed, her great black lashes settling like butterflies upon her cheeks. Her shoulders rose and fell, and then she pushed away from me.

"Zenzele," I murmured.

My chest tingled where her cheek had rested upon it. The sensation of her touch lingered ghostlike on my flesh. I ached to pull her back into my embrace.

"Quiet," she whispered, holding up two fingers.

She stepped away, looking toward the south.

As I waited, she scanned the surrounding landscape with her potent vampire senses.

There was no discernible manifestation of her power, but I had the sense that an invisible beam of energy was radiating from her mind, like a ray of light, probing the darkness around us.

Is this how her spirit touched mine that night at the lake? I wondered. Were our vampire senses just amplified versions of our normal human perceptions —or was there something more to them... something supernatural?

It certainly seemed to be the case. I could almost feel the atmosphere vibrating as she scanned our surroundings for any furtive pursuers. I could feel it in my body and my mind: a kind of throbbing.

After a moment, it faded, and she said, "No one has followed us. I was certain Palifver would send his little pet to spy on us. You must be wary of Hettut. His eyes are Palifver's eyes. But we are alone. We can speak now in private."

"At last," I sighed.

She turned to me abruptly and asked, "Why do I

dream of you? I have sensed your presence several times since the fall of the Oombai, but always from a distance, like a haunting spirit. I thought I was imagining it. I was afraid that I was going mad. Even now, when I close my eyes, your face is there."

"I have no answers for you," I said. "Perhaps the ancestors mean for us to be together."

"I do not believe in the gods of mortal men!" Zenzele retorted, a contemptuous expression flashing across her face. Her eyes met mine then, and her features softened. "Perhaps, it is some aspect of our nature which draws our souls together. Each blood drinker is made different by the *Eloa*. It could be that, by accident, we are alike in ways that attract one to the other."

"Eloa?" I asked.

"The blood which makes us gods. The Oombai called it the *ebu potashu*."

"The black blood."

She nodded. "Khronos says the Eloa devours our human souls when we are made into immortals."

"But what is it? Is it a sickness? Is it a living creature?"

Zenzele shook her head, her brow furrowing. "Khronos says that it is a god. The personification of the cycle of life and death. He says its mind is a great circle inside his thoughts, both terrible and beautiful, and in our making, we become a part of it, each joined to it in spirit."

"What do you think?"

Very carefully, Zenzele said, "I have observed that the world is very much as Khronos describes it to be. The rabbit eats the grass, and the coyote eats the rabbit, and when the coyote dies, it returns to the earth and feeds the grass--"

"And we are part of this cycle," I said.

Zenzele nodded. "In a manner of speaking.

Khronos says that mortal men have grown too clever. He says that they have escaped the unending circle. They eat the grass, they eat the rabbit, and they kill the coyote and wear his skin. The cycle of life and death has been thrown off balance, and that is why the Eloa came from the spirit world. That is why it made us a predator of mortal men. We are charged with the responsibility of restoring the balance of nature. We are the killer that men cannot outwit. We are strong so that he cannot overpower us. Fast so that he cannot outrun us. Long-lived so that he cannot outlast us."

I thought of what she had said for several minutes. "It is an enticing philosophy," I admitted. "But do you truly believe it?"

"Khronos is the first among us. He carries in his belly the core of the Eloa. He hears its thoughts. His desires are a reflection of its desires."

"That is not an answer," I said.

"It is all that I know!" she flared. "You think I have all the answers? I do not. Even Khronos was a mortal once, before he was taken by the Eloa! He has unimaginable power. He communes with our creator, but even he will admit that he does not fully understand its desires. He says it thinks in ways that physical beings cannot comprehend. He says that when it speaks to him, it is like a man speaking down to an insect. And yet, it is a part of him and he is a part of it, and we are all connected through Khronos to the primal fount."

"A living creature, then," I murmured. "With its own thoughts and desires."

"But not the thoughts and desires that concern men and women, even those who have a part of it inside them."

"Then let us discuss those mortal desires," I said smoothly, moving near to her. I pitched my voice low, hoping to seduce her. Now that we were alone, I wanted to make love to her again.

Instead, she laughed.

"Would you really have me love you?" she asked. "Khronos may destroy you when we get to Uroboros, and what then? Would you have me brokenhearted? Or perhaps you'd prefer I defy my people and suffer the same fate?"

"Of course not," I said.

"I am drawn to you, beautiful one, in ways I do not understand," she confessed softly. One hand rose to my cheek, her touch like ice, but ice had become a mother to me, a lover. "But I will not defy our kind for you. I am Zenzele, the goddess of death, the mistress of the Western Dominions. It is my duty to preserve the circle of life and death. That is the burden I've chosen to carry."

I started to protest but she shushed me.

"Like you, I was ignorant of our place in this world," she said. "I was enslaved by a loveless blood god. My mortal life was stolen from me. I suffered as you suffer for the lives I took to satisfy my appetite. But Khronos showed me a higher path. He freed me from my cruel maker. He gave me a purpose to live for and peace in my soul, and so I serve him, and he has rewarded me for my allegiance. Because I have affection for you, I will teach you our ways. I will plead your case to my god king, but if he sees fit to destroy you, I will not defy him. I cannot. I might be able to protect you from the others, but I cannot shield you from Khronos if he finds you objectionable. He is too powerful."

I nodded as if I understood, as if I agreed, but I thought to myself: she is not free. She has merely traded one oppressor for another.

2

Zenzele said that Khronos would spare me if I surrendered to him, if I adopted his philosophies as my own, but her promise was no solace to me. My people had understood the nature of the world. The cycle of life and death was a cruel and beautiful thing, but the thought of this new role I would have to assume if I wished to be accepted by their god king did not sit well with me. Yes, I was a predator. Even when I was a mortal man, I had killed to feed my belly. Legions of rabbits and deer and fish had perished to sustain my family, and I'd given very little thought to their sacrifice. I had honored their spirits, of course, as our elders taught us to, but it had never disturbed me as Zenzele's words disturbed me now. Men suffer-- in ways that animals do not-- when the life-spirit flees from their bodies. I had seen it with my own eyes too many times: their pain, their fear, their regrets. All too often I had been the cause of that suffering. Yet it was a rare thing when I did not suffer with them, even as they died. If I were to become like her, some kind of god of death... I did not believe that I could bear such pain. To kill and kill and kill... and for all eternity!

I could not!

"You are uncharacteristically silent," Zenzele said as she strode beside me through the wilderness. I knew without looking that she was worried.

The goddess of death... fretting over me!

I did not speak for several minutes. I listened to the snow crunch beneath my feet. Finally, I sighed. "Is there no way for our kind to truly die?" I asked.

"No," she answered. "Not the eternal ones. Not that I have ever seen. But why would you ask that?"

"I think that I would rather die than live forever as you have chosen to live," I said.

I expected my reply to anger her, but she answered thoughtfully, "You only believe that because you are still attached to your mortal life. You have never lived among your own kind. Your heart is still the heart of a mortal man."

"I would have it no other way."

"You believe that now, but it will not always be so. I tell you this because I was once like you." She laughed softly. "I would not feed from mortals. I drank the blood of lions and hyenas. Only predators, I promised myself. If I do this, my conscience will be clear."

She stopped, and I turned to look at her.

"But do you not see the error of that reasoning?" she asked.

I shook my head.

"Men are predators!" she exclaimed.

She smiled at me, her tiny fangs bright and white in the dark.

"Tell me: how many men have you spied in your lifetime grazing on a field of clover?"

Despite my dark mood, I couldn't help but chuckle at the image. "None."

"And how many times have you seen mortal men kill other living creatures? Even one another, often for no discernible reason, only that they feel compelled to do it. To kill their own kind. Because it gives them pleasure to kill."

I shook my head. I didn't want to answer that. She was right. And yet, there was something morally repugnant about her philosophy. These vampires piled an even greater evil upon man's wickedness and bowed down in worship of it. They called it good. Holy. There was nothing sacred about it, though! It was just more killing, more suffering.

"And so their wickedness gives us license to be even more depraved?" I asked. "To be crueler, more brutal? To kill and enslave and pillage and rape?"

"We deal with them in the manner they are accustomed," she retorted.

"Why wallow in filth? Men can be good. They can be noble and loving and fine, and so can we. We have the power to be finer! We can guide them to greater things."

"To what end?" she snapped. I could see that I was angering her now, but I couldn't hold my tongue.

"We can live among them!" I said. "I have done so without harming a single one of them. We can help one another to grow in wisdom and understanding and love."

"You give them more credit than they deserve. Watch them spread across the world unchecked? They would devour it like a disease."

"The same could be said for us."

"That is why we have the laws."

"Laws are easily broken. Usually by the very men who make them."

Her body trembled with rage, and then she sighed. Her shoulders fell and she shook her head. "You are a stubborn man," she said.

I could not see the humor in our impasse. I wanted her to recognize the truth as I beheld it, that her way was only a cycle of misery, and the philosophy of the Potashu T'sukuru a flimsy justification for self-indulgence.

"I will lead you to the true path," she said.

I shook my head. "I do not think so."

"Then Khronos will destroy you."

"I will deceive him."

"You cannot. He will see the lie in your blood."

"How?"

"See? You are like a willful child who presumes he

knows all there is to know! You know nothing! When Khronos summons you to his court, he will partake of your Eloa. He will experience your life as if he has lived it himself. He will know your thoughts as if it is he who thinks them. You can hide nothing from him. *Yahi!* Have you never shared with another blood god? Not even the one you made?"

I shook my head. I was not certain I knew what she meant. Not entirely.

"What about the mortals you have killed? You never feel their thoughts as their lifeblood pulses inside you?"

"Sometimes, like a fading echo. My vampire child Ilio has more of a talent for that than I."

"When you share with another blood drinker, it is different. It is more intense, the sharing deeper and more intimate, but not all T'sukuru are adept at it. It is like everything else we can do. Our strengths and weaknesses vary. But this is why we say 'the soul is the blood'."

I absorbed that, wrestling with my distaste at the idea-- my thoughts are my own!-- then I asked, "Why then did I not know my maker's thoughts when he changed me?"

Zenzele shrugged. "Because you were still a mortal man."

"I am doomed then," I said, and I wondered what it would feel like to have my body pulled to pieces. My limbs torn from my torso. My head ripped from my shoulders. Would I still be aware of my surroundings, or would the pain drive me to madness?

And then what?

An eternity of pain and madness.

I could flee, but I would be abandoning all whom I claimed to love. Ilio, my beautiful babies, Aioa and Irema, Priss and Valas... Everyone!

No! Better an eternity of torment than allow any

of them to come to harm!

Zenzele saw my suffering, and a terrible expression of pity came into her eyes. "Here, beautiful one, let me show you," she said softly. She stepped near to me and turned her chin to her shoulder, exposing her neck to my teeth. "Perhaps where words have failed, my life can persuade you to our cause."

"What must I do?" I asked, frightened suddenly of what I might see inside her soul.

"Just bite me and drink my blood," she said. "That is all that you have to do. The blood will do the rest."

"I do not wish to harm you."

"My flesh will heal before you get more than a mouthful."

"I do not know that I wish to be persuaded to your philosophy."

"Perhaps it will be enough for Khronos simply that you try."

I pulled her to me and placed my lips upon her neck. "I've never drunk the blood of another vampire," I said, and my breath on her smooth skin teased a ripple of gooseflesh from her.

"Don't be afraid," she whispered.

Her hand slid around my waist, then rose up beneath my arm. Her delicate fingers slid into my auburn mane, and then she pressed my face more firmly to her neck, a lover's embrace.

"It will seem like a lifetime to you, but for me: a moment of pain," she said. "And then we will hunt."

I curled my lips back from my fangs and bit into her flesh.

Her fingers tightened in my hair as she cried out, and then her blood-- her black, icy blood-- spurted into my mouth, and my entire body convulsed as if I had been struck by a bolt of lightning.

Her blood washed across my tongue, tingling, and then I swallowed, and it was like swallowing ice, and then it was inside me, *she* was inside me, and I could feel my own immortal blood coiling around her's. My stomach lurched as if our blood was warring.

Pain!

My knees buckled. Bursts of light flashed in my eyes—red, blue, green. Voices, like peals of thunder, rattled in my brain. I felt heat on my flesh, smelled dust and grass and mortal sweat.

I fell against Zenzele, my arms and legs twitching helplessly. She held me easily, our limbs entwined even as the essence of our souls entwined inside me. She put her lips to my face, to my forehead and cheek and mouth, kissing me all over, fast and light, and I could not tell where one ended and the other one began.

We were one.

We were Zenzele.

Rolling my eyes toward the heavens, I behold a sweltering sun.

3

"Zenzele!" Mother calls, her voice ringing out in the oppressive heat of the savannah.

I am squatting beside a crude shelter I have made of sticks and leaves. A hawk blinks at me from the opening, his eyes shiny and round like lithops seeds. I have named him Ombo, which means fly, though he can no longer fly. I found him flopping in the grass a short distance from our hut several days ago, his wing broken, and I have been tending to him ever since.

I jiggle the earthworm I have brought for him to eat, holding the wriggling creature between my thumb and forefinger. "Here, take it," I say, and Ombo cocks his head to one side, but he does not come forward and take the meal.

"Zenzele!" Mother shrieks, and I twitch the worm at the hawk impatiently. Mother is calling, and she punishes me when I do not answer quickly enough to suit her. She carries a little green switch with her everywhere she goes, and she swipes it across the back of my legs when I am slow. Not enough to cut into the skin, but it stings! Oh, how it stings! With nine children, and another on the way, Mother has no patience for dawdlers.

"I am coming!" I yell, and I rise from the grass like a gazelle, neck craning. I throw down the worm and wipe my fingers on my skirt. The earthworm twists in the dirt in front of the little hut I have made for Ombo, and the bird finally pops his head out of the shelter and seizes the worm in his beak. Satisfied, I run home. The shadow of my long legs—all knees and scabs—scissor back and forth on the dusty ground.

"Yes, Mother?" I pant.

Mother stands in the doorway of our home, a hut made of grass and sticks and mud. Our house sits beneath a great acacia tree. It is much cooler in the shade.

My little sister, Waceera, ogles me from Mother's hip, chewing on her chubby fist. She has been fussy today. Teething, Mother says. My little brother, Mtundu, peeks at me from behind my mother's legs.

"Help Zawadi carry this food down to your father," Mother says.

Zawadi is just inside the entrance of our hut, arranging food upon two platters-- cooked vegetables and fruit and the seared flesh of an antelope. The smell of it makes my mouth water.

"Where is he?" I ask.

"He is down by the river," Mother answers, hitching Waceera up on her hip. "Bobangi has returned to ask for your sister again."

Bobangi has come again? *I think, with a mixture of*

amusement and contempt.

He is a male from a nearby village, a people who call themselves the Msanaa. He has already come to visit us several times this season, hoping to persuade Father to let him marry my eldest sister.

Not yet, *Father always tells him. Mother and Father hope that Bobangi will get frustrated and forget my sister. Bobangi is too old for her, Father says. Not only that, Bobangi already has two wives. Patanisha would be the lowest ranking wife if she were to marry the Msanaa. His older wives were sure to be jealous. But Bobangi is persistent. He does not give up on Patanisha.*

We are Msanaa, too, only we do not live among our kind. They are a fierce people, always eager to make war with other tribes, or so Mother says, and that is why Father is not more firm with Bobangi. He is afraid to say no. He only tries to delay the man, hoping to give Patanisha a little more time to grow up.

The thought of seeing the Msanaa men is exciting, like poking a snake with a stick. The Msanaa men are dangerous, Mother says, but I think that I would like to have a fierce husband someday, a mate like one of the Msanaa men who sometimes comes to visit with Bobangi, instead of a man like my father, who is quiet and thoughtful and indulgent.

Mother and Father say I am too young to think of husbands, but I will be a woman soon. Already, my breasts have begun to bud. Soon, my uke *will bleed, and I will be old enough to bear children.*

Bobangi has come to visit many times, but sometimes he brings others with him—his sons, his brothers, his cousins. Perhaps I will catch the eye of one of them, and he will come back to ask Father for me as well. I would like to be married. I would like to have many children.

"Ma! I want to go with Zenzele," Mtundu says.

"No, Mtundu, you are too little," I reply.

He pleads with Mother to go, but she just swipes at him with her free hand. "You heard your sister!" Mother snaps, and Mtundu runs to his bedding on the far side of the hut. He is crying loudly, but it is only pretend tears. He thinks he will get his way if he cries. He usually does.

But not today. Mother is nervous. She does not like Bobangi, who walks upon the earth like it is an enemy that he has conquered. She lived in the village of the Msanaa when she was a girl—long, long ago!-- but she has grown accustomed to my father's peaceful ways. I think my father is the only man she is not afraid of.

Zawadi rises and hands me a basket of food. "Here, carry this one," my sister says. "Don't drop it."

"I won't drop it!" I say indignantly.

Zawadi is always so bossy!

"Do not tarry, or make eyes at any of the men," Mother cautions us. Waceera watches us solemnly, then begins to feed from Mother's breast. Mother winces as Waceera's new teeth nip her tender nipple.

"Don't bite, Waceera!" Mother scolds the baby.

Holding our baskets, Zawadi and I laugh, and baby Waceera releases Mother's teat to laugh along with us, her little white teeth shining.

We promise not to dally, or flash our eyes at any of the men, and then we march down the path to the big rock by the river, the place where Father goes to talk business when other men come to visit.

"Don't make eyes at any of the men!" I say in a high-pitched voice, swinging my hips back and forth.

"Don't shake your poo-maker at them either," Zawadi teases, and we both laugh.

We march down the path, both of us swinging our poo-makers back and forth in an exaggerated manner, giggling and bumping against one another. I drop some food off my platter-- whoops! Wiping the dirt off it, I put it back with the rest, and then we laugh about that, too, because the meat fell into some animal dung.

"Let's give that one to Bobangi," Zawadi whispers conspiratorially, and I nod.

"Yes! Bobangi gets the poo-poo!" I snort.

I have to wipe the tears from my eyes, I am giggling so hard.

As we near the river, we compose ourselves. Here, near the water, the short grass and gangly bushes give way to a thicket of tall elephant grass. Elephant grass is dangerous. It is high and dense, and hides all sorts of dangerous predators—snakes and lions and black-backed jackals. It is probably safe because there are zebra and antelope grazing fearlessly not too far away. The dogs that guard our home will usually start barking when predators come near as well, but still, we are cautious.

Zawadi begins to sing in a loud voice and steps into the elephant grass, following the path that Father and our visitors made through the dense growth earlier. I follow, joining her in song. Most predators will run away from people, so long as you are loud and bold and do not act afraid.

Most of them.

We make our way through the grass, singing loudly. Up ahead, we can hear our father. Father says, "No. No. I told you, Bobangi. When the dry season comes next year. She will be old enough then, and she will make a better wife for you. She is still too much of a child. She likes to play, and is lazy with her duties."

Father falls silent as we come out onto the bank of the river.

The river is just a narrow rill here at the end of the dry season. Soon the rains will come, and the river will swell, but for now the waterway is narrow and muddy, and the earthen banks are hard and scaled, like the skin of crocodiles.

Father is sitting in his favorite place at the foot of a

large gray boulder. There is a smooth, square shelf at the base of the rock. Father sometimes jokes that the spirits made that rock specifically for his butt. It is a cool and shady spot, thanks to the thorny acacia that crowd along the bank of the river. Father often comes here to watch the animals graze on the savannah. It is a peaceful place, like his heart, with a view that stretches for days and days… all the way to the great blue hills, where the savannah ends and the desert begins.

The makaya duni, *Father calls those giant hills.*

The edge of the world.

Sitting with Father are three other men. Bobangi I know, but I have never seen the other men before.

One of them is a young warrior, his body lean and wiry with muscle. He has a fierce countenance with a great number of intricate scars etched into his cheeks and chest. I feel a thrill of excitement as I take in his stern features. He has large glaring eyes and flared nostrils, a broad mouth and full lips. He sees me staring at him and grins, sliding his hand up and down the shaft of his spear. I drop my eyes, my cheeks burning with embarrassment.

"What are you doing here?" Father asks sharply. I jump to attention. He is looking back and forth from us to the men who have come to visit.

His normally placid expression is tense today, and I wonder why he is so nervous. He cannot be afraid of Bobangi. Bobangi comes all the time to beg for Patanisha. Perhaps he is troubled by the handsome young newcomer, or the other man who has accompanied Bobangi, the old one with the wooden discs inserted in his earlobes.

"Mother sends food for our honored guests," Zawadi says, repeating what Mother has told her to say. "Their journey home will be less wearisome with their bellies full."

"Put it down here and leave us," Father commands, his voice curt. "We are discussing important business."

As I kneel and place the basket of food on the ground, our guests sigh in appreciation. The smell is rich and good. My belly gurgles hungrily. I turn the platter a little so that the meat that fell in the poo is nearest to Bobangi.

"Your wife is a gracious host," the old man with the ear discs says to my father, reaching for a piece of fruit.

I rise beside Zawadi and we share a secretive smile, then I catch the young warrior staring at me again. He is naked but for wood hoops around his wrists and ankles and a decorative sash worked with bone and bright blue stones. His eyes rove up and down my body.

Feeling bold, I stare back at him, admiring his lean, strong physique, his shiny dark skin and elegant body markings. I wonder what his name is and what tribe he belongs to, but it would be impertinent of me to ask. It would embarrass my father.

I would be happy if a man like him wanted me for a wife, I think. I wonder what it would feel like to have him lay upon me, as Father lays upon Mother. To have the dark, furry organ that hangs between his thighs sliding in and out of my uke. *It must be pleasurable. Mother lets Father lay on top of her nearly every night.*

Father dismisses us and we scurry away through the thicket. As we retreat, I hear the men resume their conversation, but I cannot understand what they are saying over the rattling of the elephant grass. It sounds like Father is shouting though-- which is a very unusual thing for him to do. It makes me feel a little nervous, but men are strange. They are moved by passions that are mysterious to me.

Father should let Bobangi have Patanisha this season, *I think.* She is already a woman. *With Patanisha gone, there would be more food for everyone, and I would be second eldest sister. Also, she is lazy and bossy. All she ever does is lie around and shout orders at all the other children.*

Ah, well... it is none of my concern. I will be grown up soon enough, and then I will be the one who gives all the orders!

4

"How do I describe what it is like to devour another person's life?" I said to Lukas, sitting at my dining room table in my apartment in modern day Liege. I watched my protégé mash out his cigarette in an ashtray. He was very thorough about putting out the embers. He twisted the cigarette back and forth, grinding it until the paper turned to shreds and all its insides spilled out into the glass bowl.

He immediately lit another, and exhaled a cloud of blue smoke.

"Isn't that kind of your bag?" he smirked. "Devouring lives, I mean. It shouldn't be so hard for you to describe."

I watched tendrils of smoke curl into the air, watched them rise, dissipate. An almost imperceptible haze of nicotine and tar hovered ghostlike just a couple inches below the ceiling of the room.

Smoke always makes me think of spirits. The association between smoke and spirits is pretty universal. It's why men so often incorporate incense into their religious rituals, but ghosts are rarely anything more than memories or an active imagination. It is our pasts which haunt us. More often than the spirits of those who have pierced the veil.

I said these things to Lukas, who accepted them without comment, and then I sat staring thoughtfully out my dining room window.

"The sharing is not always so intense," I finally went on, "but with Zenzele, it was as if I were there. I was aware of myself, but only in a distant, dream-like sort of way. As her life unfolded in my mind, I often forgot myself for great stretches of time. Her mother and father were my mother and father. The love she felt for her brothers and sisters was a love that I felt for all of her siblings. That little isolated hut on the African savannah was my home. *My home...* and when she was stolen away from it shortly after, it was my heart that broke."

"It must be strange having a woman's memories rattling around inside your skull," Lukas leered. "Tell me, Drac, what was it like having your first period?"

He always retreated to crude humor when I spoke to him of emotional matters, belittling such things as soon as I related them to him.

He has no finer feelings, I thought. Either he was born without them, or they had atrophied from lack of use.

I didn't let his vulgarity annoy me, however. His emotional retardation played an important part in my schemes.

In fact, I pitied him. How gray and cold this world must be for him! A hopeless, joyless ghetto soul, his childhood dreams rotting in the gutters like dead hobos, killed just for the fun of it.

"The sharing has a simple biological function," I said, changing the subject.

Lukas cocked his head attentively, still smiling. "And what is that?"

"Self-preservation."

Lukas's forehead furrowed. I could see in his eyes that he did not understand.

"The symbiotic organism which resides inside our veins has little in the way of natural defenses, aside from the powers it grants to the mortals that it bonds with," I explained. "The sharing is a way for the Strix to protect itself from the depredations of a more powerful blood drinker. The living blood has no physical means of defending itself, so it attacks the mind of a violent aggressor with a barrage of memories. It is a psychic attack, intended to stun an assailant. Often an aggressor cannot carry through with his assault—even if he or she should recover swiftly enough—because the sharing forges a powerful emotional bond between the two. It would be like tearing out your own heart."

Lukas nodded. "Ah! I see... Cool!"

Talk of violence always got him excited.

"It is an aspect of our biology, however, which can be exploited to various ends. It is a self-defense mechanism, but it can also be used to transfer information very rapidly. To forge a more intimate bond with a companion. To search the mind of another blood drinker for the truth, if you believe that he is lying to you. What else...? Ah, yes, languages! When I recovered from my stupor, I found that I was fluent in all the tongues that Zenzele could speak, just as Ilio had learned the language of his mortal Tanti victim."

"Can it be overcome? This self-preservation mechanism?" Lukas asked.

"Oh, certainly! As I said, the psychic assault is not always so intense. It depends on how powerful the vampire is. Physically, the little ones can be overwhelmed quite easily by a vampire like myself, while a true immortal's blood will make one fall into a stupor, especially if that immortal has lived a long time. But psychologically, to kill another vampire like that—it is a ghastly affair! To watch their flesh shrivel to dust even as their soul merges with your own. It is nearly impossible to do such a thing! A *strigoi* must be exceptionally cruel to kill in such a manner."

"Did your vampire child Ilio relive your memories?" Lukas asked. "I remember you said you tried to strengthen him by giving him more of your blood once."

"No. Expelling the Strix purposefully does not trigger the self-preservation response. It is how we reproduce."

"So I won't relive 30,000 years of your life when you change me."

I chuckled. "No. It never happens during the transformation."

Lukas shuddered. "That's a relief! No offense, Drac, but one life is plenty enough for me."

"It is a terrible and beautiful thing," I agreed. "There can be no lies between two who have shared so completely. Every thought, every vile and venial act, is relived by the recipient of the blood. Every moment of horror. Every illicit desire."

I thought of the memories I held inside my mind. The memories of the ones I had shared with over the millennia. My beloved Zenzele. Apollonius. Sweet, fragile Julia, who died when Vesuvius erupted. There were half a dozen more, all dear to me. All but one. They floated in the deeper recesses of my mind like faintly glowing pearls. If I wanted, I could dive down to them, retrieve them from the dark waters they drift in, but I never do it. The pain of remembering them is nigh unbearable.

"Yet, love is the only thing that comes of it in the end," I said after a moment of reflection. "Love. Without exception."

5

"I want to go with you, 'Zele!" Mtundu pipes.

Mother has told me to gather wood for the fire.

Father and my brothers have gone hunting, and Patanisha and Zawadi are helping Mother look after the young ones.

"No, Mtundu, you are too little," I say.

Mother's eyes flick in my direction. She is grinding seeds between two stones to make meal, her forehead beaded with sweat. "Oh, take him with you!" she grunts. "He is getting old enough to help out around here. Show him how to do it." She wipes her brow with the back of her hand, then returns to grinding the seeds.

Mtundu grins at me, and I sigh.

"All right, but if he gets eaten by a jackal, it's not my fault!"

Mother flaps a hand at me dismissively. I take hold of Mtundu's arm and start walking from the hut. We leave the shade of the acacia tree and my skin tightens in the heat. In the distance, zebras are grazing on the dry grass, tails whipping back and forth. Their image ripples like a reflection on the surface of a pool. Overhead, the sky is pale blue, with just a couple puffs of clouds easing down some high current of wind.

But Mtundu looks nervous now. "I don't want to get eaten by a jackal!" he says very seriously. He glances back at Mother, his eyes large and frightened.

"I was only joking," I say soothingly. "I won't let a jackal eat you."

"You promise?"

"I promise. You better do what I tell you, though."

"I will, 'Zele!"

I look down at him and I feel my heart melt. He is such a beautiful little boy, even if he is a spoiled brat. He has large soulful eyes with long lashes, a nose like a little brown stone and bright perfect teeth. When I have children of my own someday, I hope they are as pretty as Mtundu!

I yell for the dogs as we walk away from the hut, but the dogs do not come-- not when Mother is cooking.

That's fine, you lazy hyenas, *I think.* Just don't come sniffing around me for scraps tonight!

It is another hot and dusty day. The dark clouds that gathered in the sky yesterday, after Bobangi came to visit, have moved on without weeping a single drop of rain, but that is normal for this time of year. It is the dry season. In the dry season, there is fire more than there is rain. The clouds come, but all that falls from them is lightning, which sets the dry grass aflame. In the dry season, we must always keep watch for smoke. More than once, we have had to abandon our home and flee to the big river that lies to the west.

We stroll away from home, Mtundu and I, but before we gather sticks, I stop and see if Ombo has returned. My hawk was not inside his little shelter when I checked on him this morning. I squat down and look inside, but the little hut of sticks and grass is still empty. There is no sign of him but for a couple errant feathers. I guess something has eaten him during the night. With a sigh, I rise up. I tug Mtundu's hand. "Come," I say to him, and he stumbles after me, asking what I was looking for in the little shelter.

I teach him how to gather sticks for Mother. I teach him how to watch for predators. I point out the different creatures that are grazing nearby and teach him the name of each of the different animals. I tell him which of the animals are dangerous to people, even though they do not hunt us for food. "Be especially careful of that one and that one," I say, and then I have to lift him up onto my shoulder so that he can see the elephants marching in the distance, and closer by, a lone rhinoceros. "They are very far away, so we are safe, but you must always be mindful of those two. They do not like people, especially if they have babies with them, or if it is their mating season."

"But who is that man?" Mtundu asks, pointing.

I set him down quickly and rise up on my tiptoes to

see what man he is speaking of.

Is it Father? *I wonder, squinting toward the distant figure. I shade my eyes with my hand, but I cannot tell if the loping man is our father or not. He is too far away, and his image wavers in the heat. I can only see that it is a male, and that he is dark and slim, like Father.*

"I think it is Father," I say, but I frown. I cannot tell for sure.

"I want Papa!" Mtundu cries excitedly. "Let's go see Papa!"

"Hush! He is too far away! Besides, he is hunting, and Mother wants us to gather wood. Do you want Mother to whip us when we get back?"

"No!"

"Well, she will if we do not do as she has told us. Here, carry these."

We return to our chore, walking toward the big acacias to the north. There, at the foot of the towering trees, I show him how to weave the bigger sticks together to make a travois, which will allow us to carry much more wood than our arms alone could bear. "You're doing good, Mtundu! Just don't pile too many on it," I tell him. "It will be too heavy to drag home."

"Yes, 'Zele," Mtundu says happily. My praise has puffed his chest with pride. He scampers toward another fallen branch, and I scan the horizon to the south, checking on the figure Mtundu had spotted earlier. For some reason, I am filled with a sense of foreboding. It is like the premonitions I sometimes have. The dreams that come true. Once I dreamed that the grassland was burning, and the next day we had to flee to the river. Another time I dreamed of lions, and a few days later, my brother Wahi was killed by a lioness.

Last night I dreamed that I had gotten lost, and I couldn't find my way back home.

I see buffalo and zebra, antelope and giraffe. In the distance, the elephants are still marching east. They are just tiny gray spots on the horizon. The lone rhinoceros watches me back, twitching an ear. There is no man.

Mtundu squeals in fear and I rush to him, my heart leaping into my throat.

He wraps his arms around me and points to the stick he's just thrown down. His eyes are big and round.

I laugh.

"It is just a rhinoceros beetle," I say to him.

The big black beetle is trundling across the dirt away from the stick. Mtundu must have seen it on the limb after picking it up.

"It looks ferocious, but it cannot hurt you," I say.

I tell him to go pick it up, and he clutches me even tighter, shaking his head no. "Look, I'll show you," I say, prying his arms from around my legs. I walk to the beetle and squat down. Clasping it by its thick abdomen, I pluck the insect from the ground. Its legs continue to waver as I bring it back for Mtundu to look at.

Mtundu shies away, but I say, "Don't be scared! It cannot bite you! It is just a beetle."

He looks from me to the beetle, and then he inches forward.

"It won't bite?" he asks, blinking rapidly.

"No."

I turn the insect around in my fingertips so he can examine it. Its shell is black, with a glossy green sheen. A large horn curves forward from its thorax. It is a fierce-looking creature, but no more dangerous than a butterfly, and quite helpless in my grasp. If I wanted, I could throw it down and squash the life from its body beneath my heel, but I would not do such a cruel thing.

Mtundu fetches a little stick and extends it tremblingly toward the insect's wriggling legs. The beetle grasps ahold of the stick, and Mtundu flinches. He pulls the stick away, then holds it near again. Again, the beetle grasps ahold of it. Finally, Mtundu laughs.

"I want to take it home and play with it!" he says.

"All right, but only if you carry it," I tell him. "I have to drag the travois."

He begins to nod, still smiling, and that is when he looks to the south and his smile vanishes from his lips. His eyes widen and his body stiffens, and I twist around, looking in the direction he is looking, knowing that it is something bad, and there is the slim dark man again, only he is much nearer now, near enough that I can see he is not my father, and he is running toward us--running so quickly!

It is the man who came with Bobangi yesterday, the young warrior who stroked his spear as he stared at me. I thought he was handsome yesterday, when we delivered Mother's peace bribe to the men down by the river, but I do not think he is handsome anymore. He is only scary now as he lopes toward us with his spear in his hands. I couldn't have been more frightened if I had turned to see a cheetah racing toward us.

"Run! Run!" I cry to Mtundu, but he is too scared to move, so I grab him by the wrist and begin to haul him after me.

It is like dragging a block of stone. Mtundu begins to cry shrilly as I pull him behind me, and then he falls and I am dragging him, his little brown legs leaving twin trails in the dust.

I can hear the warrior's footfalls growing louder and louder behind us—even over Mtundu's keening—and then he is right behind us, and his open palm collides into my back, and I go sprawling forward into the dirt.

He rushes past, then circles back, and I scramble around on my hands and knees and throw myself protectively over my beautiful little Mtundu.

"Hoa! You are mine now, little beauty!" the man pants as he trots back to us. His eyes are wide, his lips split into a triumphant grin.

I pet Mtundu and try to sooth him as the man's shadow falls across us. My little brother is sobbing hysterically, his tears turning to mud on his dusty cheeks. My body is trembling all over. I cannot help it. I squeeze my eyes shut and wish my kidnapper away. I know why he has assaulted us, and curse myself for being so flirtatious. I know he cannot be wished away, however, and when his hands fall on my shoulder and he tries to pry us apart, I begin to scream.

"Quiet!" he hisses, and when I do not obey, he smacks me roughly on the side of my head.

I turn my face toward Mtundu, and squeeze my eyes shut even tighter, still screaming, and he smacks me again, harder this time, making stars flash in the dark behind my eyelids.

I stop screaming. The side of my face is burning. My right ear feels as if it has burst inside. The warrior yanks me up and away from Mtundu. I fall on my buttocks, but I scramble toward my baby brother and try to scoop him into my arms.

"No! Please!" I cry as the warrior grabs me by my hair and hauls me back.

Mtundu rises to his feet and holds his arms out to me, bawling in terror, and the warrior steps forward and kicks him in the chest. My baby brother is flung back violently by the blow. His head strikes the heat-baked ground with a thud. His arms roll out limply to his sides. His eyes have turned back in his skull so that only the whites are showing.

"Mtundu! Mtundu!" I scream.

The kidnapper sweeps me into his arms. His flesh is hot and slick with sweat. I try to wriggle out of his grasp as he hitches me onto his hip and starts to carry me away. I scratch his face with my fingernails.

Go for his eyes! Try to blind him!

He jerks his head back in surprise and I wriggle loose, but I don't get far. He kicks me in the buttocks and sends me sprawling face first into the dirt, and then he makes a fist and strikes me hard in the cheek. The whole world goes dim for a moment, like a cloud has passed in front of the sun.

I try to push myself up. My arms are wobbly and weak, and then I see my blood pattering into the dirt beneath my face. Several big drops. Bright red. The thirsty ground quickly swallows them, turning black where they have fallen.

I am bleeding, *I think, but the thought is distant. It is like someone else has thought it, someone who looks like me, who kneels as I am kneeling, but who is several feet apart from me.*

My abductor lifts me and begins to trot away. I hang from his arms, too weak, too far away from myself, to fight him anymore. I am beaten. He has won. I turn my head and look back as my abductor jogs away. I see little Mtundu rise dizzily to his feet. He falls and gets up again, a tiny brown speck in the middle of the great open savannah.

Run home, baby! Run back home to Mama! *I want to cry out, but I cannot summon the strength to shout to him. I cannot seem to make my lips and tongue work.*

My face feels like it's swollen to twice its normal size, and there is something hot and wet trickling down my chin and chest.

I watch as Mtundu grows smaller and smaller.

He sees me being spirited away. He tries to follow, but he is too young, too slow. He cannot keep up. It is impossible.

Oh, my sweet Mtundu! My poor little baby! *I think.* How will he find his way back home without me?

Then the land slopes down and Mtundu vanishes into the whispering grass.

It is like he has been swallowed by the earth.

6

"Mtundu," I groaned, black tears coursing down my cheeks.

Zenzele sucked in a sharp breath and pulled me tight to her breast, her fingers in my hair. "I know," she whispered. "I know, beautiful one. It will be over in a moment. Just a moment longer. I promise."

I looked to the bright winter sky, so clear and still. The heavens were strewn with stars. There were so many of them it looked like whole galaxies had collided in the firmament, smashed together and burst apart, their twinkling guts spilled from horizon to horizon.

Then the memories swelled. They engulfed my thoughts like flood waters, sweeping me away from the present, away from my identity, and into the past of the woman who held me.

7

"What is your name, woman?" my abductor demands when I awaken.

"Zenzele," I answer, but my swollen lips make the word sound funny. I flex my jaw and wince. Even such tiny movements are painful.

"I am Onani," the man responds.

I sit upright and cast my gaze about. It is hard to see from my left eye. It is nearly swollen shut. I explore my face with my fingertips and hiss. My cheek and left brow feel enormous, the skin soft and spongy like the flesh of a mushroom. The lightest touch there stings like biting ants.

How long have I been sleeping? *I wonder.*

It is dark now, the heavens pregnant with stars,

and draped in silver moon-limned clouds. My last memory is of Mtundu, growing smaller and smaller in the distance as my kidnapper steals me away. I cried out to him one last time, telling him to run home, trying to point in the direction that he should go, but there was no hope for him—no hope for either of us! He was too far away to hear me, or to see my pointing finger. Pain and exhaustion had swept me into darkness as the savannah rose up to devour my baby brother.

The night is loud with the cries and grunts of the savannah's nocturnal denizens. I listen to hyenas laughing eerily in the dark, birds screeching and whooping and cawing, and far away, the snarls of a great cat. The calls of the great cats sound very similar to a person yawning, but it makes my blood run cold.

Lions!

"You are safe," Onani says reassuringly. He stirs the fire with a long stick. Bright embers spin skyward from the disturbed coals, flashing and then fading away.

He has built a boma from thorny acacia, constructing it in much the same manner my father does when he spots a pride of lions too near to our home. He has stacked the branches high so that they form a protective wall, completely encircling our camp. A hungry lioness would have to leap over the enclosure if she wanted to get at us, but I have never known one to try such a thing, not with a fire burning inside, not even if she were starving. Animals are instinctively frightened by fire.

Mtundu has no fire tonight, *I think.*

And no thorny walls to shield him from the teeth and claws of the beasts that roam the savannah. He is probably already dead, I think. Dead and in the belly of some hungry animal.

How long did it take some predator to spy him alone and sobbing in the middle of the grassland? Long before Mother and Father ever realized we were missing, surely! It was my fault he was dead. I was careless, childish. And now… now I belong to this man. I know why he has stolen me, and I know I will never see my brothers and sisters again. Mama, Papa, my brothers and sisters… they are all gone!

I begin to cry, and Onani looks angry.

"Stop that!" he snaps.

I try to do as he says. I try to make the tears go away, but I cannot. My head is like an old water-sack that has sprung a leak. I scrub my eyes with my hands and grind my teeth together, but the tears keep coming. They roll down my cheeks, hot and stinging.

Onani sighs loudly and turns away from me. He scowls up at the moon, listening to the lions yawning in the dark, acting as though I no longer exist. The fire crackles, its orange and yellow light refracted by my tears into a hundred glimmering sparks. I feel the absence of my baby brother, my family, my home, to the depths of my soul. It is a dark pool, and I want to drown myself in it.

Later, when the tears have run their course, Onani offers me food. He does not have much. Some dried meat. A few berries. I have not eaten since morning and I devour the food ravenously. My belly does not care that this man has abducted me, or that my beautiful little Mtundu is probably being digested in the guts of some hungry beast right now. My belly only knows that it is empty.

"Do you have any water?" I ask, swallowing the last of the dried meat.

"No," he says. "There is a small river just to the north of us. We will go there when daylight comes. You can drink then."

I nod. It is no use to complain.

Sometime later, a large animal passes near the boma. I listen as its body whispers through the grass, its breaths rasping in and out of its chest. My muscles are tense. The hairs on the back of my neck stand up, but the creature-- whatever it is-- moves on without harassing us, and my heartbeat slows to something more like its normal steady pace.

Onani looks at me and grins, the whites of his eyes very bright in the dancing firelight, and then he rises and moves to my side. Without speaking, he pushes me onto my back. He tugs at my skirt for a moment, unable to figure out the way that it is tied, and then he grows frustrated and yanks it to one side, exposing my genitals. I close my eyes as he parts my knees with his hands and rolls on top of me. His breath blows across my face, and I turn my head to one side, trying not to draw his air into my lungs. His organ is huge and hot and hard. I yelp as he prods my uke *with it.*

"Open up, girl," he laughs breathlessly. "Let me inside you."

I am too small. It will not go in.

"It's too big," I gasp, my eyes squeezed shut.

He tries again, and I cry out as the blunt head of his organ pierces me, but he can only wiggle it in a little way.

Disappointed, Onani rolls off me. He makes a low growling sound, looking up at the stars.

I pray to the spirits that he will leave me alone now. Maybe he will even be frustrated enough to release me in the morning! What good am I to him, if he cannot put his pele *inside me?*

But he does not give up. After a little while, he sits up. He sets upon the knots of my skirt again and finally solves the puzzle of them. With a triumphant hiss, he pulls my garment away and tosses it aside.

"Now, I will have what I need," he says.

He pushes my legs together and rolls me onto my side, facing away from him. He positions my body so that my knees are raised in a squatting position. I do not resist. I do not want him to hit me any more. "Relax your body," he says. "This will not hurt." He spits into his palm and smears his saliva between my thighs, and then he eases his stiff organ between my legs.

It slides moistly into the cleft of my inner thighs. Holding my hip in one of his big hands, he begins to saw his organ back and forth between my legs. After several minutes, he begins to stroke my leg and back and hair, and I feel a warm flush in my groin. My stomach flutters as his organ strokes against the soft folds of my uke, *but I do not make a sound. I will not give him the satisfaction.*

I lay there as he humps against me, staring at the dirt and the tufts of sear grass that cling to it just below my cheek. I ignore the sensations in my lower body, thinking only of my breathing, my heart throbbing slow and steady in my chest. The fire crackles and pops. Insects buzz sonorously. In the darkness beyond the boma, lions yawp and yawn.

The pace of his thrusting grows more rapid. His fingers dig into my hip, and then he stops. He grunts loudly, his body stiffening, and hot fluid gushes from his organ. I feel it pulsing out of him. I look down and watch it dribble from my thighs.

Gasping, he rolls onto his back.

I lay without moving for several minutes. I am not sure what to do. Is he finished? Will he want to do it again? I have watched Mother and Father couple, and their lovemaking lasted much longer than Onani has coupled with me. Finally I decide that he is finished with me. I sit up. Onani peeks at me from the corner of his eye, but he does not move. He looks as if he is already half asleep. I scoop the sticky fluid from between my thighs and look at it, then wipe it on the grass with disgust.

"Did you enjoy it?" he asks.

"No," I answer.

He frowns.

His fingers are laced across his chest, one knee cocked in the air. His organ is still slick, but it hangs limply between his legs now like it is ashamed.

It should be!

"When you get a little bigger," he says, "we will be able to do it in the normal manner. Until then, we will have to do it as the zozo do."

Zozo are young men who have the hair on their bodies, but who have not yet gotten married. Two of my older brothers are zozo. They get mad if anyone calls them that. When father calls them zozo, he always laughs.

"Boys do that to one another?" I ask, my lip curled back in disbelief.

He snorts. "The ones who cannot overpower a woman."

I do not reply to that. None of my brothers ever did such a thing! Not that I was aware of, anyway. I clean myself with the corner of my skirt, wiping off my groin and hands. The fluid he ejaculated between my thighs is drying quickly. It is sticky and smells like mushrooms and dead fish. I sniff it, and the smell makes me feel nauseous and slightly dizzy.

I am oddly offended that he has made light of our coupling. So he would mate with me as if I were a boy? I glare at him and his satisfied grin makes me boil over with anger.

Tonight, when he falls asleep, I will kill him, I think.

And I try.

But he wakes when I reach into his sash. He seizes my wrist as I fumble with the sheath of his knife, and I freeze in surprise and terror, and then he pulls me across his thighs and spanks me.

I retreat from him in tears when he finally releases me, my rump hot and stinging. He laughs. The humiliation is worse than the pain. And the shame--!

The shame that he has gotten the best of me again, that I am helpless, a hostage to his whims, and that he has no fear of me. I am nothing to him. A plaything.

"Glare at me all you want," he warns me, "but try something like that again and I will slice off all of your fingers. I'll cut them off one at a time-- shwip-shwip*--!" Gesturing with his hand. "Do you doubt my words?"*

I peer into his eyes, and I do not doubt. I shake my head, wiping snot from my nose.

"Speak!" he shouts.

"No," I sniffle.

Satisfied, he lies back, but he shifts his sash so that his knife is underneath his arm. He peeks at me with one eye, then, smirking, he goes back to sleep.

8

We travel north when morning comes. Just as he said, there is a river. It is nearly dried up, brown and sluggish, but I get down on my hands and knees and scoop the muddy water greedily into my mouth. The face that peers up from the surface of the pool does not look like a human face. It is misshapen, one eye swollen shut, lips grotesquely bloated. I sweep my hand through the water. Go away, ugly face! Onani hunkers down and drinks as well. When he has drank his fill, he sits back and smiles at me, breathing rapidly.

"We can only rest for a little while," he pants. "We have a long way to go today. There is a cave just on the other side of that far hill. No, that one. See? We will make camp there tonight."

"Are you taking me to the village of the Msanaa?" I ask.

He quirks his face as if he is confused by my question. "I am not Msanaa," he says. "Some of my cousins are Msanaa. My mother and your neighbor

Bobangi are brother and sister, but I am Zul. My father and I were staying with Bobangi when he came to visit you, so we followed along. Bobangi told us your father had many attractive daughters."

"Where is your father now?" I ask.

"He has gone back to stay with Bobangi. My mother is mad at him. But I am returning home."

I open my mouth to ask another question, but he waves his hand at me. "You ask too many questions! We need to continue on, or we will never get to the cave before dark."

He takes my wrist and swings me across the muddy water like a child, then leaps across himself. He waves at me and lopes forward. I watch him run, staggering behind him, and I wonder how I could have ever thought that he was attractive. He is too skinny and he has pale scars on his butt. He stops and turns back and gestures for me to hurry. What else is there to do? I know the four directions, but I do not know in which direction my home lies now, even if I managed to get away from my captor.

And without his protection, I will die.

We race our growing shadows, but we make it to the cave that he spoke off well before dark. The cave is small and damp, but there is wood already put aside, and Onani quickly gets a fire blazing. He has also speared a meerkat. He killed it shortly after high sun, so we have fresh meat to eat. I am grateful when he shares with me. I even speak the word: "Ziwazi."

No! *I think.* I am not grateful! I hate you!

But it tastes so good!

He assaults me again that night, sawing his pele *between my thighs, but after he is satisfied, he pulls me to him so that my head lies on his chest, and he falls asleep. He keeps his knife in the pit of his arm so that I cannot kill him in his sleep, but I do not think long about murdering him. I am too tired. I fall asleep, listening to the whooshing sound of his heart beating inside his chest.*

When morning comes, he rubs his pele *between my thighs again, and then we rise and continue on.*

He does not seem to be in such a hurry this day, and he talks about his family as we walk north. He has a large family, with many brothers and sisters. He says that I will be happy there. I think that I will never be happy again, but I do not disagree with him. I just nod. Nod-nod. All day long. It is easier that way.

In the middle of the day, as the sun squats on my head, he pauses to turn over a log and finds a great spider lair beneath it. A large hairy arachnid leaps at him boldly, but he runs it through with his spear. Holding it up proudly, he asks if I know how to cook the creature. Its mouthparts are still twitching.

"Of course," I say. Mother often prepared borosaabudoros *for my father. It was one of my father's favorite meals. Onani is still looking at me, and I say, "You just have to sear off all the hair when you cook them. I know how to cook! My mother taught me."*

This makes him happy, and he tucks the dead spider into one of the small pockets sewn into his sash.

Later that afternoon, we have a good scare when a cheetah bolts from the high grass not far from where we are walking, but the sleek spotted cat flashes past us without so much as glancing in our direction. We watch as the predator runs down a baby antelope. I look at Onani with a shaky smile, and he laughs. "Come," he says, gesturing with his spear, and I follow close behind him, watching the grass and low, tangly bushes with a wary eye the rest of the afternoon.

That night, I cook the spider for him, searing it the way my mother cooked them for my father. Onani nods in approval as he devours it. He does not share it with me, but I do not mind. I have gathered some berries and edible roots along the way. Besides, I've never cared much for the taste of borosaabudoros-- *the hairy eight-legs.*

9

The days that follow are a numbing monotony. We continue north shortly after rising, and make camp as the sun dives toward the hills in the west. If Onani is lucky enough to make a kill, we have meat, but most days we dine on the berries and roots and vegetation I have foraged along the way. Always, before we retire for the night, Onani couples with me from behind, sliding his pele *back and forth between my thighs. I begin to feel embarrassed that I cannot couple with him in the normal way. He seems satisfied with our compromise, however, and only treats me unkindly when I am disobedient or foolish. Every night, he pulls me against his chest, and we sleep in one another's embrace. I no longer plot to murder him in his sleep. Sometimes I think that his smell is pleasant, or take comfort in the warmth of his skin beneath my cheek. Still, when I awaken, I always expect to find myself home, my brothers and sisters sleeping beside me, Father snoring softly on the other side of the hut. If I wake before Onani has risen, I indulge myself with fantasies of home.*

I do not know how long we have been traveling together. I have lost track of the days, but Onani says we have passed into the territory of the Zul.

"We are almost home," he says, as if the home he speaks of is my home as well.

It is not my home. It is his home.

The day before we arrive at the village of the Zul, I almost die.

Onani has left to hunt while I gather wood for our fire. It is late in the afternoon, the sun bloated and red on the distant hills. It is not as hot as it has been recently. A cool breeze is blowing across the open grasslands. Low gray clouds are massing in the south. Every now and then, the belly of those plump dark clouds flicker with light, and I wonder if the rainy season has finally come around again.

After gathering wood, I wander to the far side of the acacia grove where we have decided to stop and camp for the night. I need to squat and make water. As I am voiding my bladder, I hear the dry grass rustle softly behind me. My skin prickles, but before I can turn around, I am bowled over as something powerful and hairy pounces on me from behind. I cry out as hot jaws seize ahold of my wrist and jerk me back and forth. I roll around, using my free hand to beat the creature that has attacked me. I shout at the beast as it snarls and drags me through the dirt and grass. I scream in fear and pain. I twist my body around and try to kick the creature with my feet. My thrashing raises a small cloud of dust.

It is a jackal! An old mangy one, its ribs standing out like slats. It is starved, its eyes bleary and red and crazed.

Blood seeps down my arm from the animal's fangs. I feel the bones inside my forearm twisting, straining under the pressure of its jaws. They will snap any moment. I rise to my knees and pull, tears squeezing out of my eyes. The jackal snarls and heaves back on my arm, and I tumble forward onto my belly. It drags me across the dusty earth.

"Yahhh!" *Onani cries. I see him running to my rescue, spear in hand.*

The jackal releases me, turning to snarl at my savior. The mangy old beast crouches down, the hair on its back standing up. It must be starved to stand its ground like that!

"Kill it!" I sob, cradling my bloody arm.

Onani pokes at the jackal with his spear, and the old dog snaps at the shaft of the weapon. Its eyes roll madly, and flecks of foam spray from its muzzle. With a shout, Onani lunges forward and stabs the beast in the chest. The jackal goes down on its hind quarters with a yelp, and Onani stabs it again, piercing the beast through the ribs.

The jackal dies, its hind legs twitching. Onani stabs it one more time to be sure, then comes to me and kneels. He leaves his spear thrust through the animal's neck.

"Is it broken?" he asks, inspecting my injury.

"I do not think so," I answer. My forearm is bleeding, already swelling, but I can move it. I can bend my wrist and flex my fingers.

"You are lucky," he says. "You should be more careful."

I nod shakily.

But I do not feel so lucky later. By the time the light has failed the sky, my forearm is swollen nearly double. The skin is tight and hot and painful to the touch. I am feverish and woozy.

Onani gives me his share of our food and water, his eyes large and moist with concern. "Rest here by the fire. I'll be right back," he says, and then he vanishes into the darkness.

The stars overhead seem to spin without moving. I fall into a dreamless stupor. Onani returns and rouses me. "Here, Zenzele. Open your mouth," he says, and when I obey, he shoves a wad of tree bark between my lips. "Chew on this, but do not swallow it."

The fibrous tree bark has a terrible bitter taste. I spit it out with a grimace, but he retrieves it from my chest and stuffs it back in my mouth.

"Chew it!" he demands.

I shake my head.

"Yes!"

"Ugh!"

"It will make the infection go away."

I spit it out and he stuffs it back into my mouth, then clamps his hand over my lips. I have no choice. Sobbing, I chew.

The taste makes me shudder and retch, but shortly after, my fever and the throbbing in my arm diminishes. Sometime later, I am able to sleep.

I am too weak in the morning to walk. Onani sweeps me into his arms and carries me. I put my good arm around his neck, my burning cheek against his chest, and retreat back into my feverish dreams as my captor lopes across the savannah.

"We are almost home," he pants into my ear. "My mother knows powerful medicine. She will make you well."

I only rouse a little when he speaks. I understand his words, but I do not believe that his mother will be able to cure my sickness. My forearm has swelled so much that it looks as if my skin will split open at any moment. Pain bolts through my body at every tiny movement. I tell him to lie me down somewhere-- somewhere in the shade-- and let me die. I just want to die, it hurts so much! But he ignores my pleading. All he will say is that we are almost home.

I look up at his stern scarred face. His lips are curled down in a grim, angry expression. His skin-- so dark it is almost blue-- glistens with sweat.

Past his face, the sky is full of fat gray lumpy clouds. Father says that our spirits fly up to the heavens when we die. He says that the Great Sky Spirit, who has no name, fell in love with First Woman. He loved her so much he put the spirit of a hawk inside her, so that when she died her spirit could soar up and join him in the heavens.

Does Mtundu's spirit follow us up there? *I wonder. Does he wait for my spirit to soar up and be with him, and with First Woman and Great Sky Spirit?*

I hope so.

I close my eyes and will my spirit to fly free of this pain, and it seems as though it obeys. I imagine I rise up out of my flesh and soar upon the wind, my arms outstretched like the wings of a hawk, the grassy hills tilting far below as I swoop and circle, but it is only a fever dream. It is not real.

10

I am only dimly aware of our arrival at the village of the Zul. I drift in and out of strange dreams, tormented by pain and fever so that even my waking moments seem unreal and dreamlike. The faces that swim in and out of my vision are the faces of demonic creatures, summoned by my suffering like hungry flies after sweat. They are like masks, with empty sockets where the eyes should be. When I see them, I scream and thrash in Onani's arms. "They have no eyes!" I cry. "They have no eyes!"

Onani tries to tame my flailing limbs, but I am like a wild animal. He hisses as my nails rake across his cheek. "Stop it, Zenzele!" he demands, but his voice has no authority. He is exhausted. For all his brutality, he is frightened for me. Afraid that I will die. "Mother!" he wails as he stumbles through the village. "Where is my mother?" The eyeless people run away from him. One of them points.

"Onani?" a voice calls out. "Is that my son? Is that Onani?"

"Mother!" Onani gasps, stumbling toward the voice.

A face looms out of a dark doorway, but it is no eyeless mask. It is a woman. She has a kind round face with full lips and soft brown eyes. "What is this, Onani?" the woman asks. "Who is this child?"

"She is my woman," he says hoarsely. "I stole her from the Msanaa."

"Oh, Onani! This is no woman. This is a baby!" the woman says scoldingly.

Hope shines through my misery like sunlight through storm-darkened clouds. I hold my arms out to her, and she scoops me from Onani's grasp. She is a big woman with close-cropped hair. She folds me into the cleft of two enormous dugs and carries me into her dimly lit hut.

"Get the medicine woman," she says as she lays me on a bed of soft furs. She swabs the sweat from my brow and examines my swollen arm. Her touch is light and careful, but I howl anyway. I cannot help myself. The pain is so bad I lose my grip on the waking world and slide back into the boiling darkness.

I do not know how long I lie here, only that days pass. The medicine woman comes and tends to me. She is old, the flesh of her face furrowed like the bark of a tree, her hair a white cloud around her head. She gives me a bitter infusion to drink, and wraps my swollen arm in an acrid-smelling poultice. The kind woman with the round face cares for me when the medicine woman is gone. I dream of my family, my little brother Mtundu, and then I wake, and Onani is watching over me. He pats my hand-- my good hand-- and smiles at me. I smile back at him as I drift away. It is like floating in warm water. Onani must have many sisters, I think later, when I wake again, because I am constantly surrounded by grave young women. They stare at me with round eyes and whisper to one another behind their hands. They bring me food and drink and clean me when I soil myself. Finally, in the middle of the night, the fever breaks. I wake, thinking my bladder has let go, but it is only sweat. The big woman soothes me when I try to rise.

"Shhh... lie back, little one. You are not well yet,"

she says to me. The way she speaks is strange, but I understand her words, and I lie back as she has said.

"What is your name?" I ask. The words scrape through my throat like sharp stones, and I wince.

"I am Bula, Onani's mother," she says.

"My name is Zenzele."

"I know. Onani has took you for his wife."

I nod.

"You are a pretty thing, but too young to be married just yet." She smiles at my worried expression. "Don't fret, little one. I will look out for you until you are of age. Onani will just have to be patient."

But Onani has already had intercourse with me, *I think.* We are already married. *Nevertheless, I am comforted by the woman's kindness. She has a gentle soul, like my father.*

11

True to her word, Bula intercedes on my behalf. Onani objects, quite loudly, and I hide from his anger behind her thighs. But Bula is unafraid, and he relents. The medicine woman visits and pronounces me cured of my fever. My arm is scarred where the jackal gored me, but it is no longer swollen or painful.

When I am well enough to venture out, Onani's mother allows me to roam the village freely. I explore. I play with the other Zul children. I miss my real home, my real family, but the company of Bula and her daughters helps to ease my homesickness. They treat me kindly, and I even form a friendship with one of Onani's younger sisters, a girl named Atswaan. Onani departs. He does not say where he is going or why he is leaving, but he is absent from the village for nearly the full length of the rainy season. In his absence, I grow closer to his mother and sisters. I even begin to address them as if they are my own family. Mother Bula. Sister Atswaan. One night, I realize I can no longer remember the face of my real mother and I weep inconsolably.

As I explore my new surroundings, I notice a peculiar thing. There are very few men loitering about the village. Most of the eyes who follow me through the alleys when I leave Mother Bula's hut each morning are female eyes. There are some very young boys, a few males who are old and gray-headed, but no men. I ask Mother Bula where all the men have gone, and she spares me a curious expression.

"Our men do not cohabit with us, as the men do in other tribes, Zenzele," she answers. The expression she makes is proud and wistful, both at the same time. "They only visit when they wish to copulate, or to provide meat for the bellies of their children."

"But who protects us?" I ask.

"We protect ourselves!" Bula laughs. "We do not need men to protect us!" She sighs, setting aside the basket she is weaving. "Let me tell you about men, little one. They are only good for two things: hunting and putting babies in your belly. Aside from that, all they do is fight and lie around giving orders to women, and we do not have the time or energy to put up with such foolishness. We have enough to do as it is. No... ours is the better way, my child. Let them visit, and be on their way when morning comes. Life is more pleasant that way."

I am also intrigued by the Zul practice of scarring their flesh. All the adult women in Bula's household have unique designs etched into their skin. Mother Bula's cheeks and chin are inscribed with wavy lines. She says the markings represent water. She has always had an affinity with the element, she says, when I ask her about the markings. Even her name, Bula, is a symbol of her kinship with the element of life. It is the Zul word for hippopotamus.

"What is the symbol for air?" I ask, thinking of First Woman, whose spirit was a hawk, and the big woman takes up a stick and draws in the dirt. She makes a series of V shapes, one sitting inside another. It makes me think of birds, or clouds.

"Can I be marked with this symbol?" I ask.

Bula nods. "When you are older, child," she says. "You are still two-natured. After you have had your womanhood rite, you can ask one of the elder men to put the symbol in your flesh."

A few weeks later, I wake to find my sleeping furs soiled with blood. My thighs, too. The blood, I realize, is coming from my uke*, and I wake Atswaan excitedly. "Look, Atswaan! I am bleeding!"*

My adopted sister is just as excited as I am.

"You have become a woman, Zenzele!" Atswaan exclaims. "Now you can be wed to Onani, and we shall truly be sisters!" Overjoyed, we hug one another. I do not think of my real sisters at all.

Onani, who has returned, hears the good news from one of the old men in the village. He comes to visit. He thinks he comes to claim me for his wife, but Mother Bula disappoints him again.

"You know it is bad luck to lie with a woman who is two-natured," she intones sternly. "The spirits will make her barren."

I have never told Bula that Onani and I have already coupled, though we could not do it as a man and woman do it. I see from the expression on his face, when he peeks sideways at me, that this was a wise decision. He looks ashamed. His embarrassment makes me feel ashamed.

"Then let us summon the medicine woman," he says. "She can perform the rite on Zenzele and Atswaan. They are both ready. You know Gungi wishes to be mated with Atswaan. He asks about her every time I see him."

Bula sighs at her son's impatience, but she does not object.

"What is this ritual?" I ask Atswaan later. "What does Mother Bula mean by 'two-natured'?"

Looking amused, Atswaan explains, "Men and woman are born into this world with both sexes, Zenzele. Don't you know this?"

I frown. I saw my younger brothers and sisters when they were born. They did not have two sexes. I say this to Atswaan and she shakes her head. "You do not understand. Boy's are born with their male organ enfolded in flesh, which is female in nature. Girls are born with little peles *secreted in theirs, which is male in nature." When I am no more enlightened, Atswaan pulls up her skirt and says, "Look!" She spreads the lips of her* uke *and exposes a little bulb of flesh. "See my little* pele*?"*

I peer closely. It does resemble a tiny pele... *somewhat.*

"And they cut it off?" I ask, laughing nervously.

Atswaan nods.

"This is done so that men and women are single-natured. When they are single-natured, men and women are drawn together, so that they may be whole. If they remained two-natured, they would not feel so compelled to marry. The desire would not be as powerful, or so the old ones say. Also, it is said that childbirth is easier when a woman is single-natured."

It all sounds pretty dubious to me, but I desire many children, even if it is to be Onani who fathers them. At least the men and women here live separately. The longer I stay with the Zul, the more I like their living arrangement. It is *peaceful.*

"Does it hurt?" I ask.

Atswaan flaps her hand and says, "The boys endure it without complaint."

So *that* is why Onani's organ looks so strange! *I*

think.

The day of the ritual is set. The men arrive early in the morning. They come in large groups and singly, and from every direction. After they greet their wives and play with all their children, there is a celebratory feast and then the old men get out shells filled with tinted ochre mixed with animal fat and spend several hours painting everyone's faces. There is much chanting and dancing, and the younger girls adorn our hair with flowers. Atswaan and I-- and one other village girl, a young woman named Ghinini-- are escorted, finally, to the place where the ritual is to be conducted. Onani, his face painted with yellow and red horizontal bands, grins at me as I pass, and I smile back at him, my heart racing with anticipation and fear. I hate him, and yet I love him, too. I wonder: can a person's heart be two-natured as well?

We march down a winding wooded path, leaving the celebration behind. The sun flashes in the gaps between the leaves. Birds chatter raucously. The medicine woman limps at the front of our procession, leaning on a gnarled walking stick. Four burly village women accompany us, two in front, two behind. The Zul call them "Big Mothers". When the ceremony is over, the Big Mothers will stay behind to watch over us. Atswaan glances at me, her eyes wide and anxious. Ghinini is trembling. She looks as if her courage will break at any moment. We walk until we come to the end of the path. There, a deep ravine yawns. It is like a hungry mouth. The earth is a dry yellow clay.

The ravine is surrounded by tangles of black thorn bushes and ancient acacia trees. This place has an air of secret magic. The surrounding plant life seems to tremble as we enter the clearing. It is just the wind, I tell myself, but I know in my heart of hearts that the trembling of the trees is more than just an errant breeze. I sense human voices, just fallen silent-- the voices of women, shouting out in agony and ecstasy, or a combination of both.

One of the matriarchs helps the medicine woman down the steep slope of the ravine. Ghinini descends ahead of me, then I follow. The side of the pit is dry and crumbly, and I lose my footing and slide a little before one of the older women reaches out to steady me.

Once we have descended, I expect the ritual to be done quickly, or perhaps I only wish it to be because I am frightened, but the older women instruct us to sit and then they go about making a fire. I sit besides Atswaan and we smile at one another. I wonder if she is as nervous as I. Does her heart race, and does her belly roll over and over inside her body? I look at the barren earth beneath me and I see that there are dark splotches in the soil, stains. There is a pile a woven cloth torn into narrow strips not far from the pit where the older women are building a fire.

When the fire is crackling, one of the women brings us fruit. "Eat," she says. "The juice will dull the pain."

The fruit is soft and sour-smelling, but I eat all of it, and then a second when it is offered to me. They taste retched, but I am afraid of the pain. I would choke down a third if there were any more of the fermented fruit left to eat. The rancid flesh of the fruit feels warm inside my stomach.

After a while, I go away from myself. It is like my thoughts are no longer inside my head, but float a short distance apart, looking on the scene with a strange sense of detachment. Two of the Big Mothers are boiling water over the fire while the medicine woman kneels and chants and waves her bony hands in the air. She bows her body down, forehead to the earth, and then flings herself up, arms trembling, repeating the motion over and over.

I rub my face with my hands and think how strange the sensation is. It is like there are hundreds of little spiders crawling all over my flesh. When I turn my head too quickly, my thoughts wash gray and foggy as if I am trying to see the world through a dense morning mist.

One of the older women is shaving Ghinini's head. I watch the flowers and hair land in a moist pile beside Big Mother's knees. She finishes with Ghinini, then moves to Atswaan. Atswaan's hairless scalp shines prettily when she is finished shearing her. Finally she comes to me, and I smile as she lathers my head. The suds feel good. Tingly. She smiles back and says, "Be brave. You will be a Zul woman soon, Zenzele." The stone blade scrapes across my skull with a scrrrrriiiippppp sound.

I start to reply but she is gone.

Where did she go?

I look around, confused, and see her near the fire. How did she get over there so quickly?

Atswaan laughs, and the sound is curiously slow and deep. She sounds like a giant. It is so funny hearing that deep voice booming out of her little throat that I laugh, and I have a giant's voice too.

I glance up. The sky is pink and orange.

Evening already?

Somewhere to my left, there is a deep-pitched keening sound. It goes on and on and on, and I turn my head, annoyed by it, the whole world smearing as I shift my eyes in that direction, and I see that it is Ghinini making that sound. The older women kneel at both sides of her, holding her by the arms and legs. The medicine woman is crouched between her thighs. The old woman's arms are smeared in blood-- bright red blood-- and Ghinini is screaming through her clenched teeth, her eyes squeezed shut, the muscles in her neck standing out like ropes. She is shaking her head no-no-no but the women holding her down do not release her. The medicine woman does not stop.

I blink, and Ghinini is lying unrestrained. She is trembling, her legs bound together by strips of cloth, her eyes closed. Her cheeks are wet with tears, but she is no longer screaming. It is over for her. She is a woman now.

That wasn't so bad, *I think, and I recline on the cool soil and look up at the sky. I drift away, and do not wake until the women gather around me, and take my arms and legs in their hands.*

"It is time, Zenzele," one of them say.

I nod.

I look down between my thighs and watch the medicine woman lower herself shakily between my legs. She looks tired. Her eyes and cheeks are sunken, the wrinkles of her flesh deep and black like she has begun to crack beneath the weight of her own great age. She speaks to me, but I cannot follow what she is saying. It is like her words are broken apart. They float in the air singularly, each to their own self, like the beads of a necklace that has been torn from a woman's neck. I do not feel fear until I see the knife in her hands-- long and narrow and made of glossy black stone-- and then I begin to struggle.

"Hold still, child!" one of the women hisses.

"It will be over in a moment," the one who shaved my head tells me.

The medicine woman fumbles with the fleshy folds of my uke. *Her bony fingers pinch one side of my genitals, her long dirty nails digging into the tender skin, pulling it taut, and then she begins to cut.*

I scream. I can't help myself. The pain is white hot and all-encompassing. I scream until it feels like my throat will burst, and still the old hag cuts at my maidenhood. She cuts and cuts, tossing little bloody pieces of my flesh aside as if they have no value-- my flesh!-- *and then she digs the tip of the blade even deeper, carving out my little* pele, *and I scream so loud there is not breath enough to make the sound, tears of agony coursing down my cheeks, and then it is over, finally, it is over, and they clean my bloody groin with hot water. The medicine woman rises and totters away and the Big Mothers smear my mangled sex with an odorous paste. They press my knees together and bind my thighs shut with strips of cloth, knotting them firmly.*

I try to move, and the pain drives all thought from my skull. When I awaken, the medicine woman is standing over me. "You must remain here until the sun has passed through the sky three times, woman," she croaks. "The Big Mothers will stand guard at the foot of the path. Cry out if any beasts come sniffing after the blood. I will return and check on you in the morning."

I nod, and then my thoughts slide back down the dark throat of unconsciousness.

12

I come to with a start, the pain still boiling between my thighs. I try to move my legs without thinking, and the agony that bolts through my body elicits a howl. I grit my teeth, trying to bite back any further sounds of pain. Breathing deeply, trying to master the agony pulsing in my crotch, I shift my body slowly until I am half-sitting. Propped against the crumbly bank of the ravine, I survey my surroundings. To my left, Atswaan and Ghinini lie unconscious, breathing softly. It is dark, the moon riding low in the branches of the surrounding trees, and their bindings are black with blood. The only sounds are the soft crackle of our fire and the whisper of the wind in the branches of the acacias.

My stomach trembles. My heart is racing. I sense something malevolent nearby. I know I am not imagining the threat because the night is too silent.

Even the insects have fallen still.

Cry out if any beasts comes sniffing after the blood, *the medicine woman said. Her words echo in my mind. She would not have said it if the beasts do not come, I reason.*

Eyes bulging, I scan the boughs of the surrounding trees. I hear an echoing snap-- a broken branch-- and draw a breath to shout to the women who guard us from the path.

"Zenzele? What is it?" Atswaan whimpers beside me.

"Shh! Something is moving in the trees," I whisper.

"What?" Atswaan rolls over and a guttural groan escapes her lips.

"Quiet!"

Before I can say anything more, a dark shape races through the upper branches of the encircling trees. I try to follow it with my eyes, but it is swift. It circles around, and then it leaps to the bank and slithers down into the ravine.

Even as my body jerks involuntarily with surprise, the creature stands upright.

It is a man!

But he is like no man I have ever seen. He is on the other side of our guttering fire, and the low red light gleams off his flesh, which is dark and smooth and strangely glossy. It is like his whole body has been anointed in oil.

He is tall, with a heavy-boned and thickly muscled form. He has powerful slabs of muscle for his chest. Rippling arms as big around as my waist. A flat belly banded with muscle, and a face that seems carved out of some dense and impermeable stone. He is completely naked, his male organ hanging gravidly between his legs, and as he appraises the three of us-- three helpless women, bound and injured-- his bulging eyes catch the flickering orange and red light of our fire and encapsulate it so that it appears as if there is a fire burning inside his head, its light glinting out at us through the sockets of his skull.

"A demon!" Ghinini cries, and his head jerks in her direction. He smiles, and bright white fangs show between his thick and sensual lips-- fangs as long and dreadfully sharp as the eyeteeth of the great predatory cats that roam the savannah.

I am too frightened to cry out. I have forgotten, in my terror, that we have protectors just a short distance away.

I watch as the ferocious creature inclines his head toward Ghinini, and then his nostrils flare. He sniffs loudly, his eyelids closing, then opening. Slowly. As if he is beguiled by the stench of the blood and urine soaked into the earth beneath our bodies. His face softens with pleasure, and his fingers curl-- and then he is gone!

No! Not gone! Moved, only faster than my eyes could follow.

Ghinini cries out as he crouches over her. I roll over, ignoring the pain between my legs, and watch the terrible creature dip his head into the crook of Ghinini's neck. There is a horrible crunching sound as he bites into her flesh, and Ghinini wails. He slurps at the blood gushing from her flesh as she pushes helplessly against his thick shoulders.

*"*AAIIIEEE!*" Atswaan screams. "Big Mothers! Help us!"*

The giant male's head snaps toward Atswaan, blood dripping from his chin, and then he pounces upon her.

"No! No!" Atswaan howls, battering him with her fists.

I try to aid her, but my legs are bound. I can only wriggle on the ground like a worm.

"Get away from her!" I snarl. "Sister! No! Fight him!" I grab clods of dirt and throw them at the

monster.

He pays no attention to the little rain of dirt I cast in his direction. He grabs Atswaan's flailing wrists and presses her arms to the ground, and then he bites into her neck as well.

Atswaan's face is turned in my direction, and I look into her eyes as he slurps her blood. Her eyes glitter with terror and pain as he gulps greedily from her spraying arteries. They lose focus, as if she is confused, and then the life flees from them.

"No, Sister, don't go!" I sob, heaving myself across the ground toward her.

I hear cries of surprise and fear from the edge of the ravine. The Big Mothers have arrived to answer our calls for help. The demon-man raises up from Atswaan, his lips and chin and cheeks slathered with her blood, his male organ jutting out stiffly from his lower abdomen. One of the Big Mothers lobs a spear in his direction and he catches the weapon in midair. He ducks the next one, laughing, and then, quick as a snake, he lunges toward me.

He scoops me up as more spears fall upon the place where he was kneeling only moments before-- one of them driving into the meat of poor Atswaan's thigh-- and then he leaps into the air with me, moving so fast, so hard, that I am dizzied by the force of his sudden acceleration. The trees rush up to envelope us, and then we are whooshing through the twisted branches like a wind, flying so fast that I can scarcely see more than a blur of limb and leaf. He holds me to him with one arm. His flesh is so cold and hard it is like being embraced by stone, and then he leaps clear of the grove and bounds with me into the starry heavens.

13

My thoughts are strangely calm as I dangle from the monster's arms.

Stolen away again!

I suppose I should get used to being kidnapped, only I suspect that this will be the last time I am ever abducted. The monster that has stolen me killed Ghinini and Atswaan without hesitation, and I am certain that he means to kill me as well.

I shiver from the unnatural cold of the demon-man's flesh. The wind flogs my face and shoulders cruelly as he races through the dark landscape. He moves in great leaps, the savannah rising and falling below. It would be a wonder, this flight, if not for the pain that sizzles between my thighs each time his feet hit the grassy earth and he leaps skyward again, jostling my body. I can't help but cry out each time he lands and vaults again into the heavens, and I wonder when he will finally stop and feed upon me.

But he does not stop. Perhaps his belly is full, and he has stolen me so that he might feed upon me later, when he is hungry again. I try to scratch out his eyes when I have recovered some of my strength, but he brushes my hands away from his face without the slightest sign of irritation, and so I surrender. I go limp in his encircling arms, and await my inevitable fate.

We travel east for a while, the dark grasslands blurring past below us. My captor bounds across a herd of wildebeest, crossing the great mass of dozing animals in one leap. A lioness startles when we land near her unexpectedly, but we are airborne again before she has time to scramble away in a panic. My abductor's passage eventually angles north, and then he is scaling a great escarpment of stone, a mountain, its crown swathed in mist. The moist air tingles against my cheeks and breasts as we ascend, moving higher and higher. He carries me into a cleft in the rocks near the apex of the rugged peak, and there he places me down inside a warm and fire-lit cavern.

I sprawl limply upon a mound of soft furs, trembling from the cold and the pain. There is no terror left in me now, only a fatalistic passivity. Death would be a release.

The demon-man who killed my sisters paces for a moment, his shadow quivering on the dank stone walls of the cavern. Finally, he sits on his knees. He puts his fists on his hips and looks me over. He has large, scowling features, big gleaming eyes, skin like obsidian. His hair is thick and bushy, like a fuzzy cowl.

"You bleed," he says.

I would have been surprised he spoke my tongue if not for the stupor which has come over my senses. Yes, I am bleeding. Warm, wet blood dribbles from between my thighs. So?

He makes a loud snorting sound, his thick lips twisted into an expression of disgust. He seems to come to some decision then, and he drops to all fours and crawls toward me. I do not struggle as he loosens the strips of cloth which bind my legs together, though I do cry out when he seizes my knees and forces them apart.

"Please, no!" I gasp. "Aaiiieee! It hurts!"

He does not seem to register my cries of pain. His strangely gleaming eyes are riveted to my genitals. I see his stomach convulse, and then he bends down between my thighs, and his tongue lashes across my mutilated organ.

The pain is immediate and enormous, and I shriek, the sound amplified by the stone throat of the cavern.

I struggle against him, but his hand comes down on my chest, pinning me to the ground. I try to push it away, but it is like trying to move the earth itself.

He makes a retching sound. I feel something cold and wet splatter my groin.

"Stop!" I howl, dizzy with pain. My vision sizzles with dark spots and little flashes of light. I am losing consciousness, the world narrowing, shrinking to a tiny point of light.

His tongue works its way around my wounded genitals with a moist slurping sound. It is slimy, like a fat earthworm. Slowly, the pain begins to abate. I feel a sudden flush of warmth, a sharp prickling sensation, and then the pain is gone, completely gone, as if it never existed. Pleasure, low at first, then growing in intensity, spreads throughout my pelvic area before threading its way up my body, first to my breasts, my nipples tightening to hard brown pebbles, then to my extremities. My groin throbs as if it is a second heart, and I feel the echoes of its pulsations reverberating through my body. I gasp, my thighs quaking, my toes curling. For a moment, it is like I am in a dark, womb-like place, and all there remains in the world is the pleasure, the warm, tingling pleasure.

My captor withdraws. He sits back on his knees, squinting at me. I want to grab him by the hair and pull his face back down between my thighs.

"The pain is gone," I pant. "My uke *doesn't hurt anymore."*

"I have healed your injuries," he replies, and then he rises. His organ is still tumescent. It sways back and forth like a great snake as he crosses the cavern and reclines beside his fire. I sit up, touching myself between the legs. There is no blood. No pain. Only smooth, scarred flesh, warm and pliant, still moist from his tongue.

"My teoma *has healed your injuries," he says. "But it cannot restore the flesh that was cut away from your body."*

Yes, I have already realized that. The flesh the old

woman carved from my body is still absent. There is only smooth skin and a tiny warm opening, barely large enough to press the tip of my finger inside. My pleasurable little bud, the sensitive skin that surrounded it, are gone. My explorations evoke a sharp sense of loss, a feeling that is equal parts panic and mourning.

My captor watches me fumble with myself, his expression mercurial. He seems by turns amused and disgusted, then angry and embarrassed. When I rise shakily to my feet some time later, he does not move to restrain me. "You may roam about my lair freely," he says when I glance at him questioningly, "but do not try to escape. The mountain is steep. You will fall to your death."

"But what are you?" I ask. "I have never seen your kind before. And what is your name?"

"I am Bujune," he says. "I am a blood drinker."

"A blood drinker," I repeat, and then: "Do you mean to kill me, like you killed my sister Atswaan?"

He stares at me for a long time without speaking. I see his eyes move to my breasts, my groin. Finally, he meets my gaze. He shrugs. "I do not know," he says. "Perhaps."

Then he lies back, and turns on his side toward the fire.

14

Zenzele's memories blossomed in my awareness, unfolding in my mind like the petals of some exotic flower. Every moment, every thought, every sensory experience unfurled as if it were happening to me personally, and in their revelation, yet another deeper layer of experience, her soul an infinite inwardly curling corolla.

An immortal's life... in all its entirety.

I hung in her arms, the taste of her blood still tingling on my tongue. Only a moment had passed since I sank my fangs into her neck, but in the illusory world of the Sharing, days, seasons, years shuttered rapidly by.

I aged as she aged, growing from a child to a gangly-legged teen, and from a teenager to the woman who held me, even now, tenderly to her breast. She held me, kissing me lightly on the forehead and cheek and lips as I experienced for the first time in my existence this terrible-glorious thing we call the Sharing.

Bujune was an ancient blood drinker. A babe if you were to compare him to my lifespan, but old by the standards of most of our kind. Many hundreds of years old. Tempted by the smell of blood from the Zul circumcision rite, he had come down from the mountain where he had lived for countless years in seclusion. He had stolen Zenzele, fully intending to feast on her blood, but was moved by her innocence and beauty. He healed her of the terrible wounds inflicted on her by her Zul sisters, but it was not kindness which motivated him. She evoked in him long dormant feelings of possessiveness and desire.

He was a powerful immortal, and not just physically. He was clever and stubborn and domineering. A cunning brute with impressive powers. He was not what we vampires call an Eternal, but only just. He might have persisted, even to this modern age, if he were not destroyed later by Khronos.

A vampire king commanding a great territory in central North Africa, he decided to keep the Msanaa child named Zenzele. He cared for her in his clumsy way, feeding her, looking to her safety. He was rough, and sometimes he injured her without meaning to, but he saw to her needs, and I-- I mean, Zenzele!-- felt her fear of him turn to respect, and later, as she matured, into a kind of reluctant affection.

Bujune was the Msanaa word for a male lion, and the name was certainly appropriate. With his great mane of frizzy dark hair and insouciant disposition, he reminded Zenzele very much of some indolent father lion, and she treated him as such. When she got over her fear of him, she waited on him hand and foot, more to have something to do than out of any great love for him. She forgave him for the violence he did to her adopted sister. He had explained to her the particulars of the curse that had befallen him, how it made him lust for the blood of living creatures, how terrible it was for him, and because of his misery, she took pity on him. She spent hours at a stretch babbling on about the things that concern young women. She braided his hair and made clothing for him. Sometimes she even made a game of provoking him, and if she sometimes got her ears cuffed for catching him in a bad mood, that was just the kind of thing that father lions did. Sometimes you got the tongue and sometimes you got the claw.

In the early days, he behaved in a paternal fashion toward his gangly young captive, but as she continued to mature, her feminine beauty aroused him.

He tried to put the strange feelings out of his mind at first. He had forgotten what it was to be a mortal man. Those feelings might have even frightened him a little because they had become so alien to him. But day by day-- or perhaps I should say "night by night"-- those feelings grew. He had jealously protected her, but now he felt the stirrings of other more primitive emotions. His thoughts bubbled with carnal images, memories of conquests from his former mortal life. Finally, one night, he could take no more of it. The fantasies tormented him so!

She was lying on her back beside the fire, trying to persuade him to carry her across the savannah, to help her find her long lost family. She missed them terribly, she said. She wanted to see them again. "I do not wish to leave you," she reassured him quickly. "I like living with you, but I want to see if my mother and father still live. I want to see my brothers and sisters. They probably have children of their own by now!" She sat up to see if he was listening to her, and that was when he lunged on top of her. He pinned her beneath his massive bulk, and then he raped her.

His cold, massive organ ripped into her virgin maidenhood, but it was his perfidy which did the greater damage. His betrayal of her trust shattered any love she might have felt for him.

The rape was brutal, painful, and protracted, and though he used the living blood to heal the injuries that his passion had inflicted on her, she could not forgive him. She never forgave him.

After that, he took her whenever the desire stirred in him. She did not fight him and cry out, as she did that first brutal time, but she hated him. And that hatred grew each and every time he assaulted her. She hated him for taking what she might have freely given, if only he had waited for her to desire it as well. She might have been his lover, but instead she became his prisoner.

And when he made her an immortal, that was an act of rape as well.

Zenzele knew that her companion was a thing called a blood drinker, and she knew that it was something more than human. She had seen him feed. She had witnessed his great powers. When they moved periodically from one cave to another, he took her into his arms and flew in great bounds across the moonlit savannah. But she never coveted his powers. She did not want to become a creature like him: cold, inhuman, given to strange moods and violent behavior. She only ever thought of one day returning to the place where she was born, to her mother and father and all her squabbling siblings, of maybe even having a husband and children of her own someday. Bujune had told her once that blood drinkers were incapable of bearing children, and so she held stubbornly onto her humanity, refusing every offer he made of changing her into an immortal. When he finally decided that he was going to give her the Blood anyway, she revolted. She fought him with all of her strength, a strength doubled by her panic and outrage, cursing him, calling down the wrath of the spirits, but it was not enough.

He pried her mouth open and the black blood erupted from his gullet like an evil curse. It wriggled down her throat as if it were a living creature. She could feel it coil inside her guts, stilling her racing heart before spreading out through her extremities. She watched in horror and despair as the flesh of her hands hardened and grew as cold and shiny as her captor's obsidian skin. She found her fangs with the tip of her tongue, and wiped tears from her cheeks that were no longer the tears of a mortal woman.

"Why?" she sobbed, then louder: "WHY?"

Even her voice had changed! It was no longer the voice of a mortal-fleshed woman. It had become the ear-shattering wail of a woman-shaped goddess. "I offered you companionship, and you've taken my very soul. You've taken everything from me! Now what is there for me to live for?"

He had scowled at her, incapable of understanding why she was so angry and despairing. Now they could be together forever. She would never fall ill, never grow old.

"Why do you rage at me, Zenzele?" he asked. "I have delivered you from death and sickness. I have made you my equal. I have done this out of love."

"Love?" she shrieked. "*Love?* If you truly loved me, you would have released me long ago! All you've ever thought of were your own needs, your own selfish desires. You say you've done this out of love, but love could never spawn the hatred that I feel for you now. In fact, I despise you!"

They fought-- a long and terrible battle that threatened to send their mountain lair crashing in pieces to the earth below-- but he was strong, and he subdued her, and so she continued on, for untold ages, hostage to another's desires.

Until they heard of Uroboros, the city of the blood gods.

They learned of the fabled city from a passing blood drinker.

The vampire's name was Uruk. He was a strange creature, with skin as pale as sun-bleached bone, long straight shining hair and eyes the color of the daylit sky. Their paths crossed by chance one night while Bujune and Zenzele were out hunting for blood. After a tense standoff, the two parties made peace, and he came to live with them for many moons, learning their language, dazzling them with endless tales of the exotic wonders he'd beheld in his travels.

Uruk spoke often of Uroboros, the city of the blood gods. It was a vast settlement, he said, carved from the stone of a great smoking mountain, and populated by hundreds of blood drinkers just like them, blood drinkers who had come from the furthest corners of the earth. There, mortals worshiped their kind as deities, and willingly offered their blood to propitiate the appetites of their masters. This city, he said, was ruled by a god who called himself Khronos, an eternal being who had great knowledge and magic powers. Khronos claimed to be the father of their race, Uruk attested, and standing in his presence, one was hard pressed to doubt the powerful being's claims.

Bujune was very curious about this land called Uroboros, and more than a little excited by the thought of being worshipped by mortals-- fed willingly from their very veins, Uruk had said! It appealed to his ego, and his lazy disposition.

It wasn't long after Uruk tired of their company and moved on that Bujune grew restless, and they journeyed north to see this legendary place.

15

How much more tangled shall the web of this narrative grow?

I fear it is too much already, all these frayed and wagging threads. My life's remembrances, the experiences of my soulmate, my latter day machinations... Prithee, bear with me a little longer, my dear readers, for I fully intend to weave them all together, and make of them one complete tapestry before this tale is told.

But let me return to Bujune and Zenzele for a moment before we proceed with the next-- the *penultimate*-- chapter in this, the third installment of my memoirs.

Bujune and Zenzele traveled to the city of Uroboros.

Now I do not wish to overshadow my own adventures there, so try not be frustrated if I gloss over the details of their experiences. I will say this: the denizens of Uroboros took them in, and being the first immortals to come from the continent now known as Africa, they were welcomed with much fanfare and curiosity. Khronos was unusually taken with the vampire Zenzele, being the beautiful proud warrior-woman she was-- and still is to this day. He was so enamored of her, in fact, that he destroyed Bujune within moments of tasting Zenzele's blood.

He did not even Share with Bujune. When they were summoned to his court for his blessing, as all new arrivals must do in Uroboros, Khronos sipped delicately from Zenzele's wrist. His eyelids fluttered, a soft sigh escaped his colorless lips, and then he turned and struck Bujune's head from his shoulders, sending it smashing into the wall on the far side of the great chamber.

Bujune's head struck the wall with enough force to shatter into a million glittering particles. All the courtiers who were gathered there that day scrambled out of the way, shocked by their ruler's sudden violence.

If he had been a true immortal, an Eternal, even an injury as grievous as that would not have been enough to kill the ill-fated Bujune. It would have disabled him, but he would have survived. He might even had healed without much psychological trauma, if his head were returned to his shoulders and he was given enough blood to drink. But in his creation, Bujune had fallen short of true godhood, and when his head was struck from his neck, the Strix that resided within him was unable to repair the sudden and catastrophic damage.

Bujune fell to his knees, every muscle churning beneath his dark and glossy flesh. Black tendrils erupted from the shattered stump, whipping wildly in the air. The immortal courtiers gasped or cried out in horror at the sight of those madly wavering pseudopodia, or did so moments later, when the Strix withdrew and devoured Bujune from within.

Zenzele fell back in surprise when Khronos

decapitated her master. She watched in stunned disbelief as Bujune's massive form began to shrivel. She put her hand over her mouth as chinks zigzagged down his chest and shoulders and his left arm snapped off and fell away to twinkling dust.

Bujune's torso keeled forward, separating from his pelvis with a loud crackling sound. It hit the floor with a dry crunch, bursting into granules no larger than flecks of sand.

His legs and pelvis remained upright a moment longer, still shriveling, the last bits of drying Strix wriggling upon his vertebrae, and then Khronos lashed out with one foot, sending the man's lower half swirling across the floor.

Zenzele watched with fatalistic detachment as Khronos ground the last of Bujune beneath his heel, thinking that she would join her maker in the afterlife momentarily, or worse, be bound to the will of another jealous man.

Instead, Khronos turned to her and held out his hand.

"Rise, Zenzele," he said. "I have freed you from bondage."

Trembling, frightened half out of her wits, incapable of comprehending even the concept of her freedom, Zenzele took his hand.

And so she became a free woman, and master of her own house.

16

Because their god king favored her, Zenzele was courted by the most influential clans of Uroboros, but in the end, she decided to remain clanless. Her maker was gone, she was a sovereign being, and that was how she intended to remain: mistress of a clan of one, and beholden to no other creature, save the one who had freed her from her maker.

As for Khronos, he made no demands on her save one: that she do as she pleased.

Her happiness gave him great satisfaction.

17

So what is left to tell you, my readers? That she had a brief and unsatisfactory affair with the blood drinker Palifver some time before our paths chanced to cross. That she dreamt of me long before I surrendered to her that snowy night on the mount. That she had been searching for me without knowing it, driven by her inexplicable intuition, since the fall of the Oombai. That she had subtly manipulated all of us to protect me from the rancor of her companions. From my own ignorance.

My beautiful Zenzele, my soul's mate, forgive me for the indiscretions I have and intend to set to print--here in the pages of my memoirs!

Better yet, come to me, even if my confessions have moved you to righteous fury, and save me from this terrible course that I have set myself upon.

You must know by now what I intend to do.

Zenzele, my love!

18

Gently, I pushed away from her. I stood on my own two feet. My mind was reeling, my body weak and trembling. The taste of Zenzele's blood lingered on my tongue. It lingered in my mouth like her memories lingered in my mind: foreign, alluring. For a moment, I felt as if I were two distinct and separate beings. I was male. I was female. I was Gon. I was

Zenzele. It was a maddening sensation. I shook my head, trying to clear it of this disorienting duality.

So this is the Sharing, I thought.

It was terrible and sublime, both at the same time.

I took in my surroundings, feeling as if I'd been cast adrift in time. *What strange shores have I been swept upon this time?* I wondered, and then the disturbing thought: *Is this another memory, and if so, whose?*

"Thest?" Zenzele murmured. There was amusement in her voice, but concern, too. "Are you all right?"

"That is not my real name," I said.

Too loud! Why am I shouting?

She was quiet a moment, then asked, "What is your real name?"

It was hard for me to look at her suddenly, she was so beautiful. Is this why men turn their eyes from the faces of their gods?

"The name my father gave me when he delivered me from my mother's womb... is Gon."

I looked at her breasts, the snow drifting silently toward the ground. The trees. The sky. Anything but her face!

"Gon," she said, as if tasting the word.

"It is my secret name... my *true* name. I share it with you because I love you." She opened her mouth to protest, and I insisted, "Yes, I love you, Zenzele!"

A shadow passed before her eyes, and because I had lived her life, I knew the fear that cast that shadow.

"I love you without condition," I said, stepping toward her. *Careful! Move as if she is a hare and might bolt at any moment!* "It is yours to do with as you will."

She regarded me silently for a moment, and then

she grinned, her eyeteeth very sharp and white. "I have only shared my blood with you. I have not released you from your vow, beautiful man," she said.

Her bare feet crunched very softly in the snow as she closed the distance between us. She stood on her tiptoes, put her arms around my neck. "You are my bound servant, until I see fit to release you from the bargain we have struck."

"Is not the master also enslaved?" I asked teasingly. "A tether must be fixed at both ends. By knot or by fist."

"Then you wish to be freed?" she asked.

"What if I do not?" I replied. "What if I wish to remain bound to you for all eternity?"

She laughed mockingly, her hands sliding from around my shoulders. Her fingertips trailed down my chest, my stomach, finally to my breeches. She pushed them down my thighs with a brusque motion, took my organ in her hand. "This is the only leash I need to lead a beast like you around."

I laughed, even as she pressed me to the ground.

"Palifver will urge Khronos to destroy you," she said, sinking down upon me. "I'm not certain whose tongue wields more influence with him, my old lover's or mine, but have no doubt: he will try to poison Khronos against you."

"I do not fear Palifver," I said huskily. Through her memories, I had intimate knowledge of the blood drinker. More than I cared to know! Memories of a passionate affair, their constant battle of wills, and in the end, betrayal. Once lovers, now there was only bitterness between them. I hated him, just as venomously as Zenzele did.

"I will destroy him at the first opportunity," I promised her.

"Don't even think it!" she gasped, rising and falling upon me. "You invite condemnation!"

I didn't pursue the matter, thinking to spare her from complicity. I brought my arm up, placed my wrist against her lips.

"I would have you know me," I said. "Experience my life as I have experienced yours."

Her golden eyes sought mine. There was uncertainty, fear, in those gleaming prisms.

"Do it," I urged her. "Please!"

She hesitated, then plunged her fangs into my flesh.

Uroboros

1

When we finished making love, we hunted.

Fully clothed again, we set forth, slipping through the shadowcut moonlight. Zenzele was quiet, as if lost in thought, but seemed absurdly aware of my presence. She startled each time I made some noise or crossed in front of her path. Finally, I could stand no more of it.

"What is the matter?" I whispered, and when she did not answer, I took hold of her arm. "Zenzele!"

I feared the memories I had Shared with her had offended her somehow, had extinguished the growing affection she felt for me.

She looked from the hand that clasped her upper arm to my eyes, and the coolness in her expression melted. For a moment, she seemed all too fragile, the mortal woman she might have been.

She shook her head, but then relented. "I never had children of my own," she murmured. "When I was a mortal child, all I wanted to be was a mother. To be mated and have a home full of babies! Through your memories, I know that joy now, but it has broken my heart."

"Have you not Shared with others who--?"

Zenzele shook her head. "I have only Shared with Palifver, and he fathered no mortal children."

My mortal children.

Seven millennia separated me from the offspring I had sired, but my heart still ached at the memory of them. I imagined waking from a dream to find that my children belonged to another. Yes, it would break my heart!

"Do you need a moment? We can rest for a little while, talk if you want."

Zenzele laughed. "I am fine. Only tell me... how can you stand it? It is like someone has reached inside my chest and ripped out my heart."

"My father always said 'no man should outlive his own children'," I replied thoughtfully. "Not a single one of my beautiful babies will pass from this living realm, however. Not so long as I hold them here, in my memories. If I must live for all eternity, then they shall live eternally as well. In my soul. I will never let them go."

Zenzele stared at me for a long time, as silent as the snow drifting down around us. Finally she nodded. "And now I keep them safe for you as well," she whispered. "Our beautiful babies."

I wanted to embrace her. I wanted to plant a thousand kisses on her. On her lips, her cheeks, her forehead. On her eyelids, her breasts, her inner thighs. My loins stirred like the loins of a mortal man at the thought of it, but we did not have the time.

We did not have the time!

Ha!

You'd think immortals would have no end of time, but not us. Not that night. We needed to hunt quickly and return to the slave caravan before the others grew suspicious. As Zenzele had said, I must be above reproach if Khronos was to accept me. I understood her motives now that I had Shared with her. If I found favor with Khronos, he might extend that sympathy to the Tanti. It was really the only chance I had of protecting my adopted tribe.

2

It was an easy thing to find the mortal settlement that Goro had discovered. It nestled in a narrow valley beside a frozen creek, deep in the wilderness at the foot of the Carpathians. The smell of smoke is what led us to the village, the wood they burned in their hearths to ward off the wintry cold. There were six huts, built in much the same manner the Tanti built their homes, and from the center of each snow-laden roof: a curl of gray, winding heavenward.

We crept down from the pines, flitting from one dark pool of moon-shadow to the next. It was late, and there was little chance that any of the mortals who lived below were still awake, but it is an instinctive thing with vampires to move in such a manner. That terrible, sneaking advance.

I did not want to do this.

Though human blood is delectable to me, animal blood is perfectly nourishing for our kind. A vampire can live on animal blood indefinitely. The bloodthirst will grow-- slowly, inexorably-- until the desire to feast on human blood is maddening, all but irresistible, but a vampire does not need to kill men to survive. It is only the excuse that we make to justify our loathsome acts.

It had been years since I'd fed on a mortal human being. I had not fed in such a manner since killing the fools who'd tried to steal my vampire blood: Kuhl, and his Pruss cohorts. As we approached the little village in the valley, my guts constricted and my flesh began to tingle. I was suddenly aware of my teeth. My fangs felt very large and very sharp in my mouth. The muscles of my jaws began to twitch.

I did not want to do this, but I could smell them. Two dozen mortals, their minds adrift in sleep's slow currents. I could smell their flesh and blood. I imagined I could hear their hearts beating, a soft susurration, like tiny drums.

They were only a few paces away now.

Zenzele slipped silently beside me.

"Which ones do we take?" she whispered.

"The old ones," I whispered back. "Here. In this hut."

Perhaps you think me cruel, but I wished only to spare the children here the terror of being devoured, the hardship of losing a mother or a father. The old man and woman in the tiny thatch hut we crouched beside had led a full life. They were arthritic, and, judging by the scent of the old man, soon to pass on to the spirit world.

A lesser wickedness, perhaps, but I still despaired. I did not want to do this, but I had little choice. If only the Hunger inside me were not so urgent, my hands so eager to the deed!

Zenzele nodded.

We glided to the door.

Silent as we were, the old woman woke when we slipped inside her home. Old bones rest uneasily, or perhaps it was the wisp of cold air that stole through the doorway around our ankles.

In the low red light of the hearth, her eyes glittered. Her husband lay on his side, his back to her, a fat old man with thick gray hair, snoring phlegmatically. She blinked at me in confusion, and then sudden dawning fear. Her eyes widened and her lips parted to loose a cry, but before she could yell for her mate, Zenzele struck.

The old man was a fighter, but a sharp blow to the temple sent him right back to the dream world. The old woman we killed immediately. We fed from her quickly, the two of us, and then fled back to the wilderness, our prize sagging in my arms, limbs flopping bonelessly.

The others would not like the meal we brought back to them tonight. I only hoped, in their frustration, they did not torment the old man needlessly.

As we hurried through the snowy landscape, Zenzele asked me if I still intended to destroy Palifver.

“If the opportunity arises,” I replied.

I’m not certain why I was so set upon destroying the blood drinker. Was it self-defense or simple jealousy? Was it because he threatened me and mine, or because he had once been Zenzele’s lover. I knew the man intimately, knew him through Zenzele’s memories, although the images of her life were beginning to dim, as dreams fade after awakening. I felt more like my old self, though I knew I could immerse myself in the part of her that still lingered in my psyche if that was something that I wished to do.

I knew him. Born in Uroboros into a life of privilege, the son of a high caste slave. He had found favor in the eyes of his father’s vampire master because of his beauty and because of his ruthless nature. He was made an immortal by that same clan master. Vain. Selfish. Arrogant. He was everything I despised, and so I wanted to kill him.

But Zenzele would not have it.

“This is something you must put out of your thoughts!” she insisted. “Don’t you understand the danger? Are you really so stubborn? You will have to Share with Khronos when we arrive in Uroboros, and there is nothing you can hide from him. Your desire to kill Palifver will not provoke Khronos. We all have murderous impulses, but if you act on that desire…”

We had found the tracks of the slave caravan and turned east. We followed them through the pass.

Zenzele was silent for a long while. Finally, she turned to me and said firmly, "I cannot allow it."

I raised my eyebrows, but I did not argue.

As it turned out, the question was irrelevant. When we caught up with the caravan, we discovered that Palifver had absconded. While we were hunting in the valley, he had fled east, leaving Tribtoc in command of the raiding party. He'd made no excuses, Tribtoc said, when Zenzele questioned him about Palifver's desertion. He had simply left, taking to the sky moments after announcing his intentions.

"So he thinks to race ahead of us," Zenzele glowered later in private, "to poison Khronos against you, no doubt."

"Should we give chase?" I asked.

"It would be pointless," she replied. "He has too much of a lead. He can move just as quickly as either of us. We would never catch up to him."

It was nearly dawn. We were standing outside the main tent. The old man was long dead, drained dry by the others. We were preparing to retire for the day. The camp was secure, the captives under guard.

I looked to the east. The sky there was a delicate coral pink. The sun was not yet risen, but it was just below the rim of the world, ready to spring out at any moment.

Mountains behind. Mountains to the north and south.

There was but one path for me now. East. To Uroboros. And whatever fate awaited me there.

I said as much, and Zenzele nodded broodingly.

What else could we do?

3

When we had passed through the Carpathian Mountains, our party turned south, and we journeyed through the country that is now named the Ukraine. We continued on in a southeasterly direction until we came to the land the Greeks called Tauris, which you know as the Republic of Crimea, and from there, not far inland from the northern shores of the Black Sea, to the city of Uroboros.

Uroboros was built upon the flank of a dormant volcano. The T'sukuru called this volcano Fen'Dagher, which meant "Heaven Spear". I cannot point to any modern map and tell you, "Here is the place once called Uroboros." Fen'Dagher awakened after the war of the blood gods and destroyed itself in one titanic eruption. Later, as the world warmed, the entire region was subsumed by rising sea levels. It is gone, like most of the coastal settlements of the prehistoric world, and the world of man is better for it. This, I assure you.

But in its prime, Uroboros was a fantastical sight.

Though I had seen the city through Zenzele's memories, my first view of its splendors still had the power to dazzle me... even as its horrors outraged my sensibilities.

In an age when most humans still huddled in caves or crude wooden domiciles, Uroboros was a marvel. It was a three-tiered metropolis, a towering conurbation, each district stacked upon the next, running up the side of the mountain and connected by a complex network of ramps and staircases and ladders and bridges.

At the foot of the sleeping volcano was the Shol. This was the residence of the slave caste. Here, the blood gods maintained a vast population of mortals, keeping them penned like animals behind high stone walls. Emaciated, more dead than alive, the mortals labored for their masters without rest. I knew from Zenzele's experiences that a denizen of the Shol, the lowest of the low, could expect only abuse and exploitation at the hands of his immortal overseers, but to see it for myself--! It was unendurable! For a slave of the Shol, death, whether from disease or deprivation-- or the fangs of his ravenous masters—was the only hope for release, and a quick demise the best end one dare pray for.

Hovering over the pits of the Shol, sheltered beneath a great outcrop of stone, was the Arth, the dwelling place of Uroboros's high caste mortal slaves. These mortals had found favor with the blood gods of Uroboros. They served as overseers and skilled laborers, functionaries and valets. Here, in stone structures reminiscent of the Anasazi cliff dwellings, the mortal elite resided in relative luxury. There were hanging gardens and temples of worship, markets and bathhouses. For these traitors, life was good. They were spoiled, corrupt, and spoke only in disdain of the inhabitants of the slave district below. They were no less slaves, but they at least had the prospect of advancement.

When a new blood god was made in Uroboros, the mortal who was elevated was usually from the Arth, a favored servant or a cherished lover, a functionary who had impressed his vampire master with his loyalty or cleverness. When one of their number was exalted, there were great festivals in the district of Arth. The temples ran red with blood tribute. There were games, feasts, orgies. The blood drinkers of Uroboros dangled the prospect of immortality like a worm from a hook, and the selfish, the vain, the amoral and the cruel, competed fiercely for the chance of being made into a god.

At the apex of the three-tiered city dwelled the masters of Fen'Dagher. It was from this level, called the Fen, that the city's undying rulers reined over all.

The society of the vampires was hierarchal in nature. Their population was organized into Clans, each Clan ruled by an Eternal—vampires, like Zenzele and I, who were truly immortal. The Clans were further divided into Houses, which were governed by the oldest and most powerful of the lesser immortals. Their god king Khronos held absolute power, but the Clan Masters, and, to a lesser extent, the House Mothers and Fathers, acted as a kind of unofficial senate. They were the god king's advisors, and served as administrators of the city.

Fen'Dagher was a honeycomb of subterranean chambers, and it was there, in that sunless realm, that the Potashu T'sukuru made their home.

I could see the cold creatures who ruled this realm moving up and down from their vaunted aerie as we approached the city. Some of them glided upon the zigzagging stairways that bridged their abode with the mortal districts below. Others scaled the sheer rock face like insects.

How easy it would be to think of them as gods if I were still a mortal man, I thought. And yet they had fashioned their kingdom into a kind of hell. Had I thought the Oombai wicked? The depravity of the Ground Scratchers paled in comparison to these immortal monsters!

Even from a distance, I could smell the rot and corruption of the hellish city. We approached from the west, at the foot of the mountain, in full view of the endlessly toiling mortals. Though it was night, the slaves worked by the light of greasy fire pits and countless crackling torches. From a distance, it looked like the stars themselves had been plucked down from the heavens. If not for the omnipresent stench, if not for the unending horrors, it would have been a wondrous sight.

As we drew nearer, our captives cried out at the spectacle of indignities that were soon to be enjoined on them: the starved bodies of the laborers, the brutality of the overseers, the great nadirs of rotting human corpses, mass graves where those who could no longer work were bled dry and disposed of. Even the fires, so beautiful from a distance, were fueled by human misery. The smell of sizzling human fat caused my gorge to rise. For a moment I feared my sanity would revolt. Picture in your mind Hieronymus Bosch's surreal depictions of the Inferno. That was the Shol, with its cowl of black smoke, its decay, its suffering.

I cannot bear this horror! I thought.

But I must.

For Ilio.

For the Tanti.

I knew this hell. I knew it from Zenzele's memories. What I could not fathom was how she could set her soul apart from these outrages, how she could take part in such cruelty.

As if sensing my thoughts, she looked down at me from her mount, but her eyes were hooded, her countenance impenetrable.

I knew from our Sharing that she believed there was no alternative, that Khronos's power was supreme, but I could not believe it was true, that there was no escape.

There must be a way out!

Our mortal captives balked at each new atrocity. They had to be flogged mercilessly before they would continue. They prayed to their various divinities for deliverance, for absolution, for vengeance, but their continuous rebellion only served to slow our passage through the Shol.

After gaining admittance through the outer barricades, we wound our way around the charnel pits. On the far side of the mortuary, mortal men fought to the death in a crude amphitheater, their audience, mortal and immortal alike, cheering them on lustily. We passed through areas that were being excavated, winning annoyed glances from the mortal overseers as our procession interrupted the labors of their charges. Further on, an open-air brothel, and beyond that, a district of squalid slave quarters.

There, gaunt faces peered at us from dark doorways. The smell of human waste was overpowering. In a lightless alley, a pair of immortals fed, their cheeks and chins smeared with fresh blood, their victim hanging limp and naked between them. I turned my eyes away as the blood drinkers worried the neck of the corpse, grunting and making soft wet sucking sounds. Somewhere in the maze of tenements a woman was sobbing, and in another quarter, maniacal laughter.

Mortal children appeared from some of the hovels as we marched past, racing in pursuit of our caravan. I feared the wolf Vehnfear might attack them, but the animal merely glowered at them, a low growl emanating from his breast. Keeping their distance from the ill-tempered beast, the children held their hands out in pitiful supplication, calling "Zele! Zele!" until Zenzele slipped some food discretely from her hip pack and cast it to the ground beside her mount.

The sight of the children, grubbing naked in the dirt for the nuts and roots that Zenzele had brought back for them, won black tears from my eyes. It was, for me, the most terrible sight of all.

The temperature dropped precipitously as we ascended. There were no trees to shield us from the wind when we left the Shol, not on the narrow road that snaked up the side of the mountain. The rock the winding passage was carved into was mostly columnar basalt, which looks a lot like the pipes of a steam organ, and the wind whistled in all its tiny crevices, slicing into our procession from the south, so cold and fierce that even I became uncomfortable after a while, but by then we were passing through the ramparts of the upper district, and our long journey was nearly at its end.

4

In the middle of a broad piazza, Zenzele raised her hand, signaling the caravan to halt. She slipped from the back of her mount as mortal attendants rushed out to meet us. These were men and women of the Arth, the high caste mortal denizens of Uroboros. Slaves, yes, but most of them were affiliated with one Clan or another, and some might even be given the Strix one day, made into a blood drinker by an indulgent patron—a status that was tantamount to godhood in this depraved and brutal society.

They were plump and healthy and dressed in fine warm clothing, these repulsive traitors-of-their-own-kind. I could not help but bare my fangs at them.

"Mistress Zenzele! We heard you were on your way home!" the man in charge of the group called. "What a glorious surprise on such a cold and miserable night!" I watched in disdain as the mortals groveled. A few of them even gashed open their arms so that their blood might serve as refreshments.

One such man approached me, holding out a bleeding wrist. Though I was obviously Zenzele's captive—she had put my leash back around my neck when we drew near to Uroboros—I was still a blood drinker, and he was eager to curry favor with any blood god he could. He had even painted his face in imitation of his masters. White face. Red lips.

"This must be the wild blood god from the Western Dominions," he said to Zenzele. His blood dribbled to the stone cobbles, steaming in the cold.

I was tempted to throw myself upon him. I could always claim that I had lost control. I was, after all, a "wild blood god".

As if sensing my thoughts, Zenzele gave my leash a tug. "Careful, Strudo!" she warned the man. "This one does not know our ways yet! He might just make a meal of you."

The fat man jerked back, clamping his hand over his dribbling wrist. Eyes flashing in my direction, he veered toward one of the other vampires, stuttering an apology.

"Palifver's tongue has been restless," Zenzele murmured, inclining her head toward mine.

"Let us hope he has not spoiled my prospects," I whispered back.

Her eyes darkened and her lips pressed together, but she did not comment.

More mortals were coming out to greet us. Two young men dashed around the perimeter of the plaza, lighting torches. A runner was dispatched to the Fen to inform the gods that new slaves had arrived. Before long, the courtyard was thronged with mortal and immortal alike. The blood gods had come down from their aerie, descending the long stairway or crawling straight down the face of the mountain like spiders. Our captives were forced to their feet (they had collapsed as soon as our caravan came to a halt) and were dragged one at a time to stand upon a dais in the center of the excited crowd.

There was no exchange of money. We had no concept of such a thing in those ancient days. The slaves were bartered for with the promise of goods or services, or simply claimed outright by clan leaders and other citizens of high rank, as was their right by status. Several mortal functionaries kept track of the bargains that were struck and the goods that were exchanged. They yelled out, pointing at this one and that one, making inscrutable gestures with their hands, and collecting barter. For a simple hunter-gatherer like me, the entire episode was chaotic and incomprehensible. If you'd like a modern analogy, visualize the trading floor of the Wall Street stock exchange. Yes, it was that mad! Humanity was the lifeblood of Uroboros, the coin of the realm, and that night its dark heart beat vigorously.

I watched in disgust as our captives were dragged to the auction block. Some of them were so exhausted from our long trek they could barely stand—even fortified by vampire blood.

"What do you offer for this raven-headed beauty? Look at these childbearing hips, and these fine, big udders. This one was made for bearing children," the mortal auctioneer cried out. Moments later: "Look at the size of this brute! Imagine the uses you can get out of this one, once he's been properly broke in!"

What paltry rags they still bore were torn from their bodies. The most comely, the most generously endowed, were purchased as body slaves, to be used for the sexual gratification of their masters, or employed in the brothels. They were, perhaps, the luckiest of the lot, though the sturdiest men and women were snapped up almost as quickly. Physical vitality was just as valuable a commodity as ample breasts or an impressive cock. The ugly, the diseased, the scrawny and the old were dragged back down the road to the Shol, to labor in the mines, or, if they were too weak to work, to be bled and butchered, their carcasses tossed into the charnel pits.

The slaves were poked and prodded. Their

assholes were checked for tightness. Their breasts and cocks weighed by eye and by hand. Every now and then, a vampire would step forward and demand a taste of a mortal captive's blood. The slave's arm would be forced to the mouth of the vampire, and the crowd would lean forward, almost as one, and watch avidly as the blood drinker's fangs sank into the proffered flesh.

Each time an immortal brought attention to his or herself, Zenzele leaned toward me to identify the blood drinker.

"That tall one is named Maubis. He is one of Khronos's most trusted advisors," she murmured. Later: "That one is Eyore. He is House Daunis. Very low status. Their House Mother is scarcely older than I. Topol will not cut him a deal!"

Vehnfear sidled up to her as we watched the proceedings, and Zenzele squatted to run her fingers through his pelt. The immortal animal, canny beast that he was, sensed her anxiety and licked her on the mouth to comfort her.

She turned her face aside with a smile, and the animal trotted away, tongue lolling.

"Home, Vehnfear!" she called after him, and the wolf broke into a lope. She looked up at me, still smiling. "It is almost over," she said.

5

I found myself intrigued with the Arthen architecture.

After the slave auction, we wandered around the mortal district for a while. Zenzele went to the livery to check on the horses, and then we visited the home of some minor functionary. I guess you could call the man an accountant, though commerce in that era was still a very rudimentary thing. They conversed as I examined the construction of his dwelling, wondering how stone slabs that large could be shaped and moved into position so precisely. Grooves and ridges were carved into the edges of the blocks so that they slid neatly together and held one another in place. In some spots, the seams of the stones were as narrow as a fingernail. So clever!

I wouldn't want to live there, should the earth shudder and send all those blocks tumbling down upon the occupants. I'd feel much more at home among the blood drinkers. They lived below the surface of the mountain, in a great warren of interconnected chambers, hiding from the sun like moles... or bats. Nevertheless, I lingered over the ingenious stone dwelling of the mortal Uroboran, running my fingertips along its powder-smooth surface. I'd never seen anything like it!

Zenzele indulged my curiosity for a little while, but as the night wore on, and the crowds in the streets dispersed, she grew increasingly nervous. I think she feared a confrontation with her ex-lover.

Tribtoc, Goro and Bhorg met with her briefly as I wandered through an enclosed garden. They talked in low voices while I perused the frozen flora. I could hear them perfectly fine, of course. They were talking about me. They wanted to know what Zenzele intended to do if our audience with Khronos did not go well.

"I do not know," she sighed.

"Whatever happens, we will stand with you, Zele," Goro said, and she nodded, putting her hand on his shoulder.

They departed, and Zenzele strode into the garden. She had wrapped her arms around herself as if she were cold.

"Have you seen enough?" she asked, arching an

eyebrow.

I nodded.

"Let us retire to my chambers then."

Up, up, up we climbed, until the mortal district had receded to the size of a child's plaything. My head spun when I peered over the side of the staircase. It was a sheer drop, some 1,200 meters. I wondered if such a fall would end my immortal existence, and I was suddenly, perversely, tempted to try it. I had never thrown myself from such a height.

It would be simple enough. There were no rails. I need only lean out and let the world sweep me to its breast. I probably wouldn't even feel it when I hit the ground. My cold white body would simply smash to sparkling dust, all my cares and concerns brought to nothing in an instant.

I moved gingerly toward the flank of the mountain, unnerved.

How sorely it tempted me!

"A view like this would make any creature feel like a god," I said, turning my attention to the great vista stretched out around us. It was a vast panorama of forests and mountains, valleys and rivers, and just at the rim of the world, the shores of the Black Sea. The wind swooped across the face of the volcano, making my hair whip to and fro, plucking the words from my mouth even as I spoke them.

But Zenzele heard. She spared me an inscrutable look, then continued up the roughhewn steps, her shadow in the lead, folding itself back and forth upon the risers. The sun had just breached the low mountains to the east, and its orange and pink light glinted off her smooth, black skin.

We came to a cleft in the mountainside. The stairs continued upwards, but Zenzele turned right and vanished inside the earth. The narrow passage wound back and forth for twenty-five meters or so before expanding into a broad open chamber. Torches flickered, their dancing light gleaming on the sweating stone walls. Stalagmites and stalactites jutted from the ceiling and floor like fangs. A dozen passages led off from this echoing chamber. Zenzele bowed to a passing blood drinker, a tall white creature in flowing garments, and then took one of the corridors on the left.

"This way," she said.

I followed her down the passageway, which was dank and dimly lit. At random intervals, the corridor gave access to other caverns, some large, some small. Most were the habitations of the Fen's immortal residents, their lairs stuffed with the detritus of their inhumanly long lifespans: wall hangings, weapons, tools and furnishings. Most of the residents had already bedded for the day, their mates at their sides, mortal servants sleeping lightly at their feet. Other cells were abandoned or unused. A few more were like the first juncture we had encountered, a hub from which other winding passages radiated. I was reminded of a termite nest.

"In here," Zenzele said, and she ducked through an ornate door hanging. Before I could follow, she leaned back out. I waited as she lit a torch off the oil lamp burning in the corridor, and then she disappeared again.

I pushed through the curtain.

"Home," I said as she moved around the perimeter of the chamber lighting torches.

She smiled at me and nodded.

"Home."

The main compartment was spacious, with a smaller secondary chamber, which was where she slept. Though she did not linger in Uroboros, she had still managed to amass quite a collection of personal belongings. I meandered around her quarters, examining the wall hangings and decorations. She had collected many souvenirs from the various cultures of the Western Dominions: fertility idols, war masks, weapons and religious artifacts. There were brightly colored prayer sticks, gambling bones and stone jewelry. All covered in a thin layer of dust. I picked up a large stone phallus and grinned over my shoulder at her.

"That's a good luck charm!" she said, and snatched the stone cock from my hand.

"What else would it be?" I asked innocently.

Zenzele glowered at me, tossing the "good luck charm" into the corner. She went to her sleeping area and began to prepare her bed. Kneeling down, she unrolled her furs. "Help me beat them," she said. I went to her side and held up her bedding so that she could whomp it with a small cudgel. When the dust had settled, she laid the various pieces out. She did this with little jerking movements.

"What is wrong?" I asked.

"Nothing," she said, still on her knees.

I sighed. "Do you take me for a bachelor, Zenzele?"

"Then you should not need to ask!" she snapped. Her shoulders slumped and she confessed, "I am scared, Gon. They will come for you tonight, and when they do, they will take you before Khronos, and your fate will be decided."

"You think it will go badly?"

"I saw the contempt in your eyes when we traveled through the mortal districts."

"Is there no room in Khronos's kingdom for sentiment other than his own?"

She looked up at me, eyes wide. "No!" she breathed. "None!"

I did not reply. Instead, I thought of the atrocities I had witnessed as we journeyed through the city.

Mortal men and women, worked to death in the quarries. Raped. Murdered for sport. Butchered like animals to quench the bloodthirst of their ruthless masters. Were I truly a god, I would throw the whole mountain down on these soulless fiends!

What would Khronos think if he divined such thoughts in my blood? Would he be charmed by my sentimental feelings for the mortals? Would he be indulgent of this "wild blood god"? Or would my sympathies bring down his wrath upon me?

Zenzele crawled across her bedding. "Come lie down with me," she said. "Let us sleep together like man and wife." The sight of her on her hands and knees distracted me from my brooding. I wanted to drop to the ground behind her, slide my hand over the soft curve of her hip.

She was undoing the laces of her tunic.

I disrobed and slid onto the bed beside her.

She rolled toward me, bringing the furs up over our bodies. Laying her cheek upon my chest, she murmured, "I can lower my guard when you hold me in your arms, Gon. It is a good feeling."

"Then rest with me," I whispered, trailing my finger down her cheek.

She smiled and closed her eyes.

"Tell me what you are thinking," she said softly, her lips moving against my skin.

"I miss my family," I said to her. "I miss my son. I miss my friend Valas. Most of all, I miss my granddaughters, Irema and Aioa."

Zenzele pressed her lips together, smiling faintly. She scooted closer, hugging me tight to her body.

"Still," I said, "I am glad that we have met."

"Even if it ends tonight?"

"Yes."

Zenzele was quiet for a moment. Finally, she spoke: "If it goes badly with Khronos, I will look after the Tanti for you. They will not be raided, so long as I am mistress of the Western Dominions."

"Thank you," I said, struggling to contain my emotions.

Come what may, we slept.

6

I snapped awake. Someone had stolen into Zenzele's quarters. I started to sit up, then realized it was her wolf, Vehnfear. The animal padded into her bedchamber and lay down a short distance apart.

"Hello, old boy," I said affectionately. I was fond of canines. We had shared our camp with several canine families when I was a mortal man.

Zenzele's torches had burned out, but a bit of low light was coming through some small chinks in the upper curve of the wall, and the animal's gold eyes glimmered as he stared at me. Again, I sensed an eerie, near-human intelligence in the beast's keen gaze. And he was beautiful, with gray and white patterned fur. The Strix had made a wolf-prince of the animal, regal and powerful.

He looked from me to his mistress. Finally he came to a decision. Scooting closer, he nosed my hand. I stroked his head and he lapped at my forearm. His tongue was icy cold. I laughed, and Zenzele stirred.

"Gon?" she mumbled.

"We have a visitor," I said.

She peeked over my shoulder, alarmed, then chuckled. "Vehnfear! Come here, boy!"

The wolf rose and hopped into our bedding, settling between the humps of our legs. He wagged his tail and grinned at us.

They came for me a short time later.

7

There was a disturbance in some distant corridor, one that grew in volume as it approached Zenzele's quarters. We had arisen and were waiting for someone to come for us when we heard the great warren of the blood drinkers stir to life around us. Vehnfear heard it first and rose, his hackles standing up. Zenzele stroked his back. She looked at me gravely, her eyes wide, her face drawn. I did my best to comfort her. I smiled placidly, my palms resting on my knees, trying to project an air of calm, but my stomach was churning. So much rode on the god king's approval! My fate. The fates of my loved ones. All of the Tanti.

"Gon..." Zenzele murmured.

Her door hanging was swept to one side and a wizened blood drinker ducked into the chamber. "Zenzele," he croaked.

"Master Edron!" Zenzele jumped to her feet and bowed low.

The creature was dressed in flowing robes and a large headdress, a pipe-shaped hat draped with painted wooden chits. The little wooden tablets chattered against one another when the man moved. There were several warriors in the corridor outside, and a handful of curious spectators.

Vehnfear snarled, and Zenzele stroked the beast to silence him.

"You have been summoned to the court of the god king," Edron said. He nodded to the wolf almost imperceptibly, acknowledging the animal's intelligence, which surprised me. I could feel the T'sukuru's power emanating from him like the wind off an ice floe. An Eternal! Cold silver eyes flicked in my direction and the ancient blood drinker's lips narrowed. "Khronos wishes to examine the stray you have returned from the Western Dominions with," he said.

"Of course," Zenzele nodded.

I bowed, and the Clan Master turned with a swish of his robes, leading us into the corridor with no further comment.

"Stay!" Zenzele hissed at Vehnfear, pointing her finger at him.

The wolf settled back down with a surly huff.

Edron's guards fell into step behind us as the god king's majordomo led us through the winding corridors of the Fen.

The vampire city had seemed all but deserted when we arrived at dawn, its inhabitants bedded down for the day, but it was early evening now, and the underground city was buzzing with activity.

Blood drinkers of all shapes and sizes moved busily through the subterranean chambers. If we came upon them in the corridors, they flattened themselves against the gray stone walls to let us pass, bowing obsequiously to the Clan Master, but for the most part, the denizens of the Fen paid little attention to our group. This was a city, and they had their own lives to concern themselves with. They were artisans and craftsmen, soldiers and whores. They were priests and penitents, courtiers and clowns. Few gave me even a second glance, and then only because I was in the company of a Master.

I was a tourist in hell.

I knew I was probably marching to my doom, but I could not rein in my natural curiosity. I had heard of the vampires of the east-- the great city of the blood drinkers-- from the moment I ended my self-imposed isolation, and I had wanted to see it. Now I was here, and though I found it to be a loathsome place, it was still impressive. It was still a wonder. Throngs of immortals moved about its vast chambers, their dress exotic and rich. Many of the chambers were brightly painted, and in a much more sophisticated manner than the mortal cave paintings of the period. There was a great glittering falls, the water tumbling from a chink in the roof so high up it was almost lost in the distance. Around the falls, man-made bridges circled so that the immortals could enjoy the sight up close. There were tapestries and statuary, monuments and altars. There were things I could not, in my ignorance, even figure out the intent of. Complex wood and stone objects that moved of their own accord, making monotonous clacking sounds. Troughs of flowing water that turned creaking wooden paddles. I was, by turns, amazed, intrigued, amused and even frightened.

Yet, as we moved deeper into the mountain, the inhabitants of the vampire city grew more perverse. In a vast cavern whose roof was open to the stars, some religious ceremony was being held. I watched as ecstatic mortals paid tribute to their vampire masters, slashing open their wrists and aiming the spurting wounds toward large and ornately carved wooden bowls. Blood drinkers in priestly robes slurped from the bowls ravenously, their garments dripping with the scarlet fluid. Further down, in a chamber that billowed with hissing steam, we encountered a great orgy, mortal and immortal alike, fucking and feeding. They coiled and writhed, a collective mound of twitching flesh. The air was thick with the smell of semen and sweat and hot human blood. The pools they copulated in bubbled and splashed with hot gases that had passed up from the belly of the earth. We crossed a stinking abattoir where mortals hung by their ankles like game, to be butchered and bled into crusty stone vats. The immortals working here hardly even looked up as we passed through the center of the workroom. In another chamber, vampire aristocrats lazed about shallow pools of human blood, gossiping idly. The blood clung to their flesh, dark, half-congealed, like clots. It was finally too much for me to bear. My thoughts reeled drunkenly at the nightmarish sights, the putrescent stench, of this pit of vipers. I had to lower my eyes, withdraw into my inner being.

I have always had a self-indulgent nature, and I'm ashamed to say that all this debauchery tempted me. I feared I could lose my soul in this place-- and not even notice that I'd lost it. That, to me, was the crowning horror.

That I could be one of them.

That it would be so easy.

We descended, and descended yet further, until finally we came to the royal chamber, the great court of the god king Khronos.

There, in the deepest pits of Fen'Dagher, I was brought before the father of us all.

The First One.

The original Oldest Living Vampire.

8

He was much shorter than I expected him to be.

Of course, I had only seen him through Zenzele's eyes until that moment, and so he had appeared taller in my imagination. His stature had little effect on the sense of power that radiated from him, however. It was like a high-powered radio signal, if you'll forgive one more anachronistic lapse, a humming field of energy in which his personality was embedded, transmitted to all who stood in his presence.

He had a broad, heavily muscled physique, but

more than that, he looked *dense*, as if his body were composed entirely of stone. His flesh was white, the purest white you can imagine, and shot through with curling threads of blue-- his veins. He was bald, with crude, primitive-looking features: a heavy brow, a flat broken nose, full lips and a bony, jutting chin. A deep furrow angled from his left eye to his jawline, and another marred the broad flat plane of his forehead: scars he must have received when he was a mortal man. Countless smaller scars pitted the surface of his skull, his torso, his arms. He was attired in simple garb: leggings, boots, a plaited chest-piece. His arms and shoulders were tattooed. The feature I found most disturbing, however, was his eyes. They were black.

Blank, glimmering, soulless black.

Edron led us to the center of the chamber, then gestured for us to kneel. All along the perimeter of the court, gaunt white blood drinkers stood in attendance. They stared, a few whispering among themselves, but most were silent, grim. The only sound in the chamber were our footfalls and the crackle of the torches that lined the walls above the heads of the god king's courtiers.

Palifver stood among them, Hettut at his side. He stared at me with a tiny, cruel smile, his eyes sizzling with jealousy.

I met his hot stare with ice, then turned my attention to Khronos.

"Zenzele, my lord, and the stray from the Western Dominions," the majordomo announced. He bowed and backed away.

"Zenzele, my love," Khronos said with obvious pleasure. Smiling, he rose from his throne of basalt and bone.

The floor of his reception chamber was made of volcanic stone. The igneous rock had formed a polygonal pattern when it cooled ages before, and the ancient blood drinker stepped gracefully from section to section as he approached. His shadow, multiplied by the torches, leapt and capered on the walls.

"Khronos," Zenzele bowed.

The god king of the vampires appraised me as he drew near. I found his black gaze disconcerting, but I tried not to betray my fear.

"Palifver says that you've brought us a stray," Khronos said. "An untamed blood drinker from the northern wastes. We hope that you have wet-trained the beast."

Some of the creature's sycophants tittered. Their voices echoed off the walls of the royal chamber like a flurry of bat wings.

"I'm certain Palifver has said... a great many things," Zenzele replied.

"Do not concern yourself overly much," Khronos reassured her. "I am not so ancient that I have forgotten how spurned love can poison the tongue."

With one last nimble hop, he stood before Zenzele. He held out his hands. His fingers were very long, very white, and sported long, thick, black nails. Zenzele put her fingers in his palms, and those pallid claws curled around them.

He grinned down at her, his teeth sharp and yellow, like old ivory.

"You have been gone too long, my beautiful Zenzele," he said. "The Fen is much too drab in your absence."

"I am glad to be home."

"Yes... home," he sighed. He seemed lost in thought for a moment, and then he turned to address me. "Perhaps, someday, you will consider Uroboros your home as well."

He grinned at me, waiting for a response.

"Perhaps," I said carefully.

"Good! Good!" he cried. "Tell me, stranger… what is your name?"

"Thest," I answered.

"Thest," he repeated. His jaw worked as if he were chewing the word. He turned suddenly to Zenzele. "Thest is a name used by one of the mortal tribes in the Western Dominions, is it not?"

"Yes, Khronos."

"It is not a common name," he ruminated. His eyelids fluttered, and then he made a face as if to say "ah-hah!"

"Thest is the name of one of the Tanti's deities!" He laughed at the expression of surprise on my face. "Of course I know the Tanti! I was old when the Tanti came down from the north, before they even called themselves the Tanti, when the world was gripped in fists of ice and snow and giant beasts still roamed the land!"

He looked at me with sudden intensity, and I felt his eyes boring into my skull. I imagined I could hear his thoughts in my mind—low, grinding, alien thoughts. Incomprehensible.

"But you are old, too," he said softly. He released Zenzele's hands to approach me, and I was nearly overwhelmed by a desire to retreat from him. It took all of my willpower to stay there on my knees. I wanted to scramble across the floor like a frightened child.

"Not as old as I am, but very old," he said, his eyebrows drawing together. "From before the Time of Ice, I would think. And yet, you are still very much the mortal man you once were. Interesting…"

He circled around me as he spoke. As he did, I felt that he was examining me with more than just his eyes. I had the notion that he was looking inside me, into my past, possibly even my future, with senses not much different from the strange intuition that Zenzele commanded, only more powerful, more piercing.

Several more blood drinkers entered the royal chamber. Bhorg, Tribtoc and Goro, among others, slipped as unobtrusively as possible through the main entrance. The courtiers made room for them along the perimeter of the chamber.

"Palifver said that you surrendered to Zenzele to protect the life of a T'sukuru child. He said the two of you had been living among a tribe of mortal men. The Tanti, I presume."

"Yes," I answered, turning my head to keep sight of the creature.

"Did they worship you, these Tanti?" he asked. "Is that why you took the name of one of their deities?"

"No. I lived as one of them."

"They knew what you were, and they accepted you?"

"Yes."

That caused a bit of a stir among the king's court. The god king's audience murmured in surprise and consternation.

"You are no longer a mortal man," Khronos said with a strange sort of pity in his voice, as if he were speaking to a child.

"I have begun to teach him our ways," Zenzele spoke up nervously. "He was forced to destroy his maker shortly after he was given the Blood. He has lived among mortal men all of his life. He is ignorant, yes, and stubborn, but I would like to take him into my House. I would like to give him the same opportunities that you have given to me."

"You feel an affinity with him," Khronos said to her. "You were also a stray."

"Yes, Lord," Zenzele said.

"Do you love him?"

I saw Palifver's head jerk up at that. His eyes narrowed. His fingers curled into fists.

Zenzele looked stricken. "I... am drawn to him," she said haltingly. She glanced toward me, then stuttered, "Yes... I feel... a strong affection for him."

"You have Shared?"

"Yes."

"Then he knows," Khronos said. His eyes twitched back toward me. "We will have your blood now, wild man from the north. Let us look into your soul."

9

Just a drop of my vampire blood, and his eyes rolled back in their sockets. I watched his pallid eyelids flutter, a rapid burst of motion, like the wings of a moth. His black tongue snaked out, slid across his lips. Then he opened his eyes and fixed me with his soulless gaze.

"A god of corruption, am I?" he hissed, echoing my unspoken thoughts.

Zenzele flashed a look of horror at me. Horror and despair.

"You would see mortal men rule this world in our stead?" he asked, though it was more of an accusation than a question. "You would serve them over us? Forsaking your own kind?"

"Yes!" I answered. What was the point of lying? He had tasted my blood, and through the blood: my soul.

"Mortals are weak, simple-minded, crude."

"Yes."

"Their lives are so brief. Better to spend your devotion on mayflies."

Zenzele opened her mouth to plead my case, but Khronos motioned for her to be silent.

"There is only one difference between mortal and immortal men," I said.

"And what is that?" Khronos asked.

"Their kings die!" I cried, and then I threw myself at him.

It was a desperate act. I knew that he'd found my soul offensive. Even more damning, I was glad. I wanted no part of his kingdom of filth. I had gambled my life on the slim chance that I might curry his favor, and by extension, protect my beloved Tanti, but I had lost. The only thing I could hope for now was to destroy the creature that threatened the lives of my beloved.

But how do you kill that which is unkillable?

"Gon, no--!" Zenzele shouted as I launched myself at the god king.

Khronos was close. I crossed the space to him in the blink of an eye. As the king's council rushed in to stop me, I seized Khronos's head. I could feel the terrible power pouring from his body, a palpable force, even more dreadful at this intimate distance. He was an Eternal, and so much more, but I had no recourse. I thought to tear his head from his shoulders and crush it beneath my heel. Perhaps surprise would give me the moment I needed to deliver the fatal blow, though I doubted even such a catastrophic injury could kill the fiend.

But their god king was fast. He threw me off as quickly as I laid hands on him.

As Khronos flung me to the floor, my nails raked across the flesh of his face, digging several grooves in his cold white skin. The black blood welled up out of the tissue to stitch the wounds back together almost instantly, and I brought my fingers to my mouth, hoping some of his Strix was imbedded in my fingernails. Perhaps I could divine some secret from his blood, something that might help me to vanquish the monster.

"You... DARE--!" Khronos thundered, outraged.

I tasted his blood on my nails, and then the whipstrike of his persona. His thoughts and emotions and memories flooded into my mind.

The force of the god king's psyche caught me off guard, and for a moment I was possessed. Alien images filled my vision: a world, a universe, foreign to our own, a nightmarish realm where even the fundamental laws that governed reality were antithetical to man's reason. There, all life was parasitic in nature, and the heavens were not some vast repository of far flung stars, but filled with a kind of living soup, an organic miasma. Coupled with these visions were the god king's human recollections, almost as impenetrable. I saw the warrior race that gave birth to him. I witnessed their never-ending battles. Grinding, unceasing warfare, even when he was a child. I saw him walking through fields of battle, crushing the skulls of his people's fallen foes, a boy with a large stone in his hands. I saw him as a young man, fighting with spear and blade. I saw his first kill, his first battlefield rape. I saw vast fields of war-torn corpses, the earth run red with blood while vultures feasted on the flesh of the dead and the dying. And then an Event. A terrific calamity. The long foretold Armageddon of his race's mythology. There was a flash in the heavens, so bright it turned the night to day. The ground trembled. Their forests were laid to waste. The god king set forth with a band of warriors to seek out the cause of the destruction. He found it. He found it and returned to his people a monster. But it was all too much for me, this terrible genesis, this fusion of man and not-man. It was as if I were seeing through the eyes of two separate beings, hearing two voices shouting in my skull at once, and I could do ought but reject them both, pushing them both away in an instinctive attempt to preserve my own sanity.

But before the visions faded, I saw his ambition,

or perhaps the ambition of the alien thing that was coupled to his soul: to remake the world in his image, and that was perhaps the most nightmarish revelation of all.

"Bring me his head!" Khronos roared, and I was seized by several hissing blood drinkers. They had surrounded me while I was in the spell of his blood. They wrenched me violently in one direction, then another, cursing and snarling. In a moment they would coordinate their assault and tear me limb from limb.

"No!" Zenzele shouted. I saw her rise, and then she blurred across the chamber. An instant later, she was snatching a spear from a distracted soldier's hands.

"Wait!" Khronos said, stepping toward me with a grin. "I will do it myself!"

I lunged at him, but my captors held me back. They forced me to my knees as the god king approached.

He took my temples between his hands, his nails sinking into my flesh. "Your head shall adorn my cock," he spat.

His grin twisted into a scowl. Black fluid speckled my forehead and cheeks. He made a choking sound, and we both looked down simultaneously. Even as we looked, the spearhead that was protruding from his chest vanished inside his body, scraping against his sternum. It burst back through an instant later, just above and to the left of the first hole, a ragged chunk of his heart jiggling on the tip of it.

Zenzele swung the god king in an arc, lifting him by the shaft of the spear she had impaled him with. Lips peeled back from her teeth, she set her foot against his buttocks and shoved him into the vampires who held me down.

They fell away to every side of me, knocked off

their feet by the impact of Khronos's body. I was free! I scrambled up, grabbed the first blood drinker I could get my hands on, and swung him by the arm into another group of immortals.

"Gon!" Zenzele shouted.

She had already retreated to the entrance.

I followed.

Bhorg and Goro and Tribtoc had encircled her protectively. So Zenzele's comrades intended to make good on their promise to stand by their mistress! I saw Bhorg shatter a vampire to shards with his massive hammer. Tribtoc and Goro were fighting hand-to-hand.

Where is Palifver? I wondered, scanning the room, but he and Hettut had retreated, or perhaps they were only lost in the chaos. The god king was flopping on the ground, his black blood jetting into the air. Tendrils of the oldest living vampire's whipping blood pierced the body of one of the T'sukuru who rushed to his aid, and the woman exploded into sparkling dust with a final despairing howl, drained of her vitality in an instant.

"Hurry!" Zenzele cried, and vanished into the corridor.

10

Our flight from Uroboros was, for the most part, rather anticlimactic, so I shall not bore you by recounting every tiny detail of our escape.

Since Khronos had no method of raising an alarm, we raced through the maze-like corridors of the underground city without being accosted. We knocked a few blood drinkers down in our haste, and drew a few curious stares, but aside from that, little of note occurred aside from a lot of running and some zigging and zagging.

Only the Clan Masters-- true immortals like ourselves-- would have had any chance of catching us, but even if they'd pursued us immediately, we could have easily lost them in such a densely populated metropolis. There were just too many winding corridors, too many abandoned or unoccupied chambers, and the air was too thick with the aroma of their mortal thralls to follow us by scent.

Zenzele knew a neglected route that would take us to the open quickly. It let out onto a sheer drop, she said, but we could climb down by clinging to the surface of the rock.

"Do you know how to do that?" she asked.

"Of course," I said.

We climbed down on the east-facing slope of the volcano, out of view if anyone was watching from the Fen, and well away from the mortal districts below. We leapt the last fifty meters to the treetops, then climbed to the floor of the snow-blanketed forest.

There, in the cover of the forest, I embraced my savior passionately. I put my mouth over hers, pulling her tightly to my body, running my palms across her back, her buttocks. She returned my ardor, her eyes closed. She didn't immediately answer when I asked her why she had risked her life to save me.

"Khronos will not rest now until he has destroyed us both," I said to her.

"I do not care!" she said fiercely. "I would rather die free with you than live forever in service to that monster. When I Shared with you, I saw in your memories the life I might have. I want that, Gon. I want the peace that you had when you lived among the Tanti."

We heard a crashing in the treetops. A moment later, Goro and Bhorg dropped to the earth nearby.

Zenzele pushed away from me. "Tribtoc?" she

asked.

Bhorg leaned on the handle of his great stone hammer. "He fell," the giant said. "Khronos himself laid hands on our companion. He pulled the poor bastard apart."

"And what of Palifver?"

The two blood drinkers looked at one another. Almost as one, they shrugged.

"Pity," Zenzele said, her eyes flashing dangerously. "We have unfinished business, he and I."

But she quickly forgot her vengeance when her wolf came bounding through the snow.

"Vehnfear!" she cried, dropping to one knee.

The wolf slid to a stop and let her stroke his back, wagging his tail enthusiastically, and then he trotted over to me.

"Hail, old man," I said, squatting down to embrace him, "you didn't let anyone follow you, did you?"

The animal looked over his shoulder as if he understood my words, ears pricked, but he didn't seem overly concerned. I stood and reached out with my senses, but heard no creature in pursuit of the canine.

"So where do we go now?" Bhorg asked, looking around the group.

"There is a small tribe of my people living in the Eastern Dominions," Goro, the Fat Hand vampire, said. "If this untrained blood drinker can live in peace among his mortal brothers, then perhaps so can this one. I would like to try it, anyway. I miss my own kind. It has been many seasons since I was made into this thing that I am."

"And what of you, Bhorg?" Zenzele asked. "Where do you wish to go?"

"My loyalty has always lain with you, Zenzele. Where you go, I go. If you will have me."

Zenzele glanced toward me.

"I would like to return to the Tanti," I said, "but I am afraid Khronos will expect me to do that. I do not wish to bring down his wrath upon my people. Or my vampire child Ilio. Perhaps we can go east with Goro. For a little while, at least. Draw Khronos's ire away from my mortal descendants."

"And then?" Zenzele asked, her eyebrows drawing together.

"We cannot hide from him forever," I said to her. "When I threw myself at him-- when I tasted his blood-- I saw into his soul. What I saw in your god king's mind, Zenzele... my heart cannot abide it. No, I do not intend to hide from him forever, my love...

"...I intend to raise an army against him."

Journey's Beginning

I'm afraid that is all I have time to tell you tonight, dear friends. The world has turned her back to the dark. Liege gleams outside my window in dawn's candy colored light.

The sight tantalizes. It makes me want to travel, and I intend to. I intend to embark on a long journey, and quite soon! Only I need to tie up a few loose ends first.

Lukas Jaeger being one of those loose ends.

Our good friend Lukas lies writhing on my sofa as I type this. I try to put him out of my thoughts as my fingers fly over the keys of my trusty laptop computer, but it is difficult. He screams so loud! As soon as I wrap this up, the third volume of my memoirs, I will open my computer's email program, write a quick note to my mortal agent in the United States, then attach the folder which contains this manuscript and send it halfway around the world.

The wonders of modern technology!

Every now and then, Lukas lets out a whoop or a sputtering groan. (We will not mention the other noxious noises he has been making the past hour or so!) If he weren't such a murderous bastard, I might actually feel a little sympathy for him. I know how bad it hurts when the Strix is working its terrible magic on mortal flesh and bone. It feels like hot wires being threaded through your veins, like your heart and lungs have turned to ice inside your chest, but my new companion deserves it. All of it and more!

So, no sympathy from me.

Guilt. Now that's another story. There is always guilt when one makes a new vampire. There is for me at least. Self-condemnation. Remorse. I will agonize over my decision for years. Because I know: I am responsible for every innocent life this creature takes. Every one of them. My hands will be forever tainted by the blood this man spills.

"But why?" you ask. "Why make this brutal creature into an immortal?"

First let me tell you how I did it, and then I'll tell you why.

When I finished telling Lukas of our escape from Uroboros, he sat back in his seat, his cigarette a tube of ash dangling from a slightly scorched filter. There was a satisfied expression on his face, and I have to confess, it pleased me to see that he had enjoyed my tale. His eyes were distant, dreaming, as if a part of him were still standing there on the forested slope of Fen'Dagher. He glanced out the window finally and laughed, saying gently, almost as if to himself, "It's almost daylight out. I guess we'll have to continue this tomorrow night, yes?"

"That is all for tonight," I nodded.

He ground his cigarette in the ashtray, though it had gone out several minutes ago, then glanced around the room. "So, uh... do you want me to stay here in your penthouse today... while you sleep, I mean, or...?"

Small talk in the lair of an immortal. Such banality was insufferable!

Before he could say another word, I launched myself across the table at him.

He flailed back from me, surprised, and our

combined momentum overturned his chair. We spilled onto the floor with a thud.

"What are you--? Get off--!" he grunted.

He tried to hook his thumbs into my eyes, blind me, thinking I meant to renege on our bargain, fighting for his life. His face had flushed with blood and his eyes rolled wildly in their sockets. He was looking across the floor for something, anything, he could use as a weapon, his lips peeled back from his teeth.

"Be still, you fool!" I snapped.

The ashtray--! It had fallen to the floor when I threw myself at him. He grabbed ahold of it and swung it into my temple as I tried to pry my fingers between his teeth. The dish was made of crystal, thick, too sturdy to break. Had I been a mortal man, the blow might have killed me. Annoyed, I slapped it from his hand and it went rolling across the carpet.

"Help!" he cried out, and the moment he opened his mouth, I summoned the Strix from the pit of my guts. I seized his jaws with both hands, held his mouth open, and the living blood came roaring up out of my throat.

Lukas choked and lurched beneath me, and then it was inside him.

I rose.

"Remember our bargain," I said.

The child pornographer and murderer lay very still, his eyes wide, the muscles of his neck standing out rigidly. His lips and cheek were smeared with blood where I had so roughly pried open his mouth.

A shiver passed through his body.

Very primly, he folded his hands upon his stomach. His attention had turned inward, and I knew that he could feel it, he could feel the black blood coiling inside him. Any moment now it would lance into his heart, and then it would do one of two things:

it would devour him from within... or it would make him an immortal.

I watched his face. First, a twitch. There in his cheek, right below his eye, and then his whole body contorted with pain. His back arched, and he groaned, his hands falling to his sides, fingers curling into the carpet. For a moment I was afraid that the Strix had found him wanting, that it would simply devour him, and all my schemes would come to naught.

"Gott in Himmel!" he wailed, beads of sweat squeezing out of the pores of his face.

I watched, intrigued, as the color began to fade from his flesh. His eyes dilated as the life drained out of him. All the hair on his body shifted, ever so subtly, as the surface of his skin hardened.

I watched the symbiote transform him.

His forearms whitened, then his hands, then his fingers. It was like an invisible paintbrush swiping its way rapidly down his extremities, painting them white. He grimaced and I saw his eyeteeth elongating. His jaw popped as the bones of his skull changed shape to accommodate his new fangs and increased bite radius.

Vampires can very nearly unhinge their jaws, you know, much like a snake.

He sucked in a sharp breath... and then he began to shake. Bloody tears trickled from the corners of his eyes as he convulsed violently on the floor.

So this is how it's going to be, I thought, and I believe I might have smiled a little.

Sometimes the transformation is quick and painless. I have even heard vampires claim their transformation was pleasurable. From my experience, however, it is often a slow and torturous affair, sometimes taking days to complete, and it seemed my pornographer was going to be one of the unlucky ones.

Lukas belched and then turned his head to one side and vomited. Gelid blood and the liquefied remains of some earlier meal surged across my dining room floor.

"Am I... going to die?" he gulped, when he had finished emptying the contents of his belly.

"I never promised it wouldn't hurt," I said.

He smiled, relieved, and then his body contorted in agony again. He rolled into a fetal position, groaning, and his bowels let go with a horrendous cacophony.

I walked to the dining room windows and raised them, letting in a gust of frigid winter air, then returned to the man flailing on my floor and scooped him into my arms.

"Let's put you on the sofa," I muttered. "This is going to take a while."

"Hurts--!" Lukas groaned. "So cold!"

I laid him on my couch and shifted a chair beside him. Sitting next to the writhing man, I tried to comfort him. "It will be over soon," I said, "and then you will forget this labor, as a mother forgets the pangs of childbirth."

Lukas said, *"Aaaarrrggghhhh! Bluhhhh!"*

"When the pain has passed, I will train you in our ways, as every good vampire maker should. I will show you how to hunt, and what to do with the corpse afterward so mortal men never suspect we truly exist. I will teach you how to use your preternatural skills, and then, when you are strong, we are going on a journey, you and I."

He stared at me, his beautiful new eyes twinkling like prisms.

"You are going to be a powerful vampire," I said. I examined the texture of his new flesh, consulted that intuitive faculty we all have which allows us to gauge the strength of another blood drinker. "The transformation seems to have stopped just short of true immortality, but if you are clever, and more importantly, lucky, you may live for several thousand years."

He nodded, jaws clenched, but I could see the satisfaction in his eyes. More than anything else, he had feared weakness, but that was not to be. I had made a monster of this one.

"Where... are we going?" he gasped.

"To Germany," I said. "I wish to end my life in the land that gave me birth."

His eyebrows drew together, and I smiled.

"This is the payment I exact. This is what you will give me in exchange for your immortality," I told him. "We are going to the Swabian Alb. We shall travel on foot, as we traveled in the old days, and I am going to finish telling you my story. And when we get there, I am going to find the place where I lived my mortal life with my tent-mate and our two beloved wives, and then you are going to free me from this eternal existence, which I never asked for or wanted."

He was in too much pain to speak, but I could see the question in his eyes, and so I answered it for him.

"Yes, I know. I told you that I cannot die," I said, "but that is not exactly true. There is one way that an Eternal can be killed. Only one! It is nearly impossible, but it can be done. I have seen it with my own eyes. And I believe that you, Lukas Jaeger, may be the one to do it for me."

"H-how?" Lukas panted.

I smiled, rising from my chair. "We will speak more of it later. It is late, and I have a great many things to do before I rest. Come to me when your mortal life has passed away and we will begin your instruction. For now, I bid you *adieu*."

As I bid you *adieu*, my cherished mortal readers. It is late, and I do have a great number of affairs to put to order before I embark on my final journey.

Do not worry. I intend to bring a journal with me so that I can transcribe all the details. I will make certain that my final words find their way into your hands.

Think of it as a compromise. No sentient creature really wants to die. There is a small part of me that fears what lies beyond, but I am so very, very tired of this world. It has changed too much, and I miss all those I've loved whom time has seen fit to erase from this plane of existence.

These memoirs shall serve-- as the works of all artists serve-- as a limited form of immortality. Though my soul shall be released, and I can finally join my loved ones waiting for me in the Ghost World, I shall live on in some small fashion in the thoughts of those who chance upon these recordings.

I hope it is enough to satisfy the tiny particle of my soul that does not wish to perish.

Strange, that I should feel so terribly excited!

Your friend,

Gon,

The Oldest Living Vampire

About the Author

Joseph lives in Southern Illinois with his wife, his two sons and all the voices in his head. He is the indie bestselling author of the Oldest Living Vampire Saga, as well as *Mort, House of Dead Trees* and several other horror and fantasy novels. He is currently working on his next novel.

Made in the USA
Charleston, SC
03 October 2014